One Glance From Those Moss-Green Eyes And Her Body Had Gone Soft And Pliant.

Spending a short amount of time with Marcus while she'd shown him around the bakery had been…not horrible. If it hadn't been for the secret Vanessa was hiding just one floor above, she might even have gotten him that cup of coffee and invited him to stay a while longer.

Which was a really bad idea, so it was better that he'd taken off when he had.

She had Danny pressed to her chest, content now that his belly was being filled, when she heard footsteps coming up the stairs. There was no time to jump up and hide the baby, no time to yell for Aunt Helen to run interference. One minute she was glancing around for a blanket to cover her exposed chest, and the next she was frozen in place, staring with alarm at her stunned but furious ex-husband.

Dear Reader,

I had such a good time with *Her Little Secret, His Hidden Heir,* especially since Marc and Vanessa's story is set mainly in a bakery. Writing about all the delicious goodies Vanessa and her aunt were baking up made me hungry for every single one.

So I thought it might be fun to share one of those very special recipes with you. (It's one of my personal favorites.) Turn to page six for details. And if you get the chance to try it, please drop me a line to let me know what you think!

I hope you enjoy Marc and Vanessa's story and the cookies! They're excellent with a glass of cold milk, by the way.

All my best,

Heidi Betts
www.HeidiBetts.com

HEIDI BETTS

HER LITTLE SECRET, HIS HIDDEN HEIR

For my wonderful new Desire editor, Charles Griemsman. It's been a delight working with and getting to know you this past year, and I'm looking forward to sharing many more "*Desire*-able" moments in the future.

ISBN-13: 978-0-373-73104-6

Recycling programs for this product may not exist in your area.

HER LITTLE SECRET, HIS HIDDEN HEIR

www.Harlequin.com

Printed in U.S.A.

Books by Heidi Betts

Desire

Bought by a Millionaire #1638
Blame it on the Blackout #1662
When the Lights Go Down #1686
Seven-Year Seduction #1709
Mr. and Mistress #1723
Bedded Then *Wed* #1761
Blackmailed into Bed #1779
Fortune's Forbidden Woman #1801
Christmas in His Royal Bed #1833
Inheriting His Secret Christmas Baby #2055
Her Little Secret, His Hidden Heir #2091

HEIDI BETTS

An avid romance reader since junior high, national bestselling author Heidi Betts knew early on that she wanted to write these wonderful stories of love and adventure. It wasn't until her freshman year of college, however, when she spent the entire night before finals reading a romance novel instead of studying, that she decided to take the road less traveled and follow her dream.

Soon after joining Romance Writers of America, Heidi's writing began to garner attention, including placing in the esteemed Golden Heart competition three years in a row. The recipient of numerous awards and stellar reviews, Heidi's books combine believable characters with compelling plotlines, and are consistently described as "delightful," "sizzling" and "wonderfully witty."

For news, fun and information about upcoming books, be sure to visit Heidi online at HeidiBetts.com.

CHOCOLATE PEANUT BUTTER PINWHEELS

INGREDIENTS:
1 cup butter, softened
1 cup light brown sugar, firmly packed
1 cup peanut butter (you can add more if you like
your cookies really peanut buttery)
1 egg
1 teaspoon vanilla extract
2 cups flour
1 teaspoon baking soda
½ teaspoon salt

INGREDIENTS FOR FILLING:
2 cups (or one 12-ounce bag) chocolate chips
2 tablespoons butter

DIRECTIONS:

1. In large bowl, cream butter and sugar until light and fluffy.

2. Add peanut butter, egg and vanilla. Beat until smooth.

3. Add flour, baking soda and salt and mix until dough is formed. Cover and refrigerate for 30 minutes.

4. Make filling by melting chocolate chips and butter together in a slow cooker on lowest setting or in a double boiler.

5. Remove dough from refrigerator. Roll half of it into an 11 x 17 inch rectangle on a lightly floured surface.

6. Spread half of chocolate filling evenly over dough.

7. Roll tightly from long side. Wrap in plastic wrap. Refrigerate until firm—at least 8 hours or overnight.

8. Repeat with remaining dough and filling.

9. Cut into 1/8-inch slices and bake in 325°F oven for about 8 minutes or until lightly browned.

10. Remove to wire racks to cool.

Prologue

Vanessa Keller—soon to be simply Vanessa Mason again—sat at the foot of her hotel-room bed, staring at the small plastic wand in her hand. She blinked, feeling her heart pound, her stomach roll and her vision go fuzzy around the edges.

As bad luck went, this ranked right up there with having your plane go down on the way to your honeymoon destination or getting hit by a bus right after you'd won the million-dollar lotto.

And the irony of the situation...

A harsh laugh escaped her lungs, taking with it a puff of the stale air she'd been holding onto for the past several minutes.

She was newly divorced from a husband she'd *thought* was the man of her dreams, staying in a downtown Pittsburgh hotel because she didn't know quite what to do with her life now that the rug had been yanked out from under her. And if that wasn't enough to make her wonder where things had gone so wrong, now she was pregnant.

Pregnant. With her ex-husband's child, when she hadn't managed to conceive in the three years they'd been married, even though they'd tried...or at least hadn't worked to prevent it.

What in heaven's name was she going to do?

Pushing to her feet on less-than-steady legs, she crossed to the wide desk against the far wall and dropped into its cushioned chair. Her hands shook as she laid the small plastic stick on the flat surface and dragged the phone closer.

Taking deep, shuddering breaths, she told herself she could do this. Told herself it was the right thing to do, and however he reacted, she would handle it.

This was not a bid to get back together. Vanessa wasn't sure she would want to, even with a baby now in the picture. But he deserved to know he was going to be a father, regardless of the current state of their relationship.

With cold fingers, she dialed the familiar number, knowing his assistant would answer. She'd never cared for Trevor Storch; he was a weaselly little brownnoser, treating her more as an annoyance than as the wife of the CEO of a multimillion-dollar company and *his boss*.

After only one ring, Trevor's squeaky, singsong voice came on the line. "Keller Corporation, Marcus Keller's office. How may I help you?"

"It's Vanessa," she said without preamble—he knew full well who she was. He was probably privy to more of the details about her marriage and subsequent divorce than he deserved to be, too. "I need to talk to Marc."

"I'm sorry, Miss Mason, Mr. Keller isn't available."

His use of her maiden name—not to mention calling her *Miss*—struck Vanessa's heart like the tip of a knife. No doubt he'd done it deliberately.

"It's important," she said, not bothering to correct or argue with him. She'd done enough of that in the past, as well as overlooking his snide attitude just to keep the peace; she didn't have to do it anymore, either.

"I'm sorry," he told her again, "but Mr. Keller has instructed me to tell you that there's nothing you could possibly have to say to him that he wants to hear. Good day."

And with that, the line went dead, leaving Vanessa openmouthed with shock. If hearing herself called "Miss Mason" rather than "Mrs. Keller" felt like a knife tip being inserted into her heart, then being told her ex-husband wouldn't even deign to speak with her any longer thrust the blade the rest of the way in to the hilt and twisted it sharply.

She'd known Marc was angry with her, knew they'd parted on less than friendly terms. But never in a million years would she have expected him to cut her off so callously.

He'd loved her once, hadn't he? She'd certainly loved him. And yet they'd come to this—virtual strangers who couldn't even speak a civil word to one another.

But that answered the question of what she was going to do. She was going to be a single mother, and without Marcus's money and support—which she wouldn't have taken, with or without the prenup—she'd better find a way to take care of herself and the baby—and she'd better do it fast.

One

One year later...

Marcus Keller flexed his fingers on the warm leather of the steering wheel, his sleek black Mercedes hugging the road as he took the narrow curves leading into Summerville faster than was probably wise.

The small Pennsylvania town was only three hours from his own home in Pittsburgh, but it might as well have been a world away. Where Pittsburgh was ninety percent concrete and city lights, Summerville was thick forests, green grass, quaint houses and a small downtown area that reminded Marcus of a modern version of Mayberry.

He slowed his speed, taking the time to examine the storefronts as he passed. A drug store, a post office, a bar and grill, a gift shop...and a bakery.

Lifting his foot from the gas, he slowed even more, studying the bright yellow awning and fancy black lettering declaring it to be The Sugar Shack...the red neon sign in the window letting customers know they were open...and the handful of people inside, enjoying freshly made baked goods.

It looked inviting, which was important in the food service industry. He was tempted to lower his window and see if he could actually smell the delicious scents of breads and cookies and pies in the air.

But there was more to running a successful business than a cute name and an attractive front window, and if he was going to put money into The Sugar Shack, he wanted to know it was a sound investment.

At the corner, he took a left and continued down a side street, following the directions he'd been given to reach the offices of Blake and Fetzer, Financial Advisors. He'd worked with Brian Blake before, though never on an investment this far from home or this close to Blake's own offices. Still, the man had never steered him wrong, which made Marcus more willing to take time off work and make the long drive.

A few blocks down the street, he noticed a lone woman walking quickly on three-inch heels. Given the uneven pavement and pebbles littering the sidewalk, she wasn't having an easy time of it. She also seemed distracted, rooting around inside an oversize handbag rather than keeping her attention on where she was going.

A niggle of something uncomfortable skated through his belly. She reminded him somehow of his ex-wife. A bit heavier and curvier, her coppery hair cut short instead of left to flow halfway down her back, but still very similar. Especially the way she walked and dressed. This woman was wearing a white blouse and a black skirt with a short slit at the back, framing a pair of long, lovely legs. No jacket and no clunky accessories, which followed Vanessa's personal style to a T.

Shifting his gaze back to the road, he tamped down on

whatever emotion had his chest going tight. Guilt? Regret? Simple sentimentality? He wasn't sure and didn't care to examine the unexpected feelings too closely.

They'd been divorced for over a year. Better to put it all behind him and move on, as he was sure Vanessa had done.

Spotting the offices of Blake and Fetzer, he pulled into the diminutive three-car lot at the back of the building, cut the engine and stepped out into the warm spring day. With any luck, this meeting and the subsequent tour of The Sugar Shack would only take a couple of hours, then he could be back on the road and headed home. Small town life might be fine for some people, but Marcus would be only too happy to get back to the hustle and bustle of the city and the life he'd made for himself there.

Vanessa stopped outside Brian Blake's office, taking a moment to straighten her blouse and skirt, run a hand through her short-cropped hair and touch up her lipstick. It had been a long time since she'd gotten this dressed up and she was sorely out of practice.

It didn't help, either, that all of the nicer clothes she'd acquired while being married to Marcus were now at least one size too small. That meant her top was a bit too snug across the chest, her skirt was a good inch shorter than she would have liked and darned if the waistband wasn't cutting off her circulation.

Thankfully, the town of Summerville didn't require her to dress up this much, even for Sunday services. Otherwise, she may have had to invest in a new wardrobe, and given what a hard time she was having just keeping her head above water and her business afloat, that was an added expense she definitely could not afford.

Deciding that her appearance was about as good as it was going to get at this late date, she took a deep breath and pushed through the door. Blake and Fetzer's lone receptionist greeted her with a wide smile, informed her that Brian and the potential investor were waiting in his office, and told her to go right in.

She took another steadying breath and before stepping inside sent a quick prayer heavenward that the wealthy entrepreneur Brian had found to hopefully invest in her fledging enterprise would find The Sugar Shack worthy of his financial backing.

The first thing she saw was Brian sitting behind his desk, smiling as he chatted with the visitor facing away from her in one of the guest chairs. The man had dark hair that barely dusted the collar of his charcoal-gray jacket and was tapping a tan, long-fingered hand on the arm of his chair, as though he was impatient to get down to business.

As soon as Brian spotted her, his smile widened and he rose to his feet. "Vanessa," he greeted her, "you're right on time. Allow me to introduce you to the man I *hope* will become an investor in your wonderful bakery. Marcus Keller, this is Vanessa Mason. Vanessa this is—"

"We've met."

Marcus's voice hit her like a sledgehammer to the solar plexus, but it was only one of a series of rapid-fire shocks to her system. Brian had spoken her ex-husband's name and her stomach had plummeted all the way to her feet. At the same time, Marcus had risen from his seat and turned to face her, and her heart had started to pound against her rib cage like a runaway freight train.

She saw him standing in front of her, black hair glinting midnight blue in the dappled sunlight streaming through the tall, multipaned windows lining one wall of the office, his green eyes gleaming with devilment. Yet his suit-and-tie image wavered and no amount of blinking brought him into focus.

"Hello, Vanessa," he murmured softly.

Brushing his jacket aside, he slipped his hands into the front pockets of his matching charcoal slacks, adopting a negligent pose. He looked so comfortable and amused, while she felt as though an army of ants was crawling beneath her skin.

How in God's name could this have happened? How could she not know that *he* was the potential investor? How could Brian not realize that Marcus was her *ex*-husband?

She wanted to kick herself for not asking more questions or insisting on being given more details about today's meeting. But then, she hadn't really cared who Brian's mystery investor was, had she? She'd cared only that he was rich and seemed willing to partner up with small business owners in the hopes of a big payoff down the road.

She'd convinced herself she was desperate and needed a quick influx of cash to keep The Sugar Shack's doors open. But she would *never* be desperate enough to take charity from the man who had broken her heart and turned his back on her when she'd needed him the most.

Not bothering to address Marcus, she turned her gaze to Brian. "I'm sorry, but this isn't going to work out," she told him, then promptly turned on her heel and marched back out of the office building.

She was down the front steps and halfway up the block before she heard the first call.

"Vanessa! Vanessa, wait!"

The three-inch pumps she'd worn because they went so well with her outfit—and because she'd wanted to make a good impression—pinched her toes as she nearly ran the length of the uneven sidewalk in the direction of The Sugar Shack. All she wanted was to get away from Marcus, away from those glittering eyes and the arrogant tilt of his chin.

She didn't care that he was yelling for her, or that she could hear his footsteps keeping pace several yards behind her.

"Vanessa!"

Turning the corner only a short distance from The Sugar Shack, her steps faltered. Her heart lurched and her blood chilled.

Oh, no. She'd been so angry, so eager to get away from her ex-husband and escape back to the safety of the bakery that she'd forgotten that's where Danny was. And if there was anything she needed to protect more than her own sanity, it was her son.

Suddenly, she couldn't take another step, coming to a jerky stop only feet from the bakery door. Marcus rounded the corner a moment later, coming to an equally abrupt halt when he spotted her simply standing there like a panicked and disheveled department store mannequin.

He was slightly out of breath, and she found that more than a little satisfying. It was a nice change from his normal state of being calm, cool and always in control. And nothing less than he deserved, given what he was putting her through now.

"Finally," he muttered, sounding completely put out. "Why did you run?" He wanted to know. "We may be divorced, but that doesn't mean we can't sit and have a civil conversation."

"I have nothing to say to you," she bit out. *And there was nothing she had to say that he wanted to hear.* The cruel declaration replayed through her mind, bringing with it a fresh stab of pain and reminding her of just how important it was to keep him away from her child.

"What about this business of yours?" he asked, running a hand through his thick, dark hair before smoothing his tie and buttoning his suit jacket, once again the epitome of entrepreneurial precision. "It sounds like you could use the capital and I'm always on the lookout for a good investment."

"I don't want your money," she told him.

He inclined his head, acknowledging the sincerity of her words. "But do you need it?"

He asked the question in a low tone, with no hint of condescension and not as though he meant to dangle his wealth over her head like a plump, juicy carrot. Instead, he sounded willing to help her if she needed it.

Oh, she needed help, but not of the strings-attached variety. And not from her cold, unfeeling ex-husband.

Fighting the urge to grab whatever money he was willing to toss her way and run, she straightened her spine, squared her shoulders and reminded herself that she was doing just fine on her own. She didn't need a man—any man—to ride in and rescue her.

"The bakery is doing quite well, thank you," she replied, her voice clipped. "And even if it weren't, I wouldn't need anything from you."

Marc opened his mouth, about to reply and possibly try to change her mind, when Brian Blake rushed around the corner. He skidded to a jerky halt when he saw them, looking frazzled and alarmed. For a second, he stood there, breathing heavily, his gaze darting back and forth between the two of them. Then he shook his head and his puzzlement seemed to clear.

"Mr. Keller...Vanessa..." He took another moment to suck in much-needed oxygen, his Adam's apple riding up and down above the tight collar of his pale blue dress shirt. "This isn't at all how I'd planned for this meeting to go," he told them apologetically. "If you'll just come back to the office.... Let's sit down and see if we can't work something out."

A touch of guilt tugged at Vanessa's chest. Brian was a good guy. He didn't deserve to suffer or be put in the middle of an acrimonious situation just because she despised Marc and refused to have anything more to do with him—let alone go into business with him.

"I'm sorry, Brian," she apologized. "I appreciate everything you've done for me, but this particular partnership just isn't going to work."

For a minute, Brian looked as though he meant to argue. Noting the firm expression on her face, however, he released a sigh of resignation and nodded. "I understand."

"Actually," Marc said, "I'm still very much interested in hearing about the bakery."

Brian's eyes widened with a spark of relief, but Vanessa immediately tensed.

"No, Marcus," she told him, her firm tone brooking no arguments. Not that that had ever stopped him before.

"It sounds like it might be a sound investment, *Nessa*," he retorted, arching a single dark brow and using his old pet name for her. No doubt to put her off balance. "I drove three hours to get here and I'd prefer not to turn right around and go back empty-handed." He paused for a beat, letting that sink in. Then he added, "At least give me a tour."

No. Oh, no. She definitely couldn't let him into the bakery. That would be even more dangerous than simply having him in town, aware that she lived here now, as well.

She opened her mouth to say so, linking her arms across her chest to let him know she had no intention of changing her mind, when Brian stopped her. Touching her shoulder, he tipped his head, signaling her to follow him a few steps away, out of earshot of Marcus.

"Miss Mason. Vanessa," he said, dropping formalities. "Think about this. Please. I know Mr. Keller is your ex-husband—although I had no idea when I set up today's meeting. I never would have asked him to come here if I had—but if he's willing to invest in The Sugar Shack, as your financial advisor, I have to recommend that you *seriously* consider his offer. You're doing all right at the moment. The bakery is holding its own. But you'll never be able to move forward with your plans to expand without added capital from an outside source, and if worst comes to worst, one bad season could cause you to lose the business entirely."

Even though Vanessa didn't want to listen, didn't want to believe Brian was right, she knew deep down that he was. The Sugar Shack might be her livelihood, but smart financial planning was his. She wouldn't have begun working with him in the first place if she didn't think he knew what he was doing.

Casting a glance over her shoulder to be sure Marc couldn't overhear their conversation, she turned back and whispered, "There's more at stake here than just the bakery, Brian." So much more. "I'll let him look around. Let the two of you talk. But no matter what kind of plan you two come up with, no matter what offer he might make, I can't promise I'll be willing to accept. I'm sorry."

He looked none too pleased with her assertion, but he nodded, accepting that she would only be pushed so far where Marcus Keller was concerned.

Returning to Marc, Brian informed him of her decision and they started forward again, toward the main entrance of the bakery. The heavenly scents of freshly baked bread, pies and other pastries filled the air the closer they got. As always, those smells caused Vanessa's stomach to rumble and her mouth to water, making her hungry for a piping-hot cinnamon roll or a plate of chocolate chip cookies. Which probably explained why she hadn't quite managed to shed all of her baby weight yet.

At the front door, she stopped abruptly, turning to face the two men. "Wait here," she told them. "I have to warn Aunt Helen that you're in town and explain what's going on. She never particularly liked you," she added, aiming her comment directly at Marc, "so don't be surprised if she refuses to come out while you're here."

He shot her a sardonic grin. "I'll be sure to keep my horns and tail hidden if I run into her."

Vanessa didn't bother responding to that. She was too afraid of what kind of retort might spill from her mouth. Instead, she spun and pushed her way into the bakery.

Keeping a smile on her face and cheerily greeting customers who were sipping cups of coffee, tea or cocoa, and enjoying some of her and her aunt's most popular baked goods, she hurried to the kitchen.

As usual, Helen was bustling around doing this and that. She might have been in her seventies, but she had the energy of a twenty-year-old. Up at the crack of dawn each morning, she always went to work immediately, gathering ingredients, mixing, rolling, cutting, scooping…and managing to keep track of whatever was in the ovens, even three or four different items all set at different temperatures for various amounts of time.

Vanessa was a fairly accomplished baker herself, but readily admitted it took some doing to keep up with her aunt. Add to that the fact that Helen helped her man the counter *and* take care of Danny, and Vanessa literally did not know what she would do without her.

The squeak of the swinging double doors cutting off the kitchen area from the front of the store alerted Helen to her arrival.

"You're back," her aunt said without bothering to look up from the sugar cookies she was dusting with brightly colored sprinkles.

"Yes, but we have a problem," Vanessa told her.

At that, Helen raised her head. "You didn't get the money?" she asked, disappointment lacing her tone.

Vanessa shook her head. "Worse. The investor Brian has me meeting with is Marc."

The container of sprinkles fell from Helen's hand, hitting the metal cookie sheet and spilling everywhere. Not a disaster, just a few cookies that would turn out sloppier than usual. And whatever didn't look appropriate for sale could always go on a plate as an after-dinner treat for themselves.

"You're kidding," her aunt breathed in a shocked voice.

Vanessa shook her head and crossed to where Helen stood rooted to the spot like a statue. "Unfortunately, I'm not. He's outside right now, waiting for a tour of the bakery, so I need you to take Danny upstairs and stay there until I give you the all clear."

Her fingers moved at the speed of light as she undid the knot at Helen's waist, slipping the flour-dusted apron over her head and tossing it aside. Her aunt immediately reached up to pat her stack of puffy, blue-washed curls.

Rushing across the room, Vanessa paused to stare down at her adorable baby boy, who was lying on his back in a small bassinet, doing his best to get his pudgy little toes into his perfect pink mouth. As soon as he saw her, he smiled wide and began to gurgle happily, sending a stab of love so deep through Vanessa's soul, it stole her breath.

Lifting him up and onto her shoulder, she wished she had the time to tickle and tease and coo with him. She loved running the bakery, and was very proud of what she and Aunt Helen had managed to build together, but Danny was her pride and joy. Her favorite moments of the day were those she got to spend alone with him, feeding him, bathing him, making him laugh.

Pressing a kiss to the side of his head, she whispered, "Later, sweetheart, I promise." Just as soon as she could get rid of Marc and Brian.

Turning to her aunt, who had come up behind them, she handed the baby off.

"Hurry," she said. "And keep him as quiet as you can. If he starts to cry, turn on the TV or the radio or something to try to cover it up. I'll get rid of them as quickly as I can."

"All right," Helen readily agreed, "but keep an eye on the ovens. The pinwheel cookies only need another five minutes. The baklava and lemon streusel cake will be a while longer. I set the timers."

Vanessa nodded her understanding, then with Helen bustling off to hide Danny in the small apartment they kept over the bakery, she pushed the now-empty bassinet across the kitchen and into a back storage room. Grabbing an extra white tablecloth with blue and yellow eyelet lace trim, she used it to cover the large piece of telling furniture.

Leaving the storage room, her gaze darted left to right and up and down, searching for any remaining signs of Danny's presence. A few stray items, she might be able to explain…

A rattle? *Oh, a customer must have left it—I'll have to put it in the Lost and Found.*

A handful of diapers? *I keep those on hand for when I watch a friend's baby.* Yes, that sounded plausible.

A half-full bottle in the fridge or a prescription of ear drops in Danny Keller's name from a recent infection? Those might be a little tougher to justify.

She used a clean towel to brush away some of the worst of the spilled sprinkles and grabbed the pinwheels from the oven to keep them from burning, but otherwise left the kitchen as it had been when she'd walked in. Then she pushed back through the double swinging doors into the front of the bakery…and ran smack into a waiting Marcus.

Two

Marc's arms came up to seize Vanessa as she flew through the double doors from the kitchen and hit him square in the chest. The impact wasn't hard enough to hurt, although it did catch him slightly off guard. Then, once he had his hands on her, her body pressed full-length along his own and he didn't want to let go.

It had been a long time since he'd held this woman. Too long, if the blood pounding in his veins and the heat suffusing his groin were any indication.

She was softer than he remembered, more well-rounded in all the right places. But she still smelled of strawberries and cream from her favorite brand of shampoo. And even though she'd cut her hair to shoulder-length, she still had the same wavy copper locks that he knew from experience would be soft as silk against his fingertips.

He nearly reached up to find out for sure, his gaze locked

on her sapphire blue eyes, when she pulled away. He let her go, but immediately missed her warmth.

"I told you to wait outside," she pointed out, licking her glossed lips and running a hand down the front of her snug white blouse. The material pulled taut across her chest, framing her full breasts nicely.

He probably shouldn't be noticing that sort of thing about his ex-wife. But then, he was divorced, not dead.

In response to her chastisement, he shrugged a shoulder. Her annoyance amused him all to hell.

"You were taking too long. And besides, this is a public establishment. The sign in the window says Open. If it upsets you that much, consider me a customer." Reaching into his pocket, he retrieved his money clip and peeled off a couple of small bills. "Give me a cup of black coffee and something sweet. You choose."

Her eyes narrowed and she skewered him with a look of pure disdain. "I told you I don't want your money. Not even that," she added, her gaze flickering to the paltry amount he was holding out to her.

"Have it your way," he told her, sliding the bills back under the gold clip and the entire bundle back into his front trouser pocket. "So why don't you start the tour. Give me an idea of what you do here, how you got started and what your financials look like."

Vanessa blew out a breath, fluttering the thin fringe of her bangs and seeming to come to terms with the fact that she wasn't getting rid of him anytime soon.

"Where's Brian?" she asked, glancing past his shoulder and searching the front of the bakery for her financial advisor.

"I sent him back to his office," Marc answered. "Since he's already familiar with your business, I didn't think it was necessary for him to be here for the tour. I told him I would stop in or call after we've finished."

Tiny lines appeared above Vanessa's nose as she frowned, bringing her attention back to him, though he noticed she wouldn't quite meet his gaze.

"What's the matter?" he teased. "Afraid to be alone with me, Nessa?"

Her frown morphed into a full-fledged scowl, drawing her brows even more tightly together.

"Of course not," she snapped, crossing her arms over her chest, which only managed to lift her generous breasts and press them more snugly against the fabric of her blouse. "But don't get your hopes up, because we *aren't* going to be alone. Ever."

As hard as he tried, Marc couldn't stop an amused grin from lifting his lips. He'd forgotten just what a fiery temper his little wife had, but damned if he hadn't missed it.

If he had anything to say about it, they very well *would* be alone together at some point in the very near future, but he didn't bother saying as much since he didn't want to send her into a full-blown implosion in front of her customers.

"So where do you want to start?" she asked, apparently resigned to his presence and his insistence on getting a look at her bakery as a possible investment opportunity.

"Wherever you like," he acquiesced with a small nod.

It didn't take long for her to show him around the front of the bakery, given its size. But she explained how many customers they could serve in-shop and how much take-out business they did on a daily basis. And when he asked about the items in the display cases, she described every one.

Despite her discomfort at being around him again, he'd never seen her so passionate. While they'd been married, she'd been passionate with him, certainly. The sparks they'd created together had made Fourth of July fireworks look like the flare of a wooden matchstick in comparison.

But outside of the bedroom, she'd been much more

subdued, spending her time at the country club with his mother or working on various charitable committees—also with his mother.

When they met, Vanessa had been in college, not yet decided on a major and he freely admitted that he'd been the driving force behind her *not* graduating with the rest of her class. He'd wanted her too much, been too eager to slip his ring on her finger and make her his—body and soul.

But he'd always expected her to go back to school, and would have supported her a thousand percent, whatever she wanted to do with her life. Somehow, though, she'd gotten distracted and fallen into simply being his wife. A Keller woman whose main purpose was to look good on his arm, add reverence and prestige to the family name, and help raise money for worthy causes.

He wondered now, though, if that's what *she'd* wanted. Or if she'd maybe wanted more than to be simply Mrs. Marcus Keller.

Because while he knew she was proud of the fundraising work she'd done while they were married, she'd never talked about it with this level of enthusiasm in her voice or this much animation to her beautiful features.

He also wondered how well he'd really known his own wife, considering that—with the exception of a few romantic, candlelit meals she'd prepared for him while they were dating—he hadn't even realized she liked to cook or was a world-class baker. But after sampling some of her creations, he decided that if a successful business could stand on its product alone, she may just be sitting on a gold mine.

Finishing the last bite of the banana nut muffin she'd offered, he actually licked his fingers clean, wanting to savor every crumb.

"Delicious," he told her. "So why didn't you ever bake like this while we were married?"

He didn't know if it was his tone—which he'd thought was pleasant enough; he certainly hadn't meant for it to sound accusatory—or the question itself that got her dander up, but she immediately stiffened and took a step away from him, the brief pleasure he'd noted on her face fading away.

"I don't think your mother would have appreciated me messing up her pristine kitchen or getting in Cook's way," she replied tersely. "It might have been the Keller *family* estate, but she runs the place like a monarchy."

No doubt she was right. Eleanor Keller was rather stuck in her ways. Raised in the lap of luxury and used to servants bustling around her, ready to do her bidding, she wouldn't have looked kindly upon her own daughter-in-law doing something as lowly or mundane as preparing a meal or baking desserts, regardless of how talented she might be in that respect.

"You should have done it, anyway," Marc told her.

For a minute, Vanessa didn't reply, though her mouth tightened into a flat line. Then she murmured, "Maybe I should have," before spinning on her heel and leading him away from the counter and display cases.

She pushed through a set of swinging doors painted yellow with The Sugar Shack emblazoned on them in a playful white font and led him into the kitchen. Along with a wave of heat wafting from the industrial ovens lining one wall, the smell of baking was even stronger here, making him hope Vanessa might offer to let him sample a few more items as part of his tour.

While explaining the setup of the kitchen and how she and her aunt shared both baking and front counter duties, she moved around checking timers. Slipping a thick oven mitt on one hand, she began removing cookie sheets and pie pans, setting them on a wide metal island at the center of the room.

"A lot of the recipes are from Aunt Helen's personal

collection," she confided, using a nearby spatula to transfer cookies from sheet to cooling rack. "She's always loved to bake, but had never considered opening her own shop. I couldn't believe she wasn't earning a living with her talents, since everything she makes tastes like heaven. I'm pretty good in the kitchen myself—I must get it from her—" she added with a lopsided grin "—and I guess after a bit, the two of us decided to make a go of it together."

Marc rested his hands on the edge of the island, watching her work. Her movements were smooth and graceful, but also quick and efficient, as though she'd done this a million times before and could do it with her eyes closed, if necessary.

He definitely didn't want to close his eyes, though. He was enjoying the view, struck once again by how much he'd missed being near Vanessa.

The divorce had been so cut and dry, finished almost before he knew what was happening. One minute he'd been married to a beautiful woman he'd adored, thinking everything was fine. The next, she'd announced that she couldn't "live this way anymore" and wanted a divorce. Within a few short months, the papers had been signed and she'd been gone.

Looking back, he admitted that he probably should have fought harder to make their marriage work. At the very least, he should have asked why she was leaving him, what it was she needed that he wasn't giving her.

At the time, however, he'd been busy with the company and the demands of his family and let his pride take the position that he didn't want to be married to any woman who didn't want to be married to him. A part of him, he understood now, had also thought Vanessa was just being dramatic. That she was threatening him with divorce because he hadn't been as attentive to her as she might have wanted, or that once she saw that he wasn't going to put up a fight, she would change her mind and recognize how good she had it.

But that hadn't happened. She hadn't changed her mind and by the time he'd realized she wasn't going to, it had been too late.

"Blake showed me some of your financials," he said, wondering if she'd rap his knuckles with her spatula if he tried to snitch one of the mouthwatering, fresh-from-the-oven cookies. "It looks as though you're doing fairly well."

Without bothering to glance in his direction, she nodded. "We're doing okay. Could be better. We've got a lot of overhead, and the rent for this building wipes us out most months, but we're holding our own."

"Then why are you looking for an investor?"

Finishing up what she was doing, she set aside her spatula and oven mitt, and turned to face him more directly. He noticed, too, that she straightened slightly, shoulders pulling back as though she expected a confrontation.

"I have an idea for expansion," she said slowly, obviously weighing her words carefully. "It's a good idea. I think it will go over well. But it's going to require a bit of construction and more start-up cash than we've got at our disposal."

"So what's the idea?" he wanted to know.

She licked her lips and Marc watched the delicate tendons of her throat convulse as she swallowed before answering. "Mail order. I want to start with a Cookie-of-the-Month Club subscription service that could one day be turned into a catalog business for all of our products."

Judging by the quality of the items he'd tasted so far, he thought it sounded like a damn good prospect. He would certainly consider buying a year's worth of baked goods as quick and easy holiday gifts for numerous family members and business associates. And maybe even one for himself, because he would certainly enjoy a box of The Sugar Shack's cookies showing up on his doorstep once a month.

Not that he told Vanessa as much. Until he decided for sure

whether or not he was going to invest in her and her aunt's little bakery, it was better to keep his thoughts to himself.

"Show me where the construction would take place," he said instead. "I take it you have some back storage area that you could convert, or are maybe thinking of renting the empty building next door?"

She nodded. "The space next door."

Double-checking the rest of the timers and contents of the ovens, she made her way out of the kitchen, trusting Marc to follow. They passed a narrow stairwell outside of the kitchen but tucked away from the front of the shop so that it was nearly invisible to anyone who didn't know it was there.

"Where does that lead?" he asked, inclining his head.

If he wasn't mistaken, he thought Vanessa's eyes went wide and some of the color drained from her face.

"Nowhere," she said quickly. Then, apparently realizing that he would know *something* was at the top of those stairs, she added, "It's just a small apartment. We use it for storage, and as a place for Aunt Helen to nap throughout the day. She wears out easily."

Marc raised a brow. Unless she'd aged exponentially in the year or two since he'd last seen Vanessa's aunt, he found that hard to believe. The woman might be pushing eighty, but there wasn't a bone in her body that could be labeled *old,* and for as long as he'd known her, she'd had the disposition of a hummingbird. But he let it go, deciding that if the building's second story didn't have anything to do with the bakery or his possible investment, then there was nothing up there he needed to know about.

Instead, he allowed her to lead him back through the front of the bakery and outside to the space for rent next door. Though it was locked and they were unable to enter, he could see clearly through the plate glass windows that it was half the size of The Sugar Shack, but completely empty, which meant that there would be very little remodeling necessary to turn it into anything Vanessa wanted. And if his vision of the mail order aspect of the business matched hers, he imagined it wouldn't take much more than a few computers, several packing stations, and a direct and open path connecting it to The Sugar Shack for easy access.

While he continued to peer inside, studying the structure of the connected, unrented area, Vanessa stepped back, standing in the middle of the sidewalk.

"What do you think?" she asked.

He turned to find the afternoon sun glinting off her hair, making it shine like a new penny. A flash of desire hit him square in the chest, nearly knocking him back a pace. His throat clogged and he felt himself growing hard despite the knowledge that he had no right to be attracted to her any longer.

But then, who was he kidding? They might not be married anymore, but he had a feeling it would take a lot more than a signed divorce decree to keep his body from responding to his ex-wife's presence. Something along the lines of slipping into a coma or having a full frontal lobotomy.

Tamping down on the urge to step forward and run his fingers through her mass of copper curls—or do something equally stupid, like kiss her until her knees went weak—he said, "I think you've done very well for yourself." Without him, he was sorry to acknowledge.

She looked only moderately surprised by the compliment. "Thank you."

"I'm going to need some time to look at the books and discuss things with Brian, but if you're not still completely set against working with me, there's a good chance I'd be interested in investing."

If he'd expected squeals of joy or for her to throw herself into his arms in a display of unabashed appreciation, he was doomed to disappointment. She nodded sagely, but otherwise didn't respond.

And he didn't have a reason to stick around any longer.

"Well," he murmured, stabbing his hands into his pockets and rocking back slightly on his heels, "I guess that about does it. Thank you for the tour—and the samples."

Damn, he felt like a teenager out on his first date, and the polite smile she offered only made matters worse.

"I'll be in touch," he told her after a moment of awkward silence.

Tucking a strand of hair behind one ear, Vanessa tipped her head, but said, "I'd prefer you have Brian call me, if you don't mind."

He did mind and a muscle in his jaw ticked as he ground his teeth together to keep from saying so. As much as it annoyed him, though, he understood her reluctance to be in contact with him again. He suspected that even if he offered to sink a boatload of money into Vanessa's enterprise, she might refuse just on principle. A ridiculous principle that would only cause her to end up shooting herself in the foot, but principle all the same.

Vanessa remained on the sidewalk outside The Sugar Shack, watching as Marc walked away, back toward the offices of Blake and Fetzer. Not until he was well out of sight, and she felt sure he wasn't going to turn around and come back, did she let herself release a pent-up breath.

Then, as soon as the pressure in her chest eased and her heart was beating normally again, she spun around and returned to the bakery, heading straight for the stairs that led to the second floor apartment. Halfway up, she heard some of her aunt's favorite 1940s big band music playing, and beneath that, the sound of Danny fussing.

Taking the last several steps two at a time, she hurried in

and found her aunt pacing back and forth across the floor, bouncing and hushing and doing everything she could think of to calm the red-faced child in her arms.

"Poor baby," Vanessa said, reaching for Danny.

"Oh, thank goodness." Helen sighed in relief, more than happy to hand over her squalling charge. "I was just about to give him a bottle, but I know how much you prefer to feed him yourself."

"That's all right, I've got him now," Vanessa told her, continuing to bounce Danny up and down as she moved to the ugly, beige second-hand sofa along the far wall, unbuttoning her blouse as she went. "Thank you so much."

"How did things go? Is Marcus gone now?" Her aunt wanted to know.

"Yes, he's gone."

When the words came out more mumbled than intended, she realized it was because she wasn't entirely pleased with that fact. She might have thought Marc was out of her life for good, and may have been desperate to keep him away once he'd shown up in Summerville unexpectedly, but she realized now that seeing him again hadn't been entirely unpleasant.

One glance from those moss-green eyes and her body went soft and pliant. Her blood turned the consistency of warm honey, her brain functioning about as well as too-flat meringue.

Spending a short amount of time with him while she'd shown him around the bakery had been...not horrible. If it hadn't been for the secret she was hiding just one floor above, she may even have gotten him that cup of coffee and invited him to stay a while longer.

Which was a really bad idea, so it was better that he'd taken off when he had.

She had Danny pressed to her chest, content now that his belly was being filled, when she heard footsteps coming up the stairs. Considering that everyone who knew about the second floor apartment—namely she and Aunt Helen—was already up there, she suspected she was about to get a very rude surprise.

There was no time to jump up and hide the baby, no time to yell for Aunt Helen to run interference. One minute she was glancing around for a blanket to cover her exposed chest, and the next she was frozen in place, staring with alarm at her stunned but furious ex-husband.

Three

Marc honestly didn't know whether to be stunned or furious. Perhaps a mix of both. He wondered if the *whooshing* sound in his ears and the tiny pinpricks of white marring his vision would ever go away.

It wasn't hard to figure out what was going on.

First, Vanessa had lied to him. The space above the bakery wasn't used primarily for storage and as a place for her octogenarian aunt to nap when she started to feel run-down. It was actually a fully furnished and operable apartment, complete with a table and chairs, a sofa, a television…a crib in one corner and a yellow duckie blanket covered with baby toys in the middle of the floor.

Second, Vanessa had a child. She wasn't sitting for a friend; hadn't adopted an infant after their separation just for the thrill of it or to exert her independence. Even if she hadn't been *breast-feeding* the baby in her arms when he'd walked in the room, the protective flare in her eyes and the alarm written all over her face told him everything he needed to know about her connection to the child.

Third and finally, that baby was *his*. He knew it as well as he knew his own name. Felt it, deep down in his bones. Vanessa would never have been so determined to keep him from discovering she was a mother if that weren't the case—if she didn't believe she had something momentous to hide.

Not only that, but he hadn't become the CEO of his family's very successful textile company by being stupid. He could do the math. The only way Vanessa could have such a young infant was if she'd either been pregnant before their divorce had become final or if she'd been cheating on him with another man. And despite the differences that had pushed them apart, infidelity had never been one of them—not by him and not by her.

"Want to tell me what's going on here?" he asked, slipping his hands into the front pockets of his slacks.

It was safer that way. Burying his hands—now curled into tight, angry fists—in his pockets kept him from reaching out to strangle someone. Namely her.

And though his words might have been delivered in the form of a calm, unruffled question, the sharp chill of his tone let her know it was a demand. He wasn't going anywhere until he had answers. All of them.

Out of the corner of his eye, he saw a blur of blue-topped motion as Aunt Helen bustled forward and tossed a blanket over Vanessa's half exposed chest and the baby's head. Marc didn't know which was more disappointing—losing sight of his ex-wife's creamy flesh...or of the child he hadn't known existed until thirty seconds ago.

"I'll be downstairs," Helen murmured to her niece before turning a critical glare on him as she passed. "Yell if you need me."

What Aunt Helen had to be annoyed about, Marc couldn't

fathom. *He* was the victim here. The one who had never been told he was a father, who'd had his child kept from him for so long. He didn't know how old the baby was, exactly, but given the amount of time they'd been divorced and the nine months of her pregnancy, his guess would be about four to six months.

Vanessa and her wily Aunt Helen were the bad guys in this situation. Lying to him. Hiding pertinent facts from him for the past year.

After glancing over his shoulder to be sure they were finally alone, he took another menacing step forward.

"Well?" he prompted.

At first she didn't respond, buying some time by rearranging the lightweight afghan so that it covered her exposed flesh, but not the baby's face. Then with a sigh, she raised her head and met his gaze.

"What do you want me to say?" she asked softly.

Her seeming indifference had his molars grinding together and his fingers curling even tighter, until he thought his knuckles would pop through the skin.

"An explanation might be nice." *Followed by a few hours of abject groveling,* he thought with no small amount of sarcasm, while outwardly he struggled not to let his true level of annoyance show.

"I didn't realize it at the time, but I was pregnant before the divorce became final. We weren't exactly on speaking terms then, so I couldn't find a way to tell you, and to be honest, I didn't think you'd care."

Fury bubbled inside his chest. "Not care about my own child?" he growled. "Not care that I was going to be a father?"

What kind of man did she think he was? And if she could believe he was the sort of man who wouldn't care about his own flesh and blood, why had she bothered to marry him in the first place?

"How do you know it's your baby?" she asked in a low voice.

Marc laughed. A sharp, humorless bark of sound at the sheer ridiculousness of that question.

"Nice try, Vanessa, but I know you too well for that. You wouldn't have broken your vows to have some sleazy, sordid affair. And if you'd met someone you were interested in while we were still married…"

He trailed off, a sudden thought occurring to him that hadn't before. "Is that why you asked for a divorce? Because you met someone else?"

It would be just like her. She would never have cheated on him, never been physically unfaithful. But emotional infidelity was another matter, and toward the end, he had to admit that they hadn't been as close or connected as at the beginning of their relationship.

With his brother as second-in-command, he'd taken over the Keller Corporation and started spending longer and longer hours in the office or traveling for business. Vanessa had complained about feeling lonely and being treated like an outsider in her own home—which was something he could understand, given his mother's less-than-warm nature and the fact that she'd never really cared for the woman he'd married. Hadn't she made that clear from the moment he'd first brought Vanessa home for a visit and announced their engagement?

But even though he'd *heard* Vanessa's complaints, he knew now that he hadn't *listened*. He'd shrugged off her unhappiness, thinking perhaps she was turning into a bit of a bored trophy wife. He'd let himself be consumed by work and told himself it was just a phase—that she'd get over it. He even thought he remembered suggesting she find a hobby to keep her busy in hopes that it would distract her and keep her off his back.

No wonder she'd left him, he mentally scoffed now. *He'd* have left him after being dismissed like that.

By her own husband. The man who was suppose to love, honor and cherish her more than anyone else on the planet. Boy, he'd really messed up on that one, hadn't he?

As always, hindsight was twenty-twenty…and made him want to kick his own ass.

Which meant that if Vanessa *had* met another man, Marc couldn't really blame her for leaving him in hopes of moving into a situation that made her happier than the one she'd been in with him.

The thought of another man touching her, being with her—especially with his baby growing inside her belly—made his vision go red around the edges and his mind fill with images of tearing the aforementioned male who'd dared to touch his woman limb from limb. But he couldn't *blame* her, not when so much of what had gone wrong between them was his own fault.

"Is it?" he asked again, suddenly needing to know. Though he wasn't sure what difference it would make now.

"No," she answered quietly. "There was no one else. Not for me, anyway."

He raised a brow. "What does that mean? That you think *I* was being unfaithful?"

"I don't know, Marc. Were you? It would certainly explain all those extra hours you were supposedly spending at work."

"I had just taken over the company, Vanessa. A lot of things required my attention, practically around the clock."

"And I wasn't one of them, apparently," she muttered, bitterness clear in her tone.

Marc rubbed a spot between his eyes where a headache was

brewing. He'd heard that level of frustration and discontent in her voice before, so many times. The same as he'd heard her complain that he wasn't spending enough time with her.

But what choice did he have? And why couldn't she have cut him some slack? The twenty-four-hour workdays hadn't lasted forever. Nowadays, if he was at the office past five, it was usually because he didn't want to go home. Why bother, when there was nothing much there for him to enjoy other than a soft bed and a giant plasma television?

"This again?" he ground out. "Do we really have to get into this *again?*"

"No," she replied quickly. "That's the nice thing about being divorced—we really don't."

"So that's why you didn't tell me you were pregnant?" he demanded. "Because I wasn't paying enough attention to you before the divorce?"

A furrow appeared in her brow. At her breast, the baby continued to suckle, though he could only hear the sounds, not see the child's mouth actually at work.

"Don't be obtuse," she snapped. "I wouldn't keep something like that from you just because I was pouting or angry with you. If you'll recall, we didn't exactly part on the best terms, and *you* were the one who refused to speak to *me*. That sort of thing makes it difficult to have a personal heart-to-heart."

"You should have tried harder."

Blue eyes flashing, she said, "I could say the same about you."

Marc sighed, rocking back on his heels. It was nice to know that even after a year apart, they could jump right back to where they'd left off.

No growth or progress whatsoever, and to make matters worse, there was a whole new wrench thrown into the works. One with his blood running through its veins. One that he should have been told about from the very beginning.

But arguing with her about it or getting red in the face with fury over having his child kept from him for so long wasn't going to get him anywhere. Not with Vanessa. She would simply argue right back at him and they would end up exactly where they were—in a stalemate.

Striving instead for calm and diplomacy, he said, "I guess that's something we're going to have to agree to disagree about." For now. "But I deserve a few answers, don't you think?"

He could see her mulling that over, trying to decide how much pride or privacy it would cost her to share the details of the last year of her life…and fess up to something he suspected even she knew had been wrong—namely keeping his child from him.

"Fine," she relented after a moment, though she sounded none too pleased with the prospect.

While he weighed his options and tried to decide where to start, she shifted the baby in her arms and quickly rearranged her clothing beneath the veil of the knitted throw to make sure she was completely covered.

The child, Marc noticed, was sound asleep. Eyes closed, tiny pink mouth slack with sleep. And suddenly he knew exactly what he needed to know most of all.

"Is it a boy or a girl?" he asked, his throat clogging with emotion, making the words come out scratchy and thick.

"A boy. His name is Danny."

Danny. Daniel.

His son.

His chest grew tight, cutting off the oxygen to his lungs, and he was glad when Vanessa rose from the sofa, then turned to toss the afghan over the back so she wouldn't see the sudden dampness filling his eyes.

He was a father, he thought, blinking and doing his best

to surreptitiously suck in sharp, quick breaths of air in an attempt to regain his equilibrium.

When he and Vanessa had first gotten married, they'd discussed having children. He'd expected it to happen before long, been ready for it. When it hadn't in the first year, or the second, the idea had drifted further and further to the back of his mind.

And that had been okay. He'd been disappointed, he supposed, but so had she. But they'd still been happy together, still optimistic about the future, and cognizant of the fact that they hadn't even begun to explore all of their options yet. If getting pregnant the fun, old-fashioned way hadn't worked out, he was sure they'd have discussed adoption or in vitro or even fostering.

But as it turned out, they hadn't needed any of that, had they? No, she'd been pregnant when they'd signed the divorce papers.

"When did you find out?" he asked, following her movements as she trailed slowly across the room. The baby—Danny, his son—was propped upright against her shoulder now and she was slowly patting his back, bouncing slightly.

"A month or so after the divorce was final."

"That's why you moved away," he said quietly. "I expected you to stick around Pittsburgh after we split. Then I heard you'd left town, but I never knew where you'd gone." Not that he'd intentionally tried to check up on her, but he'd kept his ear to the ground and—admittedly—welcomed any news he managed to pick up through the grapevine.

She shrugged one slim shoulder. "I had to do something. There was nothing left for me in Pittsburgh and I was soon going to have a child to support."

"You could have come to me," he told her, just barely able to keep the anger and disappointment from seeping into his voice. "I would have taken care of you *and* my child—and you know it."

She stared at him for a moment, but her face was passive, her eyes blank, and he couldn't read her expression.

"I didn't want you to take care of us. Not out of pity or responsibility. We were divorced. We'd already said everything we had to say and gone our separate ways. I wasn't going to put us both back in a position we didn't want to be in just because our reproductive timing was lousy."

"So you came here."

She nodded. "Aunt Helen had only been living here a couple of years herself. She moved in with her sister when Aunt Clara became ill. After she died, Helen claimed the house was too large for one person and she could use the company. Unfortunately, she's never met a problem that couldn't be solved—or at least alleviated—with food, so she baked and I ate. Then one day, I got the brilliant idea that we should open a bakery together. Her recipes are amazing, and I've always been pretty handy in the kitchen myself."

"Good for you," Marc said.

And he meant it. It hurt to realize that he'd never known she had such amazing cooking or baking abilities, or that she'd preferred to move away and live with her aunt in Mayberry R.F.D. over coming to him when she'd discovered her pregnancy.

He certainly had the means to care for her and their son. Even if reconciliation hadn't been an option, he could have set her up in a small house or apartment, somewhere he could visit easily and spend as much time with his child as possible.

He could have provided for her, provided for his child, in ways she could never dream of simply by running a single bakery—no matter how popular—in such a rural area.

But then, Vanessa knew that, didn't she? She was well

aware of his and his family's financial situation. While they'd been married, if she'd asked him to buy her a private island paradise, he could have done so as easily as most people bought a pack of gum.

Which was probably why she'd chosen to move away and find a way to support herself. From the moment they'd met, his money hadn't impressed her. Oh, she'd enjoyed their two week honeymoon in the Greek isles, but she'd never wanted him to give her silly, expensive things just for the sake of it. She'd never wanted priceless jewels or a private jet, or even her own platinum card for unlimited shopping sprees.

When they'd first been married, she hadn't even wanted to move into his family home, despite the fact that his brother and his brother's family resided there and the estate was large enough to house a dozen families comfortably. Possibly without any of them coming into contact with the others for weeks at a time.

Keller Manor boasted a mansion the size of six football fields with separate *wings,* for heaven's sake, as well as three isolated cottages on its surrounding two hundred acres. But Vanessa had wanted to find an apartment of their own in town, then maybe later buy a house for just the two of them and any children that came along.

Marc wondered now if he shouldn't have gone along with her on that idea. At the time, staying at the mansion had been easy, convenient. He'd thought it would be the fastest way for Vanessa to bond with his family and start feeling like a true Keller.

Now, however… Well, considering how well that *hadn't* turned out, he was beginning to think he'd made a lot of wrong decisions while they were together.

After patting the baby on the back for a good five minutes—burping him, Marc assumed—Vanessa moved to a navy blue playpen and started to lean over, presumably to lay Danny down for the rest of his nap.

"Wait," he said, reaching out a hand and taking a step forward before halting in his tracks. What was he doing? Why had he stopped her?

Because he wasn't yet ready to lose sight of his son. Or to be distracted from the reality that he was suddenly a father. A *father*. A fact that part of him still couldn't seem to comprehend.

"Can I hold him?" he asked.

She looked down at the child sleeping in her arms, indecision clear on her face.

"If it won't wake him," he added as an afterthought.

Lifting her head, Vanessa met his gaze. It wasn't fear of waking the baby that caused her hesitation, he realized—it was her fear of having him near their son, of sharing a child who had been hers alone up until now. Not to mention a secret she'd had no intention of sharing anytime soon, but that had been unexpectedly revealed all the same.

Finally, with a sigh, she seemed to reach a decision. Or perhaps come to her senses, since they both knew there was no way he'd be kept from his child now that he was aware of Danny's existence. No way in hell.

"Of course," she said, the words sounding much more agreeable than she felt, he was sure. Meeting him halfway, she carefully transferred the child from her arms to his.

The last child Marc had held who was this size, this age, had to have been his three-year-old niece. But as adorable as his brother's children were, as much as he loved them, it didn't hold a candle to how he felt now, cradling *his own* child to his chest.

He was so tiny, so beautiful, so amazingly peaceful in sleep. Marc soaked in every minuscule feature, from the light dusting of brown hair covering Danny's head to his satin-soft cheeks, to the tiny fingers he curled and uncurled just beneath his chin.

Marc tried to imagine how Danny had looked as soon as he'd been born...his first day home from the hospital...how Vanessa had looked all rounded and glowing in pregnancy. Tried and failed, because he hadn't been there, hadn't known.

A furrow of irritation drew his brows together and he knew he couldn't leave Summerville without his son, without spending more time with him and hearing every detail of the months that he'd missed of this child's life.

Drawing his attention back to Vanessa, he said, "It looks like we've got a bit of a problem here. I've been left out of the loop and have some catching up to do. So I'm going to give you two choices."

Before she could interrupt, he pressed on. "You and Danny can either pack a bag and come back to Pittsburgh with me, or you can give me an excuse to stick around here. But either way, I *will* be staying with my son."

Four

Vanessa wanted nothing more than to snatch Danny away from Marc and go running. Find a place to hide herself and her baby until he lost interest and went back from whence he came.

She knew her ex-husband better than that, though, didn't she? He would be more inclined to give up breathing or walking upright than he would to walk away from his child.

There was nowhere she could go, nowhere she could hide that he wouldn't find her. So she might as well save herself the time and trouble and just face the music. She'd composed the symphony, after all.

She'd also been prepared to tell him about her pregnancy as soon as she'd discovered it for herself. Just because things hadn't worked out quite the way she'd planned didn't mean she should disregard her moral values now.

But that didn't mean she was ready to pack up and follow

him back to Pittsburgh like a lost puppy. She had a life here. Family, friends, a business to run.

On the other hand, the thought of Marc staying in Summerville made her heart palpitate and brought her as close to suffering a panic attack as she'd ever felt. How could she possibly handle having him underfoot—at the bakery and maybe even living with them at Aunt Helen's house?

She was trapped between the proverbial rock and a hard place, both of which looked suspiciously like her ex-husband. Stubborn, stoic, amazingly handsome in a suit and tie.

"I can't go back to Pittsburgh," she blurted out, pretending the sight of Marc holding their infant son in his big, strong arms didn't tug at parts of her that had no business being tugged.

"Fine," he said with a nod, his face resolute and jaw firm. "Then I guess I'm relocating."

Oh, no, that was worse. Wasn't it? Rock, hard place... rock, hard place. Her chest was so tight with panic, she was beginning to see stars from lack of oxygen.

"You can't stay here forever," she told him. "What about the company? Your family?" My sanity?

"It won't be forever," he responded.

Looking more reluctant than she'd ever seen him, he handed Danny back to her, careful not to wake him. Then he reached into his jacket pocket and removed a slim black cell phone.

"But if you think that anything back home—with the company or my family—is more important than being here with my son right now, you're crazy. I can afford to take a few weeks away, I just have to make sure everyone knows where I am and can keep things running smoothly in my absence."

With that, he turned and headed for the stairs leading back down to the bakery, dialing as he went.

Rocking back and forth, Vanessa stared down at her sleeping son and felt tears prickle behind her eyes.

"Oh, baby," she whispered, pressing a kiss to his smooth forehead. "We're in so much trouble."

For Vanessa, having Marc "move" to Summerville felt very much like when she'd first met him.

She'd been putting herself through school by waiting tables at an all-night diner near the college campus. He'd been attending school on his father's dime, breezing through classes and spending his free time playing football or attending frat parties.

He'd walked into the diner late one night with a pack of his friends, all of whom could have been male models for some brand of expensive cologne or another. She'd served them pancakes and eggs, and enough soda to float the *Titanic*. And even though she'd noticed him—she'd noticed all of them; how could she not?—she hadn't thought much of it. Why should she, when he was just one of a thousand different customers she served day in and day out? Not to mention one of the many young, carefree men who breezed through school—and life, it seemed—while she worked her fingers to the bone and burned the candle at both ends just trying to *stay* in school?

But then he'd shown up again. Sat in her section again. Sometimes with friends, other times by himself.

He'd smiled at her. Left huge tips, sometimes a hundred percent in addition to his check total. And made small talk with her. It wasn't until much later that she realized she'd told him nearly her entire life story in bits and pieces over a matter of weeks.

Finally, he'd asked her out and she'd been too enamored to say no. Half in love with him already and well on her way to head over heels.

Those same sensations were swamping her now. Shock, confusion, trepidation... He was a force to be reckoned with, much like a natural disaster. He was a tornado, an earthquake, a tsunami swooping in and turning her entire life upside down.

Within the hour, he'd been in touch with everyone he'd needed to contact back in Pittsburgh. Put out the word that he would be staying in Summerville indefinitely, and that his right-hand men—and women—were in charge of Keller Corp until further notice.

As far as Vanessa knew, though, he hadn't told them why he would be away for a while. She'd overheard him on the phone with his brother, but all Marc had said was that the business he was thinking of investing in looked promising and he needed to stick around to take a closer look at the premises and financials.

Keeping the true reason to himself was probably a smart move, she admitted reluctantly. No doubt if Eleanor Keller learned that her cherished son had a child with his evil ex-wife, she would go into a tizzy of epic proportions. Her already just-sucked-on-a-lemon expression would turn even more pinched and she would immediately begin plotting ways to get both Marc and Danny back into her circle of influence.

But not Vanessa. Eleanor would be plotting ways to *keep* Vanessa from reentering her or her son's lives.

Vanessa imagined that where Marc took it as a given that he was Danny's father, Marc's mother would insist on having a paternity test conducted as soon as possible. She would pray for a result that proved Danny was another man's child, of course, leaving Marc free and clear.

Free and clear of Vanessa, and free and clear to marry someone else. A woman Eleanor would not only approve of, but would probably handpick herself.

She didn't verbalize her inhospitable thoughts to Marc, however. He didn't know how truly horrid his mother had been to her while they'd been married and she saw no reason to enlighten him now.

"There," he said, pushing through the swinging door into the kitchen where she and Aunt Helen were keeping themselves busy. He slipped his cell phone into his pocket, then shrugged out of his suit jacket altogether.

"That should buy me a few weeks of freedom before the place starts to fall apart and they send out a search party."

Aunt Helen was up to her elbows in bread flour, but her feelings on the subject of Marc staying in town were clear in the narrow slits of her eyes and the force she was using to knead the ball of dough in front of her.

She didn't like it one little bit, but as Vanessa had told her while Marc was making phone calls, they didn't have a choice. Either Marc stuck around until he got whatever it was that he was after, or he would drag Vanessa and Danny back to Pittsburgh.

She'd considered a third option—sending Marc back to Pittsburgh on his own—but knew that if she pushed him on the issue, it would only cause trouble and hostility. If she refused to allow Marc time with his son, in one town or another, Vanessa had no doubt it would only spur her ex-husband to throw his weight and his family's millions around.

And what did that mean? A big, ugly custody battle.

She was a good mother, so she knew Marc could never take Danny away from her on that basis alone. But she didn't fool herself, either, that the system wouldn't be swayed by the amount of money and power the Kellers could bring to bear. Eleanor alone wasn't above bribery, blackmail or making up a series of stories to paint Vanessa in the most negative light possible.

No, if there was any way to avoid a custody fight or any amount of animosity with Marc whatsoever, then she had to try. It might even mean making arrangements for shared custody and traveling back and forth to Pittsburgh or having Marc travel back and forth to Summerville. But whatever it took to keep Marc happy and Danny with her, she would do.

Even if it meant letting her ex move into her life—and her business and possibly her house—for God knew how long.

Finished filling a tray with fresh squares of turtle brownies, Vanessa wiped her hands on a nearby dish towel. "What about your things?" she asked. "Don't you need to go home and collect your personal items?"

Marc shrugged, and she couldn't help but notice the shift of firm muscle beneath his white button-down shirt. She remembered only too well what lay beneath that shirt, and how much she'd once enjoyed knowing it belonged to her and her alone.

"I'm having some clothes and such shipped. Anything else I need, I'm sure I can purchase here."

He hung his jacket on a hook near the door, where she and Helen kept their aprons when not in use, then crossed to the bassinet she'd dragged back out of the storeroom once Marc had figured out what was going on. Danny was sleeping inside, stretched out on his little belly, arms and legs all akimbo.

"The only question now," Marc said, gazing down at his son, then reaching out to stroke a single finger over Danny's soft cheek, "is where I'll be staying while I'm in town."

Vanessa opened her mouth, not even sure what she was about to say, only to be interrupted by Helen.

"Well, you're not staying in my house," her aunt announced in no uncertain terms. Her tight, blue-washed curls bobbed as she used the heels of her hands to beat the ball of bread dough into submission.

Though her aunt's clear dislike of Marc brought an immediate stab of guilt and the sudden urge to apologize, Vanessa was unaccountably grateful that Helen had the nerve to blurt out what she'd been unable to find the courage to tell him herself.

"Thank you so much for the kind invitation," Marc said, lips twisted with amusement, "but I really couldn't impose."

How typical of him to take Helen's rudeness in stride. That sort of thing never had fazed him, mainly because Marc knew who he was, where he came from and what he could do.

Plus, Aunt Helen hadn't always hated him. She didn't hate him now, actually, she was just annoyed with him and took his treatment of Vanessa personally.

Which was at least partly Vanessa's fault. She'd shown up on her aunt's doorstep hurt, angry, broken and carrying her ex-husband's child.

After spilling out the story of her rocky marriage, subsequent divorce, unexpected pregnancy and desperate need for a place to stay—with Marc filling the role of bad guy-slash-mean old ogre under the bridge at every turn—her aunt's opinion of him had dropped like a stone. Ever since then, Aunt Helen's only objective was to *not* see her niece hurt again.

Vanessa was still fighting the urge to make excuses for Helen when Marc said, "I thought maybe you could recommend a nice local hotel."

Vanessa and Helen exchanged a look.

"Guess that would be the Harbor Inn just a couple streets over," Helen told him. "It's not much, but your only other option is Daisy's Motel out on Route 12."

"Harbor Inn," Marc murmured, brows drawing together. "I

didn't realize there was a waterway around here large enough to necessitate a harbor."

Vanessa and Helen exchanged another look, along with mutual ironic smiles.

"There isn't," Vanessa told him. "It's one of those small town oddities that no one can really explain. There's no harbor nearby. Not even a creek or stream worth mentioning. But the Harbor Inn is one of Summerville's oldest hotels, and it's decorated top to bottom with lighthouses, seagulls, fishing nets, starfish…"

She shook her head, hoping Marc wouldn't think too badly of the town or its residents. Even though some parts were a little backward at times, this was her home now and she found herself feeling quite protective toward it.

"If nothing else, it's an amusing place to stay," she added by way of explanation.

He looked less than convinced, but didn't say anything. Instead, he moved away from the bassinet and started to unbutton his cuffs, rolling the sleeves of his shirt up to his elbows.

"As long as it has a bed and a bathroom, I'm sure it will be fine. I'll be spending most of my time here with you, anyway."

Vanessa's eyes widened at that. "You will?"

One corner of his mouth quirked. "Of course. This is where my son is. Besides, if your goal is to expand the bakery and possibly branch out into mail-order sales, we've got a lot to discuss, and possibly a lot to do."

"Wait a minute." She let the spatula in her hand drop to the countertop, feeling her breath catch. "I didn't agree to let you have anything to do with The Sugar Shack."

He flashed her a charming, confident grin. "That's why we have so much to discuss. Now," he said, flattening his palms on the edge of the counter, "are you going to show me to this Harbor-less Inn, or would you prefer to simply give me directions so you and your aunt can both stay here and talk about me after I leave?"

Oh, she wanted to stay behind and talk about him. The problem was, he knew it. And now that he'd tossed down the gauntlet by effectively *telling* her he knew that's exactly what would happen the minute he left the room, she had no choice but to go with him.

Which was exactly why he'd done it.

Reaching behind her back, she untied the strings of her apron and pulled it off over her head.

"I'll take you," she said, then turned to her aunt. "Will you be okay on your own while we're gone?"

The question was just a formality; there were plenty of times when Vanessa left Helen in charge of the bakery while she ran errands or took Danny to the pediatrician. Still, her aunt shot her such a contemptible look that Vanessa nearly chuckled.

"All right. I'll be back in a bit."

She headed for the door, saying to Marc as she passed, "I just need to grab my purse."

He followed her out, waiting at the bottom of the stairs while she ran up to collect her purse and sunglasses.

"What about the baby?" he asked as soon as she returned.

"He'll be fine."

"Are you sure your aunt can take care of him *and* the bakery at the same time?" He pressed as they moved past the store-front's display cases and small round tables toward the door.

Vanessa smiled and waved at familiar customers as she passed. Once outside, she slipped on her sunglasses before turning to face him.

"Don't let Helen hear you asking something like that. She's liable to hurl a cookie sheet at your head."

He didn't laugh. In fact, he didn't look amused at all. Instead, he looked legitimately concerned.

"Relax, Marc. Aunt Helen is extremely competent. She runs the bakery by herself all the time."

"But—"

"*And* watches Danny at the same time. We both do. Truthfully, she's been a godsend," Vanessa admitted. "I don't know what I'd do without her."

Or what she would have *done* without her, when she'd found herself jobless, husbandless and pregnant all in the space of a few short months.

"So are we taking your car or mine?" she asked in an attempt to draw Marc's focus away from worrying about Danny.

"Mine," he said.

Vanessa kept pace with him as he turned on his heel and started down the sidewalk in the direction of Blake and Fetzer where he'd left his Mercedes. She was still dressed in the skirt and blouse she'd worn for her disastrous meeting earlier that morning. She wished now that she'd taken the time to change into something more comfortable. She especially wished she'd exchanged her heels for a pair of flats.

Marc, however, looked as suave and at ease as ever in his tailored suit pants and polished dress shoes. His jacket was slung over one shoulder, his other hand tucked casually into his slacks.

When they reached his car, he held the door while she climbed in the front passenger side, then rounded the back and slid in behind the wheel. He slipped the key in the ignition, then sat back in his seat, turning to face her.

"Will you do something for me before we head for the hotel?" he asked.

A shiver of trepidation skated beneath her skin and she immediately tensed. Hadn't she already done enough?

Wasn't she already *doing* enough simply by accepting Marc's presence in town when what she really wanted to do was snatch up her child and head for the hills?

She also couldn't help remembering the many times they'd been alone in a car together in the past. Their first dates, where they'd steamed up the windows with their passion. After they were married, when a simple trip to the grocery store or out to dinner would include soft, intentional touches and comfortable intimacy.

She was sure he remembered, too, which only added to the tightening of her stomach and nervous clench of her hands on the strap of her purse where it rested on her lap.

"What?" she managed to say, holding her breath for the answer.

"Show me around town. Give me the ten-dollar tour. I don't know how long I'll be here, but you can't be dropping everything every time I need directions."

Vanessa blinked and released her breath. Okay, that wasn't nearly as traumatizing as she'd expected. It was actually rather thoughtful of him.

Since her mouth had gone dry, for a second she could only lick her lips and bob her head in agreement. With an approving nod, he started the car and began to pull out of the lot.

"Which way?" he asked.

It took her a moment to think of where to start, and what she should show him, but Summerville was so small that she finally decided it wouldn't hurt to show him pretty much everything.

"Take a left," she told him. "We'll do Main Street, then I'll take you around the outskirts. We should end up at the Harbor Inn without too much backtracking."

A lot of the local businesses he could make out for himself. The diner, the drugstore, the flower shop, the post office. A little farther from the center of town were a couple of fast-food restaurants, gas stations and a Laundromat. In between the smattering of buildings were handfuls of houses, farms and wooded parcels.

She told him a bit of what she knew about her neighbors, both the owners of neighboring businesses and some of the residents of Summerville.

Like Polly—who ran Polly's Posies—and went around town every morning to deliver a single fresh flower to each store on Main Street free of charge. The vase she'd provided Vanessa was front and center on the counter, right next to the cash register, and even though she never knew what kind of flower Polly would choose to hand out on any given day, she had to admit the tiny dot of color really did add a touch of hominess to every single business in town.

Or Sharon—the pharmacist at Main Street Drugs—who had given Vanessa such wonderful prenatal advice and even set her up with her current pediatrician.

She had such close relationships with so many people in town. Something she'd never had while living in Pittsburgh with Marc. In the city, whether visiting the grocery store, pharmacy or dry cleaner's, she'd been lucky to make eye contact with the person behind the counter, much less make small talk.

Here, there was no such thing as a quick trip to the store. Every errand involved stopping numerous times to say hello and catch up with friendly acquaintances. And while she'd never missed that sort of thing before, she knew she would definitely miss it now if she woke up one day and realized it was no longer a part of her life.

"That's about it," she told him twenty minutes later, after pointing him in the general direction of the hotel where he would be staying. "There isn't much more to see, unless you're interested in a tour of the dairy industry from the inside out."

A small smile curved his lips. "I'll pass, thanks. But I think you missed something."

She frowned, wondering what he could possibly mean. She hadn't shown him the nearest volunteer fire department or water treatment plant, but those were several miles outside of town, and she didn't think he really cared about that sort of thing, anyway.

"You didn't show me where *you* live," he supplied in a low voice.

"Do you really need to know?" she asked, ignoring the spike of heat that suffused her from head to toe at the knowing glance he sent her.

"Of course. How else will I know where to pick you up for dinner?"

Five

As much as Vanessa would have liked to argue with Marc about his heavy-handedness, in the end, she didn't bother. He had a nasty habit of getting his way in almost every situation, anyway, so what was the point?

She'd also reluctantly decided that, for as long as Marc was determined to stay in her and Danny's lives, it was probably better to simply make nice with him. There was no sense antagonizing him or fighting him at every turn when he potentially held so much of her future in his hands.

At the moment, the only thing he seemed to want was time with and information about his son. He wasn't trying to take Danny away from her or making threats about trying to take him later, even though they both knew he was probably within his rights to do so.

The threatening part, not the actual taking. But if she were in his shoes, anger and a sense of betrayal alone would have had her yelling all manner of hostile, menacing things.

So this afternoon when Marc asked her to show him where she lived with Aunt Helen, she took him to the small, two-story house on Evergreen Lane. It wasn't much compared to the sprawling estate where he'd grown up with servants and tennis courts and a half mile, tree-lined drive just to reach the front gate, but in the last year, it had become home to her.

Helen had given up her guest room to Vanessa and helped turn her sewing room into a nursery for Danny. She'd volunteered her kitchen to thousands of hours of trial and error with her family recipes before they'd felt brave enough to move forward with the idea of actually opening a bakery of their very own.

In return, Vanessa helped with the general upkeep of the house, had planted rows of brand-new pink and red begonias in the flower beds lining the front porch and walk, and had even taught Helen enough about computers to have her emailing with friends from grade school she'd never thought to be in contact with again.

Though Vanessa still believed there was no way she could ever truly repay her aunt's kindness in her time of need, Helen insisted she enjoyed the company and was happy to have so much youth and activity in the house again. Which, in Vanessa's book, made the tiny white house on less than an acre of mottled green and yellow grass more of a home than Keller Manor, with all its bells and whistles, could ever be.

Taking a deep breath, she checked herself over in the bathroom mirror one last time—though she wasn't sure why she bothered. Yes, it had been a while since she'd had a reason to get so dressed up, let alone get so dressed up twice in one day.

But even though jeans and tennies were more her style these days, Marc had seen her in everything from ratty shorts and T-shirts to full-length ball gowns and priceless jewels.

Besides, she wasn't attempting to impress him this evening, was she? No, she was pacifying him.

After showing him to the Harbor Inn and then letting him drop her off at The Sugar Shack once again, Vanessa had finished off her day at the bakery, closed up shop, and headed home with Danny and her aunt. While Helen had fixed dinner for herself and kept Danny entertained, Vanessa had run upstairs to change clothes and retouch her makeup.

She wasn't fixing herself up for Marc, she told her reflection. She wasn't. It was simply that she was taking advantage of a dinner invitation that included the chance to look like a woman for a change instead of a frazzled working mother struggling to be a successful entrepreneur.

That's the only reason she was wearing her favorite strapless red dress, strappy red heels and dangling imitation ruby earrings. It was over-the-top for even the priciest restaurant in Summerville, but she didn't care. She might never get the opportunity to wear this outfit again...or to remind Marc of just what he'd given up when he let her go.

The doorbell rang before she was ready for it and her heart lurched in her chest. She quickly swiped on another layer of lipstick, then made sure she had everything she needed in the tiny red clutch she'd dug out of the back of her closet.

Halfway down the stairs, she heard voices and knew Aunt Helen had answered the door in her absence. She didn't know whether to be grateful or nervous about that; it depended, she supposed, on Aunt Helen's current disposition.

At the bottom of the landing, she found Aunt Helen standing inside the open door, one hand on the knob. No shotgun or frying pan in sight, which was a good sign.

Marc stood on the other side of the door, still on the porch. He was dressed in the same charcoal suit as earlier, forest-green tie arrow straight and jacket buttoned back in place. His hands were linked behind his back and he was smiling down at Aunt Helen with all the charm of a used car salesman. When he spotted her, Marc transferred that dimpled grin to her.

"Hi," he said. "You look great."

Vanessa resisted the urge to smooth a hand down the front of her dress or recheck the knot of her upswept hair. "Thank you."

"I was just telling your aunt what a lovely home she has. At least from the outside," he added with a wink, likely because Aunt Helen had obviously failed to invite him inside.

"Would you like to come in?" Vanessa asked, ignoring her aunt's sidelong scowl.

"Yes, thank you." Marc ignored the scowl, too, brushing past Aunt Helen and into the entranceway.

He gave the house a cursory once-over and Vanessa wondered if he was comparing it to his own lavish residence, possibly finding it lacking as an appropriate place for his child to be raised. But when he turned back, his expression held no censure, only mild curiosity.

"Where's Danny?" he asked.

"The kitchen," Helen supplied, closing the front door, then moving past them in that direction. "I was just giving him his dinner."

Marc shot Vanessa a glance before waving her ahead of him as they followed Helen through the living area to the back of the house. "I thought you were still breast-feeding."

She flushed, feeling heat climb over her cheeks toward her hairline. "I am, but not exclusively. He also gets juice, cereal and a selection of baby food."

"Good," he murmured with a short nod, watching as Aunt Helen rounded the kitchen table and took a seat. "The longer a child breast-feeds, the better. It increases immunity, builds the child's sense of security and helps with mother/child bonding."

"And how do you know that?" she asked, genuinely surprised.

Danny was strapped into his Winnie the Pooh swing, face and bib spattered with a mixture of strained peas, strained carrots and applesauce. He looked like a Jackson Pollock painting as he kicked his feet and slapped his hands against the plastic sides of the seat that held him.

Without waiting for an invitation, Marc sat down opposite Aunt Helen, leaning in to rub Danny's head. The baby giggled and Marc grinned in return.

"Contrary to popular belief," he murmured, not bothering to turn in her direction, "I didn't become CEO of Keller Corp by nepotism alone. I actually happen to be quite resourceful when I need to be."

"Let me guess—you dug out your laptop and hit the internet."

"I'm not telling," he answered, tossing her a teasing half smile. Then to Aunt Helen, he said, "May I?" indicating the array of baby food jars spread out in front of her.

The older woman gave him a look that clearly said she didn't think he was capable, but she waved him on all the same. "Be my guest."

He picked up the miniature plastic spoon with a cartoon character on the handle and began feeding Danny in tiny bites, waiting long enough in between them for the baby to gum and smack and swallow.

Vanessa stood back, watching…and wishing. Wishing she hadn't agreed to go out to dinner with Marc this evening, after all. Wishing she hadn't invited him in and that he hadn't wanted to see Danny before they left. Wishing this whole scene wasn't so domestic, so bittersweet, so much of a reminder of what could have been.

Marc looked entirely too comfortable feeding his son, even dressed as he was in a full business suit. He was also oddly good at it, which she wouldn't have expected from a man who hadn't spent much time around babies before.

When Danny began to fuss and wouldn't take another bite, Marc set aside the jars and spoon, and brushed his hands together.

"I'd like to pick him up for a minute," he said, splitting his gaze between his expensive suit and his infant son, who was doing his best imitation of a compost pile, "but…"

"Definitely not," Vanessa agreed, grabbing a damp cloth to wipe the worst of the excess food from Danny's mouth and chin. "Let Aunt Helen get him cleaned up and maybe you can hold him when we get back, if he's still awake."

Marc didn't look completely pleased with that idea, but since the alternative was ruining a suit that probably cost more than most people's monthly mortgage payment, he wisely refrained from reaching out and getting covered by Gerber's finest.

"Shouldn't we go?" she prompted as he pushed to his feet and Aunt Helen rounded the table to scoop Danny from the swing.

Still looking reluctant to leave, Marc nodded and followed her back through the house to the front door. Outside, he led her to his car, which was parked at the curb, and helped her inside.

"What do you do when he's a mess like that?" Marc asked once he'd climbed in beside her.

She twisted in her seat to face him, noticing the frown pulling at the corners of his mouth. "What do you mean?"

"How do you not pick up your own child?"

Vanessa blinked, wondering if she'd heard him correctly. Oh, she heard the words clearly enough, but was that a hint of guilt stealing through his tone? *Guilt* from a man she hadn't thought understood the concept? Who'd let her walk away without a fight, with barely an explanation?

"Marc." Shaking her head, she ducked her chin to keep him from seeing the amusement tugging at her lips. "I know this is all new to you. I know finding out about Danny was quite a shock, but you have nothing to feel guilty about. He's a baby. As long as all of his needs are met, he doesn't care who's feeding him, who's holding him, who's changing his diaper."

If anything, Marc's frown deepened. "That isn't true. Infants know the difference between their parents and simply a babysitter, between their mother and their father."

"All right," she acquiesced, "but rest assured that there are plenty of times I don't pick him up right after he's eaten because I don't want him to get food on my clothes. Or worse yet, yurk on me."

"Yurk?"

"It's what Aunt Helen and I call a 'yucky burp,'" she explained, wrinkling her nose in distaste. "Believe me, once you've had soured milk or formula spit up all over you, you learn fast not to wear nice clothes around a baby and to keep a towel handy."

Without a thought of what she was doing, she reached across the console and patted his thigh. "If you're going to be in town for a while to spend time with him, get yourself some nice, cheap jeans and T-shirts, and expect them to get dirty on a regular basis. But don't worry about tonight. I didn't hold him this morning, either, because I was dressed up for my meeting with you. That's one of the great things about having Aunt Helen around. I can't do everything all by myself and she helps to pick up the slack."

Meeting her gaze, Marc wrapped his fingers around hers, holding her hand in place, even when she tried to pull it away. "I should be the one helping you with Danny, not your aunt. But don't worry, we're going to talk about that over dinner. Among other things."

* * *

Despite the threat of The Big Talk and being pinned to her chair like a bug under Marc's intense scrutiny and personal version of the Spanish Inquisition, dinner was actually quite enjoyable. He took her to the hotel's dining room, which was actually one of the more moderately upscale restaurants in town and attempted to ply her with wine and crab cakes. Of course, since she was breast-feeding, the wine was a no-no, but the crab cakes were delicious. Maybe because he let her eat them in peace.

As soon as the waitress topped off their coffees and they'd made their dessert selections, however, she knew the stay of execution was over. Marc cupped his hands around the ceramic mug and leaned forward in his seat, causing her to tense slightly in her own.

"What was the pregnancy like?" he asked, getting straight to the point, as usual.

Vanessa blew out a small breath, relieved that he was at least starting out with an easy question instead of immediately launching into demands and ugly accusations.

"It was pretty typical, I think," she told him. "Bearing in mind I'd never been pregnant before and didn't really know what to expect. But there were no complications and even the morning sickness wasn't too bad. It didn't always limit itself to mornings, which made getting the bakery open and working twelve-hour days a bit of an adventure," she added with a chuckle, "but it wasn't as terrible as I'd expected."

From there he wanted to know every detail of Danny's birth. Date, time, length, weight, how long her labor had lasted—all facts that she'd taken for granted. In his shoes, though, she could imagine how desperate she would be to learn and memorize every one of them.

"I should have been there," he said softly, staring down at

the table. Then he lifted his gaze to hers. "I *deserved* to be there. For all of it."

Her heart lurched and she braced herself for the onslaught, for every bit of anger and resentment she knew he had to be feeling...and that she probably deserved. But instead of lashing out, his voice remained level.

"As much as it bothers me, there's no going back, we can only move forward. So here's the deal, Vanessa."

His green eyes bore into her, the same look she suspected he gave rival business associates during mergers and tricky acquisitions.

"Now that I know about Danny, I want in on everything. I'll stick around here for a while, until you get used to that idea. Until I get the hang of being a father and he starts to recognize me that way. But after that, I'm going to want to take him home."

At that, at the mention of his home, not hers, Vanessa went still, her shoulders stiffening and her fingers tightening on the handle of her coffee cup.

"That's not a threat," he added quickly, obviously noticing how tense her body had gone. "I'm not saying I want to take him back to Pittsburgh forever. I honestly don't know yet how we're going to work out the logistics of that, but we can discuss it later. I'm only talking about a visit so I can introduce him to my family, let my mother know she has another grandchild."

Oh, Eleanor would love that, Vanessa thought with derision. She'd be thrilled with another grandchild, especially another *male* grandchild to carry on the Keller name. But that grandchild's mother was another story—and Marc's mother would only truly be happy with Vanessa out of the picture.

"And what if I don't agree? To any of it."

One dark brow winged upward. "*Then* I'll be forced to threaten, I suppose. But is that really the direction you want to go? I've been pretty amicable about this entire situation so far, even though I think we both know I have more than enough reason to be furious over it."

Taking a sip of his coffee, he tipped his head to the side, looking much calmer than she felt.

"If you want me to be furious and toss around ugly threats you know I can follow through on, that's fine, just say the word. But if you'd rather act like two mature adults determined to create the best environment possible for their child, then I suggest you go along with my plans."

"Do I have a choice?" she grumbled, understanding better than ever the adage about being stuck between a rock and a hard place.

Marc's smile was equal parts cocky and confident. "You had the choice of whether or not to tell me you were pregnant in the first place, and you decided not to, so…not really. The ball is in my court now."

Six

The ball was most definitely in Marc's court—along with everything else. But then, she'd known that the minute he'd walked up the stairs to the bakery's second-floor apartment and discovered he had a son, hadn't she? Her only option now was to play nice and hope he would continue to do the same.

Marc's hand was on her elbow as they left the restaurant, guiding her along the carpeted passage toward the lobby. Old fishing nets and decorative life preservers lined the walls and she suddenly realized how odd the decor must seem to outsiders.

Those who were familiar with Summerville never gave it a second thought, but anyone coming into town for the first time must wonder at the hotel's name and decor without a significant body of water nearby to back them up. Especially since the hotel's dining room didn't even particularly specialize in seafood dishes.

"Come upstairs with me," he murmured suddenly just above her ear.

Tearing her gaze from a large plastic swordfish caught in one of the nets, she flashed Marc a startled, disbelieving look, only to have him chuckle at her reaction.

"That isn't a proposition," he assured her, then waggled his eyebrows in an exaggerated attempt at flirtation. "Although I wouldn't be opposed to a bit of after-dinner seduction."

At the lobby, he steered her to the left, away from the hotel's main entrance and in the direction of the wide, *Gone with the Wind*-esque stairwell that led to the guest rooms.

"I have something to show you," he continued as they slowly climbed the stairs, her heels digging into the thick carpeting, faded in places from years of wear.

"Now that sounds like a proposition. Or maybe a bad pickup line," she told him.

He slanted her a grin, digging into his pocket for the key to his room. Not a key card, but an honest to goodness key, complete with a giant plastic fob in the shape of a lighthouse.

"You know me better than that. I didn't need cheesy pickup lines with you the first time around, I don't need them now."

No, he hadn't. He'd been much too charming and suave to hit on her the way ninety percent of guys did back then. Which was only one of the things that had made him more appealing, made him stand out from the pack.

When they reached his door, he unlocked it, then stepped back to let her pass into the room ahead of him. She'd visited the Harbor Inn before, of course, but had never actually been in one of the guest rooms, so for a second she stood just inside the door, taking in her surroundings.

Even if the large brass plaque on the front of the building hadn't identified the hotel as a historical landmark, she would have known it was old simply from the interior. The elaborately carved woodworking, the barely preserved wallpaper and the antique fixtures all would have tipped her off. Certain things had been updated, of course, to keep the hotel functional and modern enough that guests would be comfortable, but a lot had been left or restored to maintain as much of the original furnishings and adornments as possible.

Marc's room was blissfully lacking in the oceanside motif. Instead, the walls boasted tiny pink roses on yellowing wallpaper, and both the single window and four-poster bed were covered in white eyelet lace. Very old-fashioned and grandmotherly.

It was almost funny to see tall, dark, modern businessman Marc standing in the middle of all the extremely formal, nineteenth century finery. He looked completely out of place, like a zebra in the dolphin enclosure at the zoo.

But *looking* out of place and *being* out of place were two different things, and Marc didn't seem to feel the least bit out of place. Closing the door behind them, he shrugged out of his charcoal suit jacket and tossed it over the back of a burgundy brocade wing chair on his way to the brass-plated desk against the far wall.

While he lifted the lid of his laptop and hit the button to boot up the computer, Vanessa stood back and enjoyed the view. Shallow of her, she was sure. Not to mention inconsistent, considering how vehemently she protested—to herself and anyone else who would listen—that the divorce had been a blessing and she was over him. Completely and totally over him.

Being his *ex*-wife didn't keep her from being a living, breathing, red-blooded woman, however. And every one of the red-blooded cells in her body appreciated the sight of a healthy, well-built man like Marc walking away.

His broad shoulders and wide back stretched the material of his expensive white dress shirt as he moved. Dark gray slacks that probably cost more than she made at the bakery in a week hugged his hips, and more importantly, his butt. A very nice, well-rounded butt that didn't seem to have changed much since they'd been together.

Lifting a hand to her face, she covered her eyes and silently chastised herself for being so weak-willed. What was wrong with her? Was she crazy? Or catching a bug? Or were her hormones still dreadfully out of whack because of the pregnancy?

Spreading her fingers a few brief centimeters, she peeked through and knew exactly what her problem was.

Number one—she knew what lay beneath all that cotton and wool. She knew the strength of his muscles, the texture of his skin. She knew how he moved and how he smelled and how he felt pressed up against her.

Number two—her hormones probably *were* out of whack—and not just the pregnancy variety. The regular ones seemed to be turned all upside down, as well.

Which was no surprise. She'd always been a total pushover where Marc was concerned. One smoldering look and her bones had turned to jelly. One brush of his knuckles across her cheek or light touch of his lips on hers and she'd been putty in his hands.

Given how long it had been since they'd been together—how long it had been since she'd been anything more than a human incubator and a first-time mommy—it was no wonder, really, that her mind was wandering down all sorts of deliciously naughty garden paths.

And no doubt if Marc knew, or even suspected, he would take full advantage of her vulnerability and inner turmoil, so it would be wise of her not to do or say anything to give him the wrong idea. Or any ideas at all, for that matter.

Through her fingers, Vanessa watched him undo the top couple of buttons of his shirt and loosen his collar. Such a familiar habit. She remembered him doing the same thing almost every night when he got home from work. He would usually spend a couple of hours in his home office, but taking off his jacket and tie, loosening his collar and rolling up his sleeves were the first steps toward relaxing for the evening.

She lowered her hands from her face just before he picked up the laptop and turned back around. Crossing the room, he lowered himself to the edge of the bed, set the laptop beside him, and then patted the pristine white coverlet.

"Come sit down for a minute," he said, "I want to show you something."

Vanessa raised a brow. "That sounds like another bad pickup line," she told him.

Marc chuckled. "Since when did you become so cynical? Now, come here so I can show you some of these plans I worked up for The Sugar Shack."

That got her attention, allaying some of her suspicions and fears—and giving rise to new ones. Moving to the bed, she sat down, tucking the skirt of her dress beneath her to keep from flashing too much leg.

He clicked a couple of buttons, then turned the screen so she could see it more easily. "You said you want to expand into the store space next door, right? Use it for a possible mail-order division of the business."

"Mmm-hmm."

"Well, this is a quick prospectus I worked up before dinner for what I think it would cost to renovate the space, what your expenses and overhead would be, et cetera. Of course, there are a lot of aspects to the bakery business I'm sure I'm not familiar with, so it will need to be adjusted. But this gives us a rough estimate and an idea of where to start."

He got up for a second and stretched to reach the bureau,

grabbing a large yellow legal pad before returning to the bed, sending the mattress bouncing slightly.

"And this is a rudimentary sketch of a possible layout for the expansion. Counters and shelving and such."

She pulled her attention away from the document on the computer screen to the tablet he was holding out to her. She studied the drawing for a minute, picturing everything exactly as it would look next door to The Sugar Shack.

It was good. Encouraging, even. And the idea that something so simple might one day soon be a reality caused her heart to leap in her chest.

There was only one problem.

Lifting her head, she met Marc's gaze. "Why did you do all this?" she asked, passing the legal pad back to him.

"Nothing is written in stone," he murmured, setting aside the tablet and turning the laptop back toward him. "And it won't be cheap, believe me. But the expansion is a good idea. I think it's a smart move and has the potential to really pay off in the long run. Especially if you do well enough to start that Cookie-of-the-Month Club thing you mentioned."

Her heart jumped again, making her palms damp and her throat tight. It was so nice to hear someone sharing her enthusiasm about branching out with the bakery and actually supporting her ideas.

But in this case, there were strings attached. So many strings.

"That doesn't answer my question," she said softly. And then she asked again, even though a part of her was afraid of his response. "Why did *you* do all this?"

He sat back, clicking the lid of the laptop closed and moving the computer to the nightstand, along with the legal pad.

"You need a partner to pull this off, Vanessa. You know

that, or you wouldn't have gone to Blake and Fetzer for help."

Her pulse slowed and the temperature in the room fell ten degrees. Or maybe it was only her own internal temperature that dropped like a stone.

"I told you, Marc, I won't take your money."

Shoulders going back, his spine straightened almost imperceptibly, and his jaw went square and tight. A clear indication he was about to get stubborn and lay down the Law According to Marc Keller.

Mouth a thin, flat line, he said, "And I told you, Vanessa, that I'm not going anywhere. Not for a while, anyway."

A beat passed while the tension seemed to leak from his stiff form and jump across the bed into her. The last thing she needed was a reminder of Marc's refusal to leave town now that he knew about Danny, and all the fears and concerns his presence brought to the surface.

"So as long as I'm sticking around," he continued, "we might as well use the time wisely. Why not get started on the expansion and put you one step closer to your goal?"

Oh, he was smooth and made so much sense. She'd always hated that, because it put him entirely too close to being right.

Of course, he usually *was* right, at least where business issues were concerned, which was even more annoying. Especially since he knew it and often came across as just this side of smug in that awareness.

"I don't want your help, Marc."

Rising from the bed, she linked her arms around her middle and paced across the room. When she hit the closed door, she turned and paced back, keeping her gaze locked on the worn and faded carpeting beneath her feet.

"I don't want to be tied to you, to owe you for anything."

"Well, it's a little late for that, don't you think?"

She stopped, lifted her head to meet his eye. One dark brow was raised, his lips curled in a wry half smile.

"We have a child together. I'd say that ties us together more strongly than any business plan or partnership ever could."

She blinked. Dammit. There it was again. He was right and being smug about it.

For better or worse, they *were* tied to each other now until the end of time through their son. Birthdays, school events, extracurricular activities, chicken pox, measles, puberty, girlfriends, his first tattoo or piercing…

She shuddered. Oh, God, please no piercings or tattoos. That might actually be the one parental matter she'd happily delegate to Marc for a good old-fashioned father-to-son heart-to-heart.

But given how ugly and heartbreaking—at least on her part—their separation had been, it was no wonder she wasn't looking forward to sharing any of that with him. And no wonder she'd tried to keep Danny a secret to begin with. It might not have been the right thing to do, but it sure made life a lot less complicated.

"That's different," she said quietly.

He inclined his head, though whether in agreement or simply acquiescence, she wasn't sure.

"However you feel about that," he said slowly, "it doesn't change the facts. I'm going to be in Summerville, getting to know my son and make up for lost time, for several weeks, at least. You might as well take advantage of that—and of my willingness to invest money into your bakery."

Pushing up from the bed, he came to stand in front of her, cupping his hands over her shoulders. His slightly callused palms felt rough against her bare skin, his warmth seeping into her pores.

"Think about it, Nessa," he murmured barely above a whisper. His eyes, as green and lush as summer moss, bored into hers. "Use your head here instead of sticking to stubborn pride. The smart and savvy businesswoman in you knows I'm right, knows this is an opportunity you'd be crazy to pass up. Even if it is coming from your despicable ex-husband."

He said the last with a quick wink and a self-deprecating quirk of his full, sexy lips.

It was that wink and the fact that he knew how badly she *didn't* want him around but apparently wasn't holding it against her that made her stop and think, just as he'd suggested.

Think through his offer logically and reasonably, and with the level-headed, straightforward intelligence that had convinced her to take the risky financial plunge of opening The Sugar Shack with Aunt Helen in the first place. Weigh her options. Weigh her desire to expand the bakery and accept a much-needed infusion of cash and support against her desire to keep Danny to herself, keep miles upon miles of distance between her and Marc—both figuratively and literally—and maintain complete control over her business rather than sharing it with a third party who may or may not be as genuinely committed to its growth and success as she and her aunt were. Or worse yet, had the power to crush her and her business at the slightest provocation.

And there would be provocation, wouldn't there? There already was, in that she'd kept first her pregnancy and then Danny's existence from him to begin with.

For all she knew, he could be hiding his true feelings from her, being kind and considerate and generous in an effort to lull her into a false sense of security. Then the minute she agreed to take his money, to let him partner with her in the bakery and to be a part of Danny's life, he would spring the trap, taking *everything* from her.

Her business, her security, her *son*.

Did she really believe that, though? Despite the bitterness

involved on both sides of their divorce, he had never been deliberately cruel. He hadn't tried to hurt her, hadn't used his powerful influence or family fortune to leave her destitute.

Thanks to the prenuptial agreement his family—or more to the point, his mother—had insisted on before their wedding, Vanessa had left the marriage with not much more than she'd walked into it with, but she was well aware that it could have been worse.

She had friends who had gone through much nastier divorces. She'd heard the horror stories where women who had been married to extremely wealthy men were put through the wringer and kicked onto the street with barely the clothes on their backs, sometimes with their children in tow.

Marc had never been that type of man. He'd always had a very low-key personality, opting for silent fury over angry blow-ups.

Even during their marriage, he might not have been as attentive as she would have liked or taken her complaints about his family or his distance seriously, but he had never resorted to petty arguments or name-calling. A couple of times, she'd even wished for something like that, if only as proof that he still cared enough to fight. With her or for her; back then, either would have translated as caring *at all*.

But his response to marital conflict had always been to lock his jaw, slip into stony silence and go back to the office to work even longer hours that pushed them even farther apart.

Marc was also one of the most honest men she'd ever met. It would be just like him to compartmentalize their current relationship.

Anything involving Danny would remain strictly personal, and he would deal with her on a personal, father-to-mother level. Anything involving her bakery would remain strictly a business venture and he would treat it as such.

If he pulled out of The Sugar Shack, it would be only his money and professional ties that went with him, not his love for Danny or determination to be in his son's life. And on the other side of the coin, if they were at odds about something that concerned Danny, he would never pull his financial backing of the bakery just to make her life miserable.

Unfortunately, she'd never been quite as good at keeping her work and her personal life separated. She loved The Sugar Shack. It was a part of her, built of blood, sweat, tears and most of all, heart. If it failed, if something happened to it or she had to close the doors, a very big part of her would die with it.

But even more important than that, and definitely what owned a much bigger portion of her heart and soul, was Danny. She would light a match and torch The Sugar Shack down to the ground if it meant keeping her child happy and safe.

And for better or worse, Marc was Danny's father, a part of him. He was also probably the only investor she would ever find who was actually willing and able to give the bakery an influx of much-needed cash, and who apparently thought her ideas for expansion held actual merit.

Anyone else would have already jumped at the offer. But there was so much at stake for her—and for Danny and Aunt Helen.

She'd been silent for so long, she was surprised Marc didn't check her for a pulse. She also suspected she would have the mother of all headaches soon just from the strain of thinking so hard. It was as though a Ping-Pong championship tournament was taking place inside her brain.

But in the end, she didn't follow her head or even her heart. She followed her gut.

"All right," she told him, the words nearly torn from a throat gone tight with the strain of her internal struggle. "But

I don't want your charity. If we're going to do this, then I want it to be completely official and aboveboard. We'll have Brian draw up investment papers, or make it a legal loan that I *will* pay back, or however these things are normally done."

Marc smiled gently, the sort of smile a parent offers a recalcitrant child, almost as though he was getting ready to humor her.

"Fine. I'll call Brian in the morning and get the ball rolling."

She nodded slowly, still reluctant, still unsure. Gut or no gut, agreeing to let Marc become a partner in her and her aunt's business still made her hugely uncomfortable, and there was no guarantee that it wasn't a monumental mistake.

"So that's the business end of things. We'll iron out the details tomorrow," he said. Then he ran his hands down the bare flesh of her arms from her shoulders to her elbows and lowered his voice to a near whisper. "Now on to something a bit more personal."

Her first thought was that he wanted to discuss Danny again, and her heart dropped all the way to her stomach, only to jump back up and lodge in her throat. Her chest grew tight as she held her breath and waited—for the bomb to drop, for him to demand full custody or announce that he was taking their son back to Pittsburgh with him.

Instead, he tugged her close, lowered his head and kissed her.

Seven

For a moment, Vanessa stood completely frozen, eyes wide, shock holding her immobile. But then his heat, his passion, seeped into her, and she began to lean against him, his eyes sliding closed on a silent sigh.

Marc's hands slipped from her elbows to her waist, pulling her even more tightly to him and holding her there with his arms crossed like iron bands at her back. His lips were warm and firm and masterful, plundering even as he attempted to coax and seduce.

He tasted like coffee and cream, and felt like heaven. Just as she remembered.

Kissing Marc had always been pure pleasure, like a cool glass of water on a hot summer day or sinking into a relaxing bubble bath after a long, exhausting day at work.

Hand drifting up to cup her cheek, Marc pulled away just enough to let her catch her breath and meet his gaze. His eyes were dark with a desire that Vanessa knew must be reflected in her own. Whether she wanted it or not, whether she liked it or not, there was no denying the heat that flared between them. Even now, after a year of separation, after the end of their marriage.

"I've been wanting to do that all evening," Marc murmured, his thumb slowly stroking just beneath her lower lip.

She wished she could deny feeling the same way, but had to admit that the thought of kissing him again had crossed her mind a few times since their unexpected reunion, as well. Especially during dinner, while they'd stared at one another across the candlelit table.

But kissing him wasn't a good idea. Being alone with him in his hotel room for much longer wasn't a good idea.

She should leave. Put a hand to his chest, push him away and get out while she could still make her legs move.

His other hand came up to frame her face, his fingers running through the hair at her temple.

Move, legs, move.

But her legs didn't move. It was as though her entire body had turned to stone, every muscle statue-still.

"This is a bad idea," she told him, putting her thoughts into words and forcing them past stiff, dry lips. "I should go."

A hint of a grin played at the corners of his lips. "Or you could stay," he whispered, "and we can see about turning a bad idea into a good one."

Inside, she was shaking her head. *No, no, no.* Sticking around was only going to turn the bad that had already happened into much, much worse.

No, she needed to leave. And she would, just as soon as she could get her body to obey the commands of her brain.

But the connection between the two had obviously been blocked or severed or scrambled in some way. Because she didn't move. She didn't step back, or push him away, or voice further arguments against making any more monumental mistakes.

She simply stood there and watched his mouth descend once again. Stood there and let his lips cover hers, let his fingers dig into her hair and cradle her scalp. Let his tongue tease and taunt until she had no choice but to open her mouth and invite him inside.

Oh, this is a bad idea, she thought, as her own arms came up to wind around his neck, her fingers toying with the hair at his nape. *A very, very bad...*

His tongue twined with hers and she groaned, any semblance of rational thought flying right out the window. Good or bad, she was in it now, with very little might left to fight. She wasn't even sure she wanted to anymore.

Though they were already touching, he tugged her even closer, so that her breasts flattened against his chest and the evidence of his arousal pressed between her legs.

Being a woman kept her arousal from being as obvious, but it was there, without a doubt. Besides the fact that her heart was pounding and her temperature was slowly reaching the boiling point, inside the cups of her bra her nipples were turning into tight, sensitive pearls. Lower, her knees were weak and her panties were growing damp.

It wouldn't take much more of Marc's intense ministrations for him to know just how aroused she was, too. Already, his hands were wandering down her sides and over her hips, his fingers slowly rucking up the skirt of her dress until he could touch her stockinged thighs.

Her own fingers went to the buttons at the front of his shirt, slipping one after another through their holes. When she reached the bottom, she switched to unbuckling his belt and loosening the top button of his dress slacks, then tugging the shirt's tail free. Once both sides fell open, she slipped her hands under the expensive material and put her palms flat against the warm, smooth skin of his chest and stomach.

He groaned. She moaned. The sounds met and mingled, sending shivers from their locked lips all the way down her spine.

As though he felt them, too, Marc's hand went to the small of her back and followed the line of her vertebrae up, up, up. He kneaded her neck a short second before catching the clasp of her dress's zipper and tugging it down in one long *ziiiiiiiiip* of sensation.

Curling her nails into his chest, she slumped into him as wave after wave of longing rolled through her. It was almost too much to bear, melting her bones and stealing the breath from her lungs. If he hadn't been holding her, she was sure she would have collapsed to the ground in a pile of skin and rumpled red fabric.

He released her mouth, allowing her to suck in some much-needed oxygen while he tugged at her dress, letting the flowy fabric pool at her feet. Hooking his thumbs into the waist of her pantyhose, he started to skim them down her legs, following them until he knelt in front of her on one knee.

With a hand at her ankle, he said, "Lift."

She did, and he slipped both her matching red heel and the stockings off her foot.

"Lift," he said again, repeating the motion on her other ankle, leaving her standing in the middle of the room in nothing but her bra and panties.

Thank goodness she'd taken as much care choosing those as she had her dress and shoes. She'd had absolutely no notion and no intention of letting him get so much of a glimpse of her underthings, but now she was infinitely relieved that she'd made a point of wearing a brand-new matching set. A strapless red demi-bra with scalloped lace edging and lacey, boy-cut panties that covered more than enough in the front, but left half moons of bare flesh visible from the back.

From his position on the floor, Marc must have noticed the peekaboo style of the underwear, because he lifted his head and shot her a grin that could only be described as wolfish.

"Lovely," he murmured, his hands cupping the backs of her calves, then her knees, then her thighs until her thighs quivered and she wasn't sure she could remain upright much longer.

Her tongue darted out, licking dry lips. "Mothers always tell their children to wear nice underwear, just in case," she managed in a shaky voice. "Now I know why."

Marc chuckled. A low, sexy sound that beat at her insides like tiny orange flames.

"These are better than nice," he told her, cupping her bottom and pressing a kiss to the bare skin of her belly, just below her navel. "But I'm pretty sure this isn't the kind of 'just in case' they're talking about."

A noise rolled up her throat that was meant to be a laugh. It came out more of a strangled hiss.

"But you like them, right? Better than plain white cotton?"

Kissing a line up the center of her torso, he climbed slowly to his feet. "Better than white cotton," he agreed. Then when he got to her mouth, he added, "But I don't really care, since you won't be wearing them much longer."

Reaching around her back, he unhooked her bra in one quick, deft movement. Only the last-minute crossing of her arms kept the garment from falling away completely.

"Now take them off. Both of them."

The gruff order sent her stomach flip-flopping and brought goose bumps to every inch of her exposed flesh. Which, considering her state of undress, was a considerable amount.

Despite the desire coursing through her veins, however, she suddenly felt awkward and exposed. She'd come this far, even knowing it was a colossal mistake.

It wasn't wise to be alone in the same room with Marc fully clothed, let alone do what they were doing. But being with him again brought back so many incredible memories and sensory perceptions that she'd thought she would never experience again. So she'd thrown up a thick, tall wall in her brain to keep right from wrong apart. And another between her brain and her heart to keep them from playing tug-of-war while she was enjoying Marc's kisses and touch. Now here she stood, half-naked, her ex-husband telling her to drop the two tiny bits of lace and fabric that kept her from being totally naked, and her nerves were calling foul.

For a brief moment, she considered jumping back into her dress and running for the hills. But that nice, thick wall was still firmly in place, leaving just enough want to overshadow future regrets.

What she needed, she realized, was a more level playing field.

Arms still crossed over her breasts to hold her bra in place, she stepped back. Just one small step away from him.

"Not yet," she told him, the words coming out more confidently than she felt.

He arched one dark brow and the message in his eyes clearly telegraphed that if she tried to cut and run, he would chase after her.

But she had no intention of running, only of evening things out a bit so that she wasn't the only one suffering a chill from the hotel's drafty old windows.

"You're overdressed," she pointed out. "So you first."

His right brow rose to meet the left and a muscle began to twitch along his jaw. Lifting his arms to waist height, he unbuttoned one cuff, then the other. With a roll of his broad shoulders, he shrugged out of the shirt completely, letting the pristine white material float to the floor behind him.

Vanessa swallowed. Making him strip down to next to nothing had seemed like a good idea at the time, but now that his chest was bare, she wasn't so sure. The very sight of that flat stomach and those tight pectorals had her mouth going desert dry and her heartbeat fluttering in her throat like the wings of a butterfly.

Without giving her time to regroup or even brace herself for more, he moved his hands to the front of his slacks and slowly lowered the zipper. Kicking off his shoes, he let the pants drop and stepped away from the entire pile—away from the clothes and one step closer to her.

"Better?" he asked, barely a foot of space separating them while the corners of his mouth curved in predatory amusement.

Not better. Definitely not better. If possible, it was worse. Because now, in addition to feeling anxious and exposed, she was also feeling extremely overwhelmed.

How could she have forgotten what this man looked like naked? Or nearly naked, at any rate.

There were male models out there being used for Calvin Klein and Abercrombie & Fitch ad campaigns who couldn't hold a candle to a fully dressed Marc. Undressed, in only his underwear, he blew them out of the water.

Out of his underwear…well, out of his underwear, he could blow water out of the water. No one would ever ask him to be a spokesperson for designer clothing or cologne, though, because putting him on billboards would cause women everywhere to swoon on the spot. They would cause traffic accidents and hit their heads on the pavement, and those were just lawsuits waiting to happen.

When they'd been married, Marc's good looks had amused her. The fact that he turned heads and invited so much female attention hadn't bothered her in the least, because she knew that at the end of the day, he was all hers. Other women could look, but she was the only one who got to touch.

They'd been divorced for over a year, though. How many other women had gotten to touch him in that time? How many heads had he turned who'd also managed to turn his?

As though sensing the direction of her thoughts, he lifted a hand to stroke her cheek. "Cold feet?" he asked quietly.

She shook her head in denial, but inside she was thinking, *Cold everything.*

She'd left him, been the one to initiate the divorce in the first place, but even so, she didn't want to think about him being with other women. It left her more than cold; it left her shaken.

Closing the space between them, he carefully pried her arms away from her breasts, but used his own chest to hold the bra in place. He ran his hands down the insides of her arms, then linked their fingers together. Just the way he used to, the way that used to make her feel so close to him, so cherished.

Pressing his lips to hers, he whispered, "Let me warm you up." Then he kissed her and started backing her slowly toward the bed.

The backs of her thighs hit the edge of the mattress and she toppled over, but Marc followed her down, so smoothly, it felt almost choreographed. The movement finally dislodged her bra and he grabbed it by one of the cups, tossing it aside.

His chest pressed her breasts flat and abraded the tight peaks of her nipples. She moaned, wrapping her arms around his shoulders while he kissed all but about three functioning brain cells straight out of her head.

Shifting his hands to her hips, he hooked his thumbs into the waist of her panties and dragged them down. He lifted her just enough to slip them off, then quickly shed his own.

They were both blessedly naked, pressed together like layers of cellophane. Insecurities threatened to surface again, reminding her that it had been months upon months since they'd been together…that she'd gone through a pregnancy and childbirth since then…that she'd spent her first trimester in a deep depression over the breakup of her marriage and the prospect of being a single mother—and therefore had spent a good deal of time in bed with cartons of ice cream and cookie dough that never quite made it into the oven.

In addition to baby weight, she'd put on pity-party weight, and though she'd been much more disciplined since she'd stopped feeling sorry for herself, she still hadn't managed to shed all of those extra pounds. Her hips were wider than before, her stomach far from flat, her thighs a bit more well-rounded.

The only upside to her new, more curvaceous figure was her bosom. Whether it was due to the pre-baby caloric binges or the post-baby breast-feeding, the increased bra size was kind of nice. And being bigger up top helped to keep the rest of her body in proper proportion.

But whether her recent physical changes were good or bad, Marc didn't seem to mind either way. In fact, he didn't even seem to notice. Or if he did, he was enjoying them enough that he didn't feel the need to comment.

Knowing that allowed Vanessa to relax and stop obsessing. Marc's hands on her body, his mouth trailing along her jaw, her throat, her shoulder, her collarbone, were too potent to ignore for long, anyway. As was the need to touch him in return.

She stroked his back, toyed with the hair at the nape of his neck. Nibbled his ear and rubbed her cheek against the slight stubble that was growing in and would need to be shaved clean again in the morning.

His erection was pressed between them, rubbing in

tantalizing places and she arched slightly to feel even more of that rigid length against her belly and lower. With a low growl, Marc sank his teeth into the muscle that ran from the side of her throat to her shoulder. She sucked in a sharp breath, groaning at the light stab of pleasure-pain and digging her nails into the flesh of his back to repay the favor.

He chuckled against her skin and she felt the vibrations clear down to her bones.

"Stop teasing," she ordered more than a little breathlessly just above his ear.

"You started it," he retorted, words muffled as he spoke into her skin. He trailed wet, openmouthed kisses across her chest, over the mound of one breast, tighter and tighter around her nipple.

"Besides, I'm not finished yet," he added a moment before taking that nipple into his mouth and suckling gently.

Oh, mercy. Vanessa's upper body shot off the mattress, pleasure streaking through her like lightning. She couldn't even cry out, the oxygen was knocked so thoroughly from her lungs.

She clung to his shoulders, panting and writhing as he didn't just tease, but tortured. He licked and nipped and sucked at one breast before moving to the other and driving her crazy all over again.

When he finished, he lifted his head and smiled down at her. A wicked, devilish smile.

He started to lean down and she was afraid of what he might do. She wasn't sure she could take much more, whether he decided to continue his cruel ministrations to her breasts or to move lower.

Oh, no, he couldn't go lower. Another time, maybe. Another time, she was sure she would be delighted, and more than willing to reciprocate.

But tonight, it would be too much. She couldn't bear it.

So before he got any bright ideas, she linked her legs around his hips and reached between them to take him in a firm, but careful grasp. He let out a hiss of breath, lips pulling back from his teeth and his eyes falling closed.

"Enough," she told him.

His lashes fluttered and he gazed down at her. "Do you want me to stop?" he murmured.

The bastard. He knew she didn't want him to stop, he was just teasing her—*torturing* her—again.

Giving him a little taste of his own medicine, she tightened her fingers around his arousal, causing him to gasp and flex his hips.

"Not stop-stop," she clarified, as though there were really any doubt, "just wrap up the opening act and get to the big bang already."

He arched a brow, his lips splitting into a wide grin. "The 'big bang,' huh?"

She felt her cheeks heat at her choice of words. Then again, she was lying naked beneath her ex-husband, all but done with the dirty deed, as it were. Was there really any reason to be embarrassed about *anything* at this point?

Taking a deep breath and pulling her chin up a notch, she said, "You heard me."

"Well," he replied slowly, that same predatory gleam in his eyes, that same sly smile, curving his mouth, "I'll see what I can do to deliver."

It was her turn to arch a brow and adopt an overconfident expression. "You do that."

His grin widened a second before he swooped in to place a rough, hard kiss on her lips. Then he reached down to cover her hand with his. Slowly, he pried her fingers away from that most sensitive of body parts and raised her arm over her head, pinning it to the mattress.

Shifting, he settled more fully between her legs, the tip

of his erection nudging her opening. And then he slid home, slowly, carefully, his mouth still covering hers, absorbing the heartfelt moans his agonizing entry dragged from her throat.

She clutched at his hands, both of them, where they held her own flat to the mattress. And he squeezed back, groaning against her lips as his hips began to move.

Inch by inch, he filled her up, stretching muscles and tissue that had been too long unused. It didn't hurt, though. On the contrary, it felt amazingly, wonderfully perfect.

Like so many times in the past, she marveled at how well they fit together, how every part of her body seemed to be molded, sculpted, designed for every part of his body. Even with the physical changes she'd gone through over the past year, that hadn't altered.

Levering himself up on his elbows, he released her mouth, giving her the chance to bite her bottom lip and tilt her head back in growing ecstasy. He did the same, nostrils flaring as he pulled out, then drove back in, slowly at first and then faster and faster.

She lifted her own hips, meeting him thrust for thrust, letting the motion, the flesh-on-flesh sensations wash over her in ever-increasing waves. Her lungs burned, struggling for air while the rest of her body struggled for completion. Every part of her tingled, tightening in longing, in expectation.

She wanted—no, *needed*—what only Marc could give her. And while slow and steady might be good for some things, like marathons and piano lessons, that's not what she was interested in right now. She wanted hard and fast and now, now, now!

"Marc, please," she begged, wrapping her arms more securely around his neck before leaning up to nip his earlobe. Then she sank her teeth even harder into his shoulder.

His entire body shuddered from head to toe above her, his

hands grasping her waist and digging in. He pounded into her with even more force, making her cry out, making himself cry out.

Pressure built until she wanted to scream and then suddenly the dam burst. Pleasure spilled over her in a splash of heat and colorful sparks, like fireworks going off overhead.

She called his name and clung to him for dear life, absorbing the delicious impact of his final thrusts, and finally his full weight as he collapsed atop her with a long, low groan of satisfied completion.

Eight

"This was probably a bad idea," Vanessa murmured.

Marc had wondered how long it would take her to start in on her list of regrets.

They were lying side by side, flat on their backs on the lumpy, queen-size hotel room mattress. Vanessa had the sheets pulled up to her armpits, held in place over her ample breasts by both hands. He was a bit more relaxed, stretched out and letting the sheet fall where it would, low on his abdomen and across his hips.

But while he was obviously taking their minor indiscretion in stride, he couldn't disagree with her on the "bad idea" part. He wasn't sorry, since making love with Vanessa wasn't something he could ever regret or apologize for, but she was right that it hadn't been the smartest decision of his life.

He wasn't even sure what had possessed him to kiss her in the first place.

Maybe because he'd been thinking about it all night,

his eyes straying over and over again to her mouth and the luscious cleavage visible above the bodice of her siren-red sex goddess dress.

Maybe because he hadn't been able to get her out of his head since the moment he'd seen her again after such a long absence…and after pretty much determining that he would never see her again at all.

Or maybe because she was simply irresistible. For him, she always had been.

It almost didn't surprise him that they'd made a child together at the very moment that their marriage had been falling apart around them. Despite their differences and the problems that had plagued them there at the end, physical compatibility had never even made it onto the list. No matter how bad a day either of them might be having, no matter how big a fight they might have had, it never seemed to take them long to come back together and set the sheets on fire.

It was a relief to know that hadn't changed. They were no longer married, she'd hidden his son from him and neither of them had a very clear vision of what the future held, but at least he knew the passion was still there. More than passion— lust and longing and desire thick enough to land a 747 on.

His leg brushed against hers beneath the covers and a jolt of that passion times ten shot through him. She jerked away from him, letting him know in no uncertain terms that his current state of semi-arousal would definitely be going to waste.

"You're right," he said, agreeing with her earlier statement. "Probably wasn't the wisest thing to do. At least not under the current circumstances."

"There's the understatement of the century," she grumbled, rolling to the side of the bed and carefully sliding her bare legs out from under the top sheet.

She sat there for a minute, not moving, and Marc took

the opportunity to admire the short fall of her copper hair around her shoulders, the supple line of her spine, and the gentle curves of her torso from the back. She'd put on a bit of weight with the pregnancy, but it didn't take away from her attractiveness one damn bit.

If anything, it made her even more beautiful, filling her out with sensual, womanly curves in all the right places. He had certainly enjoyed exploring those curves with his hands and lips, feeling them so soft and gentle against his much harder naked length.

One corner of his mouth lifted in amusement, not only from the delectable view, but from the snarky tone of her voice. She'd always had such a way with words, and a way of delivering them that often delighted him.

It had annoyed the hell out of her when she'd been in a snit, telling him off, and would catch him grinning. Not because he wasn't listening or taking her seriously, but because he'd always loved watching her and listening to her—even when she was chewing him out.

The way she moved, pacing back and forth and waving her arms. The way her breasts rose and fell in agitation, following the cadence of her rant. What could he say…it turned him on. And nine times out of ten, their arguments had led to phenomenal make-up sex, so there was really no downside to riling her up a little more by letting her think he was laughing off her anger or upset.

In hindsight, he could see how that might have led to some of the problems that had prompted them to split. He'd never meant to deride her feelings or opinions on anything, he'd simply believed their relationship was secure enough that any differences or misunderstandings they had would blow over just as they had in the past.

How wrong he'd been. And he hadn't seen it coming until it was too late. Too damn late.

"It can't happen again," she said, still facing the other direction.

For a moment, he remained trapped in his head and thought she was talking about their divorce. That definitely couldn't happen again, and if he had it to do over, it might not have happened in the first place.

Then he realized she meant the sex. Tonight's unplanned, unexpected, but definitely not unsatisfying, indiscretion.

"Marc," she said when he didn't respond. Twisting slightly, she tilted her head until she could see him from the corner of her eye, then repeated more firmly, "This can't happen again."

Rolling to his side, he propped himself up on one elbow, letting silence fill the room while he studied her. After a minute or two, he murmured, "What do you want me to say, Vanessa? That I'm sorry we made love? That I don't hope we get the chance to do it again…frequently and with great enthusiasm?" He shrugged the shoulder that wasn't holding him up. "Sorry, but I'm not going to do that."

"What is wrong with you?" she charged, all but leaping from the bed, dragging the sheet along with her. It caught on the corners of the mattress, of course, but not before sliding from his hips and leaving him in the buff down to his ankles.

She turned, yanking at the cheap, industrial grade white cotton until it came free, pointedly ignoring his total nudity. With a huff, she yanked the quilted coverlet from the foot of the bed and tossed it over him, head and all. He chuckled, lowering it just in time to watch her wrap the sheet like a toga around her own naked form.

"We're divorced, Marcus," she pointed out, as though he weren't painfully aware of their current marital status. Or lack thereof.

She stormed around the room gathering her clothing, piece

by discarded piece. "Divorced couples aren't supposed to sleep together."

"Maybe not, but we both know it happens all the time." He waved a hand to encompass the rumpled bed and their current states of postcoital undress.

"Well, it shouldn't," she argued back, doing her best to hold up the sheet while she struggled into her underwear. "Besides, you hate me."

A beat passed while the air in the room sizzled with growing tension. "Says who?"

At the softly spoken question, Vanessa jerked to a halt and lifted her head to meet his gaze. The lower half of the sheet, which had been hiked up around her thighs while she fought with her panties, fell to the ground.

"Don't you?" she asked just as softly. "I mean, you do. I know you do. Or at least, you should. I didn't tell you I was pregnant. I didn't tell you about Danny."

His brows crossed and his mouth dipped down in a scowl at the reminder. He'd been working hard to forget that part of his reason for being in town. Or more to the point, had been willing to suspend his anger and feelings of betrayal long enough to partake of Vanessa's lovely body and enjoy the tactile sensations of having her in his arms and bed again after so long.

He took in her still half-naked form, wrapped like a Greek goddess in pristine white cotton. Sure, all of the reasons he *should* hate her were still there. And no doubt they had many issues to work out. But for some reason, at that moment, he just couldn't get his temper to flare.

"Here's a bit of advice," he told her, cocking a brow and trying not to let his frown slip up into a grin. "When someone has temporarily forgotten that they have a reason to be mad at you, it's probably better not to remind them."

"But you should be mad at me," she said quietly, holding

his gaze for a long, drawn out second before turning her back to him and continuing to dress.

Marc watched as she struggled with her bra, then let the sheet fall as she hooked the bit of lingerie behind her back. He watched the light play on the pale canvas of her skin and the smooth lines of her body as she moved.

Interesting, he thought, fighting the urge to drag her back to bed. She seemed to *want* him to be angry with her.

On the one hand, at least he knew she hadn't slept with him in an effort to cloud his mind and seduce him into forgetting that she tried to keep his son from him. On the other, she'd have been wise to do almost anything to stay on his good side at this point. To avoid acrimony, a possible custody battle or to keep him from simply picking up and taking Danny home with him, leaving her few options to get him back.

Granted, before today, he hadn't spoken with Vanessa in over a year, and the fact that she'd left him meant he probably hadn't understood her all that well to begin with. But the only explanation he could think of for why she'd remind him of what stood between them was that she *needed* something between them. A wall. A barrier.

If he hated her, he might not want to be with her again. If he hated her, he might get fed up and storm home to Pittsburgh—preferably without Danny.

Oh, they'd work out some sort of custody agreement. On that, he would insist. And he was sure Vanessa wouldn't argue too strongly against it, not now. Agreeing to let him see Danny on a regular basis or even let him take their son back to Pittsburgh for the occasional extended visit would be the lesser of two evils for her now.

But he'd been in big business long enough to know that when someone gave up something too easily, it was usually because they were trying to get or retain something even more important to them. His best guess was that Vanessa was trying to retain distance.

She'd wasted no time moving to Summerville the minute their divorce was final, and as far as he could tell, she'd been perfectly happy settling in with her aunt and making her mark on the small town through The Sugar Shack.

If Fate hadn't somehow intervened to bring him here himself, he never would have known where she'd relocated to or that she had a child. *His* child.

Oh, yes, she'd wanted distance then, and she wanted it now. And if she pissed him off—or kept him pissed off—then he'd be less likely to stick around for any length of time, wouldn't he?

Which only made him want to stick around more. He was contrary like that sometimes, a fact Vanessa was well aware of. She should have known that if he caught on to her little plan, he'd make a point of doing pretty much the exact opposite of what she wanted, just to vex her.

Of course, there was a good chance she didn't even realize she had a little plan. That she was running heavily on instinct, her current thoughts and actions more subconscious than anything else.

But it still intrigued him, and if he hadn't wanted to stick around before just to be close to the child he hadn't known existed, he certainly did now. He was even looking forward to it, considering the entertaining side benefits he'd recently discovered could be added to his stay.

Tossing back the covers, he moved to the edge of the bed and sat up. "Well, I'm sorry to disappoint you, but I don't hate you."

He pushed to his feet and walked toward her stark naked. Where she'd fought so hard to protect her modesty and stay covered, he didn't bother and wasn't the least bit self-conscious about his nudity.

When she saw him coming, she took a jerky step back, away from him, but he wasn't really after her. Bending at the waist, he scooped up the tangled ball of his pants and underwear.

"I'm not happy about what you did," he clarified, climbing into his clothes with slow, deliberate movements, "and I can't say that I don't harbor a bit of anger and resentment over it. Or that there won't be moments when that anger and resentment flare hotter than anything else."

He leaned down for his wrinkled shirt and shrugged it on, but didn't bother buttoning it, leaving his chest bare down the middle. "But we've covered that ground already. Keeping Danny from me—or the pregnancy to begin with— was wrong. That's time and an experience I can't get back. Now that I know I have a son, however, things are going to change. I *am* going to be involved in his life—and therefore in yours."

She was standing only about three feet from him, clutching that red dress to her breasts to cover as much of her front as she could. It was silly and useless, a bit like locking the barn door after the bull had already escaped, but Marc found her false sense of modesty oddly endearing.

"You should probably come to terms with that," he told her matter-of-factly. "The sooner, the better."

She simply stood there, staring at him. Her eyes sparkled like polished sapphires, but whether with fear or rage or mere confusion, he couldn't quite tell.

While he had her off balance—which was a nice switch, frankly, since she'd pretty much had him off balance from the moment he'd driven into town—he tossed another can of gasoline on the bonfire that just seemed to continue blazing between them.

"Here's something else you should probably take into

consideration," he said quietly, widening his stance and crossing his arms determinedly in front of him.

Vanessa didn't reply. Instead, she cocked her head, the tendons at the sides of her throat convulsing as she swallowed, waiting nervously for him to elaborate.

"We didn't use a condom, which means that you may even now get pregnant with our second child."

Nine

Oh, God.

Marc's words slammed into Vanessa's chest like a bullet, knocking the air from her lungs and making her literally stagger on her feet.

What had she been thinking? Bad enough she'd fallen into bed with her ex-husband faster than a star falls from the sky, but she'd completely forgotten about protection of any kind. It had never occurred to her to insist he use a condom, and since she was a new mother, still breast-feeding and with absolutely zero romantic prospects on the horizon, it hadn't been necessary for her to be on birth control.

She tried to do the math in her head, to figure out when her last period had been and when she was due again, but panic kept her thoughts in a tailspin.

And what about the breast-feeding? Wasn't it supposed to be harder to get pregnant while still nursing?

Dear God, please let that be true, because she couldn't even fathom the idea that she might actually be pregnant *again,* unexpectedly, unplanned and by her *former* husband. It was almost too horrifying to contemplate.

"I'm not," she said, as though saying it firmly and decisively enough would make it true.

Marc raised a dark, sardonic brow. "How can you be so sure."

"I'm just not," she insisted, tearing frantically at her dress until she got her feet inside and could yank it up. Never mind that it was open all the way to her bottom in the back because she couldn't raise the zipper without help. She would walk home with it hanging loose, if she had to, rather than ask him for one iota of assistance.

"And what were you thinking?" she charged, stamping a foot as she slipped it into a strappy red heel. "How could you do that—let *me* do that—without taking precautions?" She cast him an angry, accusatory glare. "I've never known you to be so irresponsible."

He shrugged, looking exponentially more casual and unconcerned than she was feeling at that particular moment. "What can I say? I was swept away by your beauty and passion, and the exhilaration of being with you again after such a long absence."

Pausing in the act of shoving on her other shoe, she tilted her head in his direction and gave a loud, unladylike snort. *"Please,"* she scoffed.

"Is that so hard to believe?" he asked, still wearing the blank mask that gave her no clue of his true emotions.

Was he upset that they'd forgotten to use protection? Happy? Angry? Excited? Confused? Nauseous?

Because she was nauseous. And upset and angry and confused. There was no happiness or excitement anywhere on her radar.

If it turned out she really was pregnant…oh, God, please

don't let her be pregnant again—not by Marc, and not so soon after Danny's birth…she would of course love the baby. Unconditionally and without question. But the difference between loving an existing child and loving the notion of carrying an as-yet imaginary one—especially under these circumstances—was like the difference between black and white, hot and cold, thirsty and drowning.

She loved Danny with all her heart and soul. She wouldn't trade him for anything, or even go back and undo the events that had led to his birth.

But she sure as *hell* wouldn't choose to be pregnant again. Not so soon after having one child, not without benefit of marriage, and not with a man she'd so recently divorced.

She was already linked too closely to Marc, thanks to his discovery of Danny's existence. But the thought of being even more closely connected to him through a second child would be a nightmare come to life.

He was almost foaming-at-the-mouth rabid about staying close to her now that he knew about Danny. Having him know from the very beginning that he was going to be a father a second time would turn him into near-stalker material. She would never get rid of him, not even for short amounts of time while he commuted back and forth between Pittsburgh and Summerville.

Oh, no, knowing Marc, he would do something ridiculous like move to Summerville himself, or insist they get remarried and then drag her back to the city where she would be trapped and miserable all over again.

No, no, no, no, no. Vanessa's head was shaking like a tambourine as she ran her gaze around the room, looking for anything she might have forgotten. Her purse, her watch, an earring…

"I think you underestimate your appeal," Marc remarked,

apparently missing the nuclear meltdown taking place inside her.

Small red clutch in hand, she shot him another withering glare before spinning on her heel and marching toward the hotel room door.

"Vanessa."

Her free hand was out, reaching for the knob, but his sharp voice stopped her in her tracks. She didn't turn to look at him, but remained still, waiting for him to continue.

"I'll see you at the bakery first thing tomorrow, eight o'clock sharp. Be sure Danny is with you."

A shudder rolled through her, and she wasn't sure if it was aversion to having to deal with him again in the morning or relief that that was his only parting remark.

With a jerky nod, she pulled the door open and started to step into the hall.

"And I'll want to know as soon as you do," he went on, stopping her a second time.

Her heart lurched in her chest. "Know what?" she asked, forcing the words past her tight, dry throat.

"Whether or not we'll be presenting our son with a little brother or sister nine months from now."

Marc wasn't at The Sugar Shack when she and Aunt Helen arrived with Danny in tow at five o'clock the next morning. Vanessa wasn't surprised, since he'd said he would meet her there at eight, and frankly, she could use the short reprieve.

It might only be three hours, but it was three hours without having to see or deal with Marc. And after last night, she needed them. Desperately.

While she and Aunt Helen bustled around readying the bakery for the breakfast opening, she tried her best to put him and the myriad of issues between them out of her mind. Not for the first time…not even for the five hundred and first time…she wondered how she'd managed to get herself into such an incredible mess.

It felt as though her life had turned into some kind of daytime soap opera, and the worst part was that she knew those things were never-ending. They just went on forever, with more and more dramatic cliff-hangers cropping up to throw the main characters into a tizzy.

Well, she didn't need any more tizzies. And she sure as heck didn't need any more drama. If she could have, she'd have canceled her own personal variation of *As the World Spins Out of Control*.

Unfortunately, those few hours of blessed freedom sped by much too quickly. Before she knew it, Summerville's early risers were filing in for a morning coffee and croissant on their way to work, or to sit and enjoy a more leisurely sticky bun with a cup of hot tea. Even before the clock struck eight o'clock, her eyes were practically glued to the front door, waiting for Marc to arrive.

But the clock did strike eight and he didn't appear. Then it struck ten after, twenty after, quarter to nine, and he was still nowhere in sight.

She should have been relieved, but instead, Vanessa found herself beginning to worry. It wasn't like Marc to be late for anything, especially after making such a production of warning her of where he would be when—and where he fully expected her to be to meet him.

She rang up an order for four coffees and a box of mixed Danish pastries with one eye on the time, trying to decide if she should bask in her apparent—and most likely fleeting—freedom, or call the Harbor Inn to check on him.

By nine-thirty, she'd not only decided to call the hotel, but if he wasn't there, intended to drive over herself to search his room, and call the police, if necessary. But before she could untie her apron and ask Aunt Helen to cover the front counter for her, the bell above the door rang and Marc strolled in, a charming smile on his face.

As hard as she tried not to notice, he looked magnificent. In place of his usual suit and tie, he wore tan slacks and a light blue chambray shirt. The shirt's collar was open, cuffs rolled up to midforearm.

Anyone else might see Marc and think he was just a run-of-the-mill guy, out and about on a beautiful summer day. But Vanessa knew better. If one looked closer, one would notice the solid gold Rolex, the seven-hundred-dollar Ferragamo loafers and the air of absolute power and confidence that surrounded him.

This was Marc's casual appearance, but as wise men knew, appearances could be extremely deceptive.

He walked through the maze of small round tables as though he owned the place, his smile turning more and more predatory the closer he came to the tall glass display case that separated them.

"Good morning," he greeted, sounding much too chipper for her peace of mind.

"Morning," she returned with much less enthusiasm. "You're late. I thought you said you'd be here at eight."

One solid shoulder rose and fell in a casual shrug. "I had some errands to run."

She raised a brow, but didn't ask because she wasn't sure she wanted to know.

"Do you have a minute?" he asked.

She glanced around, judging the number of customers at the tables and the few people who were milling in front of the display case, trying to decide which sweet was most worth ruining their diets.

With a quick nod, she moved toward the kitchen and dipped her head through the swinging double doors. "Aunt

Helen, could you work the register for a second? I need to speak with Marc."

Aunt Helen finished what she was doing and came out, wiping her hands on the front of her apron while Vanessa removed hers and hung it on a small hook on the far wall. Her aunt cast Marc a cautious, almost disparaging glance, but held her tongue, thank goodness.

Vanessa hadn't told Aunt Helen what happened with Marc the night before. She'd given a brief recap of dinner, acting as though all they'd discussed was the bakery and a potential business agreement, and that everything had remained very professional. But she hadn't mentioned word one about following him up to his hotel room or letting things get out of control. And she certainly hadn't shared the fact that her hormones had so overwhelmed her common sense that she'd allowed Marc to make love to her without any form of doctor-recommended birth control.

Knowing the whole story would only have increased Aunt Helen's animosity toward Marc. There was a time, not so long ago, when Vanessa welcomed her aunt's protectiveness and having someone to talk to about everything she'd been through both before and during the divorce.

But things had changed now. Not necessarily for the better, but in ways she couldn't avoid. Marc knew about Danny, was determined to be a part of his son's life, and that meant he was going to be a part of hers. For better or worse, she had to find a way to make peace with her ex-husband, if only to keep the next eighteen years of her life from being a living hell.

In order to do that, and also keep the peace with her aunt, she had to avoid bad-mouthing Marc. She probably shouldn't have done so in the first place, but she'd been so hurt, so miserable, that she'd had to talk to *someone*, and Aunt Helen's had been the perfect shoulder to cry on.

Marc came up behind her, laying a hand gently on her elbow. As soon as she was sure Helen was settled behind the counter, she let him lead her across the bakery and through the shared entrance that led to the empty space next door.

She thought they were simply going to use the area to talk privately, and her stomach was nearly in knots wondering what sort of shoe or bomb or anvil he would drop on her this time. But rather than stopping in the center of the empty space, he kept walking, pulling her with him to the front of the building and the glass door that opened out onto the sidewalk.

"Do you have a key for this?" he asked, pointing to the door's lock.

"Yes. The landlord knows I'm interested in renting the space and occasionally lets me use it for small bits of storage. Plus, I can let other potential renters in if he isn't available."

"Good," he replied, his warm hand still cupping her elbow more intimately than she would have liked. "I'm going to need it."

She blinked. "Why?"

"To let those guys in," he answered, cocking his head in the direction of the glass and the street beyond. "Unless you want them traipsing through your bakery and dragging all their dirty, heavy equipment with them."

Following his gaze, she blinked again, only then noticing that the sidewalk outside the empty storefront was littered with men in jeans and work shirts unloading toolboxes, sawhorses, lumber and various cutting implements from the row of pickup trucks parked at the curb.

"Who are they?" she asked in dismay.

"Your construction crew."

She met Marc's gaze and must have looked as confused as she felt because he quickly elaborated.

"They're here to clean the place up and start putting in your shelving and countertops."

"What? Why?"

Her ex-husband's expression went from being amused at her utter shock to exasperated at her apparent denseness. "It's all part of the expansion plan, remember? We've got to get this section of the building renovated for The Sugar Shack's mail-order distribution and that Cookie of the Month thing you have in mind."

Her gaze swung from Marc to the workers outside, to Marc, to the workers... She now knew exactly how wild animals felt when caught in the middle of the highway by bright, oncoming headlights.

"I don't understand," she said with a slow shake of her head. "I didn't hire them. They can't start working here because I haven't rented the space yet. I don't have the money."

Marc gave a perturbed sigh. "Why do you think I'm here, Vanessa? Aside from wanting to spend time with Danny. Don't you remember what we discussed last night?"

She remembered last night. Vividly. And she remembered his parting shot that he hadn't used a condom, she hadn't been on the pill and she might very well be pregnant with his child. Again. The rest was a bit more of a blur, especially at this particular moment.

One of the workers came to the door. Marc made a motion with his hand, indicating that he needed a minute or two more, and the man nodded, returning to his truck.

"Look, it's taken care of, okay?" Marc told her. "I talked to the building's owner about the modifications we want to make. The space will be rented in your name, and part of the agreement will include permission to make any changes we see fit to better our business. Brian is putting together the paperwork and will deliver the contracts today. I'll have him get me a copy of the key from the landlord, but for now I need the one you have."

"But…" She was starting to sound like a broken record. "If Brian hasn't talked to Mr. Parsons yet, how do you know he'll agree to let us—*me*—rent this space?"

His mossy green eyes sparkled with self-assurance. "Vanessa," he said slowly, as though speaking to a small child or particularly slow adult. "It's taken care of. The building is for rent, I told Brian to rent it. What more do you need to know?"

She was finally catching on. Or rather, finally fully absorbing the situation and Marc's deep-rooted resolve to stay in town.

"Let me guess. 'Money is no object,'" she mimicked, adopting a low, masculine voice that was clearly supposed to be his. "You told Brian what you wanted—with no limit on how much you were willing to spend—and are leaving him to do whatever he has to for you to get your own way."

Releasing her elbow, he propped his hands on his hips, letting out a frustrated breath. "What's wrong with that?" he wanted to know.

She wished she could say nothing. She wished she didn't mind that he was using his wealth and prestige to assist her in her business and help to make the bakery an even bigger success.

There had even been a time when that sort of power and cocky confidence would have impressed her. Now, though, it only made her nervous.

"I don't want to be indebted to you, Marc," she told him softly, honestly. "I don't want to owe you anything, or know that The Sugar Shack has only expanded, is only successful, because you rode into town and saved the day with the Keller family fortune."

"Why does it matter where the capital comes from,

Vanessa? The important thing is that you're getting your additional space and branching out into mail order."

Shaking her head, she crossed her arms beneath her breasts and took a step back. "You don't understand. It *does* matter, because if you come in waving your checkbook around and running roughshod over me and everyone else in this town, then it's not *my* business anymore. It's just another insignificant acquisition for Keller Corp's multimillion-dollar holdings."

Widening his stance, he copied her defensive position of arms over chest. "Don't give me that. You asked Brian Blake to look for an investor you could work with. Preferably a silent one who would be willing to flush copious amounts of money into the bakery, but not have much say on how it was run or what you did with the cash. For the most part, that's exactly what I'm doing. So your problem isn't that I'm 'waving my checkbook around,' as you so eloquently put it. Your problem is that it's *my* checkbook."

"*Of course* that's my problem," she snapped, his earlier frustrations rubbing off on her. "We've been down this road before, Marc. The money, the influence, expecting everyone and everything to fall into line simply because your name is Keller."

Uncrossing her arms, she raised her hands to cover her face for a minute, trying to collect her thoughts and her temper. Once she lowered them, her tone was more subdued.

"Don't get me wrong, I liked it for a while. I enjoyed the lifestyle being your wife afforded me. The parties, the wardrobe, never having to worry about making ends meet."

Oh, yes. After a lifetime of struggling, of working her fingers to the bone just to get by, marrying into money had been a welcome reprieve.

"But you have no idea what it was like to be your wife and live under that roof without truly being a Keller."

His eyes narrowed, their green depths filling with genuine confusion. "What are you talking about? Of course, you were a true Keller. You were my wife."

"That's sure not how it felt," she admitted softly, remembering all the times his mother had made a point of reminding her that she was a Keller by marriage only, making her feel as though she had no business even crossing the threshold of Keller Manor without a mop and feather duster in her hands.

"I'm sorry." His arms slid from his chest and he started to reach for her, then seemed to think better of it and dropped his hands to his sides. "I never meant to make you feel like an outsider."

Guilt stabbed through her at the hurt look on his face. She opened her mouth to tell him that he hadn't been nearly as big an offender as his mother, but a sharp rap on the glass cut her off, startling them both.

The same worker as before, apparently the man in charge of the rest of the crew, made an impatient face and tapped his watch. Time, as they said, was money, and he obviously wasn't making any standing around on the sidewalk. Of course, Vanessa was sure Marc was paying them well, and most likely by the hour, regardless of whether they were actively working or not.

Marc lifted a hand, giving him the *just a second* gesture before turning back to her. "I'm going to need that key before these guys decide to sledgehammer their way in here."

She licked her lips and swallowed, reluctant to do his bidding. She and Marc had been on the verge of an honest-to-goodness adult conversation. One where she'd finally almost worked up the courage to tell him the truth behind why she'd gotten fed up and left in the first place. She'd tried so many times in the past to let him know how she was being treated, how much she felt like an outcast in what was supposed to be her own home, but she'd never quite been brave enough to blurt it out.

Part of her had believed that if he loved her enough, if he understood her as much as a husband was supposed to understand his wife, then he would know what she was trying to say all the times she'd hinted at her growing unhappiness. Now, she realized that nobody should be expected to be a mind reader, especially someone of the male persuasion.

If only she had been wise enough and gutsy enough to simply tell him what was going on. Things might have turned out so differently.

But that was water under the bridge and any chance they might have had of wiping the slate clean this morning had disappeared with the carpenter's untimely interruption.

Licking her lips again, she inclined her head. "I'll get the key," she said, turning on her heel and hurrying away.

Ten

"I swear, that racket is enough to make me want to jump into this oven myself."

Vanessa raised her head from the perfect circles of pastry dough she was currently topping with raisin filling to watch Aunt Helen slide a tray of baklava into one of the industrial ovens and slam the door with a clang that only punctuated the loud, staccato sounds of construction coming from the other side of the bakery walls.

It hadn't been easy to put up with both the noise and the added traffic of having so many workers around. She'd made dozens of apologies to customers, as well as creating *Please excuse our dust* and *Apologies for the excessive noise* signs. Thankfully, no real dust or debris had made it into the actual bakery side of the building, but having the crew around all day every day didn't make it easy for folks to come in and enjoy a *quiet* cup of tea and scones.

"They'll be finished soon," she told her aunt, repeating

the line the construction foreman had been giving her for the past week. She was familiar enough with this type of thing to know that "soon" was an extremely relative term, but given the fact that they really were making amazing progress, she thought the job would likely be done in just another week or two.

"And you have to admit, it's been nice of Marc to do all of this for us."

Aunt Helen gave a derisive snort. "Don't fool yourself, dear. He isn't doing it to be nice. He's doing it for himself, and to keep you under his thumb, and you know it."

Vanessa didn't respond, mostly because her aunt was right. Without a doubt, Marc wouldn't still be in town if there wasn't something in it for him.

He wanted to be close to Danny and indeed spent almost every evening at Aunt Helen's house with them. They ate dinner together. He helped feed Danny, gave him baths and put him to bed. At his insistence, she'd shown him how to change a diaper, and amazingly, he now did that almost as often as she did. They played on blankets on the floor, and took walks, and went to the park, even though Danny was too young to truly enjoy it.

It all felt so normal, and Vanessa had to admit…nice.

But just as Aunt Helen had reminded her, she couldn't forget for a minute that there were strings attached to everything Marc did. He wanted to know his son, which was understandable and seemed innocent enough on the surface.

Beyond that, though, she knew the entire situation was steeped in ulterior motives. Or at least the potential for ulterior motives.

Right now, Marc was using the remodeling and bakery expansion as an excuse to be close to his son, and something to occupy his time while Danny took frequent naps. But what would happen later?

What would happen once he decided he'd gotten to know Danny as well as he could here in Summerville and wanted to take him back to Pittsburgh to assume his rightful place on one of the silver-lined branches of the Keller family tree?

What would happen when the novelty of helping her create a mail-order business for The Sugar Shack wore off and small town living began to bore him?

And why did she bother wondering about such silly questions, when she already knew the answers?

The past couple of weeks, Marc had reminded her more of the man she'd fallen in love with and married than ever before. He'd been kind and generous, sweet and funny. He held doors for her, offered to help her clear the table after meals and put their son down for naps.

And he touched her. Nothing overt or overly sexual that a casual observer might notice, even considering how they'd spent his first night in town. Just a light brush of his fingers now and then—down her arm, over the back of her hand, along her cheek as he tucked a strand of hair behind her ear.

She tried not to read too much into the familiar gestures, but that didn't keep her pulse from thrumming or her heart from hammering inside her chest. Aunt Helen had complained more than once that the house or bakery was too cold, but turning up the air conditioning was the only way Vanessa could think of to combat the erratic spikes in her body temperature that Marc's constant presence and attentions created.

Speak of the devil.

No sooner had the memory played through her head than Marc pushed open the swinging kitchen doors, and she nearly bobbled the spoon she was using to dollop raisin filling onto the tray.

There went her temperature again, causing her skin to flush and perspiration to break out along her brow and between her breasts. At least this time, she could blame it on the ovens and all the hard work she was putting in trying to fill an order for six dozen raisin-filled cookies by three o'clock.

"When you get a minute," he said, "you should come over and see what you think. The crew is almost finished, and they want to know if there's anything else you'd like done before they go."

"Oh." That brought Vanessa's head up.

She'd been over to the other side of the shop a couple of times during the construction, but hadn't wanted to get in anyone's way. Plus, Marc had been so on top of things that her presence and input hadn't really seemed necessary.

But now that the renovations were nearly complete, she was suddenly excited to see how it looked. To start picturing herself there, boxing up her fresh-baked delights, overseeing the extra employees they would likely have to hire. Or would *get* to hire, if the mail-order idea was as successful as she hoped.

Sparing a glance at Aunt Helen, she dropped her spoon back in the bowl of lumpy, dark brown cookie filling, and began wiping her hands clean on a nearby towel.

"Do you mind?" she asked her aunt.

"Of course not. You go, dear," Aunt Helen told her, bustling over to take over with the cookies. "I'll just finish with these, and after you get back, maybe I'll take a peek at the new space myself."

Vanessa smiled and gave her aunt a peck on the cheek, then pulled off her apron and followed Marc. The occasional bit of sanding or hammering met her ears even before they reached the entryway between the two storefronts, but it had been going on for so long that it was nothing more than background noise now, and none of her regular customers seemed to notice or was bothered by it anymore.

Marc opened the door to the other side of the bakery and pushed back the sheet of thick plastic that had been hung as an extra precaution against sawdust and paint fumes. Holding it aside, he let her duck in ahead of him.

An awed sigh escaped her lips as she straightened and took in her nearly finished surroundings. The room was beautiful. More than she ever could have imagined, even after being in on the initial stages of planning.

Shelves and countertops of various sizes and heights lined the walls, creating more work space than she ever could have hoped for. The floor and ceiling had both been redone, and everything had been painted to match The Sugar Shack so that it was obviously an extension of the bakery itself.

"Oh!" Vanessa cried, putting her fingers to her lips.

"Does it meet with your approval?" Marc asked, amusement evident in his tone.

She was sure he could tell by her shaking hands and watery eyes just how pleased she was, but still she managed a breathless whisper, "It's wonderful."

Spinning around, she slowly took it all in again, and then again, her amazement growing with each turn. She didn't stop to think about how it had come about, the strings that were attached, or how costly the bill might be when it finally came due. All she knew was that this portion of the building was hers now, her chance to grow and expand the business of her heart.

With a tiny squeal of glee, she threw her arms around Marc's neck and squeezed him tight. Almost immediately, he circled her waist, hugging her back.

"Thank you," she whispered near his ear. "It's perfect."

When she pulled away, an odd expression crossed his face,

but before she could question it, the foreman appeared at her left shoulder. She was coming to think of him as the King of Rude and Untimely Interruptions.

"I take it she likes her new work area," he said with a smile, addressing Marc.

Considering that her arms were still linked around her ex-husband's neck, that wasn't a difficult observation to make. Feeling suddenly self-conscious, Vanessa cleared her throat and stepped back, putting a more respectable amount of distance between them.

"She does seem to like it," Marc replied.

"It's more than I ever could have hoped for," she told the two men. "Even after seeing the blueprints and design specs." She shook her head, sliding her hands into the pockets at the front of her white capris to keep from fidgeting. "I never imagined it would look this good."

"Glad you're happy. If there's anything else you need, or any changes you want done, let me know. We'll be here until about four putting on the finishing touches."

She couldn't imagine anything she would want changed, but while the two men talked business, she wandered around the drastically altered space. Admiring, touching, mentally filling the shelves and working behind the counters. She loved the sculpted molding and detail that precisely matched that of the bakery and marked it as hers.

Hers!

Well, hers and Aunt Helen's. And Marc's or the bank's, since she was sure there was going to be a hefty price to pay to someone at some point.

But even though she'd resisted being tied to her ex-husband in such a way, she couldn't deny that he had given her something no one else could—or would—have, and so quickly. She never would have been able to get things done in such short order with another investor or a loan directly from the bank.

Footsteps sounded behind her on the hardwood floor and she turned to see Marc coming toward her once again.

"They'll be cleaned up and out of here in a few more hours. And the computer equipment will be delivered tomorrow, so you can start setting up then, if you like."

Vanessa clasped her hands together, just barely resisting the urge to rub them together like some sort of devilish cartoon character. She was so excited, she almost couldn't contain herself.

They would need a website…and someone to design and maintain it, since she knew next to nothing about that sort of thing. They would also need packaging, and to set up an account with a reliable shipping company, and specialty shipping labels, and possibly even a catalog.

Goodness, there was so much to do. More, possibly, than she'd realistically considered.

Alarm began to claw at her insides and her chest became suddenly too tight to breathe. Oh, God, she couldn't do this. It was too much. She was only one person, for heaven's sake, and even if she counted on Aunt Helen's help, that made them only two people, one of whom had reached retirement age twenty years ago. Which basically put her back to being only one person, who *could not* handle this type of workload alone.

"I know you have a lot to do," Marc said, cutting into her panicked thoughts and allowing a small bit of oxygen to enter her lungs again, "but before you get too wrapped up in all of that, there's something I've been meaning to discuss with you."

She took a deep breath and forced herself to relax. One day at a time, one step at a time. She'd come this far, she could make it the rest of the way…even if it took her months to accomplish what a rich and powerful Keller heir could do practically overnight.

"All right."

"There's some company business that I need to return home to deal with."

"Oh." Her eyes widened in surprise.

She'd gotten so used to Marc being around that the idea of him leaving caught her unaware. Ironic, given how badly she'd wanted him to go back to Pittsburgh when he'd first arrived. Now, though, it was hard to picture the bakery or her day-to-day life without him in it.

Shaking off that rather revealing but unwelcome train of thought, she nodded her acceptance. "Okay, that's fine. I understand you have important work back in the city, and you've certainly done more than enough while you've been here."

She stopped herself just short of thanking him, but only because she was afraid that would fall too close to…well, thanking him, when he wasn't really doing her any favors. Oh, he'd been wonderfully helpful, but not out of the goodness of his heart. Better to take what he'd so generously offered and get him out of town before he started calling in vouchers and demanding repayment in ways she was unwilling or unable to fulfill.

A slow smile started to spread across his features and her pulse jumped. That wasn't a happy smile, it was an I-know-something-you-don't-know, cat-who-swallowed-the-canary smile.

"What?" she asked, drawing back slightly in wariness.

"You think I'm going to just pick up and leave, don't you?"

She had. Or perhaps she'd simply been hoping.

"It's all right, I understand," she said again. Sweeping an arm out to encompass their surroundings, she added, "This is all amazing, a wonderful start. Aunt Helen and I can certainly take over from here."

That smile stretched further, flashing bright white teeth, and a feeling of dread washed over her.

"I'm sure you and Aunt Helen will do a great job in getting the ball rolling. But that will have to wait until after we get back."

Vanessa blinked, replaying his words in her head. The feeling of dread started to dissipate, which was good...except that it seemed to be transforming into more of an all-over numbness that kept her brain from functioning properly.

She cleared her throat. "We?"

Marc inclined his head. "I want you and Danny to return to Pittsburgh with me so I can introduce my family to my son."

Eleven

"No."

Spinning on her heel, Vanessa stalked away, leaving Marc in the rippling wake of that cold, perfunctory response. Granted, he hadn't expected her to jump with joy at the prospect of going back with him, but he'd thought she would at least be reasonable about it.

With a sigh of resignation, he followed her through the plastic-draped doorway and into the bakery side of the building. She was already out of sight, likely in the kitchen, which meant she'd been moving at a pretty good clip.

He lifted a hand to push through the swinging door only to have it push back toward him, nearly cracking him in the face. Aunt Helen's blue eyes widened in startlement when she saw him, but she didn't say a word, simply tipped up her chin and pranced off for the front counter.

No love lost there, he thought, stepping into the kitchen and finding Vanessa exactly where he expected—standing at one of the large central islands, seemingly busy and focused on more food preparation. Even if she hadn't just walked away from him in a huff, he'd have known she was agitated by her jerky movements and the ramrod stiffness of her spine.

"Vanessa," he began, letting the door swing closed behind him.

"No."

She spat the word, then punctuated it with the slam of her rolling pin on the countertop. Cookie trays, cooling racks and miscellaneous utensils clattered against the stainless steel surface.

"No, Marc. No," she repeated with equal fervor, turning on him, her white-knuckled fingers still clinging to one of the rolling pin handles. "I am not going back there with you. I am not walking into that museum you call a home and dealing with your mother, who will look down her aristocratic nose at me just like she always has. And how much more judgmental and condescending do you think she'll be when you tell her I had a child out of wedlock? The fact that Danny is yours will be irrelevant. She'll criticize me for not telling you the minute I found out I was pregnant. She'll accuse me of going through with the divorce even though I knew I was carrying your baby, depriving you of time with your child and her of time with her grandchild. Of depriving *the world* of knowing about the existence of another great and wonderful Keller descendant."

Since that was pretty much exactly what he'd accused her of when *he'd* first learned of Danny's existence, he wasn't quite sure how to respond. Especially knowing how haughty his mother could be at times.

Vanessa let out a breath, seeming to lose a bit of her steam. In a lower, more subdued tone, she said, "Either that, or she'll deny Danny altogether. Declare he's not really a Keller, because of course she's always accused me of being a tramp, anyway. Or decide not to claim him as a Keller heir because we weren't married at the time of his birth."

She shook her head. "I won't do it, Marc. I won't go through that again and I sure as hell won't put my son through it."

Jaw clenching, he bit out, "He's my son, too, Vanessa."

"Yes," she acquiesced with a short nod of her head, "which is why you should want to protect him, too. From everything, and everyone."

Releasing the rolling pin, she put one hand flat to the island, the other on her hip and squared off, a mother bear ready and willing to protect her young, no matter what. "Danny is innocent. I won't let anyone make him feel less than perfect, less than wonderful. Ever. Not even his own grandmother."

Marc put his hands to his hips and cocked his head. "I had no idea you hated her so much," he murmured quietly.

"She was horrible to me," Vanessa retorted, rolling her eyes. "She made my life miserable while we were married."

For a minute, he didn't say anything, trying to gauge the truth of her words.

Had his mother really been that awful to her, or was Vanessa exaggerating? He knew women didn't always get along with their husbands' families and that mother-in-law/ daughter-in-law relationships could often be acrimonious.

Heaven knew his mother wasn't exactly the warmest person in the whole world, even with her own children, but had she really been so cruel to Vanessa when he hadn't been around?

"I'm sorry you feel that way," he said carefully, "but I have to go back. Not for long—a few days, maybe a week. And I'd like to take Danny with me."

At that, Vanessa opened her mouth and he knew another argument was coming.

"You can't really stop me from taking him along," he told

her flatly. "He's my son and you've kept him from me—and from my family—all this time. I think I deserve to take him home with me for a while."

Cocking his head, he fixed her with an intense, no-nonsense stare. "And we both know I don't need your permission."

"Are you threatening to take him from me?" she asked in a low voice.

"Do I need to?" he responded just as softly.

Though her mouth flattened in obvious anger, he could see the pulse beating frantically at her throat and her blue eyes glittering with emotion.

"It's just for a few days," he assured her again, feeling the odd need to wipe the fear and brimming tears from those eyes. "A week at the most. And you're more than welcome to come along, keep an eye on both of us. Why do you think I invited you in the first place?"

She licked her lips, swallowing hard. "You're going to make me do this, aren't you?" she asked in a wavering but resolved voice.

"I'm going to do this, with or without you. What part you play in the situation and how close an eye you keep on Danny is entirely up to you."

She gave him a look that clearly said she didn't think the choice he was giving her was any choice at all, but damned if he'd back down or go home, even for a short stay, without his son. He'd only just discovered he was a father; he wasn't going to walk away that easily.

Nor was he willing to let Danny out of his sight for that long. It might only be a handful of days by the calendar, but he'd gotten so used to seeing his son each and every day, to spending true quality time with him, that even twenty-four hours would feel like a lifetime at this point.

The same could be said of being away from Vanessa, he

supposed, but then, his attraction to her had never been in question.

No, his thoughts now had to be for his son. And though he would never intentionally cause his ex-wife this much anxiety or upset, he couldn't honestly be sure that she wouldn't pick up Danny and run with him the minute he drove out of town.

It would mean leaving her aunt and bakery and the life she'd built here in Summerville, but she'd kept Danny's existence from him once. What was to say she wouldn't try to *steal* the baby from him this time around?

There was also the small issue of her current physical condition. Like it or not, there *was* a chance she was pregnant again, and until he knew for sure one way or the other, he didn't intend to let her get away or keep another of his children a secret from him for a year or more.

Which meant that if he couldn't stay in Summerville and keep an eye on her and Danny every minute, then he would have to take Danny with him back to Pittsburgh. Vanessa could go along or not, but the one thing he could count on was that if Danny was with him, she wouldn't be hieing off to parts unknown.

Mouth set in a mulish slant, she mumbled, "This is extortion, you know."

He raised a brow and resisted the urge to chuckle. "I'd hardly call it that."

"What would you call it, then?"

"Fatherhood," he replied. "I'm simply exerting my parental rights. You remember what those are, don't you? They're what you denied me for the past year while you kept Danny to yourself."

He hadn't meant to let his bitterness over the past slip out, but he could tell by her expression that she'd heard it loud and clear.

"I'm not letting you take Danny anywhere without me," she said stubbornly.

Her implication being that if he insisted on taking Danny home to visit his family, she would be going along, however reluctantly.

"If you can be ready by tomorrow, we'll leave around noon."

"I'm not sure I can be ready quite that early."

Marc tipped his head and gave a short nod. "Fine, make it one o'clock, then."

The last thing Vanessa wanted to do was leave Summerville and the nice, tidy life she'd built for herself to return to the lion's den that was Keller Manor. It might have been only temporary—very temporary, if Marc's promise held true— but whether it was five days or only one, every minute was bound to feel like an eternity.

Which was why she didn't rush when it came to packing for herself and Danny. She took her time discussing her absence with Aunt Helen and setting up a couple of extra employees to cover for her, wanting to make sure The Sugar Shack really would run smoothly while she was away.

Then she actually solicited Marc's help in gathering everything they would need to take Danny on even a short trip. She was pretty sure he had no idea just how involved traveling with a baby could be.

While she decided about which of her own items and outfits to pack, she put him in charge of gathering up Danny's clothes and toys. Making sure they had enough diapers and wipes, bottles and formula. Blankets, booties, hats, infant sunscreen and more.

Vanessa kept thinking up new things to add to the list, hiding her amusement when Marc would begin to grumble and reminding him that returning to Pittsburgh was his idea.

They could skip all of the fuss and muss, if he'd only agree to let her—and Danny—stay in Summerville.

Each time the topic came up, however, any mention of canceling the trip or of his going without them simply caused his jaw to go taut, and he would silently return to collecting Danny's things or securing the safety seat in the back of his Mercedes.

By one the next day—because try as she might, she hadn't been able to postpone any longer—they were standing on the curb, ready to leave. Danny was in his car seat, kicking his legs and gumming his very own set of brightly colored plastic keys, while Marc waited near the front passenger door. A few feet farther along the sidewalk, Vanessa and Aunt Helen stood hand in hand.

"You're sure you want to do this?" her aunt asked in a hushed voice.

Oh, she was very sure she *didn't*. But she couldn't say that. Partly because she'd grudgingly agreed to go and partly because she didn't want Aunt Helen to worry about her.

"I'm sure," she lied, even though her fingers were chilled inside her aunt's solid grip. "It will be fine. Marc just wants to introduce Danny to his family and take care of some business with the company. We'll be back by the end of the week."

Aunt Helen raised a brow. "I hope so. Don't let them drag you down again, darling," she added softly. "You know what it did to you last time, living under that roof. Don't let it happen again."

A lump formed in Vanessa's throat, so large, she could barely swallow. Pulling her aunt close, she hugged her tightly and waited until she thought she could speak.

"I won't," she promised, blinking back tears.

When she could finally bring herself to pull away from her aunt's embrace, she turned toward Marc and the waiting car. Though she knew he was eager to get on the road, his expression gave away nothing of his inner thoughts or feelings.

"Ready to go?" he asked in an even tone.

Since her throat was still tight with emotion, she could only nod before climbing into the front seat. Once her legs were tucked safely inside, he closed the door for her and she reached for the safety belt while he moved around to the driver's side.

Flipping down the visor, she used the tiny rectangular mirror to make sure Danny was still okay, doing her best to ignore Marc's sudden, overpowering presence as he slipped behind the wheel.

How could she have forgotten how small cars were? Even given the roominess of his sleek, black Mercedes with its supple, tan leather interior, it suddenly felt as though all of the oxygen had been sucked out of the air, making it hard for her to draw a breath.

After fastening his own seat belt, Marc turned the key in the ignition and the engine purred to life. Rather than pull right out, though, as she'd expected, they simply sat there for a moment. So long, in fact, that she turned her head to look at him.

"Is something wrong?" she asked, thinking that perhaps they'd forgotten something. Although how that could even be possible, she didn't know. They'd packed just about everything *but* the kitchen sink, as the overstuffed trunk and half-stuffed backseat could attest.

"I know you don't want to do this," he said, his moss-green eyes glittering into hers. "But it's going to be all right."

She held his gaze for a moment, feeling that lump in her throat—which had finally started to recede—swell up again. Then she nodded before turning her attention back to the view straight in front of her.

But what she was really thinking was, *Famous last words*.

Because she didn't think there was any way that this little visit to Marc's family could possibly be anything less than a complete disaster.

Twelve

Unfortunately, the drive to Pittsburgh flew by much more quickly than Vanessa would have liked. Before she knew it, they were pulling up the long, oak-lined drive to Keller Manor.

Every inch of blacktop that passed beneath the Mercedes's tires made her heart beat faster and her stomach sink lower until she started to worry she might actually be sick.

Don't be sick, don't be sick, don't be sick, she told herself, taking deep, even breaths and praying the mantra would work.

Marc pulled to a stop beneath the wide porte cochere and within moments a young man was opening her door, offering a hand to help her out, then rushing to open the rear door so she could see to Danny. Marc had obviously called ahead to let the family know he—or perhaps they—would be coming.

She'd never seen this particular young man before, but then, Eleanor Keller tended to go through household staff faster than allergy sufferers went through facial tissues. Marc's mother also liked to have someone on hand to do her every bidding at the snap of her fingers. She employed gardeners, chefs, maids, a butler, an on-site mechanic and at least one personal assistant.

How many of them Vanessa would come in contact with during her stay was left to be seen, but one thing she did know was that she would treat them a heck of a lot better than Eleanor did. She would treat them like actual human beings rather than servants or robots programmed to be seen, but not heard, and to do exactly as they were told—nothing more and nothing less.

Coming around to her side of the Mercedes, Marc popped the trunk, then tossed his keys to the kid in the short red jacket that marked him as a Keller Manor employee. It even had a gold crest of sorts embroidered over the left breast pocket.

"We aren't traveling light," Marc told him, one corner of his mouth twisting upward. "But it all goes in my suite."

Vanessa opened her mouth to correct him. Marc had brought a single overnight case with him, while all the rest of the belongings filling the car were hers or Danny's. And they definitely did not belong in Marc's rooms.

But he apparently knew what she was about to say, because he pressed his index finger to her mouth, effectively cutting off her disagreement.

"They go in my rooms," he said again, so that only she could hear. "You and Danny will be staying there with me while we're here. No arguments."

Marc might be high-handed and controlling, but just because he said "no arguments" didn't mean she wasn't going to give him one. She opened her mouth again to do just that, but he covered her lips with a quick, hard kiss.

"No arguments," he repeated a shade more sternly. "It will be better for everyone involved. Trust me on this, okay?"

She so didn't want to. There was something deeply ingrained in her since their divorce that made her not want to trust him or listen to him or even believe a word he said.

But the fact was, she did trust him. Sharing a suite with him would be awkward and uncomfortable, but considering where this particular suite of rooms was located—inside the dreaded Keller mansion—it might actually be safer than staying in a room of her own. In addition to being quite spacious, Marc's suite also happened to be the one they'd lived in together while they were married, so at least she would be in a familiar setting.

"Fine," she muttered, slightly distracted by the lingering remnants of his kiss. He tasted of mint, and she could have sworn it was of the mentholated variety, because her lips were still tingling from the contact, however brief.

"Good," he replied, looking much too pleased with himself for her peace of mind. Then he scooped Danny out of her arms, tucking him against his own chest. "Now let's go inside and introduce our son to the rest of his family."

At that, Vanessa's stomach started to pitch and roll again, but Marc reached for her hand and the warmth of his fingers clasping hers was as calming as a glass of merlot. Well, almost. She was still jittery and her breathing was shallow as they stepped through the wide, white double front doors.

Built of redbrick and tall, Grecian columns, the entire mansion looked like a throwback to *Gone with the Wind*'s Tara—pre-Civil War destruction, of course. Secretly, however, Vanessa had always thought Marc's mother was trying to compete with a much larger residence, like the White House. And was winning.

Just inside the main entrance, the foyer sparkled like the lobby of a grand hotel. The parquet floor had been waxed to a high gloss. The chandelier hanging overhead glittered with polish and a thousand bits of glass shaped like teardrops reflecting the light of another thousand brightly lit bulbs.

In the center of the floor, an enormous display of freshly cut flowers rested on a sizeable marble table. And behind that, a wide, curved staircase was only one of the many ways to get to the second floor and opposite wings of the house.

It all looked exactly as it had the day Vanessa had left. Even the bouquet, which was large enough to bring Seabiscuit to his knees, was the same. Oh, they were different flowers, she was sure; Eleanor had new ones delivered every morning for the entire house. But they were the same *type* of flowers, the same colors, the very same arrangement.

She'd been gone a year. A year in which just about everything in her life had changed substantially. But if not even the flowers in the Keller's foyer had changed, she had little hope that anything—or anyone—else under the mansion's million-dollar roof had.

They didn't have coats, so the butler who had opened the door for them moved on down the long hallway to one side of the stairwell—likely to alert his mistress to their arrival. Seconds later, he returned to help the young man who was unloading the car carry their things to Marc's suite.

A moment after they disappeared upstairs, Eleanor emerged from her favorite parlor.

"Marcus, darling," she greeted Marc—and only Marc.

At the sound of her ex-mother-in-law's voice, Vanessa's heart lurched and she murmured a quick prayer asking for the strength and patience to get through this agonizing visit with the Wicked Witch of Western Pennsylvania.

The witch in question was dressed in a beige skirt and jacket over a pristine white blouse, all of which likely cost more than The Sugar Shack's monthly profits. Her hair was a perfect brownish-blond bob and her diamond jewelry— earrings, necklace, lapel pin and one ring—all matched and were no doubt very, very real. Eleanor Keller would never stoop to wearing cubic zirconia or costume jewelry, not even on an ordinary, uneventful weekday.

"Mother," Marc returned, leaning in to peck each of the older woman's cheeks. Bouncing Danny slightly in his arms, he added, "Meet your newest grandchild, Daniel Marcus."

Eleanor's pinched mouth twisted into what Vanessa suspected was meant to be a smile. "Lovely," she intoned, not even bothering to reach out and touch the baby. She simply perused him from head to toe.

Vanessa stiffened, offended on her child's behalf. But then Eleanor's attention shifted to her and she knew she would soon be offended on her very own behalf.

"I don't know what you were thinking," Marc's mother chastised, "keeping my son's child from him all this time. You should have said something the moment you discovered you were pregnant. You had no right to keep a Keller heir to yourself."

And it begins, Vanessa thought, with no sense of surprise whatsoever. She also wasn't offended, though she knew she had every right. Probably because Eleanor's reaction to her reappearance was exactly what she'd expected.

"Mother," Marc snapped in a tone Vanessa had rarely, if ever, heard from him.

Vanessa turned her head to study him, stunned by the look of anger on his face.

"We discussed this when I called," he continued. "The circumstances surrounding Danny's birth are between Vanessa and myself. I won't have you insulting her while we're here. Is that understood?"

Vanessa watched with wide eyes while Eleanor's lips flattened into a thin, unhappy line.

"Very well," she replied. "Dinner will be served at six

o'clock. I'll leave you both to get settled. And please remember that we *dress* for meals in this house."

After flicking a disdainful glance over Vanessa's modest outfit of magenta slacks and sleeveless polka-dot blouse, Marc's mother turned on her heel and clicked her way back across the parquet floor.

Releasing a pent-up breath, Vanessa muttered, "That went well."

She meant it to be sarcastic, but Marc simply smiled.

"I told you so." Hiking a drowsy Danny higher on his shoulder, he said, "Let's go upstairs and unpack. I think Danny could use a bit of a nap, too."

Reaching out, she brushed a hand over her son's brown, baby-soft hair. "He shouldn't be tired, he slept in the car."

Marc flashed her a grin. "It didn't take."

She chuckled, because she couldn't seem to help herself. This was the Marc she remembered from when they'd first started dating, first been married. Funny, kind, thoughtful… and so handsome, he took her breath away.

Warmth suffused her as he took her hand and started toward the wide stairwell. It spread from her fingertips to every other part of her body, making her tingle, and bringing up all sorts of wonderful memories.

How could being this close to Marc again feel so good, so right, when being in this house again felt so very wrong?

Marc watched Vanessa move around his suite, getting ready for dinner. Danny was sleeping in the sitting room, in a crib that had been set up at his request before their arrival.

But it was his ex-wife's presence that had his gut clenching and his mind spinning. She looked right here. It *felt* right to have her here again.

He wasn't sure he meant *here* as in his family's home,

though. It wasn't about having her back at the Keller Manor, or even in his private suite under his family's roof.

It was about having her with him, in his bedroom, no matter where that room happened to be located.

He'd missed that. Missed seeing her things spread out on top of the bureau and cluttering the bathroom vanity. Having her clothes hanging with his in the closet, the scent of her perfume lightly permeating his work shirts and the sheets on the bed.

He'd missed simply watching her, like this, as she moved around the room getting dressed, fixing her hair, doing her makeup or choosing which pieces of jewelry to wear.

Granted, she didn't have as many of those things with her this time as she had when they'd been man and wife, but that didn't keep her from falling into the same old habits or her movements from being achingly familiar. She was even wearing her favorite perfume—probably because she'd left a bottle on the dresser when she'd moved out and he hadn't been able to bring himself to get rid of it.

Now, he was glad. He'd given it to her for their anniversary, after all. So very long ago, it seemed. But the fact that she was wearing it again, that she was here with him, and apparently still trusted him… It made him wonder if maybe they could work out their differences and give each other another chance.

"How do I look?" she asked suddenly, breaking into his thoughts.

"Beautiful," he replied, without having to think about it, without even having to look. Though he did—long and hard. Looking at her was always a pleasure.

She was wearing a simple yellow sundress and sandals, with her hair pulled back above her ears so that her natural copper curls were even more prominent. His blood stirred in his veins, arousal pouring through him, and he licked his lips, wishing he could lick *her*—like a sweet, lemon-flavored popsicle.

Her eyes turned smoky and she offered him a small, sultry smile before brushing her hands down the sides of her skirt.

"Are you sure? You know what your mother is like and I didn't really pack anything dressy. I should have remembered her rule about formal dinners."

She paused to take a breath, then blew it out and wiped her hands on her skirt again in that same nervous gesture. "Of course, I don't have very many formal clothes anymore, so I couldn't have packed them even if I'd wanted to. I thought maybe some of my old clothes would still be here, but…"

She trailed off, her gaze skittering away from his, and Marc felt a stab of guilt somewhere around his solar plexus.

"I'm sorry. Mother had them thrown out after you left. I didn't expect you to be back, so I didn't think to keep any of them."

The truth was, they'd been too painful a reminder of her. Of her desertion, of the divorce papers he'd signed willingly more out of anger than any real desire to be single again and of the happier times they'd had together before things had somehow gone terribly wrong.

He shouldn't have let his mother dispose of them, he realized that now. It had been his place to deal with them, and he probably should have tracked Vanessa down to see if she wanted any of the items shipped to her before having them carted away. But at the time, he'd just wanted them gone and had been almost relieved when his mother had declared it was time to rid the house of any reminders of his ex-wife's abandonment.

The only thing that had been left behind was that crystal decanter of perfume.

"You look beautiful," he repeated, striding across the thickly carpeted floor to grasp her shoulders. "And we're not here to impress anyone. Not even Mother," he added with a grin.

When her mouth twitched with the beginnings of a smile and at least some of the anxiety seemed to drain away from her features, he leaned in and kissed her. He kept it light, even though that was far from what he really wanted.

Just the firm press of lips to lips instead of a ravaging of tongues. Just the brush of his fingertips over the warm skin of her bare shoulders instead of his hands delving inside her bodice and beneath the hem of her skirt.

He lingered for a few precious, breathless moments, then released her, stepping back before the full proof of his desire for her became obvious. Her freshly applied lipstick was smudged and he reached out to brush a spot with the edge of his thumb.

"Maybe we should skip dinner and go straight to dessert," he suggested in a low, graveled voice.

"I don't think your mother would like that very much."

He was pleased to hear the same huskiness in her voice as in his own. It meant he wasn't alone in the passion causing his pulse to hammer and hum.

"I don't think I give a good damn," he muttered with no small amount of feeling behind the words.

"As bad an idea as that probably is, I sincerely wish we could. Anything would be better than having to face your mother again."

The corner of Marc's mouth quirked down in a frown. Was she implying that staying in the room to make love with him would be only slightly less miserable than an evening spent in his family's company? He wasn't sure he liked being considered the lesser of two evils.

Before he had a chance to reply, however, a tapping sounded on the suite's outer door.

"That will be the nanny," he said, just managing to mask a sigh of disappointment.

"You hired a nanny?" Vanessa asked, sounding both surprised and disapproving.

"Not really," he replied. "One of Mother's maids is going to sit with him for a couple of hours. That's all right, isn't it?"

Her brows crossed. "I don't know. Is she good with infants?"

"I don't know," he said, repeating her phrase. "Let's go meet her and give her the third degree."

Wrapping his hand around her elbow, he pulled her with him toward the bedroom door.

"I don't want to give her the third degree," Vanessa murmured softly as they crossed the sitting room where Danny was sleeping. "I just want to know that she's qualified to sit with my child."

"We'll be right downstairs, so you can come up and check on her any time you like," he assured her, keeping his voice equally low. "Tonight can be her test run. If you like her and she does a good job, she can stay with Danny whenever you need her while you're here. If not, we'll hire a real nanny. One you feel a hundred percent confident in."

"You're placating me, aren't you?" she asked, an edge of annoyance entering her tone.

With his hand on the knob of the sitting room door, he turned to her and smiled. "Absolutely. While you're here, whatever you need, whatever you want, I intend to see that you get it."

Her eyes widened and he knew she was about to argue. So he bent down and captured her mouth, kissing her into warm and pliant submission.

When he pulled away, his own body was buzzing with warmth, but he was far from pliant. Quite stiff and unyielding would have been more accurate.

"Indulge me," he said, brushing a stray copper curl behind her ear while the taste of her lingered on his lips and prodded him to kiss her again. "Please."

Thirteen

As always, dinner with Marc's family was exhausting. Delicious, but exhausting.

Marc's mother was her usual haughty self, and though Vanessa had always liked Marc's brother Adam and Adam's wife, Clarissa, they were cut from the same basic cloth as Eleanor. Born with silver spoons in their mouths, they'd never known a moment of true want or need. And being raised as they had been, they were extremely refined, never a hair out of place, never a wrong word spoken.

The only reason Vanessa felt kindly toward them at all was that, despite their upbringings, Adam and Clarissa weren't quite as cold and judgmental as her ex-mother-in-law. From the moment she'd married Marc, they'd treated her like a true member of the family and had seemed genuinely sorry when she and Marc had split up.

Even tonight, knowing the circumstances surrounding Vanessa's return to Keller Manor and Eleanor's obvious disdain for her, Marc's brother and sister-in-law had treated her exactly the same as they had in the past. No sidelong glances or sharply pointed questions meant to put her on the spot or make her feel insecure, just friendly smiles and harmless banter.

That alone had helped to assuage some of Vanessa's raw and rampaging nerves when she'd first walked into the opulent dining room. Of course, Eleanor had already been seated at the head of the table like a queen holding court—and her expression alone had made Vanessa feel like a bug under a microscope.

To Vanessa's relief, her former mother-in-law had played fair through the soup and salad courses, keeping conversation light and impersonal. There were a couple of sticky moments while they enjoyed their entrees, but by the time dessert was being served, Eleanor dropped her semi-polite facade and began taking potshots at Vanessa as often as she thought she could get away with it. Some of them were direct, others more passive-aggressively delivered.

But this time, Marc actually stuck up for her—something he'd never done before, not with his mother. Possibly because in the past, Eleanor's attacks had been much more subtle, and often reserved for moments when the two of them were alone so that no one else would witness her true hatred for her son's wife.

Marc had grown up under Eleanor's frosty disposition, so he was used to her testy personality and jagged barbs. Even though her mother-in-law's malicious treatment had cut her to the quick, Vanessa truly believed that much of what Marc witnessed had gone straight over his head. He was like someone raised in the city, who wouldn't be bothered by the sounds of round-the-clock street traffic the way someone would who'd been raised in the quietness of the country.

But tonight, Marc hadn't let his mother's not-so-subtle

assaults slide by. He'd caught and responded to every one, always in Vanessa's defense. And once dessert was finished, when Eleanor seemed to be working herself toward a full-blown attack, he'd announced that it had been a long day, wished his family good-night, and taken Vanessa's hand to lead her out of the dining room.

She was almost giddy with relief and unaccustomed empowerment…and was still clutching his hand like a life preserver as they jogged upstairs side by side. She felt like she had when they'd first been dating, before the realities of being Mrs. Marcus Keller had settled around her and robbed her of her happiness.

Reaching the door to his suite, they were both smiling, and she was slightly out of breath. He put a finger to his lips, signaling for her to be quiet before he opened the door.

The fact that he had to remind her to be silent made her realize how close to giggling she was. *Giggling.* Like a twelve-year-old.

Biting back the strangled sound, she kept hold of Marc's hand and followed him into the darkened sitting room. The maid-slash-nanny they'd left with Danny was sitting across the room from the crib, reading a magazine beneath the muted yellow glare of a single low-lit lamp. When she saw them, she closed the magazine and quickly rose to her feet.

"How was he?" Marc whispered.

"Just fine," the young woman answered with a small smile. "He slept the entire time."

Good news for a babysitter. Not such good news for parents who were looking forward to a full night's sleep.

"That means he'll be up in the middle of the night," Vanessa whispered to no one in particular. And then to Marc, she said, "Prepare yourself for finally experiencing the true rigors of fatherhood."

He flashed her a grin, his green eyes sparking with a blaze

of heat that had nothing to do with parental exhilaration. "I'm looking forward to it."

After slipping the young maid a couple of folded-up bills that Vanessa was sure Eleanor would disapprove of, he saw her out, then joined Vanessa at the side of Danny's crib. His hand came up to rest on the small of her back, and she had to swallow a lump of emotion at the picture they must have made. Mother and father standing at the edge of their infant son's crib, watching him sleep.

This was what she'd always imagined motherhood and family would be like. It's what she'd wanted when she'd married Marc and they'd first started trying to get pregnant.

Funny how life never quite turned out the way you planned.

But this was nice, too. Maybe not ideal, maybe not the epitome of her adolescent dreams, but it still warmed her and made her heart swell inside her chest.

"I hope he's not coming down with something," she murmured, putting the back of her hand to Danny's tiny forehead. He didn't feel feverish, but one could never tell. "He doesn't usually sleep this long."

"He's had a busy day," Marc offered just as softly. "You'd be tired, too, if this were your first big trip since being born."

She chuckled, then had to cover her mouth to keep from waking the baby. With a grin of his own, Marc grabbed her arm and tugged her toward the bedroom door.

Once they were safely inside, he twirled her around and pushed her up against the hard, flat panel, covering her mouth with his own. His arms on either side of her head boxed her in, his body pressing her flat and sending a flare of heat everywhere he touched.

For long minutes, he kissed her, their breaths mingling, his tongue thrusting, parrying, drawing her into his passionate duel. She lost her breath, her vision, her sanity, her entire world shrinking to the single pinprick of reality that was Marc's solid embrace.

When he lightened his hold enough to let her gasp for air, she blinked like a newborn foal and let her head fall back against the door while he continued to nibble at her loose, tingling lips.

"This isn't what I had in mind when you said we'd be sharing your rooms," she managed—barely—after filling her lungs with a gasp of much-needed oxygen.

"Funny. It's exactly what I pictured." He murmured the words against her skin, moving to suckle the lobe of her ear around her small hoop earring.

Somehow she didn't doubt that. But letting his mother think they were sharing a room and *actually* sharing a room—a bed—were two completely different things.

"I was going to sleep on the chaise in the other room. Or slip into one of the guest rooms when nobody was looking. This…"

She moaned as his tongue darted out to lick a line of electricity from her collarbone to the hollow behind her ear. The sensation shot through her like a shock wave, turning her knees to jelly.

"Not smart. Not smart at all," she wheezed, unsure of whether the words were actually coming out of her mouth or simply echoing through her rapidly liquefying brain.

Shifting to wrap his arms around her and lift her against his body—one hand at her back, the other cradling her bottom—he turned and strode directly to the bed.

"I think it's positively brilliant," he replied, and then dropped her to the mattress like a sack of potatoes.

She certainly didn't *feel* like a sack of potatoes, though. Not when he followed her down, covering her from chest to ankle with his hot, heavy bulk.

This time, when he kissed her, she didn't think to protest where all of this might be leading. Maybe because she *knew* where it was leading. They both did.

Or maybe because his mouth on hers, his hands on her body, drove every other rational thought straight out of her head.

With deft fingers, he untied the knot of her dress's bodice behind her neck, lowering the gauzy yellow material to reveal her braless breasts. He cupped them together, kneading, brushing the tight nipples with his thumbs until she moaned and wiggled beneath him.

He returned her moan with one of his own, then let his hands slide around her waist to the rear zipper. She rose slightly and waited for the gentle *snick-snick-snick-snick* to stop, for him to tug the full skirt past her hips and thighs. Lifting himself up, he pulled the dress completely off, then divested her of her strappy sandals, as well.

She lay there in only a pair of thin, silken panties. They weren't the sexiest thing she'd ever worn, but she thanked heaven she was past the "granny panty" phase of pregnancy and new motherhood.

Judging by Marc's expression, he approved. For long minutes, he stayed propped on one strong arm staring down at her with eyes that had gone dark and primal. A shiver stole over her at that look, at the way it made her feel.

Not helpless or vulnerable by any means. Instead, she felt powerful. That she could incite that level of heat and lust in him continued to amaze her.

It had been that way in the beginning, and for most of their marriage, but she wouldn't have expected such intense desire to still be there after all they'd been through. That it was felt a bit like a miracle, even though she had no idea how the passion they shared in the bedroom could possibly translate to their future everyday lives.

His fingers delving beneath the elastic waist of her underwear dragged her up from the quagmire of her inner thoughts, and she was more than willing to grab hold of the life rope he offered.

She let him snake the panties down her legs, laying her bare, and then wrapped her arms around his neck to pull him down for a deep, soulful kiss. With a groan, Marc ground the bulge of his still-trapped erection against her hip.

Shifting beneath him, she welcomed him into the cradle of her thighs, crossing her legs behind his waist. He groaned again—or maybe it was a growl—and pressed even closer.

There was something between them, Marc thought. Something compelling and meaningful and not to be taken for granted. And he realized suddenly that that's exactly what he'd done—he'd taken his relationship with Vanessa for granted.

He'd married her, and brought her home, and simply assumed she would always be there. How could she not be happy in a house roughly the size of Buckingham Palace on an estate that boasted a tennis court, movie theater, two swimming pools—one indoors, one out—a riding stable, gardens, walking paths, a pond...everything anyone could ever want. Add to that the fact that he had more money than Midas and Croesus combined and he'd thought there was nothing he couldn't offer her, no reason any woman would ever walk away from him.

He'd never been one to delve too deeply into his or anyone else's feelings, but these past few weeks had him thinking differently. Feeling things he'd never felt before and wondering things he'd never thought to wonder about.

Maybe money wasn't everything. Maybe situating Vanessa in his family's mansion and giving her *carte blanche* with his primary bank account hadn't been enough for her.

But wasn't that a good thing? Didn't it mean that she hadn't loved him for his money alone? For what he had or what he could give her?

He wasn't sure what to think of that, since he was rich and intended to stay that way.

What he did know was that some sort of bond obviously still existed between them.

It wasn't just the sex—although that alone was outstanding enough to give him pause. But whatever it was, still buzzing and humming whenever they were together, it warranted a few hours of serious consideration.

Was there a chance they could reconcile? Try again, start over, build something better and stronger than they'd had before?

But even if they could, should they?

It was too much to contemplate rationally at the moment, given that his mind was currently preoccupied with more immediate and infinitely more enjoyable pursuits. But he did need to think about it. Decide if what he thought he was feeling was real.

Because what he thought he was feeling was love. Love. Longing. Devotion. And a desire to once again make things with Vanessa permanent.

He groaned as her tongue swirled inside his mouth and her ankles tightened at the small of his back. The heat of her naked body burned through his clothes and suddenly he wanted them gone.

With her still clinging to him like plastic wrap, he reached between them to tug at the buttons of his shirt, his belt, the front of his slacks. She shifted when necessary, giving him the space to shrug out of his clothes with jerky movements, but never actually letting go.

Once he was as naked as she, he edged her higher on the bed, careful not to bump her into the headboard while he held her to him with one arm and rearranged the overstuffed pillows with the other. He propped a couple under her rear, lifting her so that she looked down on him and the short strands of her copper hair fell around his face, as well as her own.

Grasping her chin, he held her in place while he nibbled her lips, tracing patterns over her waist and back with his fingertips. Her skin was like the smooth perfection of an alabaster statue, all elegant dips and curves. Only where statues were cold and lifeless, Vanessa was anything but. She was passionate and beautiful, and the only woman he'd ever made love to here, in this bed.

Before their marriage, he hadn't bothered to bring women home with him, at least not in order to sleep with them. It had been easier and less complicated to limit any intimacies to their apartments or the occasional hotel room. Even with those he'd dated seriously.

After the divorce…well, the truth was that he hadn't been with another woman since Vanessa left. He'd thrown himself into his work and the company. Frankly, no one else had even remotely caught his interest in the past year. He wondered now if anyone else ever would.

Crossing his arms behind her back, he grasped her to him, flattening her full, round breasts to his chest. She ran her hands through his hair, raking her nails over his scalp and the nape of his neck, something he'd always loved. It sent shivers of arousal down his spine and blood pulsing even more heavily between his legs.

Feeling the twitch of his erection, Vanessa shifted on his lap, arranging herself at a better angle to hover just above him. She wrapped her slim fingers around his hard length and stroked him lightly for a moment before guiding him ever so slowly into her damp, welcoming warmth.

Marc hissed a breath through clenched teeth, reciting stock values in his head to keep the evening from being over much too soon. The feel of her surrounding him, of being buried inside her, was one of the most astonishing sensations he'd ever experienced. No matter how many times it happened, each was nearly a religious experience. Amazing and life-altering. Impossibly better than the time before, and certain never to be as mind-blowing again.

She fit him like a glove, snug and hot, clutching at him in a way that nearly sent the top of his head spinning off. Hands on her bare buttocks, he tugged her closer—not that there was more than the thinnest sliver of space between them to begin with. But if he could have absorbed her into him, he would have.

Her breath whooshed out as she hit his chest with a *thump,* but he didn't give her a chance to refill her lungs with fresh air. Instead, he took her mouth while he lifted her up…and down. Up…and down. Short, jerky movements at first that grew faster and more frantic as their passions built and their mingled breathing became ragged.

Marc's heart pounded beneath his rib cage, every cell in his body tightening, straining, striving for release. He fought it, wanting the feelings to last. Wanting this time with Vanessa to last.

But holding back his orgasm was like trying to hold back a monsoon. His only hope was to hang on long enough and make sure she was with him when it happened.

Reaching between them, he trailed the flat of his hand over her abdomen and slipped two fingers into her folds in search of the secret bundle of nerves that would send her over the edge. She gasped as soon as he touched her there and he felt her inner muscles clench around him.

He cursed under his breath, working to school his breathing and praying for just a little more staying power. Just a little more.

Using the pads of those two fingers, he circled the swollen

bud first one direction and then the other. Vanessa gave a long, plaintive moan, her spine bowing as she arched above him.

"That's it, baby," he panted, cocking his hips to meet her every downward thrust. "Let yourself go. Come with me."

Her body was growing taut, her movements and breathing becoming more and more frenetic as her climax approached. Marc continued to tease, continued to drive her higher and higher. Pinching, flicking, letting his nails rake across her most sensitive spot while he rocked her from below.

And then she was over, crying out as wave after wave of pleasure rippled through her, causing her to shudder from head to toe.

Marc wasn't far behind. As soon as he felt the start of her climax, he released the stranglehold on his own self-control, and followed her into bliss.

Fourteen

Vanessa awoke to early morning sunlight streaming through the half-drawn draperies and across the bed. A wide smile split her face as she stretched like a cat, feeling better than she had in a very long time.

Tilting her head, she checked the clock, then sat up quickly. Ten o'clock! How could she possibly have slept so long?

Granted, she'd had a rather rigorous evening. She and Marc had made love three times during the long night, and Danny had had them both out of bed a couple of times in between. But she still should have been up long before now, especially since Danny *had* to be awake and fussing.

Rolling to the edge of the mattress, she started to sit up only to have her hand bump something near the head of the bed. It crinkled slightly, and when she looked, she found a slip of paper lying half under Marc's pillow.

Had to go to the office, it said in her ex-husband's tall, distinctive scrawl. *Danny is with Marguerite. Home for dinner.* And it was signed, *Love, M.*

Short and to the point, which was typical of Marc. But using the L-word in a frivolous manner was not. Did he mean it? Or had it simply slipped out by habit, given their return to familiar marital intimacies?

Vanessa's heart pinched inside her chest. She wasn't sure how to feel about either possibility, so she decided not to think about it too much. At least not at the moment.

Slipping out of bed, she quickly dressed in a pair of linen slacks and a light pumpkin orange top, then made her way out of the suite and downstairs, peeking her head in several doorways as she went in hopes of finding Danny.

She found them in the library. A large blanket was spread out on the floor with Danny in the center. Toys were spread all around, and the same young maid from last evening sat at one corner, making faces and playing with the laughing child. She was definitely working overtime, Vanessa thought, making a mental note to ask Marc if she was being properly compensated.

"Ms. Keller," the woman murmured as soon as she spotted Vanessa. Pushing to her feet, she clasped her hands nervously behind her back.

"It's Mason, actually," Vanessa replied automatically. Moving toward the blanket, she knelt beside Danny and scooped him up, cradling him against her chest.

He giggled, kicked his little legs and grabbed for her hair. She chuckled in return, kissing one of his warm, chubby cheeks.

"Thank you for watching him again," she said, climbing back to her feet and taking a seat on one of the nearby sofas.

"My pleasure, ma'am. Mr. Keller said it was all right to

give him a bottle and some baby cereal, so he's been fed and burped. Changed, too."

Vanessa nodded, sending the young woman a gentle smile. Her first inclination was to dismiss the maid and take over Danny's care herself. She wasn't used to having staff on hand and underfoot anymore to see to her every need or whim. And she *was* used to taking care of things—especially her son— almost single-handedly.

But the maid looked so eager to please and Vanessa knew from personal experience how demanding Eleanor could be. She was hard enough on her children and their spouses, but with her employees, she was downright tyrannical.

Standing, she gave Danny another kiss, this one in the center of his forehead, then returned him to the blanket.

"Would you mind watching him for a while longer?" she asked as she straightened. "I'd like to get some breakfast."

The young maid looked both pleased and unaccountably relieved. She quickly moved back to the blanket and took up her post at Danny's side.

"Of course, ma'am. Take your time."

"Thank you."

As familiar as Vanessa was with Keller Manor, she was anything but comfortable inside its gates and walls. It was too big and lifeless for her tastes, reminding her of some cold, cavernous mausoleum. At times, she could swear her footsteps and voice actually echoed as if she was inside a giant catacomb.

Although she knew she could go straight to the dining room, and a servant would be there to take her order in under a minute, she instead made her way to the kitchen at the rear of the house. The kitchen staff was busy bustling around, cleaning up from the rest of the family's morning meal and preparing for the afternoon one.

"Ms. Keller," one of them chirped when she saw her.

Vanessa smiled, not bothering to correct the use of her married name. If she did that every time one of the staff reverted to the family surname, she would get nothing else done.

"Hello, Glenna. It's nice to see you again."

The older woman's smile was warm and genuine, not the usual lift of dutiful lips. "You, too, ma'am."

"How many times have I told you to call me Vanessa?" she scolded with a friendly wink.

The woman nodded, but old habits died hard, and Vanessa knew every one of the Keller staff would rather be chastised by her for *not* calling her by her first name than to accidentally slip and call Eleanor by hers.

"I missed breakfast. Do you think I could get a slice of toast and some juice?" she asked. She knew better than to try to fix something on her own. She'd done that before, when she and Marc had first been married, and learned very quickly that the kitchen staff could be more than a little territorial.

"Of course, ma'am."

Glenna bustled off to fix a tray while Vanessa climbed onto a stool right there at the center island. She could have gone off to the dining room to wait, but the room was so large and empty, whereas the kitchen felt homier and buzzed with energy. She could also do without bumping into Eleanor, which was more likely elsewhere in the house.

After taking her time with *two* slices of toast and a scrambled egg because Glenna insisted she could use the protein, Vanessa strolled back to the library. Marguerite was still there, and Danny was still playing and cooing, enjoying himself just as much as when she'd left.

She laughed herself, just looking at him. There were few things in the world as delightful as a baby's heartfelt giggle, and she never grew tired of hearing her own child expressing his happiness over some silly thing like a shaken rattle or a game of peekaboo.

Joining them on the blanket, she spent the next twenty or thirty minutes entertaining Danny and chatting with Marguerite, who turned out to be a college student trying to earn extra money for tuition over her summer break. Vanessa could certainly relate, since that's exactly what she'd been doing when she'd met Marc for the first time.

"Well, isn't this a sweet little tableau."

Eleanor's crisp tone and deceptively reproving words cut Marguerite off midsentence and sent a flush of guilt toward the young maid's hairline. She immediately jumped up, fidgeting nervously.

"You may go," Eleanor told her without preamble.

Marguerite gave a quick nod, mumbled, "Yes, ma'am," and hurried out of the room.

Vanessa was just as uncomfortable with her ex-mother-in-law's sudden appearance, but refused to let it show. She certainly wasn't going to rush to her feet like some loyal subject in front of her reigning queen.

Remaining where she was, she continued playing with Danny, fighting the morbid impulse to glance in the older woman's direction.

"You didn't have to scare her off, Eleanor," she said flatly, finally looking up at her. "She's a nice girl. We were having an interesting conversation."

If possible, Eleanor's features turned even more pinched and disapproving. "I've told you before that it's unseemly to make friends with the help."

Vanessa chuckled at that, a short burst of unexpected sound that caused the older woman's brows to pucker. "I'm afraid I don't adhere to your antiquated rules, especially since I used to *be* the help, remember?"

"Oh, I remember," Eleanor replied coolly.

Of course, she did. Wasn't that her number one complaint about Vanessa ending up married to her son? That a high and mighty Keller heir might stoop so low as to tie himself to a common, no-name waitress?

"Do you really think this is going to work out?" Eleanor continued snidely. "That you can hide my son's child from him for nearly a year, then simply bat your eyes and waltz back into the lap of luxury, trapping Marcus all over again?"

Keeping one hand on Danny's belly and rubbing him gently through the soft cotton of his teddy bear onesie tucked into a tiny pair of denim shorts, Vanessa finally turned her head to meet her ex-mother-in-law's stern, steel-gray gaze. "Contrary to your single-minded beliefs, I don't particularly consider Keller Manor the lap of luxury. You may have everything money can buy, but this house definitely isn't a home. There's no warmth here and very little love."

She paused for a moment to lift Danny against her chest before climbing to her feet. Turning, she faced Eleanor head-on. "And I'm not trying to *trap* Marc. I never was. I just wanted to love him and be happy. But you couldn't let that happen, could you?"

Shifting Danny higher on her hip, she hugged him close and continued with so much of what she'd been wanting to say for years. "God forbid Marc falls in love with a woman from the wrong side of the tracks, with red blood instead of blue running through her veins. God forbid he be happy and make his own decisions and get out from under your oppressive, all-powerful thumb."

The words poured out of her like a rainstorm, but even though a sliver of fear remained at the very pit of her belly, she also felt relieved...and stronger than she would have expected.

Why hadn't she found the courage to tell Eleanor off long before now? She might have saved her marriage. Saved herself countless tears. Saved them all months and months of misery.

Eleanor, of course, didn't take Vanessa's first act of independence at all well. Her cheeks turned an unseemly shade of pink while her eyes narrowed and her jaw locked like a piranha's.

"How dare you?" she seethed, her face turning even more mottled.

But her anger didn't faze Vanessa. Not anymore.

"I should have dared a long time ago. I should have stood up to you and refused to let you intimidate me just because you come from old money and are used to looking down your nose at people. And I should have told Marc how you were treating me from the very beginning instead of trying to keep the peace and avoid tarnishing his opinion of you."

She shook her head, sad but determined. "I was young and stupid then, but I've grown up a lot in the past year. And I have a child of my own now…one I don't intend to let you push around, or let witness you pushing *me* around. I'm sorry, Eleanor, but if you want to be in your grandson's life, you're going to have to start treating me with a little respect."

Vanessa could tell from the pinch of her ex-mother-in-law's lips that she was about as far from that happening as from flapping her arms and flying to the moon.

"Get. Out."

Eleanor spat the words like a fire-breathing dragon, as though they were two completely different sentences. Fury shook her from head to toe, and if she'd had any medical issues, Vanessa would have worried she was on the verge of suffering a heart attack or stroke.

"Get out of my house," she repeated, turning to point one long, diamond-adorned finger toward the door.

Not that Vanessa had to be told twice.

"Gladly," she said, bending at the waist to gather Danny's blanket and toys one-handedly.

With her shoulders back and her head held high, she strode past Eleanor and up the long stairwell to Marc's suite to pack her things.

Marc pulled his Mercedes in front of the house and cut the engine. Normally he would drive around to the garage, but he was only going to be a few minutes. He'd forgotten some files on the desk in his suite, and was hoping he had time to grab them, get back to the office, deal with the rest of the issues filling his long to-do list and get home again in time for dinner.

Normally, he would simply skip dinner with the family and remain at the office as long as it took to get the job done. But for some reason, his workaholic temperament seemed to have abandoned him. He barely wanted to spend the rest of the day at the office, let alone his evening, as well. Instead, he wanted to be here, at home, with Vanessa and Danny.

His mouth curved in a smile just thinking about them, and he glanced at his watch, debating how much time he could afford to spend with them before turning around and heading back into the city.

There was a taxi parked ahead of him in the driveway and he lifted a hand to the cabbie as he rounded his Mercedes, wondering what it was doing there. Perhaps his mother had visitors, though it was odd for any of her acquaintances not to have their own very expensive, chauffeured vehicles.

Bounding up the front steps, he pushed open the door and came to a screeching halt at the pile of luggage and baby items in the center of the foyer floor.

"What the hell is going on?" he muttered more to himself than anyone else.

Hearing a noise at the top of the stairs, he lifted his head to find Vanessa descending with Danny in her arms, two of his mother's staff trailing behind, arms loaded with even more of his ex-wife's and son's belongings.

"Thank you so much for all your help," Vanessa was saying. "I really appreciate it."

"What's going on?" he asked, more loudly this time.

Vanessa's head jerked up at his sharp tone or his sudden, unexpected appearance, or both.

"Marc," she breathed. "I wasn't expecting you back so soon."

"Obviously."

His brows drew down in an angry, suspicious frown as she stopped at the bottom of the steps. The two maids dipped their heads and mumbled about taking her things out to the waiting cab, then disappeared as quickly as they could.

"Sneaking off again?" he accused, not caring that his voice was cold with disappointment and betrayal.

She was leaving him again, was all he could think. He'd asked her to spend just a few days with his family—a week at the most—and she hadn't made it even two days.

They'd made love last night, more than once. Slept wrapped in each others' arms. He'd thought—stupidly, it turned out—that they had turned a corner and might actually be able to make their relationship work.

But while he'd been falling in love with her all over again, and thinking about reconciliation, she'd been planning a timely escape. Exactly the same as before.

Exactly. Because the last time she'd left him, she'd been pregnant with his child...and there was a good chance the same was true now.

"No," Vanessa said, nervously licking her lips. "I mean, yes, I'm leaving, but no, I'm not trying to sneak off. I left you a note upstairs...on the back of the one you left for me this morning."

Well, that was different, at least, he thought with a heavy dose of sarcasm.

"And a note makes up for taking off in the middle of the day while I'm at the office?" he shot back. "With my son?"

"Of course not," she returned, looking strangely not guilty. "Although when you read the note, you'll see that I explained I'm not really taking off. I'm simply leaving the estate for a hotel downtown. I was going to stay there until I had the chance to talk to you."

He cocked his head, wondering what she could be up to. But then curiosity won out and he heard himself ask, "About what?"

She swallowed hard, her blue eyes going dark and oddly blank. "Your mother asked me to leave."

His own eyes went wide in surprise. "Why?" Why would his mother ask his wife—his ex-wife, he corrected himself silently—to leave?

"For the same reason she drove me away last time— because she hates me. Or at the very least disapproves of me greatly. As far as she's concerned, I'm not good enough for you and I never will be." A small smile touched her lips as she added, "Of course, this time she was much more forthright about wanting me gone, probably because I told her off."

"You told my mother off," he murmured, trying to process what he was hearing, but growing more confused by the minute. "Why would you do that?"

The amusement that had begun to touch Vanessa's features vanished, turning her face hard and defensive.

"Because I refuse to let her push me around any longer. I refuse to let her make me feel inferior just because *she* will always think of me as a lowly waitress, unworthy of her son's misguided affections."

Marc shook his head and started forward. "This is just a misunderstanding. Mother can be distant, I know, but she's thrilled about Danny and I'm sure she's pleased to have you back at the house, as well."

He reached out to grasp her shoulders, but she took a quick, single step back.

"No. It's not a misunderstanding, Marc," she told him, her tone implacable. "I know you love your mother and I would never ask you to change that. I would never intentionally try to drive a wedge between you and your family. But as much as I love you, I can't be here anymore."

Marc's chest tightened at her words. She loved him…or claimed to, at any rate yet she was preparing to walk away and leave him. Again.

"You love me," he scoffed, tossing the declaration back in her face. "Right. You love me, but you're leaving. Again. And what about Danny? What about the child you might be carrying now? My child. Are you going to run off and hide another pregnancy from me? Keep another baby from its father?"

She blanched at that, and God help him, he was glad. He knew he was being cruel, saying things to intentionally hurt her. But damn it, he was hurting, too. He was being betrayed a second time by the only woman he'd ever loved and who'd claimed—more than once—to love him in return.

"That's not fair, Marc," she said in a small voice, tightening her grip on Danny.

"The truth hurts, doesn't it, Vanessa? Signed divorce papers or no signed divorce papers, you knew you were pregnant when you left town the last time and you didn't even bother to tell me."

Because Danny was starting to fuss at her hip, she lowered her voice, but her temper came through loud and clear.

"Don't you dare lay that entirely at my feet. I kept Danny a secret, yes, but only after you refused to speak to me. I tried to tell you I was pregnant, but you couldn't be bothered to listen."

Marc's gaze narrowed. What game was she playing at now? he wondered. If what she said was true, it was news to him—and he sincerely believed he would remember his ex-wife telling him she was carrying his child.

"What are you talking about?" he asked carefully.

"I called you. As soon as I realized I was pregnant, I called you at the office, but you said—and I quote, because I will never forget the words as long as I live—*there's nothing you could possibly have to say to me that I want to hear.* End quote."

Well, now he knew something fishy was going on. Because he'd never uttered those words, not where Vanessa was concerned.

"I never said that," he murmured quietly.

"Yes," Vanessa retorted with conviction, "you did. Or at least that's the message Trevor said he was ordered to give me on your behalf."

"Trevor." It was a statement, not a question.

"Yes."

For a second, Marc wasn't certain if the thin sheen of crimson falling over his eyes was imaginary or if he was literally seeing red. He did know, however, that his blood pressure was rising like a geyser about to erupt and his hands were fisting with the urge to punch something. Or someone.

Reaching into his jacket pocket, he pulled out his cell phone and punched the button for his assistant's line at Keller Corp. Trevor Storch picked up on the first ring.

"Yes, sir," the overeager young man answered, well aware of who was calling thanks to Caller I.D.

"I'm out at the house. I want you here in under fifteen minutes."

"Yes, sir," Trevor responded dutifully and Marc could

almost see him jumping up and rounding his desk before he'd even returned the telephone to its cradle.

Meeting Vanessa's wary blue gaze, he snapped his own phone closed. "He'll be here soon and then we'll get to the bottom of this mess once and for all."

Fifteen

The seconds dragged on like hours, the minutes like years. Vanessa stood at the bottom of the stairs while the stony silence in the foyer grew heavier and more suffocating.

Danny wasn't getting any lighter, either. Shifting him to her other hip, she started to lower herself into a sitting position on one of the wide, carpeted steps, but Marc moved forward to stop her.

"Let me take him," he said brusquely, holding out his arms.

For a moment, she hesitated, the panicked thought that if she let Marc take the baby, she might never get him back racing through her mind. But if she tried to hold on to him now, then her avowals that she wouldn't try to keep Marc from seeing their son would be a lie, wouldn't they?

Hoping Marc hadn't noticed her uncertainty, she handed Danny over, rolling her shoulders and stretching her arms to work out the kinks.

"He's getting big, isn't he?" Marc said, a small smile curving his lips. The first he'd offered since spotting her luggage in the middle of the entryway.

"Yes, he is."

She was about to suggest they move into one of the nearby parlors to await Trevor's arrival, but just then a squeal of brakes came from the front drive and a minute later the door swung open.

Trevor Storch was tall, thin and more gangly than athletic. He stood just inside the foyer, brown hair mussed, shoulders sloped and breathing hard, as though he'd run most of the way from Keller Corp's main office building instead of driving.

Before he could say anything or begin bowing, as was his usual custom, Marc handed Danny back to her and turned on his assistant, any sign of kindness or amusement wiped from his face. Watching him close in on the younger man, even Vanessa had the urge to shy away and cover the baby's face to protect him from the steam that was almost literally pouring from Marc's ears.

Raising a hand practically in Trevor's face, Marc said in a low voice, "I'm going to ask you some questions and I want honest answers. God help you if you lie to me, do you understand?"

Any hint of eager anticipation drained from Storch's face, along with every bit of his skin's natural color. No doubt he'd thought he was being summoned to Keller Manor to run some extra-special errand or to receive a much-deserved—in his mind, at least—promotion.

"Y-yes, sir," he stammered, struggling to regain his composure.

"Did Vanessa call the office last year, just after we were divorced, and ask to speak with me?"

Trevor's eyes darted past Marc's shoulder to where she was standing, rocking slightly with the baby, who was currently content with attempting to fit his entire fist into his wide-open mouth.

"Yes or no, Trevor?" Marc demanded sharply.

"Y-yes, sir," he said, returning his attention to his very unhappy employer. "I believe she might have."

"And did you or did you not tell her that there was nothing she had to say to me that I wished to hear?"

At that, Trevor Storch's eyes went as wide as golf balls and his jaw dropped like a boulder. "I...I..."

He closed his mouth, licked his lips nervously. Then he seemed to deflate, his shoulders sinking even lower beneath his black shirt and beige sweater-vest than before.

"Yes, sir," he replied obediently, "I did."

Even from her vantage point near the stairwell, she saw Marc's brows dart upward in astonishment. Until that moment, she knew he hadn't believed her. He'd thought she was lying, or at the very least had suspected she was reinventing history to suit her purposes.

"Why?" he asked, shock and confusion evident in his tone.

"I...I..." Trevor's mouth open and closed like a guppy's and the color returned to his face in two rosy spots of nervous embarrassment.

"Because I told him to."

Eleanor's voice, deep and stern and coming out of nowhere, made Vanessa jump. Danny jerked in her arms at the sudden movement and began to fuss. She bounced up and down and pressed a kiss to the top of his head to shush him, but the greater part of her attention was on her ex-mother-in-law and the bomb she had just dropped into the middle of the cavernous foyer.

"Mother," Marc murmured, turning in her direction. "What are you talking about?"

Eleanor stepped from the doorway of the very same parlor

Vanessa had almost suggested they move to before Trevor's arrival, the heels of her powder blue pumps clicking regally on the thick parquet tiles.

"After your separation, I instructed Mr. Storch to field any calls that came into the office from Ms. Mason and to inform her that you didn't wish to speak to her again, for any reason."

Marc swung his disbelieving gaze from his mother to Travis and back again. Vanessa's own heart was pounding in her chest, emotion clogging her throat until it threatened to cut off her supply of oxygen.

All this time, she'd been so angry at Marc. So hurt that he could cut her off the way he had, that he could be so cruel and uncaring with a woman he'd once claimed to love…and who was unexpectedly carrying his child.

She knew, too, that Marc had probably been equally as angry and hurt at what he perceived to be her actions after they split, if he'd been expecting her to stay in at least moderate contact, only to have all of her calls impeded by his personal assistant.

Now she realized they had both been deceived.

"But…why?" Marc asked.

Eleanor's lips thinned. "She's trash, Marcus. Bad enough that you married her and brought her home in the first place. Having her continue to contact you and hang around after you finally wised up enough to divorce her would have been beyond unacceptable. As though I would ever stand by and allow her to work her wiles and trick you into taking her back."

"So you ordered *my* assistant to block *my wife's* attempts to contact me." It was a statement, not a question.

Eleanor had known Marc all his life, while Vanessa had known him for only a handful of years. Yet his mother seemed ignorant of the resentment building in the heat of his green eyes and the clenching of his fists at his sides.

"Of course," Eleanor responded haughtily, tipping her nose another few centimeters into the air. "I would do anything to protect the Keller name from gold diggers like her."

"Her name," Marc intoned from between gritted teeth, "is Vanessa."

Before his mother could respond to that bit of information, he crossed to Vanessa and plucked Danny right out of her arms. While she floundered, unsure of what to think or do, he grabbed her elbow, ran his hand the rest of the way down her arm and threaded his fingers with hers. He marched them past the pile of her packed belongings nearly to the door, stopping a mere foot from Trevor's trembling form.

"You're fired," he told the young man in a brook-no-arguments tone. "Return to the office, clear out your desk and leave. You're welcome to work for my mother, if she'll have you, since the two of you certainly deserve each other, but I don't want to see you anywhere near Keller Corp ever again. Is that understood?"

Vanessa could have sworn she saw tears fill Trevor's eyes just before he ducked his head to stare at the tops of his shoes. "Yes, sir," he said in a watery voice.

"And you," Marc continued, turning this time to glare at his mother. "I always thought Vanessa was exaggerating when she told me how badly you were behaving toward her behind my back, because I didn't want to believe my own mother would treat the woman I loved as anything other than a true member of this family. But she was right all along, wasn't she?"

Marc paused for a moment, but Vanessa didn't think it was to allow Eleanor to respond. "You won't see us again. Not here. I'll send for my belongings and anything Vanessa might have left behind. But the company is mine. Mine and Adam's.

You're off the Board of Directors as of now and your name will be removed from anything related to the corporation."

Eleanor's nostrils flared as she sucked in a breath, and Vanessa saw the first shadow of fear cross her severe features.

"You can't do that," she rasped.

Marc's gaze narrowed, his expression every bit as unyielding as his mother's at that moment. "Watch me."

With that, he yanked open the front door and stalked through, tugging Vanessa along behind him. The two servants who had been helping her carry her things to the waiting taxi were standing beside the bright yellow car, doing their best to remain inconspicuous and out of what she was sure they assumed would be the line of fire.

"Put all of Vanessa's things in my car," he told them, transferring Danny back to her. The poor baby was probably beginning to feel like a racquetball, though from his happy gurgles, he seemed to think being passed from one parent to the other and back again was some sort of game.

Then Marc crossed to the cab and leaned in the open window to speak in low tones to the man behind the wheel. After Marc slipped him a few folded-up bills, the driver nodded, and Marc returned to her side.

"What are we doing?" she asked, still unable to believe all that had just happened.

Lifting a hand to cup her face, he said, "We're leaving. We'll stay at a hotel until I can get things straightened out at the office, then we'll head back to Summerville."

"But…"

"No buts." He shook his head, his gaze immediately softening to a lovely emerald green. "I'm so sorry, Vanessa. I didn't see it. I didn't believe you because I didn't want to admit my family was anything but perfect, that one of them would treat my wife with anything but love and respect."

His thumb rubbed slowly back and forth across her cheek, and she felt herself melting.

"If I had known, if I had truly understood what you were going through, I would have stopped it. I never would have let things between us turn out the way they did."

Her throat was so tight, she couldn't speak, but she believed him. After what he'd just done, how he'd stood up to his mother and walked away from his family home *for her,* how could she not?

"I love you, Vanessa. I've always loved you and I'm so sorry for all the time I've wasted being a blind, stupid fool."

She sniffed as happy tears filled her eyes and balanced precariously on the tips of her lashes.

He leaned in, pressing his brow to hers, and said barely above a whisper, "If I could go back and do things differently, I would never let you go."

A near-sob rolled up from her chest, causing those tears to spill over and roll down her cheeks.

"I love you, too," she told him. "And I never wanted to leave, I just couldn't live that way anymore."

"I know that," he said with more understanding than she'd heard from him in longer than she could remember.

"And I didn't plan to keep Danny a secret from you. I really did try to tell you, but after Trevor refused to let me speak to you, I was so angry and hurt, thinking the directive came from you…" She trailed off, barely certain anymore of how she'd felt or what had led her to make the decisions she had.

"I know," Marc murmured, one corner of his mouth lifting in a kind, loving half smile. He looked at their son with a father's love and pride burning in his eyes before brushing a hand over the baby's downy-soft head.

"We both made mistakes and let small issues become big ones. But we won't let that happen again, will we?"

She shook her head, doing her best to blink back fresh tears.

Framing her face with his big, strong hands, he brushed his lips lightly across hers. "I really do love you, Nessa. Forever."

"I love you, too," she tried to say, but his mouth was already covering hers, kissing her deeply, with all the passion that had bloomed between them since the first moment they'd met.

Epilogue

Two years later...

Marc strolled down the sidewalk of Summerville's Main Street, nodding and waving a greeting to friends as he passed. And he was whistling, for heaven's sake. He never used to whistle, but lately, he'd caught himself doing it more and more often.

Which just went to prove that small town life wasn't quite as dull or restrictive as he'd once believed. In fact, he kind of liked it.

Of course, he didn't think his current happiness had as much to do with where he was living as it did with *how* he was living...and with whom.

Hiking Danny higher on his hip, he continued to whistle—the theme from *Thomas the Tank Engine,* no less—and grinned at his son's hearty chuckle. He was wearing a pair of denim trousers with an official Sugar Shack infant tee and tiny yellow sneakers.

The Sugar Shack merchandise had been Marc's idea and had been an immediate success. In addition to baked goods, they now sold T-shirts, sweatshirts, baby clothes, coffee and travel mugs, and even key chains. In his opinion, it was the best advertising Vanessa could get other than plain old word of mouth.

The sneakers were because Danny was walking now…well, toddling, was more like it…and because he was starting to want to dress more like his daddy. Marc's heart gave a lurch at the thought and he squeezed his son even tighter against his side.

"We're going to see Mommy," he told the little boy, then added, "Maybe she'll give you a cookie."

"Cookie!" Danny yelled at the top of his lungs, lifting his arms and clapping over his head.

Marc laughed, wondering how much trouble he would get in when Vanessa found out he was plying their son with promises of sugar first thing in the morning. But then, she ran a bakery, so she shouldn't be surprised. "Cookie" had been Danny's first word…followed by "mama," "dada" and "cake." He was working on "baklava," but at the moment it came out more like "bababa."

Reaching The Sugar Shack's wide glass storefront, he pulled open the door to the distribution side of the business. An elderly woman was just shuffling out, so he held it for her and wished her a good day before slipping inside.

Vanessa was behind the counter, but as soon as she saw them, she smiled and started around. Her copper curls—longer now than when Danny had been an infant—were pulled back in a loose ponytail, and a pristine white Sugar Shack apron covered the front of her short-sleeve blouse and shorts.

"Cookie!" Danny cried, wiggling to be put down.

Vanessa arched a brow. "His idea, I'm sure," she murmured half under her breath.

"Of course," Marc replied. "But then, what can you expect when his mother owns the best bakery in the state? You're lucky he isn't asking for pastries morning, noon and night."

"He is, but that doesn't mean he'll get them," she answered primly.

Leaning in, she bussed Danny on the cheek, running her fingers through his toffee-brown hair, which was rather in need of a trim. They'd been talking lately about having it cut and Marc was inordinately excited about taking his son for his first visit to the barber shop. An honest-to-goodness barber shop!

When she lifted up on tiptoe to kiss him, too, he slipped his free arm around her back and pulled her in for something much longer and deeper. Trapped between them, Danny giggled when they stayed locked at the lips a bit too long and started slapping their cheeks with his small hands.

They pulled apart, and Vanessa chuckled, her face flushing a becoming shade of pink. Marc, however, was far from embarrassed; he was busy calculating how many hours were left before she closed up shop and he could convince her to go to bed early.

Too damn many, that was for sure.

"I have a surprise for you," he told her as she moved back behind the counter.

He watched her loosen the ties of her apron and slip it over her head, then dig inside a small plastic container that she kept filled with cookies just for Danny. Their son's love of sweets had prompted her to experiment with a few recipes for healthier cookies and desserts. Ones with less fat and sugar, and substitutions such as applesauce and raisin paste for the oils.

Coming around again, she handed Danny the cookie, and Marc set him on one of the high countertops to eat it, remaining close enough to keep him from toppling off.

Without the apron, Vanessa's four months of pregnancy were much more noticeable. And just like every time he saw that tiny baby bump, Marc's chest constricted with love and pride and the overwhelming relief of knowing that—even though they'd cut it damn close—he hadn't let her get away.

As much as they'd suspected it for a while, she hadn't been pregnant when they'd walked away from his family's home. Instead, they'd had some time to settle in Summerville and adjust to once again being together. Not that there had been a lot of adjustment needed, at least not on his part.

They'd bought a large, very nice house on the outskirts of town. One that had been built years before by a wealthy businessman who'd decided to move closer to the city after he and his wife divorced.

It was smaller than Marc was used to, but exceptionally large and impressive for the area. It also had plenty of room for their growing family, and came with enough acreage to afford complete privacy, as well as room for Danny and his future siblings to play.

They had also gotten remarried. At the courthouse this time, with a minimum of fuss and muss. Only Helen had been in attendance as their witness, as well as Vanessa's matron-of-honor and Danny's stand-in-nanny. He actually thought she might be coming around to liking him, but he knew he would have to prove himself all over again to be worthy of her niece's affections before he could truly win back the woman's favor.

After everything they'd been through, it had been easy to agree that another big wedding wasn't necessary. They just wanted to be together again, undoing the divorce that they both wished had never taken place in the first place.

Then they'd discussed having another child. One he would know about and be involved with from the very beginning.

"So," Vanessa prompted. "What's my surprise?" She tilted her head and shot him an impish grin, one he couldn't resist kissing off her lips.

Breaking away much sooner than he would have liked, he reached into the back pocket of his khaki chinos and pulled out a folded-over, full-color catalog. He let it fall open and held it up for her to see.

"Oh, my God!" She gave a squeal of pleasure and grabbed it up, studying the front and back covers first, then flipping through each individual page. "I can't believe it's finally ready. It's wonderful!"

It was The Sugar Shack's very first mail-order catalog, but Marc sincerely hoped it wouldn't be the last. Since leaving Pittsburgh, he'd thrown himself wholeheartedly into helping Vanessa build her business. He still drove into the city occasionally to take care of Keller Corp affairs, but was content to allow his brother to deal with the daily running of that company and the family's other major holdings.

In addition to designing the catalog, he'd set up a website for the bakery and was looking into rental spaces in other surrounding towns with an eye toward opening more Sugar Shack bakeries in multiple locations.

"I have more good news," he said while she continued to admire the pages of the catalog.

"What?" she asked, lifting her head and looking positively giddy.

He smiled in return, because he couldn't seem to help himself. "Adam and I finalized an agreement this morning to open a Sugar Shack bakery in the lobby of the Keller Corp building."

Marc expected her to shriek with joy and throw her arms

around her neck, but instead she grew quiet and simply studied him.

"What's the matter?" he asked, cocking his head in confusion. "I thought you would be happy about this."

She nodded. "I am. Everything you've done has been wonderful—more than Aunt Helen and I ever could have imagined."

"But...?"

Her mouth twisted, her eyes growing concerned. "But I worry about what your mother will think of you and Adam working together to put *my* business in the lobby of your family's company headquarters. And if we really do move back to the city one of these days the way we've discussed..."

She trailed off and he could see every one of her doubts playing across her face.

"She already knows," he told her.

Her mouth went slack with shock.

"According to Adam, she's asked about us several times, and he's been updating her. I don't want to get your hopes up—" he grinned as she rolled her eyes at the possibility "—but he seems to think she might be coming around."

Vanessa gave a disbelieving snort and he chuckled. "All right. So she'll never be the cookie-baking, story-telling sort of mother or grandmother we might wish she were, but I think walking away and cutting her out of our lives for a while showed her that I'm serious in my devotion to you. You're my wife and I won't allow anyone or anything to ever hurt you or come between us again. Not even the woman who gave birth to me."

Stepping forward, she rested her hands and then her head on his chest. "Are you sorry?" she murmured against his shirt.

Framing her face with his hands, he tipped her chin up and

met her storm blue gaze. "Not even a little bit. I don't ever want you to think that, okay? You and Danny—" he tipped his head toward their crumb-covered son "—and this tiny tyke here—" he pressed a hand flat to her growing belly "—are all that matter to me. I haven't closed the door on rebuilding a relationship with my mother, but I wouldn't trade my life now with the three of you for anything in the world. Do you understand?"

It took her a second, but she nodded slowly, and he stared into her eyes until he was sure she believed him.

"Good. Then I'll get our little Cookie Monster cleaned up while you go show your aunt the new catalog. Hopefully it will put her in a good enough mood that we can ask her to watch Danny for a while this afternoon."

"Why?" Vanessa asked.

His mouth spread in a wolfish grin and he leaned in to brush his lips across hers. "Because I'm in the mood for something sweet."

Cocking her head to the side, she narrowed her eyes, giving him a sultry, seductive look. "Well, this *is* a bakery. Sweets are what we're all about."

He gave a low growl at her wicked flirtation and nearly told her how lucky she was that Danny was with them and the bakery was fronted by floor-to-ceiling plate glass windows. Otherwise, he would be lifting her onto one of the countertops and divesting her of her clothes already.

"What I want isn't on the menu."

"So you have a special order?" she asked, batting those lashes until he felt his insides start to boil.

He nodded, mouth gone too dry to respond.

"Lucky for you, and thanks to my very business-savvy husband, we're set up to take special orders now. You may have to pay extra for shipping and handling, though."

Lips twitching, he said in a low voice, "That shouldn't be a problem. In case you haven't heard, I'm rich."

She smiled softly and reached up to wrap her arms around his neck. "So am I," she whispered.

And neither of them were talking about their bank accounts.

* * * * *

COMING NEXT MONTH

Available July 12, 2011

You can find more information on upcoming
Harlequin® titles, free excerpts and more at
www.HarlequinInsideRomance.com.

USA TODAY *bestselling author B.J. Daniels*
takes you on a trip to Whitehorse, Montana,
and the Chisholm Cattle Company.

RUSTLED

Available July 2011 from Harlequin Intrigue.

As the dust settled, Dawson got his first good look at the rustler. A pair of big Montana sky-blue eyes glared up at him from a face framed by blond curls.

A woman rustler?

"You have to let me go," she hollered as the roar of the stampeding cattle died off in the distance.

"So you can finish stealing my cattle? I don't think so." Dawson jerked the woman to her feet.

She reached for the gun strapped to her hip hidden under her long barn jacket.

He grabbed the weapon before she could, his eyes narrowing as he assessed her. "How many others are there?" he demanded, grabbing a fistful of her jacket. "I think you'd better start talking before I tear into you."

She tried to fight him off, but he was on to her tricks and pinned her to the ground. He was suddenly aware of the soft curves beneath the jean jacket she wore under her coat.

"You have to listen to me." She ground out the words from between her gritted teeth. "You have to let me go. If you don't they will come back for me and they will kill you. There are too many of them for you to fight off alone. You won't stand a chance and I don't want your blood on my hands."

"I'm touched by your concern for me. Especially after you just tried to pull a gun on me."

"I wasn't going to shoot you."

Dawson hauled her to her feet and walked her the rest of the way to his horse. Reaching into his saddlebag, he pulled out a length of rope.

"You can't tie me up."

He pulled her hands behind her back and began to tie her wrists together.

"If you let me go, I can keep them from coming back," she said. "You have my word." She let out an unladylike curse. "I'm just trying to save your sorry neck."

"And I'm just going after my cattle."

"Don't you mean your boss's cattle?"

"Those cattle are mine."

"*You're* a Chisholm?"

"Dawson Chisholm. And you are…?"

"Everyone calls me Jinx."

He chuckled. "I can see why."

Bronco busting, falling in love…it's all in a day's work.
Look for the rest of their story in

RUSTLED

Available July 2011 from Harlequin Intrigue
wherever books are sold.

THE NOTORIOUS
WOLFES

A powerful dynasty,
where secrets and scandal never sleep!

Eight siblings, blessed with wealth, but denied the one
thing they wanted—a father's love. Haunted by their
past and driven to succeed, the Wolfes scattered to the
far corners of the globe. It's said that even the blackest
of souls can be healed by the purest of love....

But can the dynasty rise again?

Praise for
Gale Force

"Rachel Caine is still going strong, throwing one curve-ball after another as she continues to shake up the status quo. She successfully maintains a sense of impending doom and escalating tension as the stakes get ever higher.... I really like this series, because it's urban fantasy that ... tell[s] something exciting and original and ever-changing."
—SF Site

"Light, wry wit keeps things from getting too heavy, but even at the funniest moments, there is an intense drama that makes this a magnetic book."
—Huntress Book Reviews

"Captivating.... Caine is a top-notch writer and her skill in weaving a mesmerizing tale is easily seen. Her characters are wonderfully dimensional, and the world they live in is solid and believable. The chemistry between these strong characters always sizzles and *Gale Force* stands out with deep and fluctuating emotions."
—Darque Reviews

"Caine jumps the reader into the middle of another epic battle, pitting Joanne Baldwin against supernatural evil unlike any she's seen before.... Fans of dynamic, fast-paced action, strong on magic and characterization, will enjoy this new installment of Joanne Baldwin's adventures."
—SFRevu

"The Weather Warden books are an addictive force of nature that will suck you in."
—*News and Sentinel* (Parkersburg, WV)

continued ...

"Another great addition to the series.... The action never stops, and like every other book in the series, this is a roller-coaster ride through all the elements Mother Nature can throw at Jo."   —ParaNormal Romance

... and for the Weather Warden Series

"The forecast calls for ... a fun read."   —Jim Butcher

"With chick lit dialogue and rocket-propelled pacing, Rachel Caine takes the Weather Wardens to places the Weather Channel never imagined!"   —Mary Jo Putney

"A fast-paced thrill ride [that] brings new meaning to stormy weather."   —*Locus*

"An appealing heroine, with a wry sense of humor that enlivens even the darkest encounters."   —SF Site

"A kick-butt heroine who will appeal strongly to fans of Tanya Huff, Kelley Armstrong, and Charlaine Harris."
    —*Romantic Times*

"The Weather Warden series is fun reading ... more engaging than most TV."   —*Booklist*

"A neat, stylish, and very witty addition to the genre, all wrapped up in a narrative voice to die for. Hugely entertaining."   —SF Crowsnest

Books by Rachel Caine

WEATHER WARDEN

Ill Wind
Heat Stroke
Chill Factor
Windfall
Firestorm
Thin Air
Gale Force
Cape Storm

OUTCAST SEASON

Undone

THE MORGANVILLE VAMPIRES

Glass Houses
The Dead Girls' Dance
Midnight Alley
Feast of Fools
Lord of Misrule
Carpe Corpus

CAPE STORM

A WEATHER WARDEN NOVEL

Rachel Caine

A ROC BOOK

ROC
Published by New American Library, a division of
Penguin Group (USA) Inc., 375 Hudson Street,
New York, New York 10014, USA
Penguin Group (Canada), 90 Eglinton Avenue East, Suite 700, Toronto,
Ontario M4P 2Y3, Canada (a division of Pearson Penguin Canada Inc.)
Penguin Books Ltd., 80 Strand, London WC2R 0RL, England
Penguin Ireland, 25 St. Stephen's Green, Dublin 2,
Ireland (a division of Penguin Books Ltd.)
Penguin Group (Australia), 250 Camberwell Road, Camberwell, Victoria 3124,
Australia (a division of Pearson Australia Group Pty. Ltd.)
Penguin Books India Pvt. Ltd., 11 Community Centre, Panchsheel Park,
New Delhi - 110 017, India
Penguin Group (NZ), 67 Apollo Drive, Rosedale, North Shore 0632,
New Zealand (a division of Pearson New Zealand Ltd.)
Penguin Books (South Africa) (Pty.) Ltd., 24 Sturdee Avenue,
Rosebank, Johannesburg 2196, South Africa

Penguin Books Ltd., Registered Offices:
80 Strand, London WC2R 0RL, England

First published by Roc, an imprint of New American Library,
a division of Penguin Group (USA) Inc.

First Printing, August 2009
10 9 8 7 6 5 4 3 2 1

Copyright © Roxanne Longstreet Conrad, 2009
All rights reserved

RoC REGISTERED TRADEMARK—MARCA REGISTRADA

Printed in the United States of America

To Ter Matthies.
For courage, for peace, for sailing on ahead.
We'll meet on the shore.

ACKNOWLEDGMENTS

Jim Suhler & Monkey Beat
Joe Bonamassa
Lucienne Diver
Charles Armitage
Katherine Gunther
P. N. Elrod
Jackie Leaf
Christina Radish
Joya Manning
Jenn Clack
Kari Phillips
ORAC
Jackie Kessler
Richelle Mead
Kaz de Winter

... and, as always, my lovely and very patient husband, Cat.

Thanks for sharing the voyage, and making all the lovely, fruity drinks.

What Has Come Before

My name is Joanne Baldwin, and I used to control the weather as a Weather Warden. These days, I can also control the forces of the earth, like volcanoes and earthquakes, and the forces of fire.

Sounds like fun, eh? Not when it makes you a target for every psycho crazy world-killing danger that comes along.

Good thing I've got my friends at my back—Lewis Orwell, the most powerful Warden on the planet; Cherise, my best (and not supernatural) friend; and a wide cast of sometimes dangerous allies who've got their own missions and agendas that don't always match up with mine.

And I've got David, my true love. He's also a supernatural Djinn, the fairy-tale three-wishes kind, and he's now co-ruler of the Djinn on Earth.

What I *don't* have is peace, because even while I walked down the aisle to get married to my true love, an old enemy totally ruined my chances for a happy honeymoon and possibly even my survival. I'm not just in danger now, I'm dangerous—to everyone I love.

I've got to go and fix this, before the whole world suffers the consequences.

Chapter One

I've had many *oh crap* moments in my life. If you know me at all, you can imagine how many of them there have been, and the rising scale of crapitude that these moments cover.

So when I say that I looked out past the Miami Harbor horizon to the east and saw the storm that was heading for us, and said a heartfelt *oh crap,* you'll understand that my concern was not so much for the state of my already disheveled hairdo, or my not-so-designer clothes, but more about survival.

And not just *my* survival. An ominous line of storm-black out there was spreading like ink, and it was already large enough to rain destruction all over Miami before it ripped through Florida's panhandle and blew apart into tornadoes, floods, deadly downbursts.

Hurricanes: the gift that keeps on giving.

I tightened my grip around a handy light pole as the wind buffeted me. Rain had already started to fall, and although it was nearly midday, it seemed very dark. I couldn't see any hint of sun overhead, not even a pale shadow through the clouds.

Chaos ruled the docks, as shipmasters rushed to secure their vessels against the unforecast storm. Tourists scrambled for shelter. Locals resignedly broke out the plywood and hammers. I'd heard that the major freeways were jammed and that the hurricane evacuation plan had been triggered, but it was never going to work. The thing was simply moving too fast, and there wasn't enough warning.

And needless to say, all this was my fault.

I mean that literally. I'm supposed to be able to control the weather, and other elements at work on this planet; I'm supposed to be able to stop things like this from happening. I'm supposed to be the hero, dammit.

It came as a bit of a shock to be both helpless and—although no one knew it yet—a villain. As the storm came roaring toward us, I knew it was my fault.

I could feel it in the burning of the black tattoo on my back, high up on the shoulder. Not the normal tramp stamp you could get (with hepatitis on the side) at any corner needle shop; mine was courtesy of an old enemy named, appropriately, Bad Bob. Bad Bob had once gotten the upper hand on me, and I was still vulnerable to him in magical ways.

Ways that I was having a very hard time controlling. The sickening thing was that as I studied the approaching hurricane, and felt the black torch on my back burn brighter, some part of me *wanted* landfall. *Wanted* to feel that awesome power rip into the fragile human community, twisting glass and metal, ripping wood and flesh, reducing all of this to a sea of wreckage and devastation.

It terrified me.

Focus, I told myself, and concentrated hard on pushing back against those impulses. I knew where they were coming from. Bad Bob was using the tattoo—no, the *mark*—to remake me in his image.

I had been denying it for days now, but it wasn't a tattoo.

It was a Demon Mark, put there by the scariest Demon alive.

And I really didn't know how to stop it.

"Jo!" A male voice bellowed in my ear, and I clawed rain-soaked hair out of my eyes and turned to look. It was my fellow Warden Lewis Orwell—the boss, actually. The CEO of magically gifted humans.

Panic didn't look good on him.

"It's not working!" I yelled back. The wind whipped the words right out of my mouth. He nodded and wrestled a yellow storm slicker around my shoulders, holding me steady while I put it on. There. I shivered in sudden relief as the rain pummeled the plastic instead of my skin, but it was just animal reaction. There was no such thing as true relief right now. "We have to get out of here, Lewis! *Now!* This thing is after us!" Me. It was after *me.*

A bolt of lightning the thickness of a skyscraper tore through the false night, arcing over the bowl of the sky. It shattered into a thousand stabbing branches. In the glow, Lewis looked worse than I'd expected—tired, of course, and unshaven, but also pallid. He'd pushed himself to the limit, and it hadn't worked.

If the most powerful Warden on the planet, connected to a network of hundreds of *other* powerful Wardens, couldn't make this thing turn its course, then we were in for one hell of a start to our day.

"Get on the ship," he yelled over the wind. "We need to get it out of the harbor, *now!*"

I looked past him to the massive floating castle of the *Grand Paradise.* "I can't believe we're stealing something the size of the frigging *Queen Mary!*"

"It's stable!" he shouted back. "I'd take a destroyer if I could get my hands on one, but this'll have to do. It's fully provisioned and ready to go. It's our only option right now, unless you want to try to take this thing here!"

Yeah, I had to admit, our options were fairly limited. Die on shore or make a run for it and hope the storm wheeled to follow, sparing the city.

Still. A cruise ship? Granted, Wardens generally don't travel cheap. That's practicality. When you have the power to control the elements of the planet—like living things, geologic forces, wind, and water—and when those elements get *pissed* about being bossed around, you'd better have some room to duck and cover. And where do you get lots of room when you travel?

First class, of course. It's not all about the free champagne. Although that's good, too.

Taking all that into consideration, commandeering the *Grand Paradise* was still over the top, even for us. The ship mostly cruised the Caribbean, but it was still enormous, and it had originally been built to give the big boys some transatlantic competition, so it was tough as hell. It was the size of a ten-story building, ridiculously set afloat. The cheery paint colors on the decks and hull made it seem even more surreal.

The problem was that up to about an hour ago, it had been boarding for its normal, tame cruise business. Granted, the storm had reversed that process, but even so, it took time to de-board three thousand passengers, not to mention the thousand or so crew members. Police were on-site, guiding the confused, angry, terrified tourists out of the boarding area and off to waiting buses to take them to shelter. It was chaos, complicated by pile-driving rain and wind, and I expected it only to get worse.

I'd been watching the steady stream of humanity with a kind of stunned, detached disbelief. As a Warden, I would never pack myself into a ship so full of people and go out to tempt fate—not recreationally, anyway. It's a fact of life: Wardens draw storms, and not just any storms. They might start out as forces of nature, but they develop their own personalities once they reach a certain level of power.

And they develop intelligence. The one thing that seems consistent about storms is that whatever their origin, they seem to really *hate* Weather Wardens.

Lucky us.

It seemed counterproductive to be boarding a ship under the present circumstances, but Lewis knew what he was doing. *He* thought that the storm was being drawn here by the high concentration of Wardens, and that was partly true, although I thought it was mostly drawn to me; it also was feeding off the natural energy created by our presence.

If we moved, it would likely follow. Bad for us, good for the millions of people in the Miami area who were looking at a worst-case-disaster scenario.

A year ago, we would never have dared try to snatch a ship like this in broad (if stormy) daylight, but times were changing. The Wardens had been around since the last spire of Atlantis slipped under the waves, but they'd existed in secret, a kind of paranormal FEMA that was noticed only when it failed. Governments rose and fell, but they all worked with us. They all funded us.

They really had no choice.

Now, though, it wasn't all hush-hush and top secret. We'd come out to the public. We'd had to; we'd pushed the secrecy as far as it could reasonably go, and in an age when every person had a cell phone and a video camera our days of operating in deep cover were long gone. We were tired of exerting energy to keep people quiet.

The new strategy—of which I'd been a part—was to just let the chips fall where they may. Less work on our part, which was good, because our ranks had been thinned recently.

The upside of coming out in public was that when we said we needed the *Grand Paradise* to save the city of Miami, the government really had to make it happen, no matter what the fallout might be later on. Even if a good percentage of the population of the world thought we were a bunch of hoodoo con artists out to defraud them.

So—there had been a whole lot of orders issued from the highest levels of government, and cash passed both under and over the table by the Wardens to make sure that everyone bought in. All that had taken time, and lawyers, and paperwork, and we'd burned up our safety margin in trying to make this happen in an expeditious fashion that didn't involve just storming the ship and pirating it away.

Hence the black morning, and the looming disaster. Sometimes, piracy is the only really efficient way to go.

Lewis took my arm and steadied me against the wind as we staggered down the harbor's spacious walkway— now crowded with confusion—toward the gangway. It still burped out passengers, though in uneven groups now rather than as a steady flow. The Wardens were clustered and ready to board. Standing at the mouth of the flapping canvas of the covered gangway was my best friend, Cherise, decked out in the latest in bright yellow hurricane-wear. She had a cute little clipboard, and she was checking off Wardens as they moved past her, flashing smiles and thumbs-up signs.

There were a total of one hundred seventeen Wardens gathered in Miami today. Not all of them would be coming with us on the *Grand Paradise*—Lewis was way too strategic to put all his eggs in one fragile, oceangoing basket—but we'd have a bigger force with us than I'd ever seen gathered in one place. Which—when you're talking about a group of people who have the ability to control the basic elements around us—is scarily impressive. Each one of us was capable of wreaking incalculable destruction, although of course we were sworn to *try* to avoid that. Our job was to make things better for humanity, not worse. Despite the wildfires and earthquakes and hurricanes, without us the human race would have been scoured off the face of the earth a long, long time ago—all because a few thousand years ago, by our records, human beings did something that annoyed Mother Nature. Nobody remembers what.

We're still waiting for her to get over it.

With enough of us aboard the ship, we were a huge, juicy target, but we could probably defuse most anything that came at us.

Probably.

I hate qualifiers.

Lewis was about to lead a whole team of Wardens (and supernatural Djinn) into the jaws of death. I was really hoping that this plan worked out better than most of my *other* life-and-death adventures.

That triggered a sudden burst of anxiety in me, not to mention a jolt of guilt. "Have you seen David?" I asked Lewis, pulling him to a halt.

My lover, David—leader of at least half the Djinn, the way Lewis was the head of the Wardens—had gone away some time ago to attend to urgent business, which probably involved some supernatural being throwing a hissy fit over being pressed into helping humans. Most Djinn had the power of minor gods and the egos to match; you could think of them as bad-tempered angels, or ambivalent devils. They weren't one thing or the other. Even the best of them could swing wildly from one end of the spectrum to the other, depending on circumstances.

As he'd left, David had told me that meant he'd be back. No time frame. I felt his absence like grief, although according to my watch, he'd only been gone for a couple of hours.

The dark part of me, the part still giggling maniacally over the approaching destruction, was glad he was gone. David could help me control the black tattoo—and of course it didn't want that.

Lewis shook his head, spraying rain in a thick silver spiral. "Haven't seen him!" he said. "Jo, we can't wait. He can reach you wherever you are, you know that. Get on the damn ship!"

I looked past the flapping canvas toward the storm front again, where lightning was ripping the sky open with vicious glee. My enemy was out there beyond this storm, with at least one hostage, and a whole lot of raw power in a form that was both invisible and fatal to the Djinn.

Bad Bob had bragged that he could kill the planet if he wanted to.

I was afraid he was right.

I was afraid he'd already started.

This was *not* the way I'd planned to take a honeymoon cruise to Bermuda.

Just when I thought things couldn't get any worse, a white-uniformed ship's officer with rows of gold braid on his sleeves came pounding down the gangway, avoiding departing passengers and arriving Wardens, to skid to a halt in front of Lewis. "Sir," he said, and nodded uncertainly to me on the off chance that I was equally important. "We have a problem."

Lewis dragged me into the cover of the gangway and pushed back the hood of his slicker. "Of course we do," he said, resigned. "What now?"

"I'm very sorry. We're doing the best we can, but several of the first-class passengers have been . . . reluctant to leave their onboard possessions. Several of them have valuable items in the ship's safe, and the hold. They won't leave without them, and—"

"I don't give a goddamn about their stuff," Lewis interrupted tightly. "I've given you all morning to make this happen. Get them off the ship, right now, or they're sailing out with us and they can take their chances. Understand?"

The officer—I wasn't familiar enough with shipboard command structure to know what he was, but I guessed maybe Executive Officer—straightened his back to full Navy-style attention, clasped his hands behind his back, and gave Lewis a long, steady stare. "Sir, I recognize that this is a matter of urgency, but we cannot permit you to endanger innocent passengers. They must be offloaded before we can put to sea."

"If we're still in this harbor in thirty minutes, you'll be sailing this ship as a fucking submarine!" Lewis snapped. "They're already endangered. They get off the boat and run for their lives, or they come with us and we do whatever we can to protect them. Those are their choices, but we can't wait for them to call their lawyers to decide." He looked past the officer to Cherise. My best friend—endearingly human, not magically gifted at all—gave us both a little half wave and kept checking off names. "Cherise! How many are we missing?"

"We're halfway in!" she shouted back. "Better tell the rest of your folks to get their beach thongs in gear!" She sounded incredibly cheerful. "Hey, I hope I get to be Cruise Director too, because this is going to be the best world-ending crisis *ever*!" Cherise was being only faintly ironic. That was the great thing about Cherise; she could find a silver lining in a coffin, six feet under, without a flashlight. She was possibly the only person I could count on who wasn't supernaturally gifted, unless good looks and a wicked sense of humor counted. Cherise was regular folks, and I loved that she could hold her own with the not-so-regular crowd I tended to attract.

Lewis skipped right over Cherise's attempt to lighten the mood. "Dammit, what's the holdup?"

"You're kidding, right?" Cherise pulled back her rain slicker hat, and her blond hair tumbled out like a flood of sunshine. She looked a little damp, but otherwise perfect, from her beach-approved tan to the hint of dark pink lipstick still kissing her lips. "Getting Wardens to do *anything* on cue is ridiculous. It's like trying to pull Shriners out of an open bar."

Those who thought Cherise shallow—which, taking one quick glance at her perfect features, perfect hair, and dazzling smile, one might—were in for a major shock once they got past her defensive dumb-blonde routine. She was a ruthlessly competent person, and if *she* couldn't get the Wardens organized, then it couldn't be done by any nonmagical means.

I knew what was going on with the Wardens, and why they weren't on board. We're an egotistical, self-involved bunch—which is, sadly, not our worst feature. Each of us tends to think he or she knows better, no matter what situation we land in. You can call it absolute power corrupting, et cetera, but I think it's more that we all have to make life-and-death decisions daily, and that tends to make you confident, bordering on delusional. That's fine if you're operating autonomously, but in groups it can get in the way. It takes a strong personality, and a stronger grip on your temper, to bend Wardens to your will even in such a simple matter as *please board the ship now or we are all going to die*.

Lewis had trusted them too much.

"Fuck," Lewis said. He had a tendency to be very Zen, but his legendary calm was showing significant cracks. "Jo, I need David back here. Can you find him?"

"I can try." I was glad for the excuse, actually. I stepped back against the billowing canvas wall, feeling the thump of rain like tiny body blows, and concentrated on the magical link that led from me to David. Up on the aetheric plane, the level of reality above the physical, the link looked like a gleaming silver rope, and it felt warm to the touch. It couldn't be seen here in the real world, but using Oversight—focusing my awareness into the aetheric, without actually leaving my body to go there—I could access it just a little.

Time to go, I whispered down the line, a pulse of power that he'd know came from me. *You're needed, mister.*

And the answer came spiraling back, a surge of meaning without the framework of actual words to define it. He was coming, but there was some kind of complication. What else was new? Seemed like neither of us could take a breath without causing, or suffering, some kind of complication.

When I focused on the outside world again, things had not gotten better. In fact, they'd taken a significant turn for the worse, because Lewis's body language had moved from frustrated to outright furious, and he was fixed on the ship's Executive Officer like a cruise missile. "What?" he growled. "What did you say?"

The officer cleared his throat. "I said that we'll need to have your attorneys draw up another set of papers to indemnify the cruise line if you sail with any—and I must stress *any*—persons who have not signed the appropriate waivers to—"

Lewis had a wicked bad temper, which was something few people had ever had reason to know because he had such a long, patient fuse. Once it blew, though, it was catastrophic; I remembered that once upon a time, it had nearly killed someone. Granted, that someone hadn't been exactly innocent, but still—it had been like using a nuclear bomb to kill shower mold. Once you pull the pin from Mr. Grenade, he is no longer your friend.

I stepped up. "Lewis," I said, and drew his focus. Some of the rage calmed in his dark eyes, but it was more of a move from full boil to simmer; the heat was definitely on. "David's coming, but it'll take some time. Why don't we go round up the stragglers? Cherise can work on evicting the first-class stowaways. She'd love that."

Cherise gave me a grin that assured me she would, very much. Give the girl a clipboard, and she became an unstoppable force. "Damn straight," she said. "You two crazy kids go have fun storming the castle. I'll go schmooze the stars. Damn, was I born for that or *what*?"

Lewis looked at her helplessly. He couldn't yell at Cherise, and he had no reason to yell at me. I motioned for the remaining target—Mr. Executive Officer Stick-Up-His-Ass—to back off, but if he saw the signal, he completely ignored it.

"The shipmaster is completely responsible for every soul on board," he continued, as if he wasn't facing imminent grievous bodily harm. "I can't permit this kind of violation of procedures to—"

"Procedures." Lewis's voice sounded almost calm, but I had a bad feeling. "Right. According to the papers I signed earlier today, you now work for me, not the cruise line. Are you aware of that?"

From the shock that flickered across the XO's face, he clearly hadn't been. He buried that quickly, though. "No, sir."

"Let me make this absolutely ... perfectly ... clear." I thought at first that I was imagining things, but then I realized that Lewis's skin had taken on an unearthly hot glow. So had his eyes. He looked about five seconds from detonation. I'd never seen a human do that. I'd rarely even seen a Djinn do it. "That storm out there doesn't care about laws, or rules, or procedures. It cares about ripping apart everything in its path. And it's coming for *us.* So Get On. The. Fucking. Team. *Now.*"

The XO took a step back. Lewis's furious glow got brighter, and I saw it reflected in the man's wide eyes.

Then he saluted, spun on his heel, and marched back up the gangway without another word.

"Dude," Cherise said in a hushed voice. "That was *hot.*"

"Down, girl," I said.

"Hey, can I help it that I find radioactive guys sexy?"

We both gazed at Lewis, who despite not having shaved, showered, combed his hair, or changed his clothes in an appallingly long time was undeniably hot, in a lanky, outdoorsy, glowy kind of way. He gave us both an exasperated look and stalked off to organize the Wardens on his own. The glow stayed on him for several seconds as he went out into the lashing rain.

"I'm surprised you didn't jump all over that," I said.

"Moi?" Cherise pressed a small, perfect hand against her breast and did a silent-movie face of astonishment. "I'd never."

"Since when?"

"I've got a sense of self-preservation. Okay, granted, it's still in the original shrink-wrap, but I've *got* one if I ever want to use it. Besides. Dude is scary serious right now." Cherise waggled her clipboard. "Want to go with me? Terrify some mundanes? C'mon, it'll be fun! And I might need you to, you know, throw a lightning bolt or something."

Well, I wasn't doing anything useful standing here worrying. I *could* follow Lewis out into the storm, but that didn't really have much appeal, his tension level being where it was. He was more than capable of scaring the Warden stragglers into line all by himself. I would only be collateral damage.

Cherise shed her rain slicker, revealing a tight baby-doll T-shirt with, weirdly, a cartoon drawing of a toaster on it, complete with toast. The toaster had some kind of bar on the side with a red glow that looked like an eye.

"Let me guess," I said, and struggled out of my slicker as well. *"Star Trek?"*

She rolled her eyes. "Do you not *own* a television? No. Not any flavor of *Trek,* and oh my God, what are you wearing? Oh honey. No."

"Shut up. It's borrowed."

"From who, a homeless person?"

"No, from the Jean Paul Gaultier fall collection."

She accepted that with a straight face. "Oh, that explains it. Homeless color-blind skank is so hot right now."

We were jabbering because we were afraid. Because the world was coming to an end, again, and sometimes whistling past the graveyard is literally the only thing that gets you safely through the experience.

And I'm just talking about Fashion Week.

I looked down at my outfit, though, and acknowledged that Cherise did have a point. The white miniskirt was too tight and too short, even by incredibly lax South Beach standards. The top would have been rejected by Frederick's of Hollywood as too trampy, and by Wal-Mart as too cheap. The shoes were plain battered deck shoes, which at least were a safe choice, if not styling.

"They have shops on board," Cherise assured me, and patted me kindly on the back.

"Cherise, do you *really* think they'll be opening the mall when we're running for our lives?"

"Why not? People got to shop. It's like breathing." It was to Cherise, anyway. "Okay, fine. I'll tell myself that it's a costume party and you came as a drowned rat."

I smacked her. She pretended it hurt. "Cher," I said, and put an arm around her shoulders. "I really love you, you know. I don't know what I'd be right now if I didn't have you around to keep me sane."

We weren't in the serious-talk business, me and Cher, but it seemed like this might be a good moment to make an attempt. She could have laughed it off; I wouldn't have been upset if she did, because I just needed to say it.

Instead, she fixed those deep blue eyes on me and said, "I don't know what I'd be without you, either. Probably nothing half as good as I am." She smiled faintly, and for just a moment, the storm lessened. Her smile was just that powerful. "Love you, too, you skanky, no-style tramp."

I smacked her again. Moment over.

We went to try to solve the first-class problem.

Chapter Two

The very rich are like everyone else, provided you classify "everyone else" as "spoiled rotten brats with vast incomes and little sense of responsibility." There are exceptions, of course, but money gets you excused from all kinds of social constraints, just as fame does, and that never does a body good.

We had a whole cadre of spoiled rotten brats holed up, refusing to leave their stash of gold bars, drugs, or folding money—whatever they had stored in the ship's hold and safe. I wondered how they'd feel using it as life preservers.

The harassed Chief Steward pointed me toward the first-class lounge area, where apparently a lot of our troublemakers had forsaken their magnificently opulent cabins and gathered to jointly declare their displeasure at being inconvenienced. You'd think that *anyone* could see it wasn't a good idea to be riding out a storm on a boat, but then again, people do dumb crap all the time, and they always seem astonished that it turns out to be dangerous. Seriously. Look at YouTube.

My first brush with the Richie Riches came in the form of a *very* famous singer, with aspirations of being an equally famous starlet. She was actually obeying orders, believe it or not, and she was on her way out, practically clawing the expensively paneled walls with frustration. She was surrounded by a milling entourage who scrambled to juggle her coffee, BlackBerry, bags, appointment diaries, and small yappy dogs. She was scowling as much as Botox would allow, and had her Swarovski crystal–encrusted cell phone at her ear.

"I'm telling you, it's *outrageous*!" she was saying. "I want a lawsuit in place before I hit the limo, do you hear me? I want to *own* this stupid ship, and then I want to use it for target practice. Just do it, Steve. And make sure that wherever I'm going, it's five star. I am *not* going to some shelter with cots! —What? I don't care what category the storm is, you find me a suite! What do I pay you for, idiot?"

I suddenly had a great deal more sympathy for the business-suited corporate drones who had no choice but to smile and take it for the paycheck. Once the flood of minions was past, I approached an immaculately white-uniformed steward who stood helplessly at the entrance to the first-class lounge, looking in.

"Joanne Baldwin," I said, and presented ID. "I'll be taking the room that Botox Diva just cleared."

He looked at me wearily. "Ma'am? Why that room in particular?"

"Because she probably left Godiva chocolates and chilled Dom Perignon, not to mention random stacks of cash in the couch cushions," I said, straight-faced. "I'll guard it with my life."

That broke the ice a bit. He even managed to produce an anxious second cousin to a smile. "You're one of them, right?" *Them* presumably being the Wardens. I nodded. "I hear you guys have some kind of, uh, magic. Would you mind . . . ?"

"What, working some on these idiots? Not sure you really want me to do that. It tends to not be so great at crowd control, unless you're trying to kill people or put them in comas. Better let me try the persuasion route first."

"Be my guest. I hope you brought horse tranquilizers." He gave me a bow and handed me the room. Cherise and I exchanged glances and stepped inside.

We stepped in it, all right. The place was complete chaos, which was odd, because it really was a room with all kinds of calm built right in. The designers had envisioned the space as a Victorian-style reading room, complete with expensively bound leather volumes and comfy couches and chairs. Nobody was enjoying the decor now, though. Middle-aged society matrons rubbed shoulders, however unwillingly, with young, vapid starlets (I might have recognized one or two of those, but truthfully, they'd all been sculpted and styled into the same person, so it didn't much matter). A thick cluster of black-clad people who I assumed were New York literary types clumped together like a dour flock of crows toward the outer edge. West Coast bling glittered in a group on the opposite side of the room. It was like a map of the wealth of America, from coast to coast—all arguing at the same time.

Another steward, looking not-so-crisp, was trying his best to calm people. They were ignoring him and all yammering away at each other, waving tickets, papers, cell phones, and BlackBerries. The din was all focused on one thing: *I'm going to sue. I'm not leaving without my (fill in the blank).*

I beckoned the steward over. He came, looking grateful that someone—even a potential troublemaker—was paying attention to him instead of shouting at full volume. I could understand why; this room full of people, at least fifty strong, had enough clout to bury the cruise line in legal red tape for years, if not generations. "We need to move these idiots out," I said. "It's time to go."

I saw him swallow whatever he was tempted to shoot back at me, and try again. "Yes, miss, I'm trying," he said, in that smoothly patient tone that only the very stressed develop after years of therapy. "I explained that if they didn't disembark, we couldn't wait for them to do so, but—"

"They called your bluff."

"Exactly." He swallowed and tugged a little at the white collar of his formal jacket. "I've tried to get the captain, but he's busy with preparations to cast off."

A woman of indeterminate age—indeterminate because plastic surgery, heavy makeup, and a forty-hour-a-week workout schedule had effectively rendered her a wax figure of herself—grabbed the steward by the arm with expertly manicured, clawlike fingers. "What are you going to do about this?" she demanded. "I demand to speak to the captain! Immediately!"

"Ma'am, I'm sorry, but the captain is occupied," the steward said, and patiently removed her grip from his uniform sleeve. "You must depart the ship immediately, for your own safety."

"Don't be ridiculous. This ship was advertised as being able to sail through a hurricane without a wineglass tipping. It's the safest place to be! I refuse to be turned out like some penniless hobo into a storm. My people say there are no hotels, and no flights out. There's nowhere to go. I'm staying."

"That's not an option," I said. "If you get your people and head toward the exit, you might still make it off the ship. Go. Right now."

She fixed me with an icy stare. "And who are you?" Her glance traveled over me, dismissing every item of clothing on me with ruthless clarity, and then summing me up and dismissing me as a whole, all over again. "Are you with the cruise line? Because if you are, I will have a word with the captain about the dress code for—"

"Shut up," I said. She did, mainly because I don't think anybody had told her that in her whole life. "Pretend there's a bomb on board. Now. What should you do?"

She blinked. "Is there?"

I stared at her, unblinking.

She lifted one heavily ringed hand to cover her pouty lips. "Is it terrorists?" Terrorists, the new monster under the bed. Well, whatever worked.

"I can't confirm that," I said, in my best poker-faced government-agent style. Hey, I learned it from television. "You should go immediately. But don't tell the others. We don't want to cause a panic."

That was an added kicker, because by being told to keep it secret, she felt privileged, and of course that convinced her. She gulped, grabbed her personal assistant in red talons, and whispered something urgent. Then they hustled off, presumably heading for the docks.

"One down," Cherise said. "Terrorists, huh?"

"The FBI can Guantánamo me later," I said. "It does the job. You take that side of the room, I'll take the other."

And so it went. About three repetitions later of the terrorists-but-keep-it-quiet story, I ran into someone who demanded to know if I had any idea who he was. I tried to control my instinctive awe and assured him I did—how could I not? He seemed to like that, and especially the whole *I'm only saving your ass because you're so special* undertone. When he strode off, trailing employees like a comet, I turned to see the steward watching me with a look that was half appalled, half amused. "What? Who is he?" I asked.

"I believe he's in the film industry," he said. "You're scary."

"You should see her when she's *really* bothered," Cherise said as she passed us, heading for her next victim. "But I hope you won't."

I felt the change in the ship before I saw the expression shift in the steward's face from nervous to outright alarmed. There was a deep, throbbing sensation coming up through the decks, transmitting itself all the way through my body.

"We're moving," I said. "Holy crap. Lewis wasn't kidding around."

"Guess not," Cherise said. We'd cleared half the room, but there were at least thirty of the first-class passengers still staging a sit-in, and we were out of time. "Maybe we can load them into lifeboats or something."

"Cher, do these guys look like they'd let us put them into lifeboats?"

"I didn't say they'd *agree*. We could, you know, knock them out or something."

"So we've moving up from threats to assault."

"Oh, come *on*. Not like you haven't assaulted anybody recently." And Cher punched me in the shoulder for emphasis.

"It wouldn't do any good," the steward broke in. "In these conditions, we don't dare launch any lifeboats, not even the new speedboat type that this ship carries. We have to have relatively calm seas or there's a significant risk of the lifeboats being compromised."

Compromised was, I assumed, ship-speak for *sunk*.

Which was kind of where we were, from the standpoint of achieving our goal.

I looked around the room again. Thirty-odd people, of which approximately a third were the rich sons of bitches who'd refused to leave, aggressively arrogant and sure that the universe cared too much about them to put them in real danger.

The others were their hapless hangers-on, employees, and family members.

I hated having innocents in the line of fire, but they'd made their choice, and now I had to make mine.

"Let them go back to their cabins," I said to the steward. "Confine them to quarters for now. If they want anything, deliver it. Don't let them go roaming around. Let them whine all they want, but do *not* let them intimidate you."

"Yes, miss." He was glad to have a clearly defined order, and he signaled to a couple of discreetly suited security men standing in the wings. They were both impressive specimens—large, muscular, with the kind of no-bullshit expressions that only men who do violence for a living could afford to wear. I figured the bulges in their coats had more to do with weaponry than with overindulging at the all-you-can-eat buffet.

The steward stationed outside was waiting for us when we emerged, and he handed me a key card and a fancy colored map with something circled on it. "Your cabin, miss," he said, straight-faced. "It's the least we can do in exchange for your help."

I remembered my earlier snarky request. "It's not—"

"Oh, yes, it is. A special thank-you from the captain. And if you can't locate any stray Godiva chocolates or Dom Perignon, please let me know. I'll bring some to you straightaway."

I shook his hand, held up the map, and waggled both in front of Cherise. Her mouth dropped open.

"You *didn't.*"

"Botox Diva's cabin." I checked the details. "Two bedrooms. Want one?"

"Maybe. And maybe I want my own swanky digs— you ever think of that?"

The steward cleared his throat very respectfully. "The captain's ordered us to close off all non-essential decks. We only have enough first-class cabins for about half of your party. The other half will get our best accommodations farther toward the stern."

Cherise gave out a sigh. "Okay, fine. I'll suffer with your guest room. You'd better not snore."

We were about halfway to the cabin, according to the map, when I felt a flutter at the edges of my awareness, like a psychic breeze. It felt cool as a mint balm to my irritated soul, and I sighed in sudden relief.

David was back.

I turned my head to see him striding down the broad hallway, heading our way. He glimmered like a hot penny, even under artificial light—silky auburn hair, worn long enough to curl at the ends, perfect bronze skin that would make a self-tanning addict weep in envy. Behind round John Lennon glasses, his eyes sparked brilliant orange, like miniature suns. His eyes were the only thing that gave him away right now as being more than human. He was dressed in well-worn, faded jeans, a white Miami-weight shirt that fluttered in the air-conditioned breeze, and a ball cap advertising a local crab shack. He'd forgone his long vintage military coat, mainly because I'd lectured him enough about the unlikelihood of anyone except terrorists and flashers wearing coats in the Miami heat. Although the idea of David as a flasher—a private-performance-only one, of course—still lingered in my mind.

His gaze was fixed on me, and he crossed the distance fast, although he didn't appear to be in a hurry. Even so, it still seemed to take forever before his hands touched me—a gentle stroke from my shoulders down my bare arms, to my wrists, then back up to cup my face. My whole body hummed and relaxed into the sensation. At close range, David's eyes were both less and more human—less human in color and more human in content. He was worried.

He had good reason to be.

"How are you holding up?" he asked me. His voice was low and intimate, like the warmth of his body near mine. "Any pain?"

"Nope," I said. "Nothing I can't handle."

His gaze held mine, searching. Waiting. I was dimly conscious of Cherise standing a few feet away, doing the awkward dance of exclusion from an intimate moment. With no key card of her own, she'd have to wait.

"I promise, if I feel anything change, you're the first to know," I told him, and put my hands on him, because I couldn't *not* put my hands on him. I stepped forward and folded myself against his chest, and his arms closed over me, holding me close. I felt his lips brush my hair, a butterfly touch that made my heart skip.

"Let me check the mark," he said. I shook my head. "Jo. Let me see it."

"It's fine."

"Jo."

I sighed and backed up a step, then turned so my back was facing him. His fingers touched my shoulder and moved down and in, pushing back the fabric and moving the strap of my bra aside to look at the *thing* on my shoulder blade.

It looked like a black torch tattoo. I knew that, because I'd spent enough time staring at it in pocket mirror reflections. It was the parting gift of my old boss, Bad Bob Biringanine—or what was left of him, anyway. He'd once been one of the most powerful Wardens in the world, but he'd gotten it illegally, the way some athletes abuse steroids. His particular poison was a Demon Mark—he'd volunteered himself as a host for a gestating Demon, and in return it had given him all the power he needed.

Until it was done with him, at least. I wasn't sure that what was currently walking around in his skin had much in common with the original Bad Bob.

Bad Bob had also given *me* a Demon Mark—unwillingly—and eventually I'd gotten rid of it. I never wanted to feel Bad Bob's sticky, foul fingers pulling my strings again; the very thought of it made my skin crawl and made me long for a shower and a steel scrub brush.

David's gentle touch slid over the black torch mark, and it was as if his fingers disappeared as they passed across the dead space of it. I couldn't feel the pressure at all. Then his touch was back, real and warm, on the other side of the numbed spot.

"It's still contained," he said. His voice was very quiet, meant only for my ears. "If you start to feel anything—"

I already had felt something—that sickening longing for destruction as I'd watched the storm. I knew it was bleed-over from the black tattoo . . . but I couldn't make myself tell him, either.

"Yeah, I know, yell for help." I hated being helpless. *Hated* it. But somehow, Bad Bob had found a way to strip away my defenses, and I couldn't fight this thing. Not on my own. David could help, at least for now. He wasn't making any guarantees long-term, though. We needed to get to Bad Bob and make the evil old son of a bitch take the thing off of me.

Or kill him. That'd work, too. I hoped. Though I had to admit, it hadn't worked too well the last time I'd thought I put him in the ground.

I tugged my bra strap back in place and turned to face my lover. No—*husband*. I had to get used to that. *Husband*. We'd had the wedding ceremony, kind of. It had been interrupted by various attacks, but I thought we were married, anyway. I just didn't *feel* married. "So, you've been AWOL most of the morning."

"Busy," he said, which was uninformative, as explanations go. His shoulders lifted and fell, as if he knew what I was thinking. "Djinn business."

Which meant none of mine. "So what's the plan? You guys coming with?"

"Some are," David said. "This is obviously our fight as well as yours. He has Rahel prisoner. Even Ashan agrees that we can't let this go without an answer."

Just as David was in charge of the New Djinn, the ones who traced their origins to human ancestry, Ashan was the Mack Daddy of the Old Djinn . . . who liked to refer to themselves as the *True* Djinn. You see where this is going, because if half the Djinn are "true," then the other half must be, well, "false." It's the equivalent of racial prejudice, among supernatural beings.

Most Djinn I've ever met are about seventy percent arrogance, twenty-eight percent altruism, and two percent compassion. David blew the curve; he was the least arrogant Djinn I'd ever met, and he maxed out on compassion. That made him incredibly hot to me, but it also made him vulnerable. Ashan buried the needle on the other end; he didn't know the meaning of altruism, and he couldn't care less about compassion. All arrogance, all the time.

He and David got along about as well as you'd expect, when they were actually talking at all.

"And is the great Ashan going to grace us with his presence?" I asked. I wasn't exactly looking forward to it.

"He'll be around," David answered, which was a typically Djinn sort of evasion. *Around* could mean anything, and nothing. "He's sending a delegation of four of his own, though."

"*Four?* He did get the memo, right? World ending, danger, et cetera?"

"Four of his most powerful," David clarified. "One of them is Venna."

Oh. Well, that was all right, then; Venna, I trusted. For an Old Djinn, she was a-okay; she even displayed an interest in regular folks, in the way a kid develops a fascination with an ant farm. She didn't consider us *equals,* but she thought we were kind of cool in a science-lab sort of way.

She liked to walk around in the guise of a child, but in no way could you classify Venna as vulnerable. Terrifying, yes. Frail, no.

David looked over my shoulder, and I followed his gaze. There at the other end of the hallway stood Venna, with three other, much taller Djinn. The expressions on the faces of the other three Djinn, whom I didn't know, were identical: pricelessly annoyed. Not here by choice, I gathered. Their smelling-something-bad scowls could have shattered titanium.

Venna, however, waved cheerfully. She was dressed

in child-sized pants and a cute little pink top with a spar-kly rainbow. She'd largely given up her predilection for dressing as Alice from *Alice in Wonderland,* but she'd kept the long blond hair and innocent blue eyes.

I waved back. Venna said something to her fellow Old Djinn, and the four of them promptly vanished, misted away on the air like a mirage. Heading for their own quarters, I assumed, if they cared about such things.

"I've brought ten of the New Djinn," David said. "In case something happens, I've also left someone at Jonathan's house who can take over as Conduit, at least temporarily."

David, in other words, had made arrangements in the event of his own death. Jonathan's house—Jonathan had been his friend, and the leader of the Djinn for thousands of years—existed in a kind of pocket uni-verse, apart from both the human world and the other planes of reality where the Djinn could travel. It was the equivalent of a defensive bunker.

If David thought this was dire enough to name a suc-cessor and stash him away in the ultimate Undisclosed Location, then things were really not at all good.

"David—" I didn't know what I wanted to say, except that I wanted it to all be okay. For *once.*

His fingers squeezed mine, very lightly. "I know," he said. "But we're in this together. For life. Whatever may happen."

He meant it.

My husband.

I blinked back a sudden irrational flood of tears and hugged him, hard, until the impulse to weep passed. "Okay," I said, and cleared my throat to bring my voice back to its normal steady range. "Want to help us out with something really, really trivial?"

"Always."

"In the first-class lounge, you'll find a couple of stewards, a couple of security guards, and a bunch of very rich jerks who don't want to take orders and are probably giving the staff a very hard time. It might speed things along if they had something more to be afraid of than their platinum card getting declined."

"You want me to intimidate them?"

"You betcha, buster."

David smiled, and this time his smile had a whole different cast to it. Dark, powerful, frightening—even to me. His skin darkened and took on a metallic sheen beneath its surface, and his eyes glowed like storm lanterns. He looked fey and dangerous and oh my God, *hot*.

"I thought you'd never ask," he said. "Point me."

We left the harbor before the storm made landfall, which was lucky for nearly everyone except, obviously, us. The *Grand Paradise* was a pretty massive vessel, but she also had considerable speed at her command. Ships didn't use old-fashioned screws anymore, but propulsion pods, and she was a lot more maneuverable than I'd suspected; we moved quickly but smoothly through the long navigation channel and out toward the open sea.

It was a good thing the ship was fast. That was all that allowed us to exit the man-made cut in time; otherwise, we'd have been boxed in, trapped like a ship in a bottle. And the bottle would have been smashed to smithereens.

Leaving port didn't mean we were free, though. Not even close. The storm wheeled like a flock of crows and came roaring after us, brushing Miami with the hem of its black skirts and probably creating another aneurysm for insurance adjusters, although it was nowhere near the destruction that could have rained down on them. The *Grand Paradise*'s engines growled and throbbed, louder than I imagined they normally would be for pleasure-cruise speeds, and we took on extra speed, crashing through the choppy seas as fast as the captain dared.

The storm gained on us.

I stood at one of the thick glass windows in the first-class lounge and watched the trouble unfolding. The storm's outer bands had spiraled over the city, but through the driving rain I could see the lights of the towers. Power was still on, and that meant things weren't so bad. Miami was tough. It would make it.

I wasn't so sure, now that we were sailing full speed ahead, that the same could be said of the *Grand Paradise*.

After a quick Weather Warden meeting, we agreed that we would attack the storm as one unit, but we'd wait until we'd lured it out well away from the mainland and any populous islands before we started screwing with it. Deeper, cooler waters would slow it down, too, which was to our benefit. The *Grand Paradise* was fast enough to keep ahead of the storm for a few hours at least, though the margin of safety would be steadily eroding. The winds inside the eyewall were ferocious.

Effectively, that meant I had an hour off, more or less, so I went to my cabin.

Considering that we were sailing off on a potentially lethal sort of mission, it was a bit surprising to find that I was enjoying the moment a little. I hadn't been on a sailing ship in a very long time, and this luxurious-cruise thing was something I hadn't even dreamed about. *Dream honeymoon,* part of me sighed. *Except for the imminent threat of total destruction,* another part warned.

Yeah, so, this is my life.

No sign of Cherise, but the downstairs shower was running. I hadn't brought any luggage, so my unpacking consisted of trudging upstairs to the second level, and slipping off my shoes. My feet sighed, and so did I. The carpet felt like clouds exported from heaven in the ultimate free-trade agreement. I tried out the bed, and it was definitely from God's own bedroom, from the body-contouring mattress to the silken sheets.

Then I sniffed myself. "Ugh," I said, and fought my way back upright. It wasn't right, subjecting this kind of luxury to the stench of my body. Besides, I'd been craving a shower for days now, and being caught in the cold, pounding rain hadn't exactly counted.

The small bath proved to have a very nice shower, complimentary robes and slippers, and a variety of expensive shampoos and soaps.

Score. I spent a blissful half hour naked and slippery beneath the massaging showerhead, washing away the sticky exhaustion. When my fingertips started wrinkling, I finally shut down the water—honestly, it was better than a ride at Disney—and belted the robe as I walked down the curving stairs to the first floor.

The room was smaller than I'd expected, but still larger than many hotel suites, and it had all the good stuff even the most discriminating guest would demand. Polished mahogany, fine carpets, luxurious furniture. Genuine artwork on the walls. I was taking a disbelieving inventory when Cher came out of her own bedroom, dressed in a matching robe, toweling her blond hair dry.

"Dude," she said. This particular inflection of that many-shaded word meant *I'm completely impressed.* "This is straight out of *Titanic.* I'm surprised they didn't pipe Celine Dion into the shower or something."

"Great. Now I'll *never* get that song out of my head," I said with a sigh. "How's your room?"

"Fantastic. Wait, check that. Why'd I get the downstairs room? Because I'm the sidekick?"

"Because you're shorter. I didn't think your little legs could manage the stairs."

She stuck her tongue out at me. Sometime in the past few weeks, while I hadn't been paying attention, she'd had it pierced. A tiny diamond stud winked impudently at me in the butter-soft room lighting. "Are you and David going to be love bunnies and keep me up all night?"

"Maybe."

"Oooh, promise? Because the porn's all pay-perview." She fluttered her eyelashes. Cher was silly and goofy and endearing, and her silliness had a point; she knew how serious all this was. How dangerous. She'd signed up to go with me, knowing there might not be any coming back from it, and she didn't even have any superpowers.

Just courage.

Impulsively, I hugged her. "Thank you," I said. She wiggled free and flipped her damp hair back.

"First grope is free, but after that, you pay to play," she said. "I'm going to jump on your bed, for payback." Halfway up the stairs, she stopped and turned back to look at me. Her face was very serious. "We're not going to die, you know. You can smile every once in a while."

I wasn't so sure about that, but I tried.

The *Grand Paradise* was a floating city. I studied the complimentary colored map as I paced the semi-spacious confines of the suite, occasionally stopping to stare out the large, very thick windows. Cher was fixing her hair, which I knew would be an hour-long epic struggle. I was content to air-dry. All the product in the world wasn't going to make my upcoming day any prettier.

The rain had stopped. The room had a sliding door and a balcony, and when I stepped out on it, salty sea air closed in around me like a hand. I felt a little stupid standing in the open in my bathrobe, but at the same time, it was a damn nice robe, and who was there to gawk? Dolphins? Let them look.

I put my hands on the cool railing and let myself float up and out of my body, which remained motionless at the rail. I moved up into the aetheric, where the forces that work on the world can be more clearly seen.

The storm, from this view, was even more terrifying. Most storms glow in the darker spectrums of power, and the worst of them take on an almost photonegative sheen. This one was all that, and a hazmat bag of toxic purple. It was also hungry, and angry. The menace and fury of it stained the entire aetheric like lethal radiation.

Bad Bob wasn't running the storm. He didn't have to. These things were sort of like the weather equivalent of a cruise missile—point, shoot, walk away. Sooner or later, they'll catch up to the target. He'd given it a taste of Warden power, and it wanted more. We were the best chance for it to indulge its cravings, and it would keep on coming.

It had a particular taste for me.

I studied the inner mechanics of the storm as I hung silently in the drifting pastel clouds far above it. I could see the bright flashes of other Wardens coming and going from the aetheric, and subtle smears of movement that I knew were Djinn, who were much more difficult to see. Humans barely registered, except as muddy outlines. The ocean itself lit up on this plane like a spiral galaxy, thick with auras and lights. All that rich diversity of life in it, trailing beautiful colors, pasts, emotions. Down at the bottom, the seafloor glowed with ancient history, steeped in bands of color and power.

Mesmerizing.

I floated weightless on the aetheric.

I felt a violent shove from behind, and turned just in time to be battered again—a flat force, like a moving wall hitting me. I bounced off and floated back. I saw nothing, but I could feel ... something. A ripple. A breath of warning ...

I twisted aside, and the shearing force just clipped me this time. That was worse, because it wasn't distributed evenly over my aetheric form; it caught my ghostly leg instead, and a bolt of pain lanced through me, odd and blurry.

I shouldn't be able to feel physical pain on the aetheric. And nobody should be able to attack like this. I'd never seen anything like it before, and I'd been around the block. Hell, I'd gotten body-slammed by the unexpected so often they'd probably named a whole wing of the Warden hospital after me.

I backpedaled, fast, and then dropped the concentration that held me so far up in the aetheric. My body was like a massive anchor, heavy without the use of power to hold me away from it, and gravity kicked in hard. I snapped and fell across thousands of miles of open water and air, and as I was pulled back toward my physical form, I saw something peculiar happen in the clouds.

I saw them turn a particularly poisonous shade of green, with jagged black edges. It was eerie and beautiful and alien, the green of a toxic emerald, and I wondered what kind of power could do that to a natural force.

Nothing I could wield, or would want to face.

I slammed back into flesh, and my knees gave way. The deck of the balcony was hard, and it hurt to hit it even though I grabbed the railing for support. *That's going to leave a mark,* I thought, but I was used to that, at least. I was more focused on the green color of those clouds, and then, belatedly, on the lancing pain that ripped through my left leg, from heel up to hip. I rose and put my weight on it, thinking it was some kind of cramp; the entire limb spasmed, shook, and gave way as if my electrical system had just cut out like a bad engine.

I clung to the railing, waiting for something. . . . It reminded me of the sensation you get when your leg goes to sleep, but I didn't feel any tingle or prickling of blood returning to feed the nerves.

It was just numb.

Come on, I thought, exasperated. The exasperation faded. The numbness didn't. I kept trying to put my weight on my leg, and it kept folding up on me like cheap paper.

Okay, now I was scared. *What the hell?* I plunked myself down on the balcony deck, legs extended, and massaged the numb leg, starting at my thigh. It was eerie. My fingers touched flesh, but that was the only feedback there was. It could have been someone else's leg entirely.

And then, with a snap, everything came back online, as if the nerve channels had just been switched on again. No slow awakening, just a sudden shock of pain and heat that made me cry out, and then it was all just . . . normal.

I stood up, clinging to the railing, and tested the leg.

It hurt, but it held.

I limped back into the living area and stretched out

on the sofa, probing my leg for anything that seemed oddly shaped, broken, or otherwise bizarre. Except for the continued random firing of pain through my nerves, everything seemed intact.

It faded, after a few minutes. I stood and cautiously walked around the room, careful to stay within grabbing distance of major pieces of furniture. *Walk it off, Baldwin.* I'd had worse. Hell, I'd had worse just *yesterday.* But it bothered me, because it shouldn't have happened. Nothing was supposed to hurt me in aetheric form, certainly not echoed down into my flesh-and-blood form.

Unsettling. It just didn't feel right.

I didn't want to, but I knew I had to mention it to Lewis. Every odd thing that happened to me increased the chances that I would end up confined to quarters, or tranquilized in the brig, if this floating casino had one of those. But this didn't seem like something I should keep to myself.

I checked the clock. I was due at the Wardens meeting.

"Cher!" I yelled to her closed door. "I'm out!" I don't think she heard over the aircraft-carrier roar of her blow-dryer.

I put on my sadly wrinkled, salt-stained, and badly-in-need-of-laundering clothes, grabbed the map, and went to wage war with evil.

Chapter Three

The map was confusing. That was all right; there were plenty of staff members around. Seems that the cruise line and the Wardens had thrown around a hell of a lot of talk about triple pay and hazard pay and bonuses, and as a result, the current passenger complement was outnumbered by its service staff by about two to one.

Which I've got to say would have been potentially amazing had I not regarded every single one of them as another weight of guilt on my conscience.

Three staff members and three sets of directions later, I arrived at the ship's movie theater. I was late, of course, but not very. The lights were up, revealing opulently layered velvet curtains in the traditional dark reds and purples on the walls, some lovely Art Deco sconces, and seats for a couple of hundred people and their snacks.

There were thirty-eight Weather Wardens on board, and as I swiftly counted heads, I realized that I was one of the last to arrive.

Lewis watched me move down the stairs toward the stage, and I knew he was noting the way I slightly favored my newly funky leg. "Did someone forget to tell you to watch your step?" he asked in an undertone. Not that anyone was paying attention. The Wardens were talking among themselves, probably arguing the finer points of weather control.

"Funny," I said. "Am I on time for the matinee of *A Night to Remember*?"

He wasn't sidetracked. "What happened?"

"I got smacked on the aetheric. Hard. And I couldn't see anybody doing it—not a trail, not a wave, nothing. No trace. And it hurt."

That got his attention. "Hurt?"

"Like, *ow, crap, damn*. And when I came back down, my leg went out on me, like a power failure. It came back, but not right away."

"Hmmmm." Without the slightest self-consciousness, Lewis got down on one knee and put his large hands around my thigh. The conversations out in the auditorium came to a stammering halt, and I felt every pair of eyes in the place turn to focus on us.

I jumped a little, and there might have been a gasp involved, but he wasn't interested in naughty groping at the moment. I felt his power slowly filter into me, rich and warm as sunlight. It followed the nerves in a slow glide down my leg, into my foot, and out.

You could have heard a pin drop in the place.

Lewis finally sat back. "I'm not finding anything except some strains in your muscles. Normal stuff." He realized that everyone was staring and, for a moment, looked completely vapor-locked about it.

I cleared my throat. "Thanks for the laying on of hands. You might want to stop now, being that it looks a little odd."

"Oh." He let go and rose to his full, lanky height. "Sorry. Didn't mean to—"

"I know." The other Wardens were *still* watching us, but after a moment they started whispering together again. Yeah, I could bet what they were whispering. "Just be glad that David—"

"That David didn't see you?" That was David, of course, arriving in a white whisper of fog that poured itself into his human form in less than an eyeblink. He sounded amused. "David did."

"I'll take it as written that you said to keep my grubby hands off your woman," Lewis said. David raised an eyebrow. "*Grubby* not strong enough?"

"Before you say that in the future, most Djinn find the concept of owning someone else slightly offensive," David said, and I could almost feel Lewis's wince. "Jo's her own woman. If she felt uncomfortable, she'd tell you."

"Yeah, she always has."

"Uh, guys?" I waved my hands. "Thanks for the macho plumage display, very attractive, but are we done? Time's a-wasting."

David smiled. He wasn't competing with Lewis; he hadn't for some time. He was possessive, on levels that he would never let anyone but me see, but he was done with jealousy. We were bonded, in his eyes, for eternity, or as long as my human body lasted. He had absolutely no reason to worry. "I came to tell you that the Djinn have completed preparations. We can begin anytime you're ready."

"Let's not delay," Lewis said, and stepped up to the edge of the theater's proscenium. "Everybody focus. We've got work to do."

There weren't five people in the world who could get thirty-odd Wardens to shut up and listen without arguing, but Lewis was one of them. I wasn't, so I shut up and paid attention, too. He'd taken his hour of downtime to shower, shave, and change clothes, and although he still looked exhausted, I wouldn't have bet against him in a fight.

Which was good, because we were about to step into the ring for the fight of our lives.

"David," Lewis said, "I need the Djinn to form a perimeter around the storm. Keep it from moving toward us. Try to hold it in place while we cut its generators." By that, I understood that he was going to do the logical thing and try to affect not the storm but the underlying forces that fed its fury. There were relatively simple ways to do it, but out on the open ocean, they also required massive amounts of power. The less energy we spent chasing the damn thing around, the better.

David nodded. "It'll stay as still as we can manage."

That wouldn't be easy, but he had at least fourteen Djinn at his command—ten of his own, four of Ashan's. I didn't think there were many things that a couple of Djinn couldn't do, so fourteen seemed a pretty comfortable safety margin.

Still. I was getting a clammy line of sweat forming along my spine. *Bad Bob knows us. He knows how we think. He's one of us.*

I wished I hadn't thought of that.

Lewis paced, because that was what Lewis did when he was under stress. He prowled the stage, talking without focusing directly on anyone, even me. "Four teams," he said. "Jo, you're heading the team that will focus on a rapid cooling of the water temperature directly beneath the storm and out to a margin of about half a mile beyond. We're shooting for a minimum drop of at least ten degrees."

Someone in the audience whistled, and it was all I could do not to echo it. Ten degrees on the open ocean? Holy crap, that was hard. The amount of force it took to effect even one degree of change in that vast amount of water was astonishing.

"Ten degrees," I said, and managed to keep the incredulity out of my voice. "All right."

"Pick your team."

David watched me as I looked out over the audience and called names. I knew most of them, and more important, I knew their capabilities. I wanted raw power, and for this, at least, I wasn't overly concerned about fine control. There wasn't a single person out there I'd name my bosom friend, but they were all solid talents. Good enough.

Predictably enough, though, someone raised a hand. It was Henry Jellico, whom I *hadn't* picked. Henry was one of the worst know-it-alls that I'd ever met, despite being an overall nice enough guy. He'd studied hard, and dammit, he wanted every single person to know it. "Excuse me, Lewis, but wouldn't it be wise to also match the cooling of the water with lowering the temperature of the exhaust process? Try matching it to the temperature of the eye to expand it outward?"

Lewis stopped pacing, but he didn't face Jellico. "I believe I said four teams," he said. "Henry, you're in charge of team two. Exhaust process matched to the core temperature of the eye. Once you've got those equations balanced, try taking the whole thing down another five degrees."

"*Five?*"

"Please."

Henry Jellico wasn't in for any picnic, either. Lewis waited as Henry picked his ten Wardens, and then chose Amanda Chavez to head up the third team, which was smaller and focused on lowering wind speed. The fourth team batted cleanup, remaining in reserve and watching for any imminent threats, and it was headed up by Lewis himself.

I sat down on the edge of the stage, my legs dangling over the lip, and lowered my head in concentration. Out in the audience, all the Wardens did the same. We looked like we were engaged in prayer; in a sense, that was what we were doing, only on a slightly more active scale.

"Anybody got an eyewall wind speed on this beast?" someone asked.

"Approaching two hundred fifty miles per hour," Lewis said. We had a moment of contemplation on that one. The storm was seriously powerful. The highest speed the Wardens had ever measured in an eyewall was two hundred fifty-five, give or take a bit. There was no such thing as a Category 6 storm, but if there was, this might have been the template. "One last thing. There's been a report that our enemies might have the ability to strike us while we're on the aetheric, maybe even causing physical side effects. Watch yourselves, and my team will deal with any attacks that come at you." That raised a few heads. "Let's get it done. The faster we're in and out, the safer we are."

I rose up into the aetheric, and the entire roomful of Wardens rose up with me. They were an army of glittering, powerful forms, shifting from the limitations of the physical to the more metaphorical shapes we registered on higher planes. I never knew what I looked like— none of us did—but I watched Henry Jellico morph from a mild little man into a bulky, muscular warrior who'd have been at home in *World of Warcraft* swinging a barbarian axe. Some Wardens didn't even keep human shapes; Greta Van Der Waal became a shining white dog that bounded and leaped through the clouds. We all had our fantasies, our true natures, and we couldn't really control how others saw us.

Lewis looked like himself. Always. He had a powerful aura, but the essence of him never changed, and that was both impressive and a bit on the scary side.

Speech wasn't possible on the aetheric—after all, no lips, tongues, teeth, or lungs—but the Wardens had developed their own methods of communication, mostly hand signals. I grabbed my team members' attention and arrowed up, fast and high, getting above the towering storm. It was like taking a glass elevator past a vertical oil spill. Nasty, and shiver-inducing. We went up almost ten miles into the atmosphere and leveled out at the top, where the storm formed a smooth dome. This was where the intake/exhaust process went on, dragging in warm air, cycling it down through the eye, breathing it out.

It was a living thing, after all, however strange it might be to our senses and logic.

The aura colors of the storm hadn't changed significantly from my first impressions—dark, shot through with photonegative spots and shapes, with livid purple around the edges. I didn't see any sign of that poisonous, otherworldly green that I'd glimpsed, though.

Good.

I felt a shudder running through the aetheric—a thicker atmosphere than the regular physical world, almost like matter caught in a phase transition from gas to liquid. Few things in the real world could stay at that balance point, but I'd always thought the aetheric was nothing *but* that—a place where everything, always, was transitional.

The shudder that ran through the aetheric came from the Djinn grabbing the storm and pulling it to a violent halt.

It fought them almost instantly, twisting, slashing back with waves of power. This was the dangerous part; if the forces got too far out of balance, things would happen that none of us could anticipate or control. We were dealing with the power of several nuclear bombs. Not the sort of thing where you want to apologize for a mistake to whatever survivors are left wandering around.

I signaled my team, and we took the express elevator back down, plunging through the storm and into the thick black water beneath it. The area directly beneath it was devoid of life; the residents of the sea that normally thronged the area had prudently departed. Good. I didn't want to be responsible for any massive fish kills, anyway.

My team—good people all—spread themselves out in an approximate rough circle near the edges of the storm's fury, and each of us concentrated on a pie-shaped wedge of the water—not that water was static, of course, which was what made this so difficult. Water, like air, was always in motion. Unlike air, it had real density, and it took a lot more effort to really make a change in it on the molecular level.

Ten degrees. Thanks for nothing, Lewis.

I'd pushed my section down a solid eight degrees, but I could sense that there were massive imbalances emerging from the change. Some of the others were having trouble managing the temperature shift at all. Nobody had hit the ten-degree mark. To make matters worse, power was collecting in odd places, like pockets of gas in a mine. That was the risk of working with multiple Wardens.

I think I sensed trouble coming—an oddly thick ripple in the aetheric, maybe—and then I saw one of my

Wardens spin helplessly out of position, losing control of her weather working. She vanished into the heart of the storm, and I felt her screaming.

Then I felt her stop.

Something was attacking us.

The fragile balances that the Wardens had built—layers of control, of forces, of risk—began to shatter like a glass tower in an earthquake. I desperately struggled to hold on to what we'd achieved. More Wardens were being attacked around me by invisible forces—battered the same way I had been earlier, but with far deadlier results. I could sense terrible things happening, but I had to hold on. *Hold on.* The strain increased. I was strong, but this was too much for any one Warden to hold on to . . . and then the storm ripped free of the Djinn holding it and began to move.

No way I could stay with it as it roared closer, heading for the *Grand Paradise*.

Something grabbed me as I faltered, but instead of bracing me, it dragged me backward, away from the fight. Up. Out.

I was just far enough away to survive what happened next.

The storm pulsed and shifted into that poisonous green color, shot through with drifting flecks of red and jagged cutting edges of black.

The power that the Wardens had been manipulating *exploded* in a brilliant burst of light, and I felt it rip through me, flaying apart my aetheric body. I re-formed, slowly and painfully, and fell with unbalanced speed back into my own body.

I jerked, gasped, and almost fell off the edge of the stage. David had me by the arms, and he dragged me backward into his embrace. He was seated on the stage, and I fell weakly against his chest. I felt broken inside, shredded, unable to think or feel.

My eyes focused slowly, and my hearing told me that people were shouting. Screaming.

Earth Wardens were arriving in the theater, summoned by emergency signal, and they were dragging limp Weather Wardens out of their seats and laying them flat for treatment. Lewis was already down there, holding Henry Jellico in his arms, pressing his palm to Henry's pale, high forehead. Henry was completely still. Lewis was gasping, shuddering, barely holding himself together.

"What happened?" I whispered. David's arms tightened around me.

"Don't try to move," he said. "You can't help them."

"But—" I tried to get my body under control, but it was like swimming through syrup. Slow and cold and clumsy. "They're—"

"Dying," David said. His voice was low and hushed, and very gentle. "Most of them are dying, and there's nothing you can do to help that now."

"No!" This time I put real effort into the struggle. It didn't matter. It wasn't David's strength holding me back—it was my own weakness. I collapsed against him again, sweating and shaking, and watched as my fellow Wardens slipped away into the dark.

I'd been right. Bad Bob knew us.

In one stroke, he'd chopped down a significant number of the Wardens who could have posed a threat to him.

And I had no idea how he'd done it.

In the end, more than half of the Weather Wardens couldn't be saved. They'd been the closest to that blast of power, or they'd been drawn into the storm's hungry maw. Their aetheric forms had been completely destroyed, and there was no soul to come back into the bodies they'd left behind. Without that, the body stuttered and died, and there was nothing any Earth Warden, however powerful, could do to stop it.

That didn't mean Lewis didn't try with every last ounce of courage he had left before he collapsed and had to be carried away.

It was a dark, silent place after that.

I sat there numbed, watching as the dead were lined up on the stage. Most of my water team had caught the blast, or been spun into the center of the storm by invisible attacks. Henry's team, which had been mirrored above, had been a little luckier, but not that much.

It was a devastating blow.

"Sons of bitches were waiting for us," I whispered. I didn't feel as shaky now, but I was still cold and weak. Someone had done me the kindness of wrapping me tightly in a thick thermal blanket, and my body heat was slowly coming back.

Cherise was holding my hand. I don't know who'd called her, but she'd appeared before David had let go of me, and I hadn't been left without human contact since. I wondered if they were afraid I would just dissolve without it, like those poor bastards we'd just led to their deaths.

David had gone to see to Lewis, though I doubted that there was much that could be done for him, either. He was strong. He would survive.

It was our mutual curse, seemed like. Being strong.

"Somebody pulled me out," I said. "Was it David?"

Cherise's thumb rubbed lightly over my knuckles, and she squeezed my fingers. "I don't know. He's not so sharey right now." Even Cher's usual defiant good cheer was gone, replaced by a sobriety that was new to me. "You just sit and rest."

"The storm—"

"It's moved off to the west," she said, which surprised me. "At least, that's what the bridge crew told me."

"You were on the bridge?"

She raised an eyebrow, and an echo of the old Cherise came bouncing back. "Honey, there are *men in uniform* on the bridge." She let it fade again. "It looks like we're in the clear. For a while, anyway. Let yourself recover a little."

I nodded, still feeling numb, and for no apparent reason, burst into tears. Cherise rubbed my back and murmured things that I didn't hear, a comforting sound like rain on the window. I wasn't the only person having a breakdown. At least three of the other Wardens had already been removed from the room, unable to stop crying and shaking.

"You should go lie down," Cherise said. "Nothing you can do here, babe."

She was right, but with Lewis flat on his back, the Wardens needed a leader, and by default I was it. I wiped my eyes, took a deep breath, and shook my head. I unwrapped the blanket and stood up.

Cherise took my arm, balancing me on my feet before stepping away and letting me go it on my own.

I found a knot of uniformed crew members outside in the theater lobby, whispering together. They fell silent when they spotted me—fear, or respect, I couldn't tell and didn't care. I suspected my blue eyes held something terrible, because none of them would look at me directly.

"What can we do, miss?"

"Body bags," I said. "I assume you have some on board. I'll also need some medical assistance, as we have some very traumatized people. Bring tranquilizers."

They all exchanged startled glances. One of the female stewards nodded and stepped away to a phone. The response time for the medical staff was impressive, but then again, it wasn't like they had lots to occupy them right now. I followed the gurneys, doctors, and nurses into the theater, and went to consult with the next most senior Warden in the room.

That was a Fire Warden named Brett Jones. Brett was a big man, solid; I'd heard he played professional football, once upon a time, but he'd taken retirement before it had left him too busted up. He nodded when I approached him. The Fire Warden contingent of our little war party had been kept out of danger so far, but I could see that the losses had affected him just as deeply as they had me.

"What went wrong, Jo?" he asked. He sat me down next to him, angling to face me as much as a man that big could in theater chairs. "Nobody can give me a decent explanation of what went on up there."

"I'm not sure I can, either," I said. "There's something on the aetheric. I can't see it, but I can feel it, and it can hurt us. That's how it started. Then the storm itself—it was like it converted our power into something else. It *changed*, Brett. I've never seen anything like it."

"I have," said a childlike third voice, and we both looked up to see the Djinn Venna leaning over a seat in the next row, staring at us with unearthly calm blue eyes. "Do you want to know what it is?"

We exchanged looks. "Uh, if you don't mind?" Brett said. He knew what Venna was, and he was nervous. So was I, but for different reasons.

Venna's small, pointed face screwed up into a frown. "If I minded, why would I have offered?"

"Forget it, Ven. Tell us."

The frown smoothed out into a bland mask. "You shouldn't order me, you know."

I felt a savage bite of anger. "It's been a bad day. And I'm not too concerned about your fragile Djinn feelings right now. You'll live."

From the disbelieving stare Brett was giving me, I could tell he couldn't quite grasp that I was sassing a supernatural time bomb of power this way, but I really didn't care. Venna wasn't going to hurt us, and I didn't want to play ego games.

She let it pass. "A long time ago, there was a thing that happened. It doesn't matter what it was, but it left a kind of scar between the highest plane of our existence and another place. A bad place."

"The place where Demons dwell," I said. "Right?"

"Oh no," she replied. "Much worse than that. The Demons love aetheric energy, but really all they want is to eat their fill and go back where they belong. No, this is a place the Demons fear. We don't know what lives there, but it came through, once."

"Came through," Brett repeated. "What happened when it did?"

"The universe died," Venna said. "I told you it was a long time ago."

I stared at her, speechless. So did Brett. So did everyone else within earshot of this bizarre conversation.

She tilted her small head sideways. "What?"

"Um—even *you* can't be that old, Venna."

"I'm not. I read about it."

"Where? At the Djinn Bookmobile?"

"Of course not." She kicked her feet, just like a regular kid at the movies. "In the stars. In the dirt. In the water. It's all around us. You can't see it?" She answered her own question with a shake of her head. "Of course you can't. Even most of the Djinn can't see back that far. What we are wasn't always *this,* you know. Everything in the universe recycles. Universes expand, contract, explode again. But this wasn't from our universe. It was bad."

"I'm—not sure how this is going to help us," Brett said.

I was. "You're saying that what's on the aetheric, what took over the storm, it's what came through last time?"

"No. I'm saying that it *started* this way, before. With the storm, and the power, and the ghosts."

"Ghosts." It was my turn to repeat her words. "On the aetheric."

"You can't see them, can you?"

"What kind of ghosts?"

"I can't see them either," Venna said, "but they're angry. They don't like Wardens."

"Do they like the Djinn?"

"They don't notice us, really. At least, not so far."

This was interesting, but it wasn't getting us where I needed to be. "Venna, I need a way to stop this. Is Bad Bob behind it?"

"He was," she said, and her eyes went unfocused and distant. "He opened the door, but he's not interested in what's coming through. Chaos is what he wants. It's what he's getting." She snapped back to focus with such suddenness that I flinched. "You can stop it, but not if he keeps the gate open. You need to stop *him*, and then you can worry about the rest."

"What about the storm?"

"You can't hurt it. You can only survive it."

Kind of like this day. "Venna," I said, and looked right into her eyes. Not a comfortable experience, really. "Can you kill Bad Bob for me?"

She considered the question for a long, silent moment. "No," she said. "I could hurt him, but he could hurt me just as much. His power cancels mine in many ways, and I think he might just be worse than I am."

"You mean he could kill you."

"No, he probably couldn't. But I wouldn't like what was left of me, in the end, if I won." She said it without much emphasis—just a calm assessment of her chances, nothing to be afraid of. "It's better if you do it, anyway. Humans. You don't have the same vulnerabilities that we do."

It was *very* odd to hear a Djinn talk about human strengths instead of considering us slightly less useful than a soiled tissue.

Of course, she ruined it by adding, "And you're much more easily replaced."

Lovely. "Does *he* have any vulnerabilities?"

"Of course. He can still die," she said. "He can still feel pain. Part of him is still human. A small part, but it remains, and it feels things the way humans do. The way you do."

I felt the ship's speed lurch, accelerating. Some of the ship's staff looked startled.

That wasn't standard procedure, obviously.

"I sped us up," Venna said. "We were moving too slowly. I don't want the storm catching us again. It would be inconvenient."

Maybe, but now I could feel the thudding impacts of waves through the ship, and the very slight rolling had increased to a definite wallow. A ship this large damp-ened the usual motion of the sea, but in waves this high, at unnatural speed, we were going to be in for a rough ride.

I glanced at Brett, who was already looking distinctly uncomfortable. "Better get the ship's stores to break out the giant economy-size Dramamine."

He nodded. "Anything else?"

"Yeah. Bad Bob was a Weather Warden, when he still had just his regular set of powers. Fire may be our best bet to overcome him—it's his biggest weakness. You get your guys ready. I want original ideas, something he can't anticipate or plan for." I chewed my lip for a second. "And whatever your plans are—don't tell me about them. I'd rather you keep it in your team."

Whatever he thought of that, Brett nodded and left me. I sat, watching the dead Wardens being loaded into body bags, then trundled away on gurneys.

I looked at the faces of the survivors. Almost all the Wardens had gathered now, except those with specific duties related to the voyage or standing lookout up on the aetheric, and they all had a similar expression.

They were measuring themselves against the body bags.

I stood up and walked to the stage. I didn't go up, just stood in front of where the medical team was working. Venna turned in her seat to watch me, and all the Wardens did as well.

"Okay," I said, "I'm not going to lie to you. We knew this trip would be tough, and today we got clear evidence of that. We made a mistake, and it cost lives, but those lives were not wasted. It's the duty of Wardens to give their lives in the protection of others. It's part of the oath we all took when we signed on to this job." I paused and made sure that sank in. "Now we know things we didn't know before, and couldn't know without triggering that trap. It sucks, yes, but our enemies aren't playing around. They want us dead, every single one of us. Every Warden and every Djinn. Once we're gone, there's nothing standing between them and the defenseless human beings of Earth. Once humans are gone, they'll strip this planet clean of every single thing with a connection to the aetheric—every animal, plant, insect, and bacterium. They'll devour all the aetheric energy they can get, and then they'll leave. It's what they do."

The only sound in the theater was that of body bags being quietly zipped behind me.

"The Wardens were formed to save people," I said. "For thousands of years, we've tried our best to do that. Sometimes we've been better at it than others. Sometimes we've outright sucked, like lately. But we *can* save people. We *have to.* We're Wardens, and we cannot give up. Ever. Agreed?"

A few of them murmured or nodded. Wintry, unwilling agreement, but at least it was a start. "So what now?" asked one of the Earth Wardens, holding the hand of a still-trembling and shell-shocked Weather Warden survivor.

"Now we get ready to kill us a Demon," I said. "And if you've got any good ideas, start talking."

Sometime later—hours later, in fact—I realized that I was hungry, and so tired I was likely to doze off even if Bad Bob himself showed up and asked me to tango. Food wasn't an issue; the ship's staff brought us buffets, mountains of sandwiches and chips and drinks, entrées steaming in silver trays, sliced cheeses and elaborate desserts. I guessed we were getting first-class treatment. It tasted good, although I didn't linger after I got a turkey sandwich into my system.

I grabbed a ship's map and tried to find my way back to my cabin. The effort was marginally successful. Hallways were clearly labeled, but faded into one another with dizzying regularity. Add in the other decks, and I could see that I'd be getting lost for some time to come. That was something I really couldn't afford. You never know when you might need to get somewhere in a real hurry.

Following my map led me down a maze of corridors, mostly deserted . . . whole decks were empty and lifeless now. Somehow, my exhausted brain betrayed me during some turning, and I found myself in an area that didn't match up to my less-than-expert map reading.

A housekeeper was just coming out of one of the cabins, and I tapped her on the shoulder. She turned, smiling. She was a cinnamon-skinned young woman with black hair pulled back in a sleek, lacquered bun, and warm chocolate eyes. Not very tall, but graceful. I could see her as a dancer, somehow, moonlighting as a maid.

"Miss?" she asked. "Can I be of assistance?" She spoke excellent English, though I could tell it wasn't her mother tongue.

I held out my hand. "My name is Joanne Baldwin. I'm one of your—ah—special guests. You're on staff, right?"

She looked at my outstretched hand, at my face, and slowly took my fingers to shake. "Hello, Miss Baldwin. But I'm not staff. I'm crew."

"There's a difference? Call me Joanne."

"We're not allowed to use the first names of guests, miss," she said. "Yes, staff would be the people who work in guest relations areas. I'm a cabin stewardess. We're crew, not staff." She read the expression on my face, and smiled. "Ships are very tightly regimented, miss. We all know our duties and where we fit."

"Trust me, the rules are going to be shredded on this trip. So I'm Joanne, and you are . . . ?"

"Aldonza Araujo," she said, and her handshake grew a little more firm. We were about the same age, I thought. "Aldonza, miss."

I gave up temporarily on forcing informality on her. "I'm looking for my cabin. I know I'm close, but—"

She got my cabin number and showed me the route by tracing a French-manicured fingernail on the map. I'd mirror-imaged my route, and I'd somehow ended up on the opposite side of where I should have been. Port, not starboard, in nautical terms. "I'm afraid you'll have to go around this way," she said.

I frowned down at the map. "What about this way?" It was marked in featureless gray.

"Those are service areas, miss. You can't go that way."

"I'm pretty sure that for us there is no such thing as off-limits. We're not regular guests. You know what I mean?"

She did, but her smile instantly froze solid. "I—I am sorry, but I can't—we're not allowed—"

"Aldonza." I interrupted her gently enough, but firmly, and took her hand in both of mine. "You signed the waivers, right? The Wardens explained to you what kind of risk was involved in staying on this ship?"

She nodded mutely. I could sense that she wanted to pull away from me, but also that her curiosity was burning a hole in her head. Instead of asking, she just waited.

"The fact is, we're not going to be regular passengers," I said. "Think of us as policemen, or military personnel. We don't need coddling, but we do need to know every-thing about this ship we can, from the technical stuff to the most insignificant details. It could mean the difference between life and death for everybody on board if things get worse."

I watched that sink in, but Aldonza still shook her head in refusal. "I can't let you in, not without someone telling me I can. It's strictly against regulations."

"Okay, you can tell me how to get there, and if I happen to stumble accidentally into the crew areas, then it's not your fault, right?" She hesitated. "Please, Aldonza. It could be important. I promise, I'll talk to Security and to the Chief Engineer too, but in my experience, the bosses don't know everything. They *think* they know everything. You are the guys who really understand the ship."

She actually laughed, covering her mouth with her hand, as if too loud a sound was definitely Not Done in the posh areas, at least not when wearing a uniform. "That's true," she agreed, but she sobered from her brief burst of laughter far too quickly. "It's not possible for you to go through the crew area without being seen and stopped. The ship has lots of surveillance. Cameras everywhere. We all know each other. We have to, living in such close quarters. If they don't know you and you're in off-limits areas, they'll call security and escort you out." She was shaking her head again, clearly talking herself out of even trying it. "We have very good security people. It's not worth the risk. Talk to the captain or the Executive Officer."

I tried to imagine any of the security people being prepared to deal with even a middle-grade Warden, much less somebody like me or Lewis or the Djinn. I failed. "Okay," I said, because Aldonza clearly was feeling more and more uncomfortable. "I suppose it's a bad idea anyway. I'll take the long way around.—But, just for future reference, what do the crew-area doors look like?"

Aldonza blinked. "I thought you knew."

Huh? My confusion must have registered, because she looked behind me at a simple door with a swipe card lock labeled PRIVATE.

"Oh," I said. "Right. Thanks."

She clearly thought I was crazy, and she wasn't about to get fired over it. From the glances she threw back at me as she moved down the hallway, she was trying to make sure I wouldn't do anything wrong—at least not before she was safely away from the scene of the crime.

Couldn't really blame her.

I pretended to read my map, waiting until she'd had plenty of escape time. I marked the location of the crew door on it and noted the locations of the surveillance cameras, too.

I *could* pop the door right open, with a relatively minor pulse of power. I *could* fritz out the cameras, too.

But the truth was, I could do that anytime I needed to, and right now it wasn't my first choice. I just wanted to reach my soft, expensively appointed bed.

I looked up at the surveillance eyes focused on where I stood, sighed, and took the long way around.

I *still* got lost. This huge floating palace was like some creepily deserted amusement park—all the lights were on, but there seemed to be a faintly sinister edge to everything. It was made to be inhabited, to be full of life and fun and conversation, and instead there was just fear. The few people I spotted were staff (crew?) going about their business.

I somehow ended up on the Grand Promenade, or at least that was what I read on the map. It was the big railed expanse looking out over the ocean. Overhead, the sky was nail gray, and the water looked just as hard and unfriendly, with sharp-edged waves. The *Grand Paradise* was big and heavy enough to cleave its way through like a knife, even at the labored speed we were moving.

The promenade was deserted, too. I stood in the clammy wind for a while, watching the endless rolling of the waves, and then I yawned and felt my eyelids growing even heavier.

So tired.

At least, I was tired until I felt a hot, seductive tingle on my back, just over the shoulder blade. That jerked me back to full alert like a jab from a cattle prod.

I didn't make any more stops on my way.

Safely in the bedroom—no sign of Cherise downstairs—I sat down, closed my eyes, and focused on David. I can't really describe the connection between the two of us; the ceremony and the vows—even though our wedding had been interrupted by Bad Bob's attack, and technically not really finished—had pulled us together, bound us in ways that even now I couldn't understand, except that it made it easier to call him when I needed him.

When I opened my eyes, David was forming out of the air in a swirl of gray and gold. There was something blank in his eyes this time, as if I'd taken him away from something both terrible and important. He'd been with Lewis. I wondered how bad it was.

Then he took a deep breath and willed it away, whatever it was.

"The mark is burning," I said, without any preamble at all. He took on human form and flesh and sat down next to me. He felt warm as summer, and he smelled faintly of spices and real, human sweat, deliciously male. His fingers unbuttoned my cotton camisole and pushed it down my arms, and then he unhooked my bra and slid it off. There was no seduction in it, or at least not as much as I'd have liked; he was very focused on the job at hand.

When his fingertips pressed on the black torch mark on my back, we both gasped. He spread his whole left hand over it, and the heat spread, increased to an agonizing burn that felt as if it should come with the sound of sizzling. His right arm went around me, holding me up, keeping me from fighting him to get away from the pain.

With shocking suddenness, the fire turned to ice, a chill that ripped all the way through me, and I shuddered. When I exhaled, my breath frosted the air in delicate feathers that vanished in seconds.

I couldn't feel the mark on my back anymore, and that was a huge relief. But, as David trailed his fingers over it, I realized that I could feel less of the area around it, too. The numb spot was growing.

I turned to look at him, and caught the unguarded pain in his face before he could hide it from me. He was tired, and he was anguished. Worse, he was despairing.

"Stop that," I said. "What's happening?"

"It's getting larger," he said. "I had to expand the containment to keep it within the boundaries. You can't push yourself this hard."

"I know that, and yet I'm not seeing I have much of a choice. How's Lewis?"

He didn't want to tell me, but I think he knew I wasn't about to let him slip away without an explanation. "Fighting his guilt," David finally said. "He blames himself for the deaths. He feels he made a tactical error."

That wasn't unexpected. "He made the right choices at the time. We had to give it a try."

"I know. He's afraid that he rushed into it. He's afraid that he allowed personal issues to color the decision."

"That'll be the day," I said, and then wondered what that meant. "Personal, how?" Please, let it not be about me.

"Rahel," David said softly. "He can feel her suffering, just as I can. Bad Bob is making sure we can feel it."

Bad Bob had a Djinn named Rahel in his clutches—one of David's New Djinn, and someone I could almost call a friend. He could do whatever he wanted to her—the curse of a Djinn being bound to a bottle, of having her will taken away. And she couldn't fight back. The nightmare dimensions of that stretched on and on into the darkness, because I knew how sick Bad Bob's imagination had been even years back. God only knew how much worse he was these days, with so much Demon in his body that I wasn't even sure the old Bad Bob was still around in any form I would recognize.

Rahel had done me some very kind favors in the past. She was never to be trifled with, or underestimated, but unlike a lot of the Djinn, she did care, however remotely, about the fate of individual humans—and the fate of the human race.

David, as her connection to the power source of Mother Earth, would feel every injury done to her. I wasn't sure, but I thought that her connection to Lewis was more about personal feelings than old-fashioned lines of fealty. She liked him. He liked her. Maybe it went deeper than that. He'd never felt the need to tell me, and I didn't ask. I had thought their relationship was more of a hookup than love, but I could have been wrong.

I put my hand on David's cheek and looked him full in the face for a long, long moment. "How bad is it with her?" I asked him. I didn't want a kind evasion. I didn't want anything but the truth, the whole truth, nothing but the truth, and he could sense that from me. "Is he going to destroy her?"

"Eventually," he said, and gently took my wrist. "There's nothing more I can do for Rahel just now. She would want me to focus on those I can help."

"You've done all you can for me, too."

"Yes," he said, and I could see he hated to admit that. "I'm slowing it down, but that's all I can do. It's deep, and it's still growing. But I intend to keep trying. I'm not giving up, not on either of you."

He wasn't saying anything we didn't both know, but I could hear the frustration in his voice, and the anguish. I slipped my arms around his neck and the two of us cuddled close for a moment. His lips found mine, long and lingering.

"You're tired," he murmured. Like the gentleman he was at heart, David slipped the bra back up my arms, turned me around, and fastened it for me. He even buttoned up my camisole. "I want you to rest."

I was more used to him undressing me. This felt . . . warm. Intimate in a way that seemed more personal than unbridled passion. It was the kind of thing a husband did for a wife—an everyday kind of gentleness.

It made me crave him so badly.

"David?" My voice came out very small. "I can't sleep. Will you stay with me? Just for now?"

His arms wrapped around me and his head rested on my shoulder. I felt a shudder go through him, some emotion I couldn't name. When he looked up, the intensity of it was enough to shatter my heart.

"I'll stay," he said, and eased me down onto the bed. "I'll stay as long as you're awake."

"Big promises, Mister Big Shot," I said. "What if a cat

gets stuck up a tree in Peoria? I bet you'd go running off
to the rescue."

"You know how seriously I take a vow. Unless I made
one to the cat, you're my priority." He tapped me gently on the nose, and there was humor in his face now.
"Clothes off or on?"

"Oh God, off. Off off off."

We were naked before our backs hit the mattress,
thanks to David's wondrous Djinn fabric-vanishing
powers. The duvet settled over us like snowfall, but
it was warm beneath it, so warm, and when his lips
touched mine it was a dreamlike kiss, damp and gentle
and sweet. I rested my head on the pillow of his arm
and moved in closer, drawn without a word being spoken. His fingers brushed hair from my face and feath-
ered it back, then lingered on my cheek, drawing heat
down to my chin.

"Please," I whispered. "Please make all this go away.
Just for a while. Can you do that?"

"I'm only a Djinn," he said. "Not God Himself. But
I'll do what I can."

His lips brushed their heat down, taking all the time
in the world, pausing in unexpected and vulnerable
places. The inner aspect of my forearms. My wrists. The
delicate skin just beneath my breasts. He began to suck,
drawing my blood to the skin with slow deliberation. He
left a map of visible kisses down my body, a slow and
thorough awakening of my entire body that made me
writhe silently, sheets fisted in my hands.

Oh, I forgot. I forgot *everything*.

Gradually, his mouth became demanding. Challeng-
ing. Nips of his teeth, strokes of his tongue. My control
slipped, and I made a tortured sound in the back of my
throat, rising up to meet him. I didn't want seduction

right now. I wanted to be ravished, and he could feel it echoing out of me like a ringing bell.

I could tell the exact second that his control slipped gears. His body language shifted, tensed, and he raised his head and looked at me. My already quickened pulse jumped, because the look in those Djinn-bronze eyes was feral. *Wanting.* I sat up and met him halfway through the space and devoured his mouth, hungry and desperate, full of feverish need and frantic energy. It fed back through the link between us, striking like lightning through a grounded circuit, shorting out whatever defenses we'd kept built between us.

When I pulled back, David's eyes were no longer bronze. They were fire, with pupils of absolute darkness. *Mine,* I thought incoherently. *Mine.* I didn't know if that came from me or from him. It had the force of a Djinn emotion, something vastly more complex than simple human possessiveness.

David growled and put a hand on my chest and pushed me all the way back full length on the bed. He followed, not quite putting his weight on me. Brushes of his hot skin teased and tortured us both. He ran his palm lightly over the rising tilt of my left nipple and flicked his tongue over the right, and the difference in sensations made me gasp. His hand was light, delicate, and burning hot; his mouth was heavy, demanding, and deliciously wet. I bit my lip and felt my whole body shudder in response. I heard an answering sound from David—need, lust, love, wordless reassurance.

We were both on the knife-edge of control. David had never fully let his Djinn instincts out to play before, not like this. I think he'd been too afraid—afraid of hurting me, afraid that I'd be shocked by the depths of his needs and desires.

I knew better. I put my hands around his face and held him still for a moment, staring deep into those inhuman eyes.

And then I nodded. No words, and none necessary.

His skin took on a dusting of gold, and then darker shades, until he seemed more metal than flesh—but it was flesh to the touch, warm and soft and firm. He tasted like exotic spices—cardamom, saffron, wild honey from the rocks. Everything about him was different, and yet everything was exactly the same.

His hand slipped lower down my body, into the slick folds between my thighs. The sensation was overwhelming—burning and cooling at the same time. His thumb pressed and stroked while his long, lovely fingers slipped within. His mouth closed over mine, cinnamon-hot, and I sucked his tongue and tasted fire.

Ecstasy to the power of infinity.

The old, wild magic spiraled up inside of me, exultant, slow pulses that built on each other. *Yes, God, yes . . .* When I came I did it silently, rigidly, holding the awesome force of it inside and giving it to David through the link between us.

It drove him beyond human disguises, and light exploded in the room. I heard him gasping, struggling to stay with me in flesh, because flesh was what we both needed just now.

He solidified again into skin, hot and firm against me. I rolled over and up to my hands and knees, and felt the fiery stroke of his hands over my back, down my hips, between my thighs . . .

I gasped and dropped my head to the pillow as the relentless pleasure of him filled me. Nothing mattered in that moment—only the need, the all-encompassing need to *feel*. Every thrust traveled through my body in shattering waves, as intense as any sensation I'd ever known. I heard David whispering in that liquid, sibilant language that I knew must have been his native tongue, the language of fire, of Djinn. I didn't know the words, but I heard the music—dark, delicious, and utterly abandoned.

He knew just the right spot to hit to shatter me completely. I screamed as another orgasm flooded me like boiling light. It spilled into him, triggering a matching explosion that rocked us both to the core.

The room was full of light.

I caught my breath to hold on to the pure, silvery perfection of that moment, riding the waves, feeling them slowly and gently diminish.

We hadn't said a word, not in English. David still didn't. He continued to move inside me—slow, gentle strokes—and kissed the small of my back. It was the gentlest gesture after such an aggressive, passionate coupling, and it promised me, without the luxury of words, that whatever boundaries we found ourselves crossing, he would always lead me back.

David eased down next to me on the bed, flushed and glowing and triumphant. Human, and not.

So much power and control, made vulnerable through me.

I felt a tingle of heat in my back. *No. Not now.* It faded, more like a warning than an attack.

I curled into David's body and recovered my breath. Despite everything the past few hours flooded back, bringing guilt and regret. *What right do I have to be happy?* I had none. Maybe I never would. *That wasn't safe.* I couldn't surrender control like that, not with Bad Bob's mark on my back. What if he'd taken advantage of that moment to strike? What if he'd taken control?

"Jo." David's voice was rough, not quite steady. When I looked up into his eyes, I recognized the expression. "I see I can't make the world stop for long. And you think too much."

"I was just thinking what a terrible risk that was," I said. "Because—"

"Because of the mark."

I nodded. He lifted himself up on one elbow and looked down at me, golden skin still shimmering in the light, flushed in all the right places.

"I know," he said, and trailed his fingertips over the line of my collarbone. "But you're my wife, and no matter what the risks might be, that matters more to me."

"I love you," I whispered. "But you need to be careful. Especially with me."

His smile was warm enough to light every candle in the world. "I was, at first. But I fell in love with you instead. Now there is no safety from you."

I burrowed close to him, and his arms wrapped around me, and for the moment it was all quiet. All peace.

"For as long as we live," he said, and kissed the top of my head. "Which means forever, if I have any say in it."

Chapter Four

It wasn't heaven, but it was damn close. For the next couple of hours I slept, curled in David's protective arms, feeling safe for the first time I could remember. The motion of the ship was rhythmic and soothing, and for a little while the world did go away, after all.

I could almost—*almost*—believe it was a honeymoon cruise.

Right up until Cherise threw open the bedroom door and stood there, panting, staring at us with eyes that didn't really see us at all.

"You'd better get out here," she said, as David sat up. I did too, swiping hair back from my face and grabbing at the thousand-thread-count sheets as they threatened to slide away. Cherise, shockingly, didn't seem to notice any of that—not even David's exposed chest, which frankly should have at least gotten a double take, or a stare, or a patented Cherise come-on.

She just delivered her message and dashed away.

"That's not like her," David said, swinging his legs out of bed. "Is it?"

"Nope. Clothes?"

"Closet." He was already heading there. He pulled

open the door and inside was a rainbow of choices, some for him, some for me.

"Underwear?" I asked.

He raised eyebrows. "Is it absolutely necessary?"

"Right now? Yes."

"Top drawer." He nodded toward a delicate-looking dresser, something that would have made *Antiques Roadshow* stars buzz with excitement. In it, I found new bras, panties, stockings—pretty much anything I might need, or crave. Or David might crave. I picked out something plain and put it on. As I turned, David threw me a shirt and pants. Jeans, and a navy blue shirt that clung in all the right places.

He was dressing too, the old-fashioned way. As a Djinn, he could have easily just gone the magic route, but I stole a few precious seconds enjoying the sight of him wiggling into Joe Boxers, which might have been intended, from the smile he gave me.

Even with mutual appreciation, it took us only about a minute to dress, and then we headed down the stairs.

Cherise was there. So was Lewis. He was self-contained again, only the shadow of trauma left in his dark eyes.

"I need you," he said bluntly. He turned and walked out of the cabin, moving fast. David and I exchanged a look and followed.

There was a dead body in the hallway. I stopped when I saw her, shock slamming through me. She looked like she'd been turned to crumbling clay, or ash—lifeless, a mockery of something that had once been real and vital.

"God," I whispered, and slowly crouched without touching the corpse. Lewis knelt on the other side of it. "Who—?"

"That's the problem," Lewis said. "I don't know. I think she's one of the Djinn."

I looked up at David, who was staring down at the two of us with a frown. He focused on the body on the floor.

"That isn't a Djinn," he said. "I don't know what that is."

He realized, then, what he was saying. Djinn couldn't *not* know, in the normal course of events; they could spool back the history of things. They saw *time*—it was a real sense to them, the way touch and taste were to humans.

The only way he couldn't know who this person was, was if this was a Djinn and the Djinn had been murdered by Unmaking, the special new weapon of Bad Bob Biringanine.

Antimatter. It was deadly to the Djinn in all kinds of hideous ways.

The next thought came to me with sickening speed and impact. *He had access to the ship.*

I snapped a lightning-fast glance at Lewis, and saw that this was not news to him. He'd already come to the same conclusion, presumably well before he'd come to summon us. David's reaction was just his confirmation. "Fuck," I said. "He's been here, on board, or at least he's gotten one of his minions through our defenses. We should have known. Our early warning system—"

"Clearly isn't working," Lewis finished. "Which means he, or any of his people, could be here. This place is big enough to hide an army if they didn't want to be found."

"But if hiding was the point, why leave this poor lady right here in the open?" I asked. "They could have hidden her anywhere. Her Conduit wouldn't even know she was missing." Which was the awful part of it. David, as Conduit for the Djinn, had a personal connection to each and every one he was responsible for. Ashan had the same connection to his half of their numbers. Bad Bob's weapon of choice did worse than kill; it *erased*. The Djinn couldn't recognize their own dead, or the weapons that killed them. The moment the victim died, it ceased to have ever been.

My nightmare was that it might be David lying here, with another Djinn staring at him in that same annoyed confusion, not even remembering his existence.

There was something so chilling in it that I had a hard time wrapping my head around it.

"That's not a Djinn," David murmured. He wasn't trying to convince us, only himself. "It *can't be*." We'd been through this. He understood, intellectually, what was happening, but this was a kind of phobia for the Djinn—a blind spot that left them vulnerable, one that couldn't be overcome by knowledge or experience. It wasn't seated in the rational parts of their brains.

"Count your people," Lewis said. He said it quietly, a little regretfully, as if he didn't really want to know, either. David continued to stare at the corpse.

"Counting myself," he said, "fifteen Djinn are on this vessel." In other words—exactly the number we'd started with.

I exchanged a baffled stare with Lewis. "You're sure?"

"Of course I'm sure. Ten of my people, myself, and four of Ashan's. Fifteen."

"Then where did this one come from?"

He couldn't answer that. It was like his brain locked up and refused to produce an answer. Instead, he shook his head, stubbornly unable to get past the paradox.

"Maybe Ashan sent another Djinn," I said. "A new one."

"You're sure this isn't one of his four?" Lewis asked.

"I'm sure." I'd seen the four of them, and Venna had been the only one representing herself as female. While the Djinn *could* change sexes, in my experience they rarely did it without a damn good reason. "This is insane. Can you get Ashan on the line and ask him?"

David's attention went elsewhere, but only for a moment, and then he shook his head in the negative. "Venna's coming," he said. Before he finished the sentence, I caught sight of Venna's sparkly pink shirt at the end of the hall. She didn't seem to be in a hurry, but in the next breath she was there, standing at David's side.

"What's this?" she asked, staring down at the dead Djinn with academic interest. It was creepy.

"We were hoping you could tell us," Lewis said. "Anything?"

She studied the body intently, then shook her head. "No. I don't know what it is."

I cleared my throat. "Radiation?"

"Nothing dangerous left on the body," Lewis said. "It looks as if she died the same way the other Djinn did, from antimatter poisoning—but there's no residual energy. She's just—dust."

There wasn't any way to resolve this, not through the Djinn, in any case. "Thanks," I said to Venna. "Don't worry about it."

She didn't give it a second thought. She skipped off down the corridor as if stepping around dead, dust-and-ash bodies was an everyday occurrence.

"I'll be back," David said abruptly, and misted out before Lewis or I could protest. He was deeply bothered; I could see that, but there was no way I could help him. He'd have to come to terms with this, or not, in his own time.

"So what do we do?" Cherise asked. I'd almost forgotten about her. She was standing a few feet away, arms wrapped around her chest as if she was fighting off a chill. "We can't just leave the poor thing out here. God. I can't believe this is happening. This is just *awful.*"

Lewis and I looked at each other, and I knew he was thinking the same thing I was: the way the body had disintegrated into dust and ash, I wasn't sure moving her was much of an option.

But it seemed like the only decent thing to do was to try.

"We'll save a sample," Lewis said. "Maybe we'll find some kind of clue if we analyze it in detail. But Cherise is right—we can't leave her here. And there doesn't seem much reason to store the body."

No, because we both knew the body was going to disintegrate as soon as we started trying to move it.

We retrieved a shower curtain and repurposed it as a body bag. There was something very disturbing about having pieces of the dead Djinn break off and float away as we went about it, but we managed to get her scraped onto the makeshift bier and carried her away. Cherise didn't follow. She stood there, staring at the flecks and smears that littered the carpet. It looked like a spilled ashtray.

"Nobody even knows her name," she said. "That is just so—sad."

Burial at sea was the best we could give our nameless victim. As Lewis and I tipped the crumbling remains over the railing, I felt we ought to say something, anything, but nothing came to my mind.

It did to Lewis's, though. "You may be forgotten," he said, "but you won't go unavenged. I promise you that. We'll find out what happened to you."

Her corpse disintegrated almost instantly in the pounding waves, returning to the embrace of nature. I hoped that the vast intelligence that made up this world remembered her, named her, gathered her close.

I hoped that her life had mattered to some human, somewhere, who still had fond thoughts of her.

White spray was soaking my thin shirt and leaving my skin cold and stiff. Lewis's warm hand touched my back. "Inside," he said. "There's nothing we can do here."

"I'm tired of hearing that," I said. "I'm really tired of being helpless. Aren't you?"

Turning, I caught the flash of outright rage in his eyes. "Yes," he said. "And we're not going to be helpless much longer, I promise you that. Come on."

He stalked away from the rail.

I followed.

"Where are we going?" I called, as Lewis's long legs pulled him several steps ahead of me. The hallways were narrow, even in these upper-class areas, but they were nicely appointed, with paneling and original artworks, some of them by artists I recognized. He wasn't giving me time to sightsee. I hustled past the art so fast that it could have been clown paintings, for all I knew.

He didn't answer.

When our little mini-parade came to the less exclusive areas, the design standards changed. Still nice but less art, more lithographs. Cheaper carpeting, and the wood was trim, not wall. I glimpsed a sign that said we were heading for the Main Gallery, whatever that was.

"Lewis, dammit, slow down!" I wasn't slow, but he was acting like this was an Olympic event. "Where are we going?"

We turned a corner and stepped out into upper-middle-class opulence. Maybe even nouveau riche opulence. There was a waterfall in the middle of the open space that spilled a graceful, sinuous wave over curved rock three stories tall, with lush tropical vegetation carefully complementing the lines of the design. Five levels of decks, all with railings circling this part of the ship. As I looked over, I saw that two of the dining areas were below, at the foot of the waterfall—one casual, one formal. All eerily vacant at the moment, except for some staff—I guessed they were staff—taking advantage of the slow moments to grab themselves lunch and drinks. A few Wardens were wandering around in groups of two or three, rubbernecking while they had the luxury of not being marked for death.

Somewhere in the back of my mind, Celine Dion was singing again, dammit. Well, one thing was certain, my heart would *not* go on, not if this voyage went badly, and I wished she'd just shut the hell up.

Lewis turned, leaning on the rail, with the waterfall as a backdrop. Its hissing rain formed white noise around us.

"I wanted to go someplace we could talk uninterrupted," he said. "And someplace it would be harder to overhear."

"You think someone's watching us?"

"I don't think we can assume that our enemies are on the beach perfecting their tans." He shook his head and leaned against the railing, weight on his elbows. Mist from the impossible waterfall behind him made pearly rainbows around the lights. "I'm sorry. I didn't want to do this. I really tried." He sounded genuinely dispirited and angry about it, whatever *it* was.

"What are you talking about?"

"We're fighting shadows," he said. "We're guessing

and flying blind. I didn't want to have to use the resources I knew we had."

"What kind of resources?"

He didn't answer me, not directly. "I've been thinking
about Paul."

The name hit me hard, in unguarded places. Paul had
been my friend, my mentor in many ways, and somebody I'd thought I could always count on in a pinch.

But he had betrayed us, and I'd killed him for it. I
hadn't meant to do it—it had been in the heat of battle,
and my real enemy had used him as a human shield. I
didn't know when Paul had chosen the wrong side, or
how, or why; all I knew was that at that last, desperate
minute, he'd been standing next to Bad Bob, and that
had destroyed him.

I'd destroyed him.

"I'm wondering," Lewis said, "if Paul was really planning to funnel information back to us. He could have betrayed Kevin and Rahel anytime he wanted. He didn't. I
think he was trying to do the right thing. Maybe he was
still on our side after all."

Did he think that made it any better for me, carrying
around the memory of his death? "I hope so," I said. I
really did. I'd much rather Paul died a hero.

"And now," Lewis said, "I'm wondering the same
things about you. Whether you're really on our side . . .
or not."

I took a deep breath. It'd be too easy to turn this into
a blame-fest, and the last thing we needed right now was
to gouge pieces out of each other over nothing. Lewis
was so exhausted I suspected he'd welcome a fight, just
to keep his pulse moving, but I'd hurt enough people
recently.

"You don't think I'm loyal?" For answer, Lewis

reached over and put his hand on my numbed shoulder. I shook him off with a little too much anger. "Screw you, Lewis. I'd *die* for these people. Hell, I *have* died for them!"

He held up a hand to stop me. "No offense, but in a certain sense, if I tell you what I'm thinking or doing, I may be whispering it in Bad Bob's ear. You know that, don't you? Can you guarantee me it isn't true, or it won't be tomorrow?"

That was a cold, hard slap of reality, and I smarted from the impact. He was right, of course—the black torch on my back might be controllable for the moment, and I might be convinced that I was my own person, beyond Bad Bob's reach for now, but I couldn't really *know*. I also couldn't guarantee that it would stay that way five minutes from now, much less tomorrow.

"So now I'm the enemy," I said, and tried to keep my tone as dry as a good martini. "Fine. You know a good Demon tattoo-removal guy? And can we work in a day spa visit, while we're at it?"

He didn't laugh, and he didn't take the opportunity to lighten up. "I wanted to tell you that if I think you're slipping away, I won't hesitate. I'll kill you. I'll have to. Understand?"

I did. There was no room for misunderstanding in this. We both knew the stakes, and we both knew the consequences.

"Yeah, I understand," I said. "You're sure you can take me if you have to?"

"I can," he said. "And I will."

I took a deep breath. "Okay."

"The problem is, it would probably kill us both in the end, and we both know that's not a good outcome."

"I promise not to fight back."

"You can't promise. That's the problem, isn't it?"

"So what are you asking me, Lewis?"

"I want to put in a fail-safe. I need your cooperation."

Fail-safe.

This was something I'd heard about, rarely. It was generally used on Wardens who'd demonstrated behavioral problems—those who were mentally unbalanced. A crazy Warden was a very dangerous thing, and fail-safes were sometimes the only way to be absolutely sure you could stop a Warden before it was too late and the body count was too high.

I'd never thought I'd be facing the possibility myself.

"Fine," I said, and my voice sounded thick and strange to my ears. "Do it."

"I also need your consent."

I rolled my eyes. "Didn't I just say *do it*?"

His smile was very thin, and not at all happy. "I need you to say more than that. Informed consent."

"What, you think I'm going to sue? Fine, here's the cover-your-ass speech: I hereby authorize you to put a fail-safe switch in my brain, to be under your sole control, which you can use to shut me down if I present a clear and present danger to those around me." I heard the sharp, angry edge in my voice and tried to moderate it. "I give you permission to kill me. How's that for consent?"

He gazed at me with compassion, and a good deal of resentment. "You know I hate this, right?"

"Yeah. I'm not a big fan of the concept either, but I get why it's necessary, so let's get it done before David finds out what you're thinking about."

We probably looked like we were just meditating together, in front of the peaceful roaring waterfall. Two friends, standing calmly together, getting our Zen on.

Lewis held out his hands, palms up. I put mine over them, palms down.

I had to stand there, open and horribly vulnerable, as Lewis's Earth power moved slowly through my nerves, climbing my arms, my shoulders, lighting a bright fire at the base of my neck and spreading out over the cap of my head.

It sank in like a net of light. I couldn't *see* what he was doing, but I felt it—a sharp, bright spark deep in my brain, quickly contained. My whole body jerked, and my eyes flew open, but I couldn't see anything.

It took several seconds for my vision to come back. Just shadows at first, then smears of color, then a gradual definition to the edges of shapes.

Lewis's face, intent and focused.

He sighed, and I felt the power drain away from me, heading toward my feet. It was a little like being embarrassed in slow motion, a wave of heat traveling through flesh until it terminated through the soles of my shoes.

"Done?" I asked. He nodded. "How does it work?"

"It's a signature switch. I'm the only one who can trip it, and I have to do it a certain way, in a certain sequence."

"And if you do, it's lights-out in my head? Instantly?"

"Yes," he said. He sounded beaten and very, very tired. "Lights-out."

"No pain, though."

"Very little. About like a pinprick. It's over in about three seconds."

"I can't believe we're even talking about this," I said. "What's to stop me from undoing it, especially if I go all Team Evil on you? And once I know, Bad Bob could know. He could just disable the kill switch."

"I know," Lewis said. He looked very sad, and very

guilty. "That's why I had to get you off alone before I did this. I needed to be sure I was the only one who knew about it."

I didn't get it. "But *I* know about it."

He just stood there watching me, and the look in his eyes was intensely strange. "I need to say this," he said. "Just this one time. I love you. I've loved you for half my life, it seems like. And I always will love you, even though I know it's not possible for you to love me back. If you hadn't met David, it might have been— things might have been different. But I know when I'm beaten."

I was stunned. Lewis, of all people, was not a confessor. He didn't blurt out his emo secrets, not to anyone, *especially* not to me.

"I . . . have no idea what you want me to say," I said. "You know how I feel about you, you're—you're *Lewis*. God, why are you telling me this *now*?"

"Because I can. Because you won't remember anything about it thirty seconds from now," he said, and reached out and touched his finger to the exact center of my forehead.

"No—"

The world exploded into jagged shards.

What the hell had I just been saying?

I'd somehow managed to hypnotize myself by staring at the waterfall for too long. I shook off the blurring fascination and gave Lewis a doubtful look. "Jeez, I just spaced like mad," I said. "I'm really tired. What was I saying?"

Lewis was leaning on the railing, staring into the falling curtain of water. "You were saying you'd die for us," he said. "For the Wardens."

You'd think I'd remember *that*. "Damn straight I would, bucko. Anything else?"

He seemed tempted to say something, but then he shook his head and shifted gears. I could tell from the way his body language changed, from contemplative to decisive. "Yes. I want a thorough check of every Warden. Make sure there are none of Bad Bob's crew in our particular woodpile. When you're done, interview the passengers and crew. I want everybody, absolutely everybody, checked out by you and David."

So much for sweet, sweet bed rest. "That's going to take all night."

"Oh, at least. Let me know if you find anything."

"You are *such* a bastard." I sighed. "Is that all? Want me to build the Sistine Chapel out of paper clips in my spare time? You know, you didn't need all this hush-hush privacy to tell me to do your scut work."

"I know I didn't," he said. "I just wanted to show you the waterfall."

I glanced at it. "Pretty," I said. "Anything else, O Lord and Master?"

He continued to lean on the railing, staring into space. "That'll about do it."

I walked away, still wondering why the hell he'd dragged me here. Maybe he'd been about to ask me something personal. Maybe he'd been about to declare his undying love for me. *Yeah, like that would ever happen.*

Whatever it had been, he'd chickened out, and I could only think that was a good thing, given the circumstances.

I had a lot of work to do.

Sitting the Wardens down for their loyalty checks was easier than I figured it might be—mainly because they were shell-shocked after the disaster of trying to control the storm. Even the Fire Wardens, notoriously temperamental, and the Earth Wardens, notably hippie-nonconformist, decided to play nice.

I found nothing. If any of them were lying about their allegiances, it was beyond my ability—or David's—to discover. If Bad Bob and his crew could go that deep cover, there was no way we were coming out of this alive, so I decided not to worry about it.

That left some thirty-odd rich folks who were confined to their cabins—hopefully—and a whole bunch of ship's staff and crew.

It was going to be a long stretch. Luckily, I had David along with me, which meant he was paying more attention to my energy levels than I was, and after thanking the last eerily compliant Earth Warden and shaking hands, he steered me in the direction of the only open restaurant.

"I'm not hungry!" I protested. He raised his eyebrows. "I can't eat now. I've got work to do. Besides, I ate at the buffet when we had the meeting."

"You ate a turkey sandwich. Before you dumped all your energy into the attempt to control the storm."

David had a point—I'd burned profligate amounts of power, all day long, and now that I thought about it, my muscles had that oddly shaky feeling that meant I was about to crash. My head hurt, too.

I tried rejecting the whole problem again, but David knew when to press, and before I knew it, we were taking the big, sweeping gallery stairs down to the restaurant. It was called Le Fleur D'Or, and it was one of the smaller eating places on the ship—kind of an intimate date-type restaurant, with lots of dark woods and plush carpeting.

The hastily printed menu featured sandwiches, which I figured wasn't the usual fare. The place (and the staff) looked more used to handling lobster and exotic salads than BLTs. They couldn't resist foo-fooing them up by cutting crusts off the bread and making little triangles, but a sandwich is still a sandwich, even if it's on challah bread. I think I ate a dozen, making sounds that probably would have been more appropriate in bed than at the table.

David didn't need to eat—Djinn don't—but they *like* to eat, to take advantage of all the human senses they assume in human form. So he had some kind of pasta thing and a glass of red wine. Could Djinn get drunk? I'd never really considered the question before. I tried to imagine David intoxicated; he'd probably be a sweet, sloppy drunk, not a mean one, I thought. He'd be throwing his arms around Lewis and mumbling about how much he loved the guy in no time.

Well, maybe not, but it was an intriguing fantasy.

"Thanks," I said, pushing back from the crumb-dusted plate and swigging half of my iced tea in convulsive gulps. "I didn't know I was that bad off."

"You've got limits," he said. "You should learn to pay attention to them occasionally."

"Hey, that's not fair. I see the blur as I blow past them."

He came around, pulled my chair back, and handed me up to my feet in a courtly Old World gesture, very appropriate to this hushed, romantic restaurant with its subdued violin music. He combed his fingers through my curly hair in a slow, gentle gesture that left it straight and shining in the wake of his touch. "I was thinking more of actually staying within them."

"Funny. So where do we start with the rich folks?"

David turned to the waiter still hovering near the table, eager for any chance to break out of his boredom. "Do you deliver room service?"

"No, sir, the cabin stewards do that."

"Do they ever tell you about the difficult passengers?"

That got a big fat silence. I could imagine that passenger gossip was one of those major disciplinary no-no things.

"We won't say who it came from," I promised, and gestured to David, rubbing my fingers together. He reached in the back pocket of his pants, pulled out a wallet, and peeled off a hundred-dollar bill, which he placed on the table as a tip.

The waiter's eyes widened. "Cabin seventeen in first class," he said. "If you're looking for the biggest jerk."

"That's what I'm talking about. Mr. Prince?"

David offered me his arm in another of those dashingly gallant gestures. "Mrs. Prince," he said. "Cabin seventeen it is."

Cabin seventeen was located only a few doors down from my own spacious digs. As we headed in that direction, I saw Aldonza, the cabin stewardess, closing the door to room 22. She had a tray of used dishes balanced in her hands. I waved. She gave me a professional, polished smile in return, as impartial as a Swiss banker.

"Aldonza," I said, "can I ask you a question?"

"Yes, miss," she said, and tried not to stare at David too openly. "Of course."

She was carrying about twenty pounds on that tray, and she was a slight little thing. As I glanced at David, I saw he'd already reached the same conclusion. He reached out and took the tray from her, despite her shocked gasp.

"To the restaurant?" he asked. She gave him a stunned nod.

"But, sir, you can't—"

He could. David was quite enjoying being free of the Djinn secrecy restrictions; he misted away with the tray in full view of Aldonza, and her pretty face went pale with shock. She crossed herself and murmured something in Spanish.

"He's okay," I promised her. "More like an angel than, you know, the other thing." She stared at me blankly, shaking her head as if she simply wanted the whole thing to go away. "I need to ask you about one of your guests. Cabin seventeen?"

That snapped her out of her fugue state. Color flooded back into her face, and then she made a visible effort to stay calm and professional. "Mr. Trent Cole," she said.

"Nice guy?"

"I can't talk about my guests, miss." Her lips twitched. "Not even about you and the angel."

"Eh, don't worry about us. You can talk all you want. We've been on CNN." She snorted, then covered her mouth with her hand as if she was appalled at her bad behavior. I winked. "Look, about Mr. Cole—I'm about to go talk to him. Anything you can tell me about him that might help me decide if he's a threat or not?"

She hesitated, and I could see the good-girl/gossip-girl conflict being played out for a solid three seconds before the gossip girl pulled a smackdown. "He has a gun," she said. "I saw it. He put it in the pocket of his bathrobe. He doesn't like anyone coming into his room, and he's very rude. He doesn't let me do any cleaning, and that makes it so hard, because he can complain that I'm not doing my job, and if a passenger makes a complaint like that I can be fired and left at the next port—"

Man, when Aldonza decided to talk, it was hard to stop her. "What kind of a gun?" I asked. She looked puzzled. "Small? Big? Revolver? Automatic?"

"Big. An automatic."

"Okay. I just want to know what we're dealing with," I said. "Aldonza—did Mr. Cole threaten you? Hurt you?"

From the rigid set of her posture, I thought he had, but she shook her head. Maybe not even her gossip-girl side could voice that complaint. At least, not to a mere passenger.

"Okay," I said. I felt David coming back, and saw her eyes shift and widen as he whispered into existence behind me. "Thank you very much for your information. David—" I did the finger-rubbing thing again. He produced his wallet, Aldonza got a hundred-dollar bill, and as we walked away, David handed me the wallet. "What?"

"I just thought it might be more convenient," he said. "In case you want to bribe anybody in cabin seventeen."

"I want to intimidate the holy living shit out of cabin seventeen," I said. "How would that be?"

He gave me a slow, evil smile. "You only love me for my ability to terrify."

"And your ability to produce money out of thin air. That's important, too."

"I'm glad I'm well-rounded."

"In oh so many ways."

Mr. Trent Cole, aka Cabin Seventeen, decided that he wasn't going to submit to answering any questions, no matter how nicely we asked. In fact, Mr. Cole wouldn't even open his door.

Yeah, like that was going to keep us impotently standing outside.

"We're not Housekeeping," I called through the door. "Open it or we're coming in anyway."

"Like hell you are! I know my rights!" Mr. Personality screamed back at me.

David moved me out of the way—my own personal Djinn shield—and put a single finger on the surface of the glossy wooden door. When he pushed, the lock snapped and shattered like glass.

Nice. I liked the economy of his violence.

He stepped over the threshold, and Trent Cole fired three bullets into his chest, point-blank. He did it like a guy who'd had practice, but when David didn't fall down—didn't even flinch—Cole's expression turned from murderous to completely confused.

David stepped forward, took the gun (Aldonza was right, it was a big black semiautomatic), and handed it to me. I dumped it in the ice bucket on the bar, after burning my fingers on the barrel. If David was bothered in the least by someone trying to kill him, he didn't let it show in his cool smile, or the absolute ease with which he stiff-armed Mr. Cole toward the sofa.

Cole met the cushions at speed, and toppled like a tortoise onto his back, an awkward position at best. He was dressed in one of the ship's fluffy robes, his big feet shoved into slippers that flopped around hilariously as he tried to right himself. He struggled up to a sitting position as David shut the door behind us and repaired the lock with a minor pulse of power.

There was a bottle of Perrier-Jouët champagne sweating on the coffee table, along with two full flutes of sparkling liquid.

"I see we're in time for happy hour," I said, and settled myself in the tapestry armchair across from the sofa. I poured myself a glistening flute and then appropriated the second one for David. We sipped. Mr. Cole, a bulky sort, grabbed at the flapping hem of his robe to avoid giving me a Full Monty as he swung his feet to the floor. David settled himself in one of those intimidating poses the Djinn had perfected several millennia ago, literally guarding my back.

Cole, uncertain what to do, leaned back on the sofa. Slowly. "You can't just barge in here," he said. "I've got rights, whoever you think you are."

The champagne really was excellent. "You think those rights include shooting anyone who walks through your door?" I asked him. I craned my neck a bit to look up at David. "Speaking of that, you okay, honey?"

"I'm fine," he said. He held out a fist. I opened my palm, and he dumped three perfect bullets into it. "Souvenirs."

"For me? Thanks." I fluttered my eyelashes at him, and got a slow, hot smile. We both loved this part. I focused back on Cole, who was staring at us like we were straight out of a big-budget special-effects movie. "You need these back? Maybe you recycle?"

He shook his head. I put them in the pocket of my jeans. You never know when you'll need a good bullet.

"Now," I said. "Thanks for seeing us, Mr. Cole. We'll only be a minute. First question: Why do you feel the need to go all Wild West Show on friendly visitors? Bonus question: Why are you still on this ship? Because I think anybody who doesn't have to be here must have a really good reason to be staying."

Trent Cole was not accustomed to answering questions of any kind, much less from a plebeian like me. He struck me as nouveau riche, probably something to do with hedge funds or stocks or porn. Someone who had a lot of cash and was tremendously impressed with it.

He kept darting admiring looks at David. I was familiar with that. I just wasn't so familiar with seeing it in a man.

"I was just defending myself," Cole said. "I'm sorry. I got rattled."

While he was speaking, I allowed myself to drift just a bit out of my body so I could examine him in Oversight. His aura was muddy and indistinct—so, a genuine regular human-type guy, no surprise there—and bloody around the edges with guilt and nerves.

"Rattled?" I repeated. "You looked pretty calm to me. Good grouping on your shots."

"Center mass," David supplied. "Very well aimed."

Cole looked from one of us to the other, then fixed on David. His whole body relaxed. "You're wearing a vest, right? Of course."

For answer, David unbuttoned his shirt and displayed part of his bare chest.

"David, stop teasing the man," I said. *And me.* "Mr. Cole. Look at me, please." He did, not with any great pleasure, and I deepened my focus to get a better look at the inner Trent.

Not a terribly good experience.

"You're protecting yourself," I said aloud. "That's why you didn't leave the ship. You know you're an obvious target if you do. You're running from something."

He flinched, but he didn't move otherwise. "What the hell are you talking about?"

"Do you know a man named Robert Biringanine?" This was the money question, but I got nothing from him. Just a continuing roil of anxiety and fury. He didn't know Bad Bob, at least not by name.

David took his cue. "He looks like this." And he transformed himself into a perfect replica of Bad Bob, from his flyaway white hair, bloodshot blue eyes, and pug-Irish nose to his bowlegs. In fact, it was *so* good that I pulled in a startled breath and clenched my fingers on the arms of the chair, then deliberately relaxed. It was just an image, nothing more, and David dismissed it with a flick of his fingers when Trent Cole shook his head.

"Okay," I said, and tried to slow down the fast beat of my heart. "Who's after you?"

"None of your business," Cole barked.

"It is if you plan to go around shooting anybody who looks at you funny on this ship," I said. "Let us help you. There's no need to be afraid. Not now."

Cole stared at me with a perplexed look on his face. Clearly, I wasn't fitting the pigeonholes he was trying to stuff me into. I was used to that, actually.

"Who *are* you?" His gaze leaped from me to David, and then back again. "Are you with the government?"

"Yes," I said. In fact, that was sort of true. And sort of not.

"I'm calling my attorney. He's kicked the ass of everybody in the Justice Department, from the attorney general to the janitorial service. He'll make short work of you two jokers."

Cole reached for his cell phone.

It disappeared. Cole stared at the place where it had been, slapped his hand around, and looked at me with comically big eyes. "What the hell?"

David opened his right hand, and there was Cole's cell phone. "If you want it back, play nice," he said. Cole's mouth dropped open, and he surged to his feet.

"Hey, fucking David Copperfield, give that back!" His face turned brick-red, which I was pretty sure wasn't an indication of his general good health. "You sons of bitches, my life is in that phone!"

"Then I hold your life in my hand, don't I?" David pointed out mildly. "Sit."

I wasn't sure if it was a suggestion or an order, but Cole's ass hit the sofa cushions pretty quickly. His high-blood-pressure blush was already fading, as he realized that his biggest problem might not be in retrieving his contact list and scandalous text messages. "What the hell do you people *want*?" From Cole, that actually sounded kind of subdued.

"We want to be sure there's no more trouble," I said. "So we'll be taking your gun. Anything else contraband in here we should know about? Purely for safety?"

His gaze flicked away from me, racing toward the sweeping staircase, and then returning just as fast. In the aetheric, his aura whispered a fast rainbow of anxiety and guilt. I sat back and looked up at David, who nodded and disappeared, taking Cole's cell phone with him.

"What—" Cole's mouth had dropped so far open that I could see all his impressive dental work. I guess he'd figured out that David might share a first name with a famous magician, but he was far, far more impressive. "What *are* you people?"

"Who said we were people?" I smiled coolly at him. That flummoxed him for a full ten seconds.

"Look, I'm not some terrorist or something, I'm just— Okay, I took some money. A lot of money. From some people I worked with. And they're trying to get it back from me, that's all. It's just business."

Business mob-style, I gathered. Which explained why he wanted to hole up in his suite with a warm gun, and why he hadn't disembarked with the others. A common criminal.

I could live with that.

David ghosted back into view behind me and dropped a hand on my shoulder. I twisted to look at him.

"Boyfriend," he said. "Up in the bedroom. He had this." David deposited another gun in my lap, a match for the semiautomatic we'd confiscated from Cole. "Do you want to take a look?"

"Why, is he naked?"

It's hard to get a complete double take from a Djinn, but I managed. "I didn't notice," he said. Which was, no doubt, a crushing blow to Mr. Cole. I was sad for him. "What do you think? Pass?"

"Pass," I said. "Whatever problems he has aren't any concern of ours. Mr. Cole, we're done here. I'll be taking your guns with me, though. If you have intruder problems, David will be happy to come to your rescue." I batted my eyelashes again. David didn't look pleased with being volunteered. "Thanks."

"Thanks for what?" Cole asked, mystified. I walked over to the bar and retrieved the second pistol from the ice bucket. Nicely cooled down.

"Not shooting me, too," I said. "That would have been awkward."

"No," David said. "That would have been fatal for Mr. Cole."

I gathered that Mr. Cole was a man of few boundaries, but he recognized that one, and he nodded. "It won't happen again. Sorry. Eh—what's your name?"

"I'm David Prince. Her name is Joanne Baldwin," David said. "But you can call her Mrs. Prince."

I got a shiver out of that. A nice one.

We left Cole on the couch, still grappling with the utter destruction of his worldview.

All in all, not a bad first interrogation. Then again, my standards are pretty low. If I survive it, it can't be *that* bad.

Chapter Five

After Mr. Cole, the others seemed meek as kittens. Spiteful, furious, spitting, hissing kittens with needle-sharp claws and biting teeth. Each cabin seemed to come with its own particularly darling set of divalicious problems. Take Holly Addams, the model. . . . She had two employees, one of whom was solely occupied in making her disgusting-looking smoothies whenever she got hungry. They must have been made out of cardboard and water, because she had less body fat on her than your average piece of dry bone. She also had a trunk full of illegal and controlled substances, which explained why she hadn't left the ship when ordered. Her employees were just hapless and cowed. I tried not to traumatize them any more than I had to.

Three bankers in a row, two male and one female, all of whom had refused to leave out of lapdog-like devotion to star clients. These were rich people in their own right, but they'd gotten that way by single-minded dedication to that art of brownnosing, and they weren't about to stop the habit of a lifetime now. No connection to Bad Bob that I could find for them, their assistants, or (in the case of one of them) his mistress, who was ensconced in the downstairs bedroom.

And then we ran into Cynthia Clark.

"*The* Cynthia Clark?" I asked Aldonza, who was still hustling clean towels around the hallway. She nodded. "Isn't she making a movie?"

"She was," Aldonza said. "But she quit. I don't know why. Now she's here."

Cynthia Clark was an old-school star—glamorous, beautiful, icy cool. If Grace Kelly had ever had a rival, or Audrey Hepburn had ever worried about being upstaged, she was the source of their anxiety. Her 1960s-era films were classics. So were her '70s efforts. By the '80s she'd transitioned from starlet roles to tough matrons, and *still* did it better than anyone else.

Then she'd had a well-publicized marital disaster, some alcoholism, some rehab, and a whole lot of plastic surgery. Now she looked frozen at the age of fifty, although the twenty-year-old ice was beginning to crack under the strain.

She occupied cabin thirty-two, along with a European maid and a personal trainer, who I suspected doubled as another kind of workout partner.

I knew the minute we entered the cabin that something was off. David did, too. No bullets flying, no obvious signs of danger, but there was something very wrong with the feeling of the whole place. I couldn't put my finger on it.

Maybe Miss Clark had been in the middle of a knock-down, drag-out fight with her assistant. That would have explained the feeling of tension and anger that saturated the air.

Miss Clark was seated, like Mr. Cole, on the grand sofa, but she was wearing a pair of pencil-legged white pants, very '60s nautical, paired with a blue-and-white-striped knit shirt. Her eyes were the same blue as shallow

Caribbean waters, and if her hair was dyed that lustrous shade of blond, I couldn't tell. Even with the makeovers, she had seriously fierce DNA at work.

I felt as if I should genuflect before taking a seat in the side chair that she offered with a gracious nod. David remained standing, but he didn't resort to the intimidation stance this time around. More of a tranquil stand-at-ease type of thing.

Clark's trainer and maid busied themselves in another part of the room. I barely registered them as background noise, because La Clark simply drew every bit of attention to herself just by sitting there.

"Thank you for seeing us, Miss Clark," I said. "My name is—"

"Joanne Baldwin, yes, I know," she said. She had a contralto voice, and she used it the way a master musician uses a violin, conveying all shades of meaning in one brilliant stroke. "You represent these Wardens I've been hearing so much about. And your companion?"

"David Prince," he said.

"You're one of the ... Djinn?" She tried the taste of the word, and I could tell she liked it. When he nodded, Clark's eyes drifted half closed, and she sat back against the cushions, studying him. "Extraordinary. I thought there were no surprises left in the world, but here you are. Like something straight out of a fairy tale. The old kind, of course. The frightening ones."

She offered us coffee, tea, drinks. Neither of us felt thirsty, but I accepted a delicate little teacup steaming with French Roast, just to make this more of a social call. Being able to say *I had coffee with Cynthia Clark* didn't factor into that decision at all. Well, not much.

Clark blew on the surface of her own brew and studied us both with X-ray eyes that had reportedly once made Steve McQueen swoon. "How can I help you?" she asked.

"Just a few questions, and then, I promise, we'll certainly be out of your way," I said. "First, can you tell me why you didn't leave the ship before departure, as you were asked to do?"

"Well, you're direct," she murmured. "How very refreshing. It's all a bit embarrassing, I suppose, and it's going to make me seem like a horrible tyrant. I was terribly tired, and I left strict instructions not to be disturbed for any reason prior to departure. I'm afraid my employees might have taken those instructions a bit too literally. When I finally rose for breakfast, I was informed of the evacuation order, but it was too late for us to make our arrangements and leave."

There was something odd about Clark's aura. It seemed very calm, swirling with neutral blues and soft golds, but it also felt *artificial.* "What kind of arrangements? I'd think you'd want to get out as quickly as possible."

"I really can't go into details," she said. "But it was entirely accidental that we ended up staying here, on the ship. We won't be any trouble to you. I'm quite content to stay in the cabin." She gave me a cool smile. "It's so difficult to find privacy these days out in the real world."

I wondered, because a curl of hot magenta drifted over her aura. Resentment, maybe. She wasn't the It Girl anymore when it came to the paparazzi, and she knew it. It probably took a great deal of effort to get herself photographed at all, except in retirement magazines talking about how she was "still young at sixty-five."

"Routine questions, Miss Clark. We just want to be sure we're aware of any problems that might come up," I said.

"Such as?"

"Oh, I don't know . . . Trouble between you and another passenger, maybe a stalker? Business disagreements?"

"Alas, I don't have that many enemies, Miss Baldwin. I'm sure I'd feel much more important if I did. No, I have no fears, and I'm sure that none of my little party represents any sort of difficulty for you."

I wished I could figure out what was bothering me. She just didn't seem . . . *right*. Was she scared? No, not really, but when I concentrated on her aura, I saw flecks like floating ice. I wasn't sure what it meant, but I *was* sure that it wasn't normal.

I let the silence go on too long. "Is that all?" Clark asked, suddenly a good deal less welcoming. "I have a strict meditation schedule. Yoga. It keeps me toned and flexible. I highly recommend it."

"May I speak with your employees?" I asked her.

"No," Cynthia Clark said. Just the one word, cold and final. I blinked and glanced at David, who was staring at Clark with very dark eyes. I didn't know what he was seeing, but it wasn't good. Not good at all.

Then he looked from Clark to where her two employees stood at the other end of the room.

"Jo," he said, and touched my shoulder. "You should go."

"I— What?"

"Now." The touch turned into a painful squeeze. *"Now."*

I stood up, but it was too late. I barely sensed the snap of power coming before it hit me like a pile driver to the chest—not just on the physical plane but on the aetheric, too. I knew this sensation.

It had hit me before. It had killed a whole lot of my friends.

The blitz attack sent me into the air in a tumbling, twisting heap. I flew across the cabin and slammed into the solid wall with a wood-cracking thump. I hardly had time to process the shock of pain before pressure closed around me, deep as the black depths of the ocean, and drove all the air from my lungs. I felt my entire nervous system flickering, overloading, on the verge of burnout. There was an unearthly shrieking roar in my ears, like a mental institution on fire, and everything felt *wrong*, so wrong.

I fought. I flailed, trying to throw it off, but I couldn't, because there was nothing to grab hold of. I blinked away darkness and saw David moving like a streak of light toward the two at the far end of the room, but he was too far. It was happening too fast, unbelievably fast. . . .

I was going to die, and he wouldn't be able to stop it.

You can stop it, Joanne. All you have to do is let go.

The thought bubbled up on some black, greasy tide from the depths of my soul. It was solid as a life preserver in a storm, and I grabbed it, desperate to stop the pain, the shrieking, the sickening and inevitable feeling of every cell in my body being crushed into slime.

You have to let go, it told me. *Let go, Joanne. You can save yourself if you choose.*

With the weight of mountains on my chest, with my entire body screaming for release, with my bones turning to powder inside and my nervous system frying like a burned-out bulb, I believed it was the only choice.

Then I felt the eager, hot twinge of the black mark on my back, and I *knew* where that thought was coming from.

No.

Time had proceeded only a tiny fraction of a second.

David hadn't even reached the far end of the room yet, although the Djinn could move at the speed of thought. I was being crushed into greasy paste by a force so vast it felt like Earth herself had landed on me, and the idea of waiting an instant, a single breath, for help was almost impossible.

Save yourself. You can. It's easy.

Yes. All I had to do was shatter the containment that David had put around the black torch, and it would burn away all my problems.

Forever.

I held on. I don't know how; it wasn't inner strength, it wasn't courage, and it wasn't anything I could be proud of. Maybe it was just paralyzing terror. The instant passed, and even though I felt death's breath on my lips, the taste was all that lingered; David reached Cynthia's personal trainer, and that man—whoever, *whatever* he was—had no more time for killing me.

I gagged in a trembling breath, rolled on my side, and sobbed in agony. My nerves continued to burn, and the entire circuit board of my brain seemed on the verge of overload. I hadn't been hurt that suddenly, that *deeply*, in a long time. The taste of mortality is ash and blood, and I coughed until I could stop gagging on it.

Getting up was like free-climbing the Empire State Building in a hurricane, but I used an overturned table for support until I could feel my legs. They weren't quite right, somehow. Most of me wasn't, at that moment. This was going to hurt later. A lot. For a long time.

I forgot all of that when David screamed, "Jo! *Cover!*"

Fire rolled out from him, blistering white, and I lunged for the sofa, where Cynthia Clark still sat frozen in shock by the explosion of violence. I shoved her down into the cushions and threw myself on top of her. I couldn't reach the other innocent in the room—her personal assistant—but I extended the fastest, hardest shield of interlocked molecules I could over the woman's prone body. She'd sensibly dropped to the floor and curled into a ball on the rug.

No time for any other defenses. Whether David had called the fire, or his enemy had, it filled the room like an airburst of napalm. I felt the back of my clothes and my hair smolder, and smelled instant, toxic charring of plastics and carpet and furniture. The flame would have incinerated all three of us if I hadn't shielded us; mortal flesh would have burned off like flash paper.

It *had* burned the flesh off of David's opponent.

The blast flamed out, leaving a thick swirl of smoke, and I raised my head to see my Djinn lover facing a skeletal, blackened *thing* that was certainly not human, never human—something that should be dead, and yet was still standing. It wasn't a Demon, though it had some characteristics that reminded me of the way a Demon's bones curved and spiked.

It looked like it was made of glass. In fact, only the smudges and soot that clung to it made it visible at all. I blinked and clicked into Oversight.

It was *invisible* on the aetheric.

Ghosts, Venna had named them.

The forerunners of the end of all things.

David let out a wordless roar of fury and fastened his hands around the creature's throat. He was glowing like liquid gold, dripping with living fire.

But where he touched this thing, his fire went out. And darkness began to creep up his arms. No, not darkness—oh *God,* I knew what that was.

Ash, and dust.

He was being destroyed, just like the Djinn who'd died in the hallway. The touch of this thing was toxic to them. That Djinn must have come across it somehow, maybe even been sent by Ashan to warn us of the danger—and it had killed her.

It had *erased* her.

Just as it was trying to do to David.

"Let go!" I shouted, and rolled over the top of the couch to land on my feet. I staggered, but I didn't have time for weakness. "David, back off!"

David didn't want to, but he did, breaking away and lunging to his left as I strode forward, gathering up raw power in both hands. As I moved, a silver sword formed in my grip—not metal but ice. Hard as steel, reinforced with a binding that left the cutting edge as thin as a whisper.

If this thing could survive David's heat, I wanted to see how it felt about chills.

The blade hit, bit, and cut, slicing through fragments of muscle and cooked skin, through crystalline bones that glowed blue where the ice slashed.

I chopped right through its neck. I paused, holding in my follow-through, to see what would happen.

The creature's head stayed on. As I watched, it wobbled a bit on the skeletal column of glassy vertebrae, then settled back into place.

It smiled with needle-sharp crystal teeth. If it had ever been human, other than a casual disguise, it certainly wasn't playing at it now. This was something out of a big-budget nightmare, and I took a step back from it, fast.

"David, get everybody out!" I yelled. I could sense this thing orienting on me, predator to prey. The last thing I needed right now was mortal trip hazards and speed bumps; it was going to be all I could do to protect myself, much less Cynthia Clark and her employee.

I sensed David grabbing up the noncombatants and hustling them to the door.

The creature facing me opened its mouth and flicked a tongue like a whip at me. It was more like an icicle than living tissue, but it moved like a cobra. The end was as sharp as a needle, and I barely avoided the stabbing turn of it in midair. A return stroke with my ice-knife passed through the tongue without any effect at all.

Damn. I couldn't hurt this thing, at least not with these weapons.

I retreated. I changed out ice for steel and tried again. This time, I sliced a piece out of the tongue, which fell to the floor and writhed like a slug in the sun. Whether that hurt the creature or not, it charged me, and I tried to make like a matador. That didn't help. It had reach and speed, and what had been its fingers in human form were now claws, diamond-sharp and lightning fast.

I felt the slices like chilly tugs on my side, but there wasn't any pain, not at first. I didn't allow myself to look down, I kept moving, turning, keeping myself away from the razor-edged whirlwind that was hissing through the air in pursuit.

Then I hit a corner, and there was nowhere left to run. I slashed, trying to slow it down, but the creature was just too damn fast, and too damn powerful. It smashed through the shield I put up. I didn't have time to try any Earth powers; fire wouldn't work, and weather tricks wouldn't buy me more than another fragile breath.

I was going to lose.

A small, white ball of light hit the thing from the side and plunged beneath the crystalline structure. It lit the creature up like an arc light from within. I couldn't even estimate the heat; it felt like a nuclear bomb compressed to the size of a baseball, forces well beyond my ability to summon, much less command.

All I could do was duck and cover. Again.

The creature shrieked in that horrible, soul-destroying range again and became a photonegative blast of flame that cooked everything within a foot of it—but not an inch beyond. The inverse flame became white flame, then reversed itself into a tiny, glittering spark ... and the creature was gone except for a shower of glittering crystalline powder.

A wave of intense pressure passed over me and shoved me hard into the corner.

The white ball of light expanded into a softer glow, and as the wave passed over me I squinted into it and saw the Djinn Venna standing where the creature had been, her pink HELLO KITTY sneakers buried in half an inch of crystal powder.

She looked worse than I had ever seen her: pallid, trembling, *afraid*. She sank down into a crouch, just a frightened little girl, and I couldn't help but move toward her. I picked her up in my arms, and she shuddered and buried her face in my chest.

Her warmth changed, cooled, became gentle against my skin. I felt my wounds starting to heal, though very slowly. My body began murmuring a shocked report of damages, but I told it to be quiet. Shock felt nice, at the moment. Soothing. I'd take whatever comfort I could get just now.

David reached us a second later, wrapping his arms around us both. "All right?" he asked, and looked into my eyes. He didn't like what he saw there, clearly, but he liked what he saw in Venna a whole lot less.

I didn't blame him.

"It's one of them," Venna said. "One of the ghosts. It didn't belong here. It can't *be here.*"

The confidence of the Old Djinn in their well-ordered universe had just been shattered, and beings that had never feared much in their long, long lives looked into the abyss that humans faced every day—the dark chasm of uncertainty of the future.

"It's okay, Venna," I said, and smoothed her long blond hair. "You did great. Ghost or not, you completely kicked its ass."

"I can't do it again." Venna looked at David and took a deep breath. "It took part of my ass with it. And I don't think I can get any of that back. Maybe ever."

Cynthia Clark hadn't boarded with a personal trainer, as it turned out. In fact, she didn't remember a thing about the entire incident. There didn't seem to be much point in trying to convince her that she'd been hypnotized into covering up for some otherworldly demonic glass monster. She wouldn't even believe that David and I hadn't set her room on fire deliberately, so I figured the whole monster thing was right off the table.

I staggered away to the nearest public lounge while David tried to settle things to everyone's satisfaction. I was checked out by a small army of Warden medics and Lewis himself—none of whom were happy with me, or my descriptions of events, come to think of it—and eventually was told that I was in no imminent danger of death or coma, but healing was a long way off.

I was still lying there, feet up, grateful to be breathing, when I spotted Aldonza hurrying past, rolling a luggage cart. She did a quick jerk of surprise when she saw me, and loitered. "Are you okay, miss?" she asked, which told me just how terrible I looked. "Can I get you something?"

I didn't raise my head from the leather pillow. "I'm okay, Aldonza. Sorry about the cabin."

"The cabin?"

"Miss Clark's cabin. It's—ah—kind of a mess."

Aldonza got a blank, terrified look on her face and hurried on. I could hear her horrified cry all the way down the hallway.

A half hour later, a whole phalanx of stewards rolled by, carting La Clark's salvaged baggage and armloads of expensive clothes. They were moving her to a new cabin.

They moved her into mine, as it turned out. I didn't find that out until I struggled up from my temporary resting place and met Cherise in the hall, dragging her suitcase and looking half-mournful, half-impressed. "Did you know that *Cynthia Clark* is going to be sleeping in your bed?" she asked. "That's kind of awesome, in a sucky kind of way. Anyway, we're down the hall, and *Moses on a motorcycle,* what the hell happened to you, bitch?"

I was better, really I was. I was limping—broken bones had been repaired into merely cracked and hurting bones—and I was singed and bloody and looked like some Halloween fright mask, but hey, I was breathing, upright, and thinking straight again. "You should see the other guy," I said, and coughed. It turned into a lung-bursting hack like a fifteen-pack-a-day smoker's. I could still taste that awful taint of death, even though I thought that it was all in my head now.

"Uh, thanks, I faint at the sight of gross anatomy. Come on, sweetie. You need a bunk."

I didn't argue about it. I'd been inclined to think I could walk it all off until I'd walked about ten feet, and then priorities had shifted again, drastically.

Rest seemed like a very good idea. I accepted Cherise's support, staggering the rest of the way to our new cabin.

"Ouch," Cher sighed, as the door swung open on a cramped little room with two narrow beds facing each other. "Looks like we've been bumped to coach. Or maybe servants' quarters."

"Don't care." I sank down on the closest flat surface—luckily, it had a mattress—and covered my eyes with my forearm. I needed to think. *How* had that creature gotten on the ship? And why? Was it just biding its time, waiting to kill as many Wardens as possible?

Had it killed the nameless Djinn we'd found in the hallway?

Most importantly—were there *more*?

David had sensed it, though not with any accuracy. Venna had been able to nuke it, though only at a drastic cost to herself.

We just couldn't fight an army of these things, and I had the sense that these were just incidental players in Bad Bob's upcoming melodrama.

Crap. Why did this keep happening to me?

"Jo?" The mattress dented on my left side as Cherise perched on the edge. "You crying?"

"No," I lied. "Fuck." I swallowed hard. "I can't do this. *We* can't do this. We're sailing away into the middle of nowhere with a bunch of innocent people and we're all going to die, Cher. I can't stop it. God, we've screwed this up."

"Hey." She moved my arm away from my eyes and looked down at me with such gravity that she didn't look like Cherise at all. "What's going on?"

"Did you hear me? We just about got our asses kicked!"

"But you didn't," she said. "You told me before we got on this ship that it was going to be hard, and people were going to die, because you can't go to war if you don't expect casualties. You didn't want me to come with, remember. You wussing out on me now, Rambette?"

I sniffled. "No."

"Good, don't even. You're a Warden. You don't let *anything* stand in the way of what you think is right. You have the most lustworthy guy I've ever seen madly in love with you. You have fabulous hair. You're strong and beautiful and smart and evil pees itself when it sees you coming. So don't you fold up on me, Jo." Cherise's mask slipped, just a little. "Because if you do, I don't think I can keep it together on my own."

"Bullshit," I said. "You're way tougher than me." I hugged her. "I'm just so tired. I just want to rest."

"Then rest," she said, and let go. I settled back on the bed. "But don't you dare think you're not up to this. You're a hero, babe. Heroes don't wuss."

"Do they whine?"

"Only to their bosom sidekicks." She flashed me her bosom to prove she had the cred. Cherise, motivational speaker to the stars.

I managed a weak laugh. I didn't feel like a hero, not at all. I didn't think Venna did, either, and I *knew* David didn't. He was too worried for me, and his anxiety was feeding mine, like a deadly and accelerating loop.

I took some deep breaths. Then I took some more, and let myself drift away from the pain and fear. I imagined myself floating in water, in a sparkling blue pool, with calm clouds whispering by overhead. The sun was warm and soft and kind, and I had on the perfect blue bikini that David liked so much.

The *Grand Paradise*'s rocking motion lulled me into

a mindless calm, and as I hung there, suspended, I felt
my body reaching for relief. It healed itself, bit by bit,
cell by cell, using power drawn from the energy around
me. The temperature of the cabin lowered in response,
and I heard Cherise get up and check the thermostat,
then break out the blankets. One settled over me, thick
and soft.

"You okay?" Cherise whispered. I didn't open my
eyes.

"Yep," I murmured. "Check it: Heroes don't wuss."

I was hoping that Venna had been wrong about her
damage. I mean, shock, right? But no. Venna had been not
just injured but *diminished* by the battle in Clark's cabin.

When David told me that, sitting on the edge of my
narrow bed in much the same way Cherise had earlier, I
could tell that he was trying not to give away how much
it disturbed him. He had on his *just-the-facts-ma'am*
face, and he'd damped down the link between us to a
low hum, suggestions of emotion, nothing more.

That was as close to cutting himself off from me as he
could manage, since our wedding ceremony had joined
us together on that powerful level.

I didn't like it.

"She's all right," David told me. He was looking at me,
but not—eyes unfocused, and miles away. "Physically . . .
aetherically . . . she's all right, she's just . . . less than she
was. As if pieces of her had been burned away."

"Or eaten," I said.

"You're thinking of an Ifrit," he said, and the focus
sharpened in his eyes. "That wasn't an Ifrit." No, it definitely had *not* been an Ifrit. Those were Djinn, badly
damaged and transformed, yes, feeding on their own
kind, but still recognizably of the Djinn DNA family.

This thing . . . not so much.

"What if it was part Ifrit?" I said slowly. I struggled up to a reclining position, with my pillow bracing my aching back. "Part Demon, too? Some kind of hybrid?"

"That would be bad," David said, very softly.

"Yeah, it'd suck like an industrial-strength Hoover. Demons are hard to kill; Ifrits can consume pieces of other Djinn, right?" As I understood it, Ifrits were the result of damage occurring to a Djinn's ability to process energy from the aetheric. Starving and desperate, they did what any living creature might do to survive; they turned cannibal, stealing energy from their own kind. Dark, nightmarish vampire Djinn, usually with a nearly complete lack of higher mental faculties. Maddened by hunger.

Marry that to a Demon, and you've got a truly terrifying weapon against the Djinn, not to mention anyone else who gets in the way, like Wardens.

In a word, one of Venna's ghosts—invisible, deadly, and adaptable.

"Can she recover?" I asked, thinking again of Venna. David gave me a highly suspect shrug. "Check that—can she recover in time to do that again?"

"I don't know. I'm not her Conduit."

"Cop-out."

"Hey!"

"You know. You may not be able to help her, but you know whether or not *Ashan* can help her."

"Ashan isn't saying much," David said. "You know how he is."

Oh, I knew. We'd hit the same brick wall when trying to help another of Ashan's Old Djinn, a particularly arrogant specimen named Cassiel who'd pissed the old dude off and been cast out to fend for herself for her troubles.

She hadn't *quite* become an Ifrit. Instead, she'd decided to go the less conventional route of binding herself to the Wardens for her daily dose of life energy . . . and I wasn't at all sure that had been a good idea, still. Thank God, she wasn't here with us, causing trouble. Wherever she was, I hoped she was doing better than we were.

Ashan had refused to talk about that incident, too. He wasn't, in general, the chattiest of all my many enemies. He'd read the guidelines for villainy, the first one being *Don't monologue.*

"Is she staying?" I asked. Because Venna being Venna, she could stay or go, exactly as she pleased. In her place, I'm not sure I wouldn't have gone off to the Djinn Day Spa for the next several millennia, and left us human idiots to our own devices.

"Of course she's staying," David said, and smiled just a little. "Venna's more like you than she'd like to admit."

"Apart from being cuter."

"Debatable."

"I don't have any HELLO KITTY shoes."

"Could be remedied." He lifted my hand to his lips, and I shivered at the gentle touch, not to mention the look in his eyes. "I'm sorry about earlier. I realized I wasn't helping you recover. It's hard to remember how much we share now. I don't want to add to your problems."

"You were worried," I said. "Hell, join the club. We have T-shirts and free-drink coupons. Open bar every Wednesday."

"Come here." He folded me in his arms, and I let out a long sigh. Most of my remaining tension went with it. "You did very well back there."

"What, getting myself backed into a corner to be

chopped up by the walking meat slicer? Yeah, spectacular job. Mom would be proud."

"I don't think many humans could have stood against it at all," he said. "Fewer still would have tried. I talked with Venna about how she destroyed it. She vibrated it. I think you could do the same?"

"Vibrated—" Of course. Crystalline structure in its bones and claws and teeth. Strong, but hit it with the right oscillated frequency, and you could hurt it, maybe destroy it. "I'd need to experiment to get it right. I don't suppose you have any remains . . . ?"

For answer, he reached in his pocket and pulled out a single crystal tooth, about the size of a small switchblade. He held it in his palm for a moment, weighing it, and then handed it to me. "Careful," he said. "Sharp."

He was right; it still held a wicked edge. I wrapped it in handfuls of tissue paper from the box on the nightstand and put it in my own pocket for later study.

"Do we know if there are more on board?" I asked. "Because we really don't need another ugly surprise."

David got up and opened the cabin door. In walked another Djinn, a brawny, bald-headed sort who looked like he might have moonlighted on a cleaner bottle from time to time. His skin was a dull metallic gray, and his eyes were the color of rust.

He looked around the sparse cabin with an expression like he'd bitten a bug in half, then dragged over the small side chair. Cherise wasn't in at the moment, for which I was grateful; she'd gone off in search of medicinal ice cream. I could imagine her running commentary on this scene.

"This is Lyle," David said.

"Seriously?" I blurted. They both shot me an odd look. "I mean, come on. *Lyle?*"

Lyle smiled. He'd filed his teeth into sharp little points. "You got a problem with that?" He had a surprising Deep South accent, slow and warm. It didn't sound artificial, as if he was mocking me, either.

Another oddity.

"Uh, no, no problem," I said. "It's just not exactly the kind of name I'm used to hearing from supernatural beings. A little too—"

"Human?"

"Country," I said. "Not even a little bit rock and roll."

David decided it was time to intervene before my conversational skills cost me a bruise or two. "Lyle became a Djinn during one of the World Wars."

"Which one?"

"They come so close together," David said. "First?"

Lyle nodded. "I kept my human name. A lot of Djinn don't bother. Sorry it doesn't meet with your approval, Warden."

"No, you're not," I said, and he smiled again. This time, he'd put away the scary teeth, and his dentition was blindingly white and perfectly human-normal.

If anything, that was weirder.

"Lyle was checking for energy signatures," David said. "Did you find anything?"

"Yes. Weaker than the one you two tripped across, though, and well hidden." Lyle's rust-colored eyes darkened just a shade. "They're hiding as humans."

"How many?"

"Two."

"Two *more*?" My throat threatened to close up around the words, and Lyle sent me a sharp look. I needed to work on my poker face. "What do we know about them?"

"They're wearing skins," Lyle said. "The skins used to be people, so they have history and weight in the aetheric. They took care not to kill the skins. I think they knew it was a good disguise. Good enough to fool most Djinn, even."

He was trying to describe something that I was trying equally hard not to imagine. "These people—can we save them?"

"Not people," Lyle said. "Like I said, they're just skins now. Nothing inside."

I wished he hadn't said that. Or at least, hadn't sounded so matter-of-fact about it.

"Why haven't they attacked us already?" I asked. "They probably know their big brother's gone, right? What are they waiting for, the all-you-can-eat-buffet light to go on?"

"They're definitely waiting on some type of signal, if they haven't struck at us yet," David said. "They can afford to bide their time. We don't even really know what they're capable of doing, not yet."

"No," I said slowly. "They did strike already. They killed the Djinn we found in the hallway outside my old cabin. We just don't know why, because we can't figure out who she was or what she was doing at the time."

It was the perfect dead end, and it was wasted on David and Lyle, who looked at each other as if silently thinking that I'd gone just slightly nuts. *Humans,* Lyle's shrug said. *Who knows what goes on in their tiny heads?*

"We need to backtrack and figure out why they felt threatened by that Djinn," I said. "Or why they had to stop what she was doing. David—" He was still giving me that blank look. "Never mind. I'll figure it out. Anyway, one good thing about it—they're probably worried about how we managed to kill their strongest monster already." I swallowed. "Please tell me that it was the strongest one."

"It was," David said. I heaved a deep sigh of relief.

"We should kill them now," Lyle said.

"How? Just one of them was capable of nearly killing me, fighting David to a standstill, and halfway destroying Venna," I said. "So I'm not feeling real good about our chances with taking on two of them at once. Any other options?"

Lyle cocked one thin eyebrow. "Swim back to shore."

"Just run away."

"Unless you want to wait for them to strike first."

"You weren't serious about the running away, right?"

"Oh, he was," David said.

Lyle nodded. Lyle was turning out to be the least confrontational supernatural being I'd ever met. Under normal circumstances, that would have been a refreshing change, but considering that I wanted a bunch of fire-eating, hard-charging badasses to back me up right now . . . not so much.

We both looked at David, who seemed to be half a world away. He dragged himself back with an effort. "We bide our time," he said. "It's too dangerous to go after them right now. Venna can't be used against them again, and we need to know more than we know now. Joanne—"

"Yeah, got it. Find out the right frequencies to do damage, and get everybody up to speed on the info, quietly. Oh, you probably should tell me just who I'm avoiding, here. Not Wardens?" Because I'd hate to have missed that in my initial checks.

"No," Lyle said, relieving me of screwups. "One is

crew, an engineering mate below passenger decks. The other is hiding as a stowaway in the ship's hold. He will be difficult to reach, and harder to trap."

"Let them hide for now," David said. "Watch them. Any change, any indication something's happening, report it as soon as you can. If they try to sabotage the ship—"

I hadn't even thought of that, and the idea twisted me deep in the gut. "Could they?"

"Of course. But not easily, and probably not fatally. With the Wardens and Djinn aboard, most damage can be repaired immediately." David sounded a lot more confident than I felt at the moment. I guess I was glad somebody was. "If you need help—"

Lyle gave a very human-sounding snort. "Why would I?"

"Because Joanne's right," David said. "One of these things nearly won against two Djinn and a powerful Warden. Don't let your confidence blind you to the possibility of losing spectacularly." At that moment, I thought he sounded a whole lot like his predecessor, Jonathan—calm, acidic, absolutely in control. And Lyle must have thought so too, because he inclined his head a bit and looked contrite.

"Their names," I said.

"What?" Both Djinn looked at me.

"The people. I'd like to know their names."

"Why does it matter?" Lyle asked. "They're skins. I told you, they're empty."

"You also told me the skins used to be real people. Real histories. Families. Friends." I held his gaze. Good thing I'd had practice with that, because Lyle had the eerie Djinn thing down pat. "I want to know because it's the only way we can honor their memories."

He seemed to understand that. "The engineer's mate is Jason Ng. He joined the crew twelve years ago. He had a wife and three children in New Orleans, and a mistress in Brazil. The other was once named Angelo Marconi, from Naples. His sister owns a restaurant there. His family thinks he's still away at school."

"School," I murmured. "How old—"

"He is dead, Warden."

"How *old*?"

"The skin is sixteen," Lyle said. "I'm sorry. But you can't let what they're wearing fool you into hesitating. You know that, don't you?"

I knew. I also knew that if push came to shove, if I had to stand there and sling fire at a sixteen-year-old boy, I wasn't going to be very good at it.

But I knew someone who would be.

I found Kevin Prentiss on the ship's main promenade deck, standing at the railing. He was watching the thick gray foaming clouds and the iron-colored water with its lacings of white, and he looked—as always—like a punk streetwise kid who needed to learn the concept of personal hygiene.

The difference these days was that Kevin had pulled himself together, to a greater extent than I'd ever thought possible. He'd earned himself some respect from his fellow Fire Wardens. He'd learned something from his apprenticeship to Lewis. He still looked greasy, but it was mostly hair product and deliberately baggy clothing. He had at least a handshake acquaintance with regular bathing.

However, Kevin *still* hated me. The look he sent me as I approached was a shot across my own personal bow, warning me to steer clear. I ignored it and took up a post at the rail beside him, leaning on the wood and bracing myself against the rise and fall of the deck with my feet well spread.

"You look like shit," Kevin said, and flipped half a lit cigarette into the air. Before it hit the water, it had burst into flame. Nothing but ash to litter the ocean. "Congratulations on the improvement."

"Well, you know me, I'm all about the cutting-edge fashion trends."

"What, beat to shit is the new black?" Kevin abandoned the ocean to turn and face me. He still needed a haircut, but his pimples were mostly gone now, and he'd filled out while I wasn't looking, turning from a skinny beanpole to something closer to lean and hungry. I supposed some girls went for that.

Like Cherise, now that I thought about it. The kid was legal age. I knew she'd originally been attracted to him because he was needy, broken, and bad; I also knew that she'd been the perfect foil for him, to remind him that he had better things inside.

Kevin liked to put on the badass hat, though. And always would.

He studied me out of the corner of his eye. "You want something," he said.

"Why would you say that?"

"Because you never talk to me unless you want something."

"So not true," I said. I held my breath for a second, then let it out. "Okay, I want something."

He didn't even have to waste his breath on an *I told you so.* "Big or small?"

"Pretty big."

"And I'd do it for you because . . . ?"

"Because you're a good man, somewhere deep underneath all that greasy stupid kid disguise," I said. "Because you want to be, or you wouldn't be out here on this insanely stupid trip. And because you don't want anything to happen to Cherise."

He straightened up. He was getting taller all the time, and now his body language reminded me less of skate parks and more of Lewis in a really foul mood. "You should never have dragged her off with us."

"I didn't. Cher goes everywhere with her eyes wide open, you know that. I'm just saying that of all of us, she's the least able to defend herself if something bad happens, so she's a good reminder note, because we both care about her."

Kevin muttered something impolite under his breath that I pretended not to hear, and turned back to glare at the ocean. Steam rose from a couple of waves before he got himself back under control. I was impressed. A few months ago, he'd have vaporized a few metric tons of ocean in a fit of pique.

Of course, *not having* a fit of pique would be better still, but baby steps.

"What do you want?" he asked, in a different kind of tone than before. Actually asking for information instead of confronting. Good for him. And good for me, of course.

"I want you to make friends with a Djinn named Lyle," I said. "Pick a team and stay alert. You may have to react quickly."

"Lyle?" Kevin let out a braying laugh that got whipped away by the fiercely driven wind. I licked my lips, and tasted salt and metal. "You're shitting me. Okay, never mind, I won't even ask. React quickly to what?"

"He's going to be keeping watch on a couple of people who aren't supposed to be here." I reached out and grabbed Kevin's shoulder, turning him toward me. "Kevin. Pay attention. This isn't a joke. These two are very, very dangerous, even to the Djinn. Even to you. So don't get cocky."

"Me?" He gave me a look so ironic it was practically tipped over into sincerity. "You're not telling me something. Or, like, anything."

"I told you they're dangerous."

"How, toxic body odor? Really sour attitudes? Can they kill me with their brains?"

I gave up, and held on to the rail as the ship took a particularly hard dip into the water, almost a bounce. The waves were getting thicker and deeper, and the storm behind us was finding gangs of friends to our port and up ahead. It was going to hit us sooner rather than later.

"They're not human," I said. "They're fast, they're deadly. Think *Alien,* made out of indestructible crystal, only with human skin."

"Wouldn't that be *Terminator* or something?"

"Enough of the movies. This isn't funny, Kevin, it's serious. The one in the ship's hold is wearing the body of a sixteen-year-old boy." There, I'd said it.

And he understood it. "And that's easier for me, right? Because I won't see him as just a kid. I see him as more of an equal."

I nodded unwillingly. "I'm not putting you out there alone," I said. "But I know you. I know you won't hesitate if—"

"If I have to kill somebody who looks like he just got passed up for his junior prom? Yeah, I'm definitely that guy."

I didn't answer that, because there was a new note in his voice: self-loathing. Kevin hadn't lived an easy life.

He was more pragmatic than most kids I'd ever met, and tougher, too. But that didn't mean he wanted to be, even though he wore his damage like a badge of honor.

"I'm sorry," I said, finally. "I wish I didn't have to ask you."

"I wish I wasn't the go-to guy to kill monsters dressed as teens, but there you go." He shrugged. "At least I've got experience."

And that was the heart of it, at last. I'd come to Kevin because I'd seen him kill without hesitation, and without remorse. Granted, he'd had plenty of personal hatred built up, but it took a special kind of detachment to do what he'd done and never suffer much guilt about it. He mostly resented the fact that we all knew about it—not that he'd been forced to do it.

"I'm not your pet psycho." I flinched, because Kevin could have been reading my mind. "But yeah, I'll find Lyle and do this. Just don't put me on speed dial the next time you have to push a school bus off a cliff or something. So. What's our approved monster-killing technique?"

I pulled the tissue-wrapped crystal tooth out of my pocket. "Let's find out." The thing glittered like a diamond in the dull light.

We took the fragment with us, found a crew member to open up the gym for us, and moved equipment to get clear floor space for our experiments. Kevin took to the scientific method with enthusiasm, because there's nothing a teenage kid likes better than trying to destroy something that's indestructible. Kevin tried so many kinds of fire that even I was impressed with the variety and breadth of control he had over it, especially since he didn't kill us in the process.

Except that nothing worked, and eventually Kevin

tried stomping on the thing in frustration. That didn't work so well, either.

"Let me," I said, and crouched down across from where the glittering crystal shard lay between us. Kevin mimicked me from about four feet away.

"No fair using Earth powers," he said. "I'll call bull-shit."

"You'll be working with an Earth warden, idiot," I said. "Watch and learn. I'm going to start with super-low frequencies and work my way up. You watch the structure with me. If you see any response at all, tell me."

"If I'd known this favor of yours would mean sitting around watching you use a vibrator, I would've said hell yeah earlier—"

"Bite me," I said. He flipped me off. I ignored him—mostly—and paid attention to the structure of the crystal.

It took the better part of an hour, but we pinpointed the frequency range that had the greatest effect on the thing. I couldn't get to Venna's epic pulverizing effect, but I figured that anything that cracked and shattered the bone would do. At the very least, it would distract the holy living hell out of the enemy.

"Yeah, that's great," Kevin said, as I wrote down the numbers. "Big problem. I can't do that, genius. It takes a tree hugger."

"And I'll get one for you," I said. "But I wouldn't call her a tree hugger if I was you. She'll make your face grow backwards if you piss her off." I wrote down the name—Maida Manning. Three hundred pounds of extremely sarcastic Earth Warden who wouldn't take any of Kevin's bullshit. Maida also had a vicious sense of humor. I could see a beautiful friendship developing, unless of course they managed to kill each other first.

I'm so public-spirited.

"Give her this," I said, and handed him the written instructions. "Tell her I'll give her a raise if she manages to not kill you before you kill the bad guys. But whatever you do, wait for Lyle to give a signal to move. Got it?"

"Of course I've got it. I've got an IQ above your dress size." He paused. "Then again, it might be the other way around. I mean, do they even *make* dress sizes in the hundred and fifties?"

Cherise was having a terrible influence on the kid. I decided that one of us really needed to stay focused on professional dignity, and so I settled for a rude gesture instead of a comeback.

"Score," he said. He walked away, just another bad-attitude teen from his messy, uncombed hair to his dragging, world-weary sneakers.

It takes a special kind of courage to know your own darkness, I thought. I wished he didn't have to be such an expert, but as long as he was, I had no choice but to take advantage of his skills.

Lewis was going to take my head off for it, too.

Chapter Six

Passengers—even me—weren't allowed on the bridge. Apparently, that only happens in the movies, or to Cherise. I helped Lewis get through the rest of the passenger and crew interviews in neutral, nonsecure locations. No real surprises: a couple of drug smugglers, some embezzlers, and a few people who had raided the cabin steward's closet for illegally obtained soaps and pillow mints. Other than that, we were clear of evil influences ... except for the two we already knew about.

And me, of course. I was acutely aware that the tingles from the numb area on my back were coming with more and more frequency.

By late evening, I was feeling exhausted and even more sore than I'd anticipated. Cherise forced sandwiches on me, and then a glass of scotch, and I dozed off curled up in the corner of a sofa in the first-class-lounge area, listening to half a dozen Wardens debate the logistics of creating a clear course for us to follow. I was wishing that David would drop in, but I knew all too well that Lewis had other plans in motion—plans that specifically excluded me, thanks to the Bad Bob mark on my back. Need to know, and all that.

So I napped.

Lightning flared, startling me, and when I opened my eyes, I was somewhere else.

No . . . I realized that I *wasn't* somewhere else. My body was still huddled on the sofa, still watched over by Wardens and Djinn alike. Protected.

But I was *also* standing in a small concrete room with bare, dusty floors and a few battered old chairs held together with wire and tape, and it was nowhere near the ship that still held my physical form.

It's not real, I thought, but it felt damned convincing.

The door opened on howling darkness, and I could feel the blast of sea-salted air that rolled through the room to stir up debris.

When the door closed, a bandy-legged old white-haired man moved into the pallid circle of overhead light.

Bad Bob, in the flesh. At least, I presumed it was flesh. I was starting to wonder how real the real world actually was, in relation to what my former boss could accomplish these days.

"Look who dropped in for a visit," Bob said, and pulled up a rickety chair. He flopped into it—risking total collapse of the ancient wood—and sat there smiling at me as if I were a favorite niece come for the holidays. Honestly, that was the worst thing about him. You couldn't really tell how crazy he was at a glance.

Or how vile.

I could hear the wind howling and it grated on me, and I wanted to lift my hands to cover my ears—only my ears weren't physical. *I* wasn't physical. I was a spirit in the aetheric, and there was simply no way that Bad Bob could see me, or that my spirit could walk around like this in the real world. Surely this was a dream. No, a nightmare. Except it felt real, from the gritty concrete floor under my feet to the demented shrieking of the storm winds outside.

"I thought I'd give you guys a chance to surrender," I said. My voice sounded distant and disembodied, and I wasn't sure he could hear it until his smile widened. He was an evil old man, but he still had a charming smile. It went well with his apple red cheeks and blunt little nose. "I'd hate to skip the niceties. Courtesy is so important."

"You're playing my song, sugar," he said. "You're also playing my game. I wonder why?"

I smiled to match him. "Guess."

"If I have to. Well, you found my little friend on board your ship—I felt him shuffle off this mortal coil. Good for you. Bet you can't do that again, though." He studied me with those fluorescent eyes— almost Djinn eyes, these days, brighter and more intense than they'd been in the old days when he'd been my boss, a genuine Warden hero. "I have to hand it to you, I figured you guys would argue until doomsday about what to do about me," he continued. "Seriously now, a *cruise ship*? I didn't see that coming. Beautiful. I thought maybe a yacht, or a freighter. But putting all those people in the line of fire? You're growing a pair, sweetness. I like that."

I waited. Bad Bob always had liked to hear his own voice more than anyone else's.

"But you know what I think?" he continued, right on cue. "I think it's so showy that it's desperate. Like dressing up in neon and waving look-at-me flags while blaring Tchaikovsky's Fifth. You really should study magicians. Misdirection, that's the key to a good trick."

"You think I'm tricking you?"

"You're not that subtle," he said, which stung because it was true, mostly. "But there's somebody else on board that ship who is."

We both knew that he was talking about Lewis. "You've still got a chance to end this peacefully," I said. "Let Rahel go. Give up. It doesn't have to be Armageddon: Atlantic Edition. We can find a way to make this work, Bob. Or whatever you are."

"I'm still Bob," he said, and winked at me, just the way Bad Bob would have back in the old days. "I'm just Bob plus. And I don't think we're going to come to any nice, peaceful settlement, princess. This isn't about dividing up territory or setting boundaries. This is about me, wiping all of you off the face of the earth, and then my friends coming in to take everything else. It's nature's way, you know. The strong eat the weak. The many eat the few. And I am about to eat *you*."

He smiled, opened his mouth, and his jaws gaped hideously wide, like a snake's. If this was a nightmare, it was a first-class effort out of my very darkest subconscious.

I stepped back from him.

His jaws re-formed and closed. The Cheshire Cat smile remained. "Don't look so scared," he said. "You wouldn't believe the stuff I can do with my tongue. Bet I could make you forget all about that wimpy little Djinn boy you're so taken with. Give me a chance— No? All right, then. I guess I'll just have to settle for something else. Thanks for being so accommodating and wandering on over here, by the way. I figured you might, sooner or later. The torch has that effect on people. It just draws people to me, whether they like it or not."

He took two steps forward, thrust out his hand, and put it all the way through my ghostly, insubstantial chest. Unsettling, and a little uncomfortable, but I actually felt a little spurt of triumph. *Not as easy as you thought it would be,* I was about to say, when I realized that he'd reached to a very specific place.

To the ghostly mark on my back. The black torch. His fingertips brushed against it beneath my translucent skin—I could feel it, even if I couldn't see it happening.

All of a sudden the room was far too small, like a trap, and I wanted to leave this place, *now,* before something happened.

Too late.

I felt my physical body, still far away on board the ship, writhing in its sleep. I felt the hot tingle of the black torch begin to spread across my shoulder blade.

I'd lost David's containment, and because I was asleep, he might not know it.

Bad Bob removed his hand from my chest, shook it as if he was flicking something nasty off his fingers, gave me a feral grin, and walked away. I struggled to figure out what was holding me here, in this place, pinned like a bug to a board. *The mark.* He was right. Until I figured out how to turn it off—if I could—he could keep me here, out of my body. I knew that the longer I stayed out, the worse it was going to be when I got back.

I remembered the Wardens, lost in the storm. If my spirit was shredded, my body would just . . . stop. And they would never know why.

Outside, a truly ferocious storm raged. I felt the hot, damp blast of hair burst into the room, stirring grit and pushing the rickety sticks of furniture in random fury. Lightning flashed like strobes, turning Bad Bob's pale hair and face into a fright mask.

He reached outside, and when his hand came back through the doorway, it was holding a spear. I recognized the thing—it was thick, and it sparkled with bursts of something that wasn't color, wasn't darkness, wasn't anything human senses could identify or codify. He'd refined his weapons, I saw. This spear had started out life as a small chunk, grown in the dying body of a Djinn, and Bad Bob had given it enough care and feeding to make it a seven-foot-long, wickedly pointed expression of his own appetite for destruction.

The Djinn called it the Unmaking. It was, as best I understood the physics of it, stable antimatter, capable of destroying anything he wanted to destroy.

Including removing Djinn from the fabric of the universe.

"Oh, Bob, that's just sad," I said. His grin broadened. "Seriously, why can't your type ever grow a discus for a weapon, or the world's largest potato? How come it's always so—phallic?"

Bob ignored the opportunity to banter, and stepped out into the storm. He looked up at it, into the heart of it. I knew what he was seeing—the raging engine of destruction, the primitive mind forming behind it. This was a living thing, this storm—a predator, yes, but a natural one, like a tiger or a puma.

He ground the butt of his spear against the dirt, and a blinding pulse of something that wasn't light, wasn't heat, wasn't *right* went up from the pointed end of the spear into the storm.

Again.

Again.

With every thump of that weapon against the earth, I felt the world itself shudder. On the aetheric, muddy red waves spread like blood from a mortal wound.

The force emitted from the spear had a sickening feel to it, and the color—if you could call it a color—was a poisonous, pallid thing, like the glow given off by decay.

The storm's lightning suddenly flashed, but it wasn't light.

It was *dark*. Photonegative energy, but here on the

real world. He'd infected the storm itself, made it a force for destruction far different from any natural predator.

And then it flashed that unearthly emerald green.

"Almost ready," Bad Bob said, and reversed his grip on the spear. Handling that much anti-energy couldn't have been pleasant, even for him; I could see the skin blackening and flaking away where his hand touched the surface. "Ready for the cherry on top?"

He pointed the spear down at the ground, and drove it in. It went deep, even though he didn't use any real force—as if it tunneled greedily on its own.

I felt the earth shriek in real pain beneath my ghostly feet, and the whole building shook. Grit filtered down in feathery whispers, and then the *real* lurch came.

The building exploded as force traveled up through the ground, pulverizing layers of granite into dust. The cinder blocks of the walls buckled, ground themselves into powder against each other, and the ceiling crashed in a twisting, tearing mass of wood and metal that was snatched away by the wind.

Nothing touched me.

I stood exactly where I had as the building disintegrated around me, ripped away by the howling Category 5 winds. The ground lurched like pounding surf underneath me.

Bad Bob rose up into the air, holding to the end of his spear. He kept rising.

The spear grew, and grew, like some poisonous tree with its roots sunk deep.

He broke it off at ground level. It shattered at the stress point with a musical, glassy sound I heard even above the shriek of the storm.

A palm tree toppled and rolled toward me. Through me. Bad Bob landed on the rippling earth in front of me, appallingly normal in this terribly destroyed setting, and used the remaining part of his spear as a walking stick. *Thump. Thump. Thump.* It echoed through me like the beating of Poe's telltale heart.

Around us formed a little circle of clear air, stable ground, like the eye of the hurricane. It expanded, and other people appeared out of the chaos. Wardens, once upon a time. I recognized many of them, at least by face if not by name. His pets, his converts to his righteous war against the Djinn—not that Bad Bob cared a bean about killing the Djinn to benefit humanity. Oh no. Bad Bob cared only, and always, about his own ends, and whatever these pathetic, deluded people thought they were getting out of fighting on his side, they were bound to be disillusioned.

I assessed numbers. Might as well, since I was stuck here. It did occur to me that Bad Bob was showing me only what he *wanted* to show me, of course, but for all that, the guy who keeps showing off will eventually show you something he doesn't intend to.

Bad Bob was one hell of a chatterbox.

Sixty of them. My spirits sank, which was no doubt what he'd counted on. He had numbers. Of course, we had more, but add to that Bad Bob's Demon-derived powers and the neat trick of handheld antimatter that the Djinn could neither recognize nor defend against, and we were well on the train to Screwsville.

"You still think you can win?" he asked me. I didn't answer, because I wasn't sure I dared tell a lie right now, and a lie was all I really had. "Scared little Jo. It was always going to end like this, you know. You against me, and you never could take me."

"I did take you," I said. "You sadistic old bastard."

He lost his smile and pointed the spear at me. "Wonder what happens if I give it a taste of you in your aetheric form?" he said. "Bet it'll hurt like fuck."

"Bet you don't want to be around when I survive it and come to kick your sorry ass off the face of the planet."

He laughed and grounded the butt of the spear again. "I always did like that about you. You got sand, I'll give you that." He leaned forward, eyes avid and wet. "Fight me, Jo. I love it when you fight me. It won't matter in the end, but it'll be damn fun. You thought by dragging the Wardens away from all those innocent people on shore you'd save lives, but I think you just made my job a whole lot easier. See? You were already working for me. And now you're going to *really* draw your paycheck, peach."

"Like hell," I said.

He blew me a kiss. Back on the ship's sofa, my body continued to twitch and writhe. Cherise sat down next to me, putting a hand on my forehead, then calling for help.

The sensation of her hand against my skin was just enough to form a link—a way back. I pulled. The black mark felt like Velcro, sticking me here to this spot, but I ripped and tore at it, struggling, and with a hissing snap I came free.

I called lightning.

A white blast of energy erupted out of the clouds overhead—clean, pale energy, not the poisoned kind he'd poured into the storm—and struck me squarely in the top of my insubstantial head, flooding through my form in a splintered glowing ladderwork, then blasting out into the ground.

It shattered the remaining connection that held me at Bad Bob's command, and I flew backward through the screaming darkness, whipping past pitch-black writhing ocean, over half-seen bits of island, into calmer seas.

Into the massive, smugly sailing bulk of the *Grand Paradise*.

Into my body, with a lurch like a slap.

I came awake with a gasp that felt like a shriek. My back was burning, on fire, and I tried to lunge to my feet. It felt like my entire nervous system cut out, faulty wiring shorting and sparking.

I pitched off the sofa to the carpet and got a taste of rug.

Cherise was instantly on her knees beside me, trying to cradle me in her arms. I couldn't let her touch me. Everything felt wrong, strange, bad, vile . . . and I wasn't sure that it wasn't contagious.

"No," I panted, and crab-crawled back to jam myself against the bottom of the sofa. "No, leave me alone!"

"Help!" Cherise shouted. That got the attention of some passing crew members. A passing steward—I still didn't know his name, but he was the one who'd been trying to manage the First-Class rebellion before we'd set sail—shoved aside the coffee table and reached down for me. "Miss, are you all right? Should I get medical help?"

I wrapped my hand convulsively around the white lapel of his jacket, and where my fingers gripped the fabric, it started to smoke and hiss.

He exclaimed and tried to claw his way free. I couldn't let go. My hand didn't seem to be *mine,* exactly; it was moving, and I could feel what it was doing, but it was holding him in place.

Part of me wanted to destroy him. A big part of me, and it was growing larger as the broken containment on my back allowed the poison from the torch mark to flood into me. The dam was breached.

I was being swept away.

The steward struggled, panted, yelled for help, and finally managed to slip out of his jacket, which remained clutched in my fist as it burst into full smoking flame. I heard other voices—Wardens?—in a rising babble. Somebody tried to tamp down the fire that was bubbling up from my fingers, but I couldn't stop it. All my nerves were fried, useless; all my control had gone with them.

The jacket caught the rug on fire.

Someone hit me with a good old-fashioned fire extinguisher, but as soon as the icy foam stopped blasting, fire erupted from *both* my hands, crawling up my arms like snakes, twining around my body in living veils of flame.

I could feel other things happening inside me now—fire was always the easiest of powers to call, because it was virtually unstoppable even in natural form, but now I could feel my other abilities stirring, too. Something inside me was rifling through my mind, my soul, shuffling aside unwanted things to find the most devastating things on offer.

I was an open doorway, and *something was reaching through.*

I think I might have screamed, but if I did, it was just in my head. My body stood up, dripping flame as my clothing burned away, leaving me draped in living energy. I could see myself reflected in the lounge windows—a pillar of fire, a pagan goddess, naked and primal. My hair didn't burn, but it rose and fluttered on the waves of heat created from my skin.

My eyes were Djinn eyes, flaring gold, and where I touched, things blackened and smoked and charred into ruin.

"Back!" someone snapped to the growing cluster of onlookers, and a hardened bubble of air formed around

me, thick as steel. The fire erupting out of me consumed
the available oxygen in seconds, then began to gutter
and fail as its fuel ran out.

I felt nothing, except that all-consuming heat exploding from the black torch on my shoulder. It seemed to be
getting worse, not better, as if someone had injected me
with acid. If I'd had control of my voice, I'd have been
begging for it to stop.

The cold, blackened part of me inside still had control, but it allowed me to collapse into a naked, smoking
heap inside the air bubble. I struggled to breathe, but
there was nothing left to fill my lungs that wasn't toxic.

Someone stepped up on the other side of the bubble.
Lewis.

The darkness in me took over, but it did it in a hor-
rifyingly clever way.

I lifted my hand and slapped my palm flat against the
bubble, pleading for mercy. My fingernails were turning
a delicate robin's-egg shade of blue. I must have looked
completely pathetic and weak.

I wasn't. Not at all.

There was something very strange in the way he was
looking at me. Something my grandmother used to say.
Tombstone eyes . . .

Lewis's head snapped around, not fast enough, and
something collided with him. A streak of bronze light
that froze into the form of David, on the other side of
my invisible prison.

I watched Lewis's lips move. He was yelling at David,
telling him not to be a fool, not to fall for it. *He knew*.

He needn't have worried. David might be passionate,
but he was no kind of a fool. He crouched down and
put his hand flat against mine, separated by five inches
of thickened, impenetrable, interlocked molecules. His

face was a mask, his eyes dark and secretive, but not quite managing to hide his fury—at me, at himself, at Bad Bob for putting us here.

I smiled, tasting his despair—it felt *good*.

The talisman burned into my back hit a white-hot peak, and I felt my Weather powers flooding out of me, battering at the prison holding me. Lewis was incredibly strong, maybe the strongest Warden who'd ever lived, but I was damn close on this front. I hadn't always been, or at least I hadn't always known it, but I was afraid that very strength was going to be my undoing now . . . because I could feel my powers eating away at the force he'd set up to keep me contained. Once it broke, there was no telling what I'd do. What I *could* do. Possibilities raced through my mind, each worse than the last— poison gas drifting through the sealed corridors of the ship, killing everyone it touched. Or maybe I'd just blow a gigantic hole through the bottom, sending this beautiful floating coffin down to join other famous wrecks. I could almost see that one—the foaming rush of the sea through the shattered hull, the rooms filling up, all these people trapped and dying . . .

God, I wanted to do it.

I couldn't let this happen. I couldn't be the cause of so much death.

Bad Bob had done one thing for me, thanks to this little exercise in hellish torment; he'd shown me how to break loose. I wasn't trapped in my body; my body existed separately from my spirit, connected only by random impulses and autonomic functions. I pulled away and stretched to the limit. I arrowed up into the aetheric, feeling the bond stretch and pull, thinner and thinner. At the top of the aetheric, there was a flickering white milky light—the boundary of another world above that one. Another plane of existence. The Djinn could pass through it. Humans couldn't, not even Wardens.

I touched it, trailed ethereal fingers against the barrier, and looked down. Distances and heights didn't mean the same things up on the higher planes, but in this sense they did—there was a form of gravity, and momentum, and forces that translated from the aetheric back to the physical.

I let go, turned, and put all my power into an accelerated dive back to my physical body. Instead of letting myself *fall*, I *raced*, gathering as much force along the way as I could. Pulling it directly from the aetheric, like the wake from a speedboat. I'd never tried this; I knew that there were Earth Wardens who had, who'd managed to get a power boost through this technique. It wouldn't last, and it came at a heavy cost, but it was at least something to try.

They never told me how bad it would *hurt,* though.

Hitting the physical form of my body had a psychic shock wave, like slamming head-on into a bank vault at eighty miles per hour. Then the aetheric wake slammed in behind me, temporarily compressing me inside.

I blew it out through the mark on my back, channeling it through the black lines. It overloaded within an instant, shocking the mark into silence, sending it back into its containment state.

I raised my head and looked David in the eye and mouthed *Help*. I didn't know if he'd believe me or not—I almost hoped he wouldn't—but without him, I knew that sooner or later this was going to end in my death.

My whole body was trembling, anoxic, on the edge of unconsciousness. I couldn't create oxygen from the toxic soup of molecules left inside this bubble; I'd have to break the shell, get some kind of feed from the outside.

Or maybe I'd die. That wasn't a bad solution, all things considered. Not my fave, admittedly, but it would save innocent lives, and—

David's outstretched palm pushed through the hard shell of air. Stress fractures formed as white cracks around his fingers, and then he broke through, and a rush of delicious air fanned my hair back from my face. The bubble disintegrated. I dropped facedown to the floor.

A weight settled on top of me—David, straddling me. Slamming his hand down on top of the black mark, and if I'd thought that sucker was painful already, this was a thousand times worse, so bad that I couldn't stop screaming, writhing, trying to claw my way out of the pain.

"I'll kill you!" I was screaming. And worse. And I meant it.

Lewis took my wrists and held me still. Somebody else grabbed my flailing legs and anchored them. It was like old-style surgery without the benefit of anesthesia, this feeling of something vital being cut out of me, bloody and dripping . . .

And then it stopped.

I collapsed, sobbing helplessly. I couldn't feel David's hand on my back. I couldn't feel anything from the nape of my neck to my waistline; it had all gone icily numb.

"Mother of God," someone among the onlookers murmured, and the tone was so appalled that I wondered just what he was seeing. I didn't care. It was enough that it didn't hurt, just for a few precious breaths.

"Get the medical team," Lewis said. His voice sounded strangely rough, low in his throat. When I turned my head and focused on him, his eyes were red, lids swollen. There were tears tracking down his cheeks.

He was still holding my wrists in a brutally tight grip.

"I'm okay," I said. I wasn't. I felt hollow and odd, as if I was floating several feet from my own emotions. "Hey. Don't worry. I won't go nuclear on you." I didn't think I had anything left, anyway. "I'm losing, you know. Can't hold it."

Lewis let go, very slowly, and swiped his arm across his eyes. He sat back on his haunches, and his gaze moved away from me, up and behind.

Locking eyes with David, presumably.

I felt David's warm hand touch the back of my neck. "Don't move," he said. He sounded almost as odd as Lewis. "I need to tell you something."

This didn't sound positive. "What?"

"The mark. It's gone."

Wasn't that good? "And?"

There was a short, heavy silence. David said, "It burned off your skin, all the way down to the bone in places. I've tried to close the wound, but—"

"It won't let you," I finished for him. That explained the emergency numbness covering my entire back, and the shocked trembling of my muscles. I felt cold, too. My body was trying to marshal its resources against a life-threatening crisis. "It doesn't matter, the mark's still there. It's buried inside me. I can't burn it out. Was anyone hurt?"

David let out an uneven breath. "Other than you?" I felt his weight ease off of me, and then he moved into view, kneeling next to me. Lewis moved out of his way. "No. You didn't hurt anyone. You fought it off."

"No. Not really." I swallowed and tried to order my drifting, scattered priorities. "I saw Bad Bob. He has sixty former Wardens with him. I can tell you where."

"Jo—" That was Lewis again, soft and almost regretful. "We can't believe you now. You understand that, don't you? You can't know that any of what you saw is real. He could have put it there. He's a manipulative son of a bitch. Even if it was true, he'll move before we can get there."

"He knows," I said. "He knows we got one of the skins. He'll be activating the others. You have to move, *now*. Stop them."

Lewis tore his gaze away from me. "David, I'm going to need you."

"No," David said.

"If this ship goes down, she still dies. Is that what you want?"

David's eyes flashed—not fire, not bronze, but white-hot, like the flash from the sharp edge of a diamond. "I'll give you all the power you need. I'll assign Djinn to you. But I won't leave her. Don't ask me again." The edge to his voice scared me, and I reached out to touch his hand.

"No," I said. "I'm not dead, I'm just massively screwed up." I sucked in a deep breath. "Help me sit up."

David didn't like the idea, but he saw that if he didn't, I'd flail around and do it anyway, probably hurting myself even more. "Wait," he said. "Bandages."

I suppose the medical team had arrived, because I was lifted up to a sitting position, my arms were raised, and I got wrapped up like a mummy, from waist to just under my armpits. It was a very odd sensation—I could feel every bit of the pressure and texture on my front and sides, but the bandages simply disappeared when they touched my back.

It took care of half the problem that I was naked in the middle of a crowd. Somebody brought in one of the cruise line's fluffy guest robes, which took care of the other half once I'd gotten it on and belted.

When I faltered getting up, Cherise ducked in and braced me, arms around my waist. David held me up on the other side. "I'd carry you, but—" I understood. There was no way for him to do it without putting pressure on my ruined back.

"It's fine. I can walk." I wasn't sure I could, but damned if I wasn't going to try. As I stood there catching my breath and my balance, though, I took a look around.

I'd pretty much managed to trash the first-class lounge. The sofa was a skeletal wreck, burned through to the springs. The carpet where I'd been standing (or lying) was melted and blackened into a tangled knot of ash and acrylic fibers. Add to that the still-lingering smoke that curled blackly around the room, seeking exits, and the general reek of burned flesh . . . Yeah. That security deposit was gone for good.

"Sorry," I apologized, to no one in particular, and concentrated on putting one foot in front of the other on the way out of the room.

I heard a dull *boom* from below us, somewhere in the bowels of the ship, and looked at David's tense expression.

"It's not your problem," he said.

Whether it was or not, he wasn't going to let me claim responsibility of any kind.

"Are we sinking?" I asked.

We were sitting on my narrow bed—me lying on my stomach, David propped on the edge, looking down at me. The ship was rocking much worse than before, slamming into waves with such force that I swore I could hear metal groaning somewhere in the bowels of the vessel. Of course, that was stupid; big as this thing was,

I'd never know if something was going catastrophically wrong. The iceberg that had killed the *Titanic* hadn't even knocked over glasses in the dining room.

Of course, the *Titanic* hadn't been wallowing in massively turmoiled seas, beset from all sides, and between being driven toward an even worse predator. We were like a whale being stalked by a school of sharks. Sooner or later, they'd take out enough bites to make a difference.

"No," David said, and stroked my hair. "No, we're not sinking."

"You think the mark's gone," I murmured, and closed my eyes. "It's not. I can still feel it." My mind kept wanting to shut down, lock itself off, focus on summoning up its strength for healing, but I couldn't seem to let it go.

David shifted. He probably touched my shoulder, or at least the bandages over the open wound, but I couldn't feel anything. "I know," he said. "I can see it on the aetheric."

"It's bigger."

"Yes."

"I said I'd kill you, didn't I?" He didn't answer. "I meant it. I really did, David. The only thing that's stopping me is the containment. You understand?"

"I do." He brushed fingers gently over my forehead. "It's not your fault."

"It will be," I said. I felt a distant, inescapable grief, but like everything else, it was arm's length from me. I really couldn't *feel* anything. "How's Kevin doing?"

David was silent for a long enough minute that I had to fight to stay awake to hear the answer. "He's doing well." My lover sounded surprised. Well, I supposed I was a little bit surprised, too. Pleasantly so. "One of the skins has already been destroyed. They're hunting the other one in the hold. They're getting close."

"No problems?" It was odd to be worried by that, but I was. Things never went that easily, did they? Not in my experience.

"If there are, it's for someone else to handle," he said. "Rest. We'll see to things."

He seemed confident. I went over that in my head like a string of worry beads, and finally said, "You did warn Lyle, right? Not to take the skin on directly?"

David frowned. "I don't know what you're talking about."

"Don't you remember?" I rolled over on my side to stare up at him. "These things are lethal to Djinn. David, you have to pull the Djinn back. Let the Wardens handle this one."

"I will."

Was he just humoring me? It was understandable if he was; I wasn't sounding overly competent just now. Too tired, too sick, too much in shock. Besides, I was compromised. Even burning the tattoo right off my body hadn't destroyed the link between me and Bad Bob. I wasn't sure anything, short of my horrific and gruesomely painful death, would. That meant I couldn't really count on my mind being my own, or be sure that Bad Bob wasn't hooked into me like some kind of long-distance spy bug. I'd be perfectly placed for that kind of duty. He could use me, and there would be nothing—*nothing*—I could do to stop him.

Bad Bob could use me as the hammer to shatter the entire Warden organization, not to mention the Djinn. Through my link to David, I compromised their safety, too.

"Jo." David must have known what was going through my mind, because his tone and his touch were both gentle. "You're alive. Don't underestimate your ability to come through this. I don't."

"You want to be there, with them."

"My place is here."

"Your place is at the front of the battle. You're not Jonathan. You don't sit things out." I couldn't quite suppress a smile. "Being the Boss of Bosses doesn't really suit you, you know. You're more of a hands-on guy."

"I'm not sitting anything out. I'm a Djinn. I don't have to be physically present to make things happen, you know."

My brain drifted away, randomly connecting things. Wardens didn't have to be present to make things happen, either, although for Fire and Earth Wardens it was certainly a whole lot easier to be in close proximity—which was why Fire Wardens had a tendency to die fighting their fires. . . .

My eyes opened. "David," I said. "Who's with Kevin?"

"Don't worry, Lewis sent a whole team. Kevin's only part of it." He thought I was worried about Kevin. I struggled to sit up, but my arms felt like wet spaghetti. David helped me. "What?"

I didn't know exactly, but I *felt* something. "I need to get to them. Right now." A building anxiety. A conviction that something was very, very wrong. My arm's-length emotions were rapidly closing in on me.

"No. You're not going anywhere," David said. He was right, horribly right; I couldn't summon up the energy to make it off the bed, much less carry on to a fight. But my heart was pounding, my palms sweating, and I could feel dread boiling up from the pit of my stomach. "What is it?"

"*I don't know!* It's just—"

The whole ship shuddered beneath us. I looked at David, horrified, remembering the lessons of the *Titanic* all too clearly. I could see the same thing reflected in his face.

"Stay here." He flared white and disappeared.

The *Grand Paradise* groaned like a living thing and heeled ponderously to starboard, rising and then settling back to vertical. Our little cabin didn't have the luxury of a balcony, but it did have a small reinforced porthole. I dragged myself off the bed and shoved aside the single guest chair to reach it.

I was staring at water. That wasn't possible. The deck we were on was far above the waterline—six stories above it, probably. How could I be looking at the water?

Were we sinking?

There was chaos outside. Shouting, screaming, rich people boiling out of their cabins and demanding to see the captain, which was their standard response to everything from being out of toothpaste to a terrorist attack. I kept myself upright by sheer force of will, edging along the wood paneling, heading for—what? I didn't know. I just knew I needed to get there.

Two people were in my way. I blinked, because quite frankly, the last two people I expected to see holding on to each other were the cabin stewardess Aldonza and movie princess Cynthia Clark. Their body language wasn't what I expected, either—no subservience from Aldonza, no arrogance from Clark. They were just two women, staying together for support and comfort.

They turned and looked at me with identical expressions of surprise that turned into concern.

"What the devil happened to you?" Cynthia Clark

asked, and grabbed my left arm to support me. "Mrs. Prince?"

That still sounded odd to me. "Oh, hell, call me Jo. Everybody does," I said. I felt sick and dizzy and a little bit high. "Aldonza. I need a door to the crew area. Right now."

"Yes, Jo," she said. Finally I'd made her give up the formality. Just in time for disaster. "This way." She took the lead, glancing back to make sure we were struggling along in her wake. The ship seemed to be wallowing more and more now, side to side. Lights were flickering.

I looked at Clark, taking the bulk of my weight, who seemed composed despite all the chaos around us. "Thanks," I said.

"You seem to be one of the people who can make sure we survive this," she said. "It seems reasonable to be sure you get where you're going."

"Can I have your autograph?"

She smiled, and even now I couldn't see the strain. What an actor! "Maybe later," she said. "I'll have my assistant drop some photos by. I hope I can sign them: *To the woman who saved my life.*"

"Well, if you can't, I'll let you off the hook for the headshots," I said. I was shaking off my shock and weakness, though not quickly; I felt more alert, steadier on my feet. Good enough for shopping, maybe, if not fighting evil.

Too bad I was heading for the latter.

The subdued, elegant lighting in the hall flickered again, buzzed, and then died. After a heart-pounding five seconds of absolute blackness, emergency lighting clicked on with a hiss—glaring white halogens, not flattering to anyone's complexion, much less when people are distorted with terror. And somewhere in the back of my mind, I kept seeing water rising, rushing through corridors....

"Yeah," I muttered to myself. "Wish I'd never seen that damned movie."

Aldonza paused at a simple metal door labeled PRIVATE, with a key card reader to the side. She swiped a card that was hanging from a pull cord at her side, but nothing happened. Of course. Emergency regulations—all electronic locks would have popped, allowing for easy evacuation. I grabbed the knob and turned it, and opened the door on a different world.

It was as startling as opening up a broom closet at the Ritz—all of a sudden, there was no expensive thick carpet, no indirect lighting, no artwork. Just metal, some indoor-outdoor carpet for traction, and plain fixtures that wouldn't have been out of place on a fish trawler. Aldonza stepped over the watertight lip of the door and gestured me inside. Clark tried to go with us, but I stopped her with an outstretched hand. "No," I said. "Get to the lifeboat stations. The captain's probably going to try to get you off as quickly as possible."

"In this storm? How?"

"Trust me. He'll find a way." I shook her hand. "Love your movies, by the way. Sorry about incinerating your cabin."

"These things happen," she said, deadpan. "And I hope you find a way to stop this before it goes any further."

Me too, I thought, but I didn't even really know what I was heading toward in the first place.

Aldonza shut the watertight door and spun the locking mechanism. Nobody would be getting in that way, not now.

"Come on," she said, and offered me her shoulder. "You want the hold, yes? Where your friends went?"

I nodded, and off we went.

The hallways here were narrow industrial constructions, and as we passed larger open spaces they were uniformly workmanlike. A TV lounge area big enough for a few dozen, with comfortable but un-fancy Sears-style furniture. A computer area with banks of monitors and keyboards. A mess hall with all the charm of mess halls everywhere.

The place was deserted. "Where is everybody?"

"Duty stations," Aldonza said. "Organizing the passengers."

All of them? I supposed that made sense; we were heading down now, flights of narrow stairs descending into the emergency-lit bowels of the ship. Stairs. Lovely. *Feel the burn, Baldwin.*

I wondered where David had gone.

"One more," Aldonza murmured, when I had to stop for trembling breaths. "You're sure you want to do this?"

"No choice," I said, and coughed. "Let's go."

The bottom of the stairs opened into another hallway. This one held crew quarters—four narrow bunks to a room, top and bottom on each side, with small lockers in the middle on the far wall. Most had homey touches—photos of family, home, friends. Magazines to read, or books. Colorful nonstandard blankets and pillows.

Aldonza stopped.

"What?" I asked. She let go of me and took a step back. I braced myself on the metal wall, looking first at her, then down the hall.

Lights were going out, one by one, marching up the corridor toward us.

"Which way to the hold?"

"That way," she said. "Straight on, then go left when you must turn. The crew entrance to the hold is there."

"Get out of here," I said. *"Run."*

She stared at me in confusion for a few seconds, then she must have seen what was happening inside me.

She backed away and ran.

And I went toward the darkness.

And the darkness went into me.

Chapter Seven

The danger sign was that I felt . . . better. Calmer. Steadier.

I shouldn't have, not at all. I was operating on threads, and yet suddenly I felt assured, in control, and *powerful*.

The containment was leaking. Leaking badly. I was starting to turn around again, and I needed to do what I'd come to do before that happened.

I wasn't totally blind. Earth Wardens can sense heat, shapes, all kinds of frequencies not usually accessible to other regular folks (or Wardens), and with my night vision, I could see the hallway, the cool shapes of closed doors, and a long empty stretch.

The hallway ended in a blind T-shaped intersection, and I turned left as Aldonza instructed. At the end was a big double-sized watertight door with all kinds of warnings and crew restrictions blazoned next to it.

I spun the wheel and pulled. The air on the other side felt heavy and thick, unpleasantly stale. No fire, at least. And no ocean flooding in, which made me wonder why we were sitting so low in the water.

The hold was massive, a cave of treasures that would have taken months to map and explore. Cargo containers were stacked in neat, symmetrical rows that glowed cool greens and blues in my night vision.

And I saw the bright red and yellow flicker of bodies up ahead.

None of them were moving.

I struggled with a fiery hot pulse of primal satisfaction, of pleasure. I pushed it back.

I limped ahead, stopping for breath when I had to, and the scene slowly came into focus. There, near the center of the hold, were cages where I supposed duty-free items like liquor and expensive perfumes were kept. There was a massive freestanding safe, too, which no doubt held all those precious goodies the rich passengers had been so loath to leave behind. I wondered how much of it was drugs.

Standing, sitting, or lying in a circle near the safe were bodies. Some had the white-hot glow of Djinn, some the merely warm spectrum of human flesh, but none of them were moving by so much as a breath.

Still alive, though.

Not for long, the darkness inside me whispered, and purred. I felt it stretch its claws.

I limped as close as I dared before I felt something tingling along the edges of my nerves. There was some kind of energy field here that I really didn't want to encounter directly.

This was the team, Wardens and Djinn, that had come here to fight the skin. I didn't sense the signature of the one they'd been hunting at all, though. Instead, I saw a broken heap of crystal, and some slagged flesh.

Score one for the good guys. So what had gone wrong?

Kevin was standing only a few feet from me, frozen in midstep. Up on the aetheric, I could see his fury boiling like lava, so he was aware, if unable to move.

"Hey!" I yelled. One of the Djinn—Lyle, with his lead gray skin and rust-colored eyes—was closer to me than the others. "Lyle, can you hear me?"

"Yes," he said. He couldn't move, but he could speak.

"What's happening?"

"We are all that's holding the ship out of the water," he said. "We have to hold our concentration, or the forces won't balance. This deck will collapse. The ship will sink."

Instead of merely being frozen, the Wardens were in danger of being smashed, because there was a force *below* us, rising up from the blackest, coldest depths of the ocean . . . and it was pulling us down.

That was why the ship was riding low in the water. It was caught in a downward suction, like a ball at the end of a vacuum hose.

If the Djinn let go, it wasn't just the team of Wardens who were fatally screwed.

We all were.

Good. This time, the darkness pooled in my guts, warm and velvety, and I had to choke back a sob. It would be so easy to let go. So utterly easy.

There was a grating sound in the hold, something scraping over metal. I crouched down, making myself as small a target as possible, as the voice echoed off of metal, wood, and immobile bodies. I heard the shuffle of footsteps, and saw an odd shape moving among the stacked cargo and luggage. It had the outward shine of a human form, but it was like a superimposition—beneath it lay something dark and twisted.

The skin. It had created some kind of decoy, which was what the pile of glass was not far from Kevin, for the Wardens to chase while the rest of the plan had gone into motion.

Great. We might have killed the powerful one first, but this one was the *clever* one.

The skin ducked behind a parked, covered Porsche, then flitted around some hanging chains and weights, more like nightmare than human form.

It paused long enough in the glow of an emergency light for me to get a good look at it. The body it wore was one of those fresh-faced kids who looked like they'd be more at home in a television ad for soap than running around murdering people. He was almost as pretty as a Djinn.

"Angelo," I said. "Angelo Marconi?"

It just looked at me. I could see now that Lyle was right—it was literally just skin, stretched like a Halloween mask over the darkness inside.

Like you, laughed my dark side. *Like you are becoming. Not long now . . .*

The skin flitted out of the light and into the darkness.

I had no idea what I was going to do if it came to power-on-power, because I was barely staying on my feet.

Ten feet away, the frozen statue garden of Wardens and Djinn glowed steadily in my night vision. I caught a moving glow, much cooler than the others, blue instead of yellow or white.

Angelo darted into the middle of the standing figures. I switched back to regular sight, and saw him put his hands on one of the Djinn. One of Ashan's, who snarled and struck back with invisible force that bounced off of Angelo's body like the impact from a water balloon.

Angelo's skin blackened, crisped, and flaked away, revealing the crystal underneath, as the Djinn fought him. I felt the ship lurch sharply downward as the Djinn's attention was pulled away from the task of holding the opposing forces in balance.

The Djinn began to turn a soft ashy gray. Rotting from the outside in, the way the Djinn who'd died outside my room had ended her life.

I settled my back against the cold metal of the safe. If I was going to do anything at all, I didn't want to worry about falling down while I was about it. If what Venna had said was right, this thing was the forerunner of something much bigger, something that devoured on a universal scale. I thought about all those lifeless planets spinning in space that our telescopes and probes had found. How many of them had once been like us? How many had fallen prey and been wiped clean of life?

Why fight it? It's nature. You are all aberrations, a momentary mistake in the plan of the universe. Let go.

The ship bounced and settled deeper in the water. I heard the almost-human groan of the metal around me. It couldn't withstand this strain, not for much longer.

And neither could I.

I closed my eyes, visualized the frequencies I needed, and began to set them up in a tightly enclosed ring around the skin and his Djinn victim.

Nothing happened.

The Djinn struggled now, no longer interested in maintaining the balance, but he'd waited too long. He couldn't break free of the crystal claws that were digging into him, siphoning away his power and his life. He was losing.

I shifted frequencies.

The Djinn shrieked in unworldly agony as his body began to crumble away. The dark part of me met that with trembling eagerness, drinking in every agonized second of it.

I shifted frequencies again, blind to everything but the dance of molecules, the music of the energy being expended and absorbed.

Come on . . .

It wasn't strong enough.

Venna had been able to blow her victim to kingdom come, but she was Venna, a power of the ages. I was just a wounded, exhausted Warden up against something I didn't understand.

I was losing.

The Djinn who'd screamed was no longer recognizable as a Djinn at all. It was a pile of disintegrating ash and dust, sliding away from cohesion to scatter on the deck.

And I felt everything slipping away inside.

The ship groaned again, and I saw metal buckling, vast rivets ripping out of place, and the first jets of water blow through into the open space of the hold.

We started sinking again.

The skin turned to the next Djinn. Lyle.

I felt the shift of power in the room. The water stopped rushing in. The metal sealed and strengthened.

Where David walked, the world mended around him.

"No," I whispered, but he wasn't going to stop, not for me. Not this time.

He wasn't going to allow Lyle to die.

Another watertight door opened on the other side of the hold, and a swarm of Wardens poured in, led by Lewis. In seconds, they had the skin surrounded.

But the skin had its claws buried in Lyle's chest, like some giant parasitical tick.

I switched frequencies one more time. Lewis saw what I was doing, and joined me; the other Earth Wardens quickly supported us, creating a resonance that was so powerful it began to shatter glass and crystal stored in the crates. Someone's eyeglasses broke under the strain.

I felt feedback—the exact frequency that this creature's bones sang to. I began to focus harder, refining the sound until it was at a lethal intensity. I could *see* the waves now, a standing well of ripples in the air around the creature, battering it from all sides.

"Jo, let go!" Lewis shouted. "Drop out!"

I couldn't do that. Instead, I reached inside and came up with more power than I'd thought was hiding down in the empty storehouse of my gifts.

Because it felt so *good* to kill.

The vibrations ramped up into a shriek of power, and instead of Lyle dissolving into ash, the skin that had been Angelo Marconi blew apart into glittering crystal dust.

Lyle sagged and hit the deck, too weak to continue, but David stepped into his place and froze, concentrating.

The ship leveled out—still fighting the downward force but no longer being pulled down.

As quickly as it had come, the extra power I'd found was gone. Vanished. I was just me again, frail and fragile and ready to drop. If Angelo hadn't been a pile of ragged flesh and demonic parts on the metal floor, he'd have had an easy meal of me.

Lewis reached me a few seconds later, as I slid down to a sprawl against the safe. "I told you to step out!" he snapped, and touched my forehead. "Damn it. What the hell did you do?"

I struck out at him. I couldn't help it; his anger woke the beast inside, the one that had patiently stalked and laughed and waited.

I couldn't hold it back anymore.

I burned him.

If it had been anyone but Lewis, I'd have killed him; I wasn't pulling punches, and the fire that boiled out of me onto him was thick, plasmatic, and clung like napalm. It flickered with a sickly green tint.

Lewis reacted instantly, stepping back from me and concentrating all his will on putting out the fire before it could eat him up. He succeeded, but my attack left him with nasty third-degree burns on his hands and arms.

I laughed.

David called another Djinn to take his place in the fragile power structure that held us above the waves, and flashed across the hold toward me. As he did, Lewis blocked him. "No," he said. His voice was ragged with pain. "Don't touch her."

David looked like he was considering touching Lewis, in a very hostile manner, but he took the advice. He pulled in energy and ignited a small golden ball of light in the palm of his hand. It was cozy, warm, and gave me a false sense of security. The glow woke shades of orange and red in his eyes, made his face into the image of a classical bronze god.

Next to him, a faint mist formed in the air. It didn't bother to take human form, and it didn't need to; there was a *feeling* that came with it, oppressive as the ocean depths, and just as cold.

The Air Oracle. She—or he?—was the Djinn equivalent of an archangel, both supremely powerful and unknowable. Even as Conduit for the Djinn, David couldn't order an Oracle; he could only petition.

He'd obviously petitioned, and now the Air Oracle was here, looking at me out of a body that barely registered in the world at all. There was communication going on between David and the Oracle. It wasn't civil, from the look on David's face.

This was a perfect moment to see just what I could do with all this *power*.

As I summoned it up in a roiling boil inside me, thick and hot and dizzying, the Air Oracle's attention focused on me with a snap, and I was driven to my knees.

The Oracle seemed surprised that I hadn't been driven into tiny little fragments identifiable only by DNA. *Very* surprised. *You're going to get a lot more shocks, bitch,* I thought, and smiled.

David was far sneakier than I gave him credit for. Instead of coming at me directly, he used his link to me, sending a massive burst of power through the aetheric connection between us.

It blew me out of my body. I fell, stunned, and waited for the end. The Air Oracle was no friend of humans in general; I was no better than the slime at the edge of a pond to her. But she didn't act.

She just left.

David bent and took me in his arms as if I weighed less than my equivalent in feathers. His lips brushed my temple. "Forgive me," he said. "It's better if you sleep."

Before I could even think about protesting, all the light winked out, and I was drifting away into warm, dark, safe eternity.

When I woke up, it was because David could no longer afford even the small pulse of energy it was taking to keep me unconscious.

I swam up out of the thick darkness to the sound of alarms, screaming, and the gale-driven shriek of wind. The air smelled of metal and salt and fear.

Heavenly, that smell.

I opened my eyes on darkness, but in the next second a lightning bolt split the sky above me in half, miles across, like a hot purple zipper letting in the darkness.

It lit up low, thick, black clouds that fired rain down like arrows from the battlements.

I was on my back on the deck, reclining in a white padded chair that was made for lounging. It slid hard to starboard, and I jerked and rolled off and to my feet before it slammed into the promenade railing. My bare soles hit cold, wet wood, and I shivered. I was soaked to the skin. How had I gotten here? And why? And what the *hell* was going on?

Nothing good, obviously. The deck was thick with uniformed crew and a chaotic swirl of passengers. It was too dangerous out here, but that didn't seem to be stopping anybody; I wondered why they hadn't taken refuge inside, but some practical knowledge finally kicked in, and I knew.

Either the crew understood that there was an excellent chance that this ship was going down, or there was something below that was even more dangerous than the storm. Either way, not good news for me or anybody else.

"Jo!" Cherise. I barely recognized my best friend, because I'd rarely seen her look this—well, bedraggled. Drowned-rat wet, pale, and shivering with cold. "God, I thought you'd never wake up. Come on!"

She dragged me off in some random direction. No one had told her that I was prone to irrational bursts of killing fury, I supposed. *Good.* That would make it easier.

"We need to get to the lifeboat—"

My senses were coming back online, all of them,

and in Oversight I saw the thick red streams sweeping around us, closing in.

The storm that Bad Bob had dispatched, the one powered by the Unmaking he'd pulled out of the spear, was almost on us, and it was devastating.

Cherise's words were lost in a fresh blast of wind, a gust so flat and hard that it slammed her bodily against the metal wall. I suppose that in better times I might have tried to help her. Instead, I just clung to a metal stanchion and watched her struggle.

I saw one of the heavy lounge chairs topple right over the railing and disappear as the ship lurched to starboard again. We were heeling around, getting hammered by churning waves like a punch-drunk boxer.

The ship was still stuck in one spot, anchored by the suction coming from deep beneath the ocean. I could feel it, and it was growing stronger, not weaker.

The Djinn were losing the fight.

"Hang on!" Cherise screamed, and another gigantic wave crested and fell, pounding us with spray like nails. "We have to get off the ship, *now*!"

How exactly that was going to be accomplished I had no idea, but I nodded. In the brief lull between lashing waves, we staggered to the next handhold. Along the way we ran into more castaways. I barely recognized a sopping-wet Cynthia Clark, who surely hadn't been this miserable since she'd made that epic disaster movie with Gene Hackman, back in the day. I also recognized Cho Chu Wing, one of our Weather Wardens. Cho was a tiny little thing, skinny as a restaurant greeter. She'd managed to keep herself mostly together; her black hair was pegged back in a tight ball, and only random strands of it clung to her damp face. She'd worn a storm slicker, neon orange, and beneath it she seemed to be drier than any of the rest of us. She waved us frantically toward the bow of the ship. As we slipped and fought our way through blinding spray and stinging, whipping rain, we gathered Weather Wardens in ones and twos, until there was a tight knot of them linking arms together, like a rugby team in a scrum.

I stood apart from them. Remote, even in the midst of my fellow Wardens.

"We need to get a bubble!" Cho screamed. "Focus on giving us clear water for a hundred feet in every direction!"

That wasn't as hard as it might seem; it was basically wave cancellation, which is a fundamental principle of the physics of anything that moves as a unit—sound, water, a rippling flag. You need to find the specific frequency of the wave and cancel it out, and move the energy elsewhere. Normally that was the tricky part; bleed-off energy could destabilize everything, and whip up a whole mess of side problems you'd never anticipate.

In this melting stew of uncontrolled energy, another few mega joules in the wrong place would hardly matter.

"Tornado!" someone screamed, and I looked up to see the approaching black arms of the hurricane sweeping in like scythes. There were bulbous eruptions forming in the trailing clouds, swelling and then narrowing into cones. Forming tornadoes have a lazy look, almost tentative; they bob and weave and seem impotent at first, until they get their strength consolidated.

I'd never taken time to admire their elegance before. *So beautiful. So deadly.*

Cho was shouting something at me. She wanted my help.

Well then.

I gave it. I gave it to the tornado, and laughed as it gobbled up power like a greedy shark.

Cho must have realized what I was doing. She stepped up and gave me a sharp elbow to the back of my neck, sending me reeling into another Warden, who put me down on the deck and pinned me, yelling for Djinn.

My pet tornado collapsed—no great surprise, they always were fragile constructs, by the very nature of the physics that drove them—and the waves that battered the *Grand Paradise,* heeling her violently from one side to the other, eased to merely heavy instead of psychotic. I felt the waves' pounding rhythms begin to ease, like a racing heart slowing as adrenaline faded.

"You can't stop it," I told Cho, who was taking advantage of the breathing space to stare into the heart of the storm. "Everybody dances with the devil."

I knew the storm was watching too, this monster of a thing that Bad Bob had imbued with life and cunning and cruelty, and a particular kind of insanity. I could feel it gathering itself, studying us. *Planning.*

It could feel that I was an ally, if only it could reach me. I could have done more, but I felt lazily content to wait.

No hurry. I was enjoying the panic too much to end it quickly.

The ship lurched—not side to side, but *down,* as if a giant hand had suddenly grabbed the hull from beneath and pulled it straight down. The ship sank like an express elevator, and I watched the ocean pour in over the railings on the decks below, then come for us in a foaming, deadly rush . . .

. . . and then the force let us go, and the ship's buoyancy popped us violently straight up like a cork from a rubber band. I don't think the *Grand Paradise* quite came out of the water, but there was a sickly sense of utter stillness as momentum fought gravity and gravity's patient pull won.

The ship crashed back into the water and settled. We were sprawled like ninepins all over the deck—Wardens, crew, staff, hapless passengers. The screaming sounded thin and lost.

"We're loose!" one of the Wardens shouted. "Get everybody on the lifeboats!"

"No!" Cho snapped. "We're getting control! We'll stand no chance at all in the smaller boats!"

"Are you?" I asked. "Getting control? I don't think so!" It felt like the kind of adrenaline rush you get from hurtling down a mountain on skis, straight for a killing drop, knowing it may destroy you but there's nothing so beautiful as that moment when death means nothing, nothing at all . . .

The Warden holding me down—I realized it was Kevin, as I focused on his face—gave me a solid right cross, trying to put me out. "You'll have to beat me harder than that," I told him, very seriously. "Come on, Kevin, dig deep. Hurt me like your stepmother taught you."

He went pale, and I felt his grip on me loosen. Too easy. I threw him off, not particularly caring where he landed, and stalked to Cho.

Before I reached her, we all staggered as a massive subsonic *boom* rocked the decking.

Far beneath the *Grand Paradise,* the seafloor collapsed into a massive trench, sending a crush of seawater flooding downward to fill the sudden mile-deep gap. For a moment, a significant section of the sea dipped into a concave bowl—not by much, distributed over such a huge and adaptable area, but enough.

And a wave formed, rushing over the depression, gathering strength and speed and energy.

Rushing straight at our port side. It would take a minute to get to us, maybe more—not much more, though. We were in deep water, not shallows; that was the only thing that might save us. To survive, the ship had to turn into the wave.

I needed to stop it from turning.

"Jo." That was Cherise, laying her hand on my shoulder. "Jo, stop."

I turned to look at her, and I saw fear ignite in her eyes. "Oh God," she breathed. "Oh my *God*—"

She was so fragile. So *easy*.

Cherise's fear was like incense rising on the air, and I wanted more of it. All of it.

Every last, red drop.

She raised her chin, and the fear faded.

"This isn't you," she said. "And I think you can stop it, Jo. You're the hero."

She was wrong. I wasn't the hero now—if I ever had been. What I'd done to Lewis was proof of that. What I'd *tried* to do with the tornado.

Part of me still liked Cherise, but it was a small part, and it was getting smaller all the time, like a tiny island of color in an inky flood.

I didn't hurt her. I'm not really sure why.

I felt the shudder beneath my feet, as the *Grand Paradise*'s enormous bulk began to make its ponderous, city-blocks-wide turn toward the wave that was sweeping closer.

I looked up, drawn by a pulse of power, and saw Lewis and David standing on a balcony above us. Arguing.

David tried to turn away.

Lewis grabbed David by the fabric of his shirt. His lips moved.

David disappeared. No misting, no sense of transition, just . . . gone.

And Lewis didn't look surprised. I was—not just by David's sudden vanishing act but by the sensation that rippled through me, liquid and hot and wrong.

What just happened?

Lewis shoved something in his pocket as he vaulted the balcony railing. He landed flat-footed, keeping his balance on the still-lurching deck with one hand on the railing. "Get everybody inside!" he yelled. "Everybody!"

Cherise turned and began pushing people to the nearest entrances. People seemed more than motivated to follow instructions, for once—in fact, there was a traffic jam until officers began funneling people to other doors.

I didn't follow. I stood at the railing, hands folded, calm and content. It was all unraveling around me.

All I had to do was enjoy the ride down.

The ship had managed to slew around at an impressive rate, but the waves kicked up as the Wardens' fears eroded their concentration. It significantly slowed our progress.

Lewis joined me at the railing, far enough away that it indicated he knew what a risk it was to be near me.

"Where's David?" I asked. I looked over at him, noting the healing burns on his hands. I wondered if it hurt. I certainly hoped so.

"Where you can't hurt him," Lewis said. "I know what's happening to you."

I shrugged. "So you know," I said. "Can you stop it?"

"Do you want me to stop it?"

I laughed. That was probably enough of an answer.

On the horizon, there was a mountain. One big rising mass, heading for us. At this rate, we didn't have another minute. Maybe thirty seconds, I was guessing.

Maybe less.

"The ship will capsize," I said. "You can't turn fast enough. Where are the Djinn?"

"Gone," Lewis said. "For their own protection. We're all alone now."

David wouldn't have run, not to save himself. He was foolish that way. "You've done something." He didn't deny it. It was big, whatever it was; it was more than likely an unforgivable sin. But Lewis was the sort to make that choice, if he had to. Or thought he had to. "Something to David?"

He didn't answer me directly. "We're going to capsize, even if that wave doesn't hit us broadside." And it probably would. We just didn't have enough time to hit it bow-first.

"You could turn it," I remarked. He locked stares with me, and his eyes were bleak, tired, and frightened.

"No, I can't," he said. "You can."

I smiled. "I won't."

I felt the front of the ship dipping down, and then rising, more like a speedboat than a giant of the seas.

Lewis seemed very calm. Very tall and still, hair ruffling in the wind. There was a glow about him, a power that I couldn't remember seeing before.

As the mountain of water roared down at us, I turned and walked calmly toward the nearest door.

Cherise and one of the white-coated officers waved me urgently on. Cher grabbed my arm and pulled me over the high threshold, and the officer slammed the door shut and turned the locking mechanism.

"Hatch twenty-three sealed!" he shouted into his

radio, in the high-pitched voice of utter panic. I took a moment to look around. It was a bar, large and casual, but all the bottles and glasses had been stowed away, and the place had an unfinished look to it. The room was packed with refugees, some of whom were gazing longingly at the bar as if they wondered where all the rum had gone. I spotted Cho Wing and three other Wardens, all seeming tense and expectant. They knew what was coming. The civilian passengers seemed confused and a little bored.

The bridge officers assuredly knew that their worst fears were coming true; they could see it from their windows.

Cherise was chattering at me, trying to get me to take cover. I shook myself free. She gave me one last, despairing look, then wedged herself in a corner and tipped an armchair over herself.

I heard the wave coming, even through the steel plates. I felt the rumble of it.

The bow of the *Grand Paradise* lifted sharply, and kept rising, rising. Tables and chairs started sliding, and people screamed and clung to whatever was within reach, stable or not. I heard glass crashing; that was probably unsecured stock somewhere under the counters.

A huge wooden cabinet, designed to look primitive and rough-hewn, began to topple down from one wall. There were six people beneath it. I watched with placid interest.

Cho yelled a warning. One of the Earth Wardens flung out a hand and stopped the falling cabinet.

Disappointing.

A racing bite of energy spread over me like a hot blanket of fire, concentrating on my back and then flowing down my arms and into the core of my body. I went down to one knee, bracing myself as the horizon continued to rise toward the sky. People slid past me, screaming, flailing. I didn't pay much attention.

"We're going over!" someone shouted amid the chaos and crashing furniture. We were still climbing. The floor passed a forty-five-degree upward angle, heading for vertical, and I felt the whole ship slip sideways, twist, and start to tumble out of control.

We were falling.

Then we stopped falling, and the ship's torturous descent changed, smoothed, and entered an eerie kind of calm. The ship slowly drifted back to a stable, horizontal line, but it didn't feel like we were in flat seas. It didn't feel like we were in the water at all.

I rose and walked to the large picture window that commanded a view of the promenade.

Lewis was standing just where I'd left him, at the railing, and his glow was Djinn-bright, the color of soft morning sunshine against the blackness of the storms. Yes, the storms were still there, whipping around us in a frenzy, but we were floating in a bubble of force that stretched all around the ship in a perfect sphere. *Ship in a bottle,* I thought, and for just an instant I was too angry to think properly. No Warden could do this, not alone.

Not even Lewis.

We were floating on the storm in our own little self-contained pocket universe of calm sea and air.

I tried to unlock the watertight door, but it seemed stuck. I sent a snap of Earth power from my fingertips out through the metal, realigning the surfaces, and when I turned the handle again, the door slid smoothly open.

"Jo!" Cher was right behind me. Her eyes were huge and frightened. "What's happening?"

"I'll find out," I said, with utter calm. I felt alive inside, manic with glee, but I didn't want her to see that. "Wait inside."

"But—"

I slammed the door between us and hit it with the heel of my hand, hard enough to make a hollow *boom*. "Lock it!"

I heard the heavy clash of metal engaging, and then I turned toward Lewis, standing like a misplaced figurehead at the rail.

He opened his eyes. I could see the energy spilling out of him, a raw wound that split him open to the core.

He was bleeding on the aetheric. Bleeding himself to death.

"How?" I asked, and leaned on the railing. He didn't answer me. Couldn't, perhaps. His nose was bleeding, and his eyes were flushed red under the stress of what he was doing. Fifteen Djinn and four times as many Wardens hadn't been able to stop the storm, but Lewis was somehow fighting it, toe to toe.

Not winning, though.

Not hardly.

"You'll kill yourself," I commented. "For God's sake, Lewis, what does it matter? What does any of it matter? Just let go. The ship will get torn apart. People will drown. Life will go on, for a while, until it doesn't." I shrugged. "Just let go. It's that easy."

Lewis let out a gasping sob. His knees buckled, but he held fast to the railing.

He held the bubble of force against the storm.

"You aren't doing this alone," I said. "But you didn't have time to get the other Wardens to help. And even if you did, they're not capable of this kind of power. Not alone—" I paused, because I finally worked it out. "But you're not alone, are you?"

Lewis's breath was coming in short, desperate gasps now. Nobody could sustain this, not even the most powerful Warden in the world.

Not even one with a direct connection to the aetheric.

Which was what Lewis had. He'd always been close to our temperamental Mother Earth, but this was beyond that, way beyond. The power that poured through him to fill this shell of force was like a geyser, tapping directly into the heart of the planet herself.

Only the connection between Lewis and a Djinn Conduit could do that.

He'd claimed David. He'd put David in a bottle and made him a slave, and he was using him to open this portal directly into the lifeblood of Earth, to save the ship.

It would burn Lewis out before David, but not much before.

They'd both die.

Some part of me was screaming inside, begging me to stop it. But that was the very last tiny foothold of the old Joanne drowning in a sea of darkness.

I closed my eyes and sighed. All I had to do was . . . wait.

I felt a warning tingle in the still, calm air, and as I looked up, I saw a tornado striking down at us from the clouds that writhed overhead. Lightning snaked around it, living barbed wire, and it hit the curved surface of Lewis's protective bubble around the *Grand Paradise* and began to probe for weaknesses.

Then it bombed us.

I saw the metal shape hurtling down at us through the oddly clear eye of the tornado, that empty funnel space where the cold air and the warm air cycle to fuel the beast's engines. I didn't know what it was at first— wreckage, maybe a mass of siding or a barn, or—

No. That was a *ship*. A whole, intact *ship*. A small fishing vessel. The black-painted bottom was heavy with barnacles, and as lightning flared brighter I saw the name on her rusty bow—*Abigail*.

There were living men on board. I could see their terrified faces at the railing as the ship dropped toward us in free fall, her weight turning majestically in the air and driving her nose down like the tip of a spear.

"No," Lewis moaned, but he didn't drop the shield. He couldn't.

The *Abigail* hit his protective bubble and exploded into shrapnel, scrap, and bodies. I flinched—instinct, not sympathy. The ship's fuel tanks burst, slopping marine diesel in a wave across the invisible wall.

Lightning ignited it, and flames sheeted over us in a semicircle. It didn't last long. Nothing to burn once the diesel had flamed out.

The wreckage of the *Abigail* was gone in even less time, along with her crew. Even if there'd been a chance of saving them—which, after the fury of that crash, I doubted—there was no way to reach them without dropping our own protective shield.

Bad Bob really was bringing his A game.

The tornado's sloppy mouth slithered over Lewis's shield for another few seconds, and then it withdrew up into the clouds. Not gone, just reloading. I could see this storm sweeping its way from Bad Bob's location to ours, picking up ammunition along the way, like a boy collecting stones to throw. Congested shipping lanes out there. Naval vessels flying under various flags. Pleasure craft and yachts and sailing ships and cruise ships smaller than this one . . .

Lewis's strength gave out, and he lost his grip on the railing. He fell to his knees. I could feel David's agony rippling through the connection between us. This was tearing them both apart. Lewis's body was surrendering under the strain.

I reached out and put my hand on his sweat-matted hair.

Finally, he turned his head and looked at me. Just one look, not very long. Bone-deep exhaustion in him, and just a tiny trace of regret.

"Jo, you have to stop yourself," he said. "Please. Stop yourself."

"Too late," I told him, and took control of the bubble away from him.

It was a shock, how much power was involved. Even with the enormous flood pouring in from the storm, from Bad Bob himself, the force that hit me was staggering. A normal Warden, no matter how accomplished, would have been shredded in seconds.

Lewis collapsed limply on the deck, rolled away, and began to crawl slowly.

I rolled him faceup, and held him in place with a foot on his chest. I turned my face to the storm, looking into the abyss.

Nietzsche was right—it also looked into me.

"Stay put," I said to Lewis. "I want you to see this. You used to be an altruist, but I watched you change. You turned into such a realist, with all your cold win/lose/ draw equations. You just never thought you'd acutally lose, did you?"

Lewis reached in his pocket and pulled out a small glass bottle. It was sturdy, one of those pocket travel samples of men's cologne. Designed to be break-resistant, but still meeting all the glass-only requirements of a Djinn containment bottle. The cap, of course, was off, because Lewis had been accessing David's powers.

I saw him struggle with the choice. That was a no-win scenario.

He eventually did the moral thing, and tried to smash it against the deck. It didn't break.

"Where are the other Djinn?" I asked. Lewis shook his head and collapsed, panting. He was holding the bottle in a death grip. "Let me guess. I have a good idea of how you think. You ordered David to send them all away, to a place of safety. Maybe Jonathan's house."

Lewis nodded, eyes tightly closed. I wondered why he wouldn't look at me. I wondered what he *saw*.

"I'll bet you told yourself it was temporary," I said, and took my foot off of Lewis's back to crouch down next to him, staring at his face. "You'd let him go as soon as the emergency was over. But that's not human nature, Lewis. We don't work that way. We take power, and we keep it. We don't give it up. Someone has to come along and take it from us, usually violently." I smiled softly. "There's always another goddamn crisis, baby. Don't you get that?"

He didn't want to look at me. I wondered what was so terrible about my face; I felt positively great. Better than I had for ages.

Finally, Lewis got up his strength to ask, "What are you going to do?"

"Take this ship where it was going anyway," I said. "Directly to Bad Bob. The difference is, most of you will be dead by the time it arrives, I'm afraid." I paused, waiting to feel some kind of regret. Nothing came. The last little bit of me was slipping under the waves, and I really couldn't even care.

Lewis rolled over on his side and wiped blood from his nose and eyes, still avoiding my gaze. His pupils were huge, like those of a man who'd never left the darkness.

"Well?" I asked, and cocked my head. "What are you going to do about this little situation? Aren't you going to stop me?"

He coughed. It sounded wet and deep, like something had broken deep inside him. "No."

"Really."

"You're the one with the hero complex, not me."

"And what are you?" He didn't answer. "Oh, that's right. You're the one who doesn't have to feel good about himself to know he did the right thing. Then live up to it, Lewis. You can stop me. You've got the answer in your hand."

His fingers closed around the bottle.

David's bottle.

"Come on," I whispered. "Let him out. You know you want to. Wouldn't it do your heart good to make him come after me? Wouldn't that be *fun*?"

"Stop."

"Make me."

The look on his face made fires ignite deep inside me. Tasty. "No."

"It's too late to get all noble on me now, Lewis. You put a Djinn in a bottle. Worse, you put *a Conduit* in a bottle. Don't you think that's going to piss the Djinn off? The last war was about them wanting their freedom. This one's going to be pure revenge, and they won't care about who's innocent and who's guilty. Congratulations. You've single-handedly destroyed the Wardens."

"I'm not the one who made the Djinn ... vulnerable to capture," he said. He had to stop for breath. "You knew marrying David ... would do this. Vows. You didn't care."

A wave washed over the bubble above us, leaving a thin, lacy film behind. It was like looking through my mother's kitchen curtains. The storm outside raged on, but it was losing some of its fury. It knew I'd won.

We'd won. Me and the storm, together.

"I'm a selfish bitch," I agreed. "I tried, okay? I did the good-girl thing. I fought the good fight, and where did it get me? *My skin burned off, Lewis.* Nobody was telling me so, but I was never going to get better, was I? I'm damned if I'm going to walk around with no fucking skin the rest of my life so that I can feel all good about adhering to my strict moral code." I took a deep breath and tasted ozone from the storm's whipping frenzy. "It's just power. Doesn't matter where it comes from, or where it goes."

"And you can quit any time you want."

My tone hardened. I still didn't like being mocked. "Fuck your intervention. I'm the one still standing."

Lewis's fingers tightened around the bottle. The one holding the only thing that *might* stop me. I'd known from the moment I walked out on the promenade that it was going to come down to this.

I smiled.

And he surprised me. "No. I'm not calling David. Not just for his sake—for yours. If you live through it, I don't want you having that on your conscience."

"I'm not Bad Bob," I said. "I love him."

He coughed blood. "You kind of loved me, too. Look how that turned out."

I slapped my hand down hard next to his head. Hard enough to split the wood. Overhead, the storm shrieked harmony to the howling rage inside me. *"Call him!"*

"No way in hell."

All he had to do was get David out in the open. That was all I wanted. I slapped the deck again, and again, and again. Splinters jabbed deep, and I left primal bloody handprints behind.

It felt so *good*.

Lewis opened his eyes and locked stares with me at point-blank range. "No," he said, very softly. "This isn't going to happen the way you want."

I looked up. There were other people out on the Promenade now—Wardens, arraying themselves against me.

Cherise, standing with them, like an actual person who mattered. They all wore identical tense, focused expressions . . . the look of soldiers just before the battle.

I looked down at Lewis and smiled a real, warm, sunny smile. "We'll see," I said, and stood up to put my hands on my hips. "We'll see about that."

Then I walked away to get some air.

Nobody stopped me as I walked.

In time, I felt the last whispers of power click into place, locking me into the storm. We were one now—a symbiotic dark engine, generating our own power. Our own reality. The storm and I were one.

Easy, I told it. *Easy, for now.*

And the winds began to slow. It could bide its time.

So could I.

I waited until the winds died a bit, then let go of the bubble of force that Lewis and David had built at such cost.

I ended up on the port side of the ship, in a bar—preciously named Arpeggio's—where some of the non-Warden guests and crew were still gathered. Tables and chairs had been righted. There'd been some minor injuries, but not even a broken bone, remarkably. I supposed we'd gotten off light, unlike the crew of the *Abigail*.

I bellied up to the serving bar and perched on one of the high chairs. There were three guys behind the bar.

One was cleaning up broken glass. The other two were taking orders. A lot of people were drinking. I didn't blame them at all.

"What'll it be, miss?" the server asked me, and gave me a smile so even and white that he should have been in a commercial. It faded quickly. Even across the other side of a ship the size of a small city, word traveled fast, and it clicked in quickly who—or what—I was. The room went quiet. He cleared his throat nervously. "Anything to drink?"

"Cyanide?" I was trying to be charming, but I could see from the alarm in his eyes that I was somehow missing the target.

"Fresh out, miss," he said weakly. "Some other poison, perhaps?"

I gave up. "How about a vodka tonic?" That was my sorry-for-myself drink, and this seemed an ideal place to throw a ten-minute pity party. He turned away, mixed the drink, and put it on the coaster. I sipped. It was excellent. "I'm surprised the bar is open."

"Anything to keep people calm." There was more than a touch of febrile panic in his eyes now.

"Be sure to save some for yourself." I smiled, with teeth. "You're going to need it."

He poured himself a shot of whiskey and downed it without a pause, then fled, leaving me in possession of the entire bar's contents. I sipped my vodka tonic and took a self-assessment as pretty much everybody else followed the bartender's lead and got the hell out of Dodge.

My back didn't hurt anymore. It also wasn't numb. It felt normal, natural . . . and as I angled around to get a look in the still-intact bar mirror, I saw the shadow of a black form under the new skin.

A torch, embedded instead of tattooed.

Much, much larger.

One or two of the ship's staff hadn't fled with the rest. One stern-looking woman poured me a second vodka tonic without being asked. "On the house," she said. "If you can get us out of this and home, you're welcome to drink the place dry."

I drank it all in a gulp, and said, "Two things. First, if I want to drink this place dry, you definitely haven't got a thing on board this floating sewage plant that can stop me. Second, you're not going home. Get used to the idea."

Then I tossed a twenty on the bar and resumed my stroll. I paused at the big, flat stern of the ship to gaze out over our churning gray wake. Nothing in sight, not on any side, but open water and storm.

I leaned on the railing and opened myself up through the darkness, searching. It didn't take me long to find the wellspring of that black flood. It was directly to starboard, and close.

Maybe a day away, if that.

"I'm coming," I whispered into the dark. "You're getting what you wanted, you evil old bastard."

I felt Bad Bob's chuckle inside me like lips against skin. "Knew you wouldn't let me down, little girl," he said. When I shut my eyes I could see him standing beside me in ghostly outlines. "You bring me the ship and the Wardens. That's a good start to our work. From then on, no limits. No limits at all."

"On my way," I said, and broke the connection with him. I used my Earth powers to lock out the computer controls of the ship and put in the destination.

Then I went in search of more vodka.

*   *   *

By early morning, the black torch mark was a bold swirl beneath my skin, stretching from the flame at the nape of my neck to the elaborate scrolled cap, just below the flare of my hips. The flames at its top weren't just black ink anymore. They were real fire, moving silently beneath the translucent covering of my flesh. It was the ultimate tribal stamp, declaring who and what I was to anyone with the courage to look.

It should have frightened me, I guess. Instead, I admired it for a moment, then picked up the hair dryer and began to make myself presentable for the day.

An hour later, I strode out from the cabin—perfectly put together. My hair was curly and tumbling glossy black down toward my waist. I wore a skimpy aqua-blue top with cap sleeves that bared most of my midriff, and low-rise jeans that hugged every curve. David had stocked the closets with anything I might want, for any conceivable mood or occasion.

I decided today was Seduction Day.

I ran into Cherise and Kevin in the hallway. They were talking with that suppressed urgency of two people trying to keep a secret, and they stopped when they saw me.

"What?" I put my hands on my hips and raised my eyebrows. "Not enjoying the three-hour tour, Mary Ann? Of course, that makes him Gilligan. It fits."

Cherise didn't smile. I'd never seen her not-smile at a *Gilligan's Island* joke before. "We should talk," she said. There was a faint quiver in her voice, and I saw her take Kevin's hand for support. "Maybe back in the room?"

"Maybe you should get out of my way and stop bothering me," I said. I let it lie there for a few seconds, then lightened it up with a grin that felt strange on my lips. "I mean, you're between me and breakfast. You know how dangerous that is."

"Don't," Kevin said.

"Don't what?"

"Don't you fucking dare threaten her. She's trying to save your life." Kevin stepped in front of her, or tried to. Cherise hauled him back and gave him a look that would have frozen Lake Michigan. "Sorry." Insignificant as she might be, Cherise wanted to fight her own battles. Well, I could have told him that.

"I just want to talk," Cherise said, returning her attention to me. "Please."

She didn't demand anything, and I knew that if I pushed it, she'd back down. And I was tempted to push, very tempted, not so much because of her—Cherise really wasn't on the radar anymore—but because the simmering, furious violence in Kevin was addictively delicious. All I had to do was hurt her, and I could drink my fill.

Not yet, I told myself. *Don't enjoy yourself too much.*

"Please," Cherise repeated.

"Jeez, okay, don't beg," I said. "Just you, though. Not him."

Kevin held up his hands in surrender, a sour look on his face. "Dude, like I want to spend time coddling your self-involved evil-turning ass." His glance at Cherise said something different, though. "Be careful."

"*I'm* going to hurt her? I'm not the one with the body count, Kevin," I said. He flinched, just a little. "Why don't you loiter out here looking menacing while you wait? Maybe you can beat up cabin stewards, just to keep in practice."

He flipped me off, but that wasn't original for him. I took Cherise's arm, and we headed back to the cabin.

She locked the door behind us. I raised my eyebrows as I settled on my unmade bed. "Oooh," I said. "Is this going to be hot girl-on-girl action, or what?"

"Shut up." Cherise hugged herself and stayed where she was, between me and the door. "Something's really wrong with you."

"Oh yeah? You think?" I leaned back against the hard cabin wall and crossed my arms. "You've been drinking Lewis's Kool-Aid about how bad I am, boo-hoo. But I understand why you'd go that way. He's still got an open position for girlfriend-slash-wife, so hold out for the brass ring, kid." She gave me an uncomprehending stare. "Wouldn't be the first man you've screwed for fun and profit."

"Would you *shut up*? God, you can be such a bitch! Since—since your back thing happened, you've been changing. Slowly at first, but then it got worse, and now you're—" Cherise made a helpless gesture that encompassed everything about me, from head to toe. "Look at you."

I looked down. "What?" Granted, the clothes might be a bit sluttier than my usual, but I liked them, and besides, it was a cruise ship. South Beach rules of conduct and dress.

"It's not the outfit, Jo. It's *you*. It's the look in your eyes, the kind of smile you give people. The way you think about them." Cherise swallowed and ducked her chin to avoid eye contact. "When you think they're not looking, it's like you're examining pieces of meat—like they're not people at all. You never did that before."

I deliberately relaxed again. "Yeah? You're sure about that? Maybe you just never caught me at it before."

"No. I know you, and this—this isn't you. Looks like you, feels like you, sounds like you. It's in your skin, but it's not the Joanne Baldwin I'm friends with."

I didn't know why this should wake a feeling of anxiety in me. Pale and faint, yes, but still . . . I wanted to make her feel better. "People change," I offered.

"Not this much. Not this fast. You let something inside you."

I tried to explain—again, I wasn't sure why I bothered, except that the genuine warm concern in Cherise's eyes actually reached something in me, something I'd thought long drowned in darkness. "It's just giving me access to power. Like having a Djinn at my command, only—better. Faster. You're going to have to get used to the fact that I can't be Miss Congeniality anymore. This is war."

"Jo, the war's over. You lost. You're a casualty."

I came up from the bed in one sinuous motion and took a step into her space. "You know what's really over? This conversation. I'm leaving."

"You have to go through me first."

"Can do."

"What? You're going to hurt me?" Cherise—tiny little Cherise, with her perfect tan and perfect teeth and glistening hair. Funny and sexy and quirky. "Go ahead."

Frustration erupted inside me. It burned from the torch on my back under my skin, traveling lines and ladders of nerves, and I felt fire tingle at the ends of my fingers. *"Move."*

"Make me, bitch."

I wanted to, oh God, I did. Instead, I bared my teeth. "You know what you are?" I asked, low in my throat. "You're nothing. Even among human beings, you're a worthless failure. Model? A model is just some girl who strips for cash—a body for hire. A walking mannequin with a shelf life of about five minutes. Take away your looks and you've got nothing to sell. Who's going to love you then, the Human Torch out there? Face it, without tagging along to somebody *better,* you're nothing, peach. You used to be *entourage.* Now you're not even that."

The color faded out of Cherise's face, leaving the tan like some eerie overlay, and I saw a real spark of fear in her clear blue eyes.

It turned hot.

"Why'd you just call me *peach*?"

Of all the things she could have said, that was the one that stopped me in my tracks. *Peach. Sweetness.* Bad Bob liked expressions like those, mockingly sentimental, used to wound. He'd used them on me all the time.

I took a step back. My hands locked into fists, and I felt the fire from the torch on my back flare hotter. It didn't like me doubting myself.

It didn't like me *thinking.*

"It's just another kind of Demon Mark," Cherise said. "Remember? Remember how that felt? You told me about it, how it made you feel so powerful, so free—"

"Shut up." My voice didn't have much force to it.

"He's using it to destroy you. You've *got to stop.* You're going to destroy everyone and everything you love."

I closed my eyes. Images flashed across the darkness—David, the first time I'd seen him, a dusty stranger on the road. David, naked in morning light, looking at me as if I was the most glorious thing he had ever seen.

Lewis, standing against the storm, and compromising himself and his beliefs to find the strength. Not asking for my praise or my applause. Knowing I might kill him for it.

Cherise, without the power to light a match, signing on because it was the right thing to do.

Everything I loved was right here, on this ship, and I was destroying it.

And I still couldn't care.

"You understand," said a little-girl voice from behind me. "That's good. I wouldn't want you to die without understanding that it had to be done."

Venna stood behind me in her Alice pinafore, perfect and shining and eerie. I looked from her to Cherise.

"How the hell did you hook up with the Djinn?"

She shrugged. "Diplomacy. Ain't it a bitch?"

"And so am I." But I didn't strike at either one of them. Instead, I sat down on the bed and crossed my legs into the lotus position. It was a bit of a tight fit, in the jeans.

I stared idly at the far side of the cabin—Cherise's side—where she had beauty products lined up in thick clusters on the shelf. All kinds of things—tubes of makeup, lipsticks, eye shadow compacts.

Bottles of expensive perfume, just the right size to hold a Djinn.

Venna smiled. "I'd kill you first," she said, and there was absolutely no doubt in my mind that she meant it. "There wouldn't be enough of you to summon the sharks."

I held up my hands. "Can't blame me for thinking about it."

"Oh, I can," she said. "I most certainly can. But it would be amusing to see you make the attempt. Your vows with David gave humans access to the New Djinn, not my kind." She was studying me with alien, utterly cold intensity. "But I think I understand you. If someone offered you poisoned water in the desert, would you rather die of thirst, or take longer to die of poison?"

She really *did* understand. "If I hadn't taken the

poison, I'd be dead already. None of *you* were offering anything else," I said. "Alive, I can always turn myself around, right? Go to rehab, some twelve-step thing?"

Venna's eyes turned black. "I've heard this excuse from others," she said. "Most recently from Lewis, as he violated our most basic trust. There will be an accounting, when this is done. No Djinn—not even our younger cousins—will be imprisoned by your kind again. Expedience is not excuse."

I shrugged. "So? Are we throwing down, MiniMe, or are we done now? Because I don't really think even you can stop me now. Or that you're allowed to try." Venna's presence was waking a kind of utterly unsettling hunger inside me; she had so much *power,* and I had a bottomless appetite for it. If she fought me, she'd expend power.

If she lost, I could take it all.

Venna said, "There is only one person who can save this ship. You, Joanne. If you wish."

"Well, I don't. I'm taking it to meet Bad Bob, and what happens from there doesn't really concern me."

Cherise covered her mouth with both hands, appalled and shocked. That was funny. Had she really not seen that coming?

"They won't allow you to do this so easily. They'll fight," Venna said. It sounded like she was analyzing the next move in a Grand Masters chess game.

"Hope so," I said, and slid off the bed to stretch, yawn, and shake my hair back over my shoulders. "Fun time's over, girls. I need to do some work now, so I'm going. You can either move out of the way, or I can walk over your bleeding corpses. That's metaphorical for you, Venna, but you get the point."

Neither of them moved. Cherise looked uncertainly

at Venna, but for the little girl Djinn I was the only thing in the world holding her focus.

I walked right up to her. She looked up into my eyes with eerie, ancient eyes, and then moved out of my way.

"You can't do this," Cherise whispered.

I used a casual punch of power to slam her across the room, into a wall, and she tumbled limply to the floor.

Bleeding.

"You're not completely his," Venna said, as I opened the cabin door. I looked back. She was standing in the same place, still calm and self-contained. "Do you want to know how I know?"

"Do tell." I drummed my fingernails on the wood of the door impatiently.

Venna's gaze flicked to Cherise, and then back. "You didn't keep your threat. She's bleeding. She isn't dead."

"Yet," I said. "I thought that as a Djinn you'd understand the importance of timing."

Chapter Eight

As I sat in Arpeggio's deserted bar-cum-breakfast-nook, munched my command-ordered bagel and light cream cheese, and sipped coffee, I wondered what Cherise would report to Lewis—assuming Lewis was still in any shape to be reported to. Nobody bothered me, not even other Wardens.

The few fellow diners who'd endured my presence got up and left, quickly, when Venna appeared in the middle of the room, clearly and utterly alien in the way she looked and moved. She sat opposite me at the polished wooden table, a glass of orange juice in front of her, and stared at me with impassive intensity.

"I thought we were done," I said. I sipped my coffee. It was bitter, dark, and exactly what I needed.

"For the sake of what you were, I thought I would try once more." That was irritatingly superior.

"You can run back and tell Lewis that I'm done with pretending to care about every little life that stubs its toe, every goddamn kitten up a tree. I've spent my life bleeding for humans. I've died for them. Enough. If that makes me evil, then fine. I am."

Venna said nothing. She drank her juice like a little girl, two hands wrapped around the glass for stability, and it left her with a faint orange ring around her lips that she tried to lick off before wiping it away. "Cherise is right," she said. "You are more like us than them now."

"Let me sum that up with *ewwwwww.*"

She stared at her empty juice glass. It filled up, welling from the bottom of the glass. She emptied it again.

"Was that supposed to be a metaphor? Sorry. Don't get it." I ate the last bite of my bagel and pushed my chair back to stand as I swigged the dregs of my coffee. "Bother me again, and I'll seriously inconvenience you." From the pulse of power inside me, it was entirely possible that I could really hurt her.

"You didn't ask," she said.

"Ask what?"

"Anything. Why the staff of this ship are still willing to make your bagels when their world is crumbling around them." Venna shrugged again. "You don't ask anything, because you don't care anymore. It means nothing to you. It's very Djinn."

"I'm not Djinn."

"No," she agreed. "You're becoming something else. It's—interesting."

"But not good."

"No. Not good at all. Not for anyone, really."

I didn't care. Some part of me could not *wait* to blow past these conventional, stupid rules.

And some tiny, whispering part of me was mourning that very thing.

"I won't see you again," Venna said. "Not until this is over. I'm sorry. I liked you. It would have been better if I'd killed you."

I put my hands flat on the table. "So? Do it now."

"I can't," she said, which was surprisingly honest. "And I won't. That's for your own to do, not me."

She finished another half glass of OJ, then misted away without another word.

I thought she looked a little grave, and a little sad.

I got up and stiff-armed the door out onto the promenade.

The *Grand Paradise* had left the storm behind during the night, although it was following us like a pit bull on a leash, obedient to my every wish.

The ship cut a rapid, hissing passage through the still-high waves, making for the destination I'd identified. *Home,* part of me said. Not the best part.

Sunlight flooded the promenade, glittering on drops of spray, turning the place into a gallery of diamonds. Watertight doors had opened all up and down the length of the ship. Wardens who'd been gearing up for the fight of the century, or at least the storm of the century, were left wondering what to do. I didn't seem to be much of a threat, standing at the railing and enjoying the day.

Nothing but sun and fresh wind now. It was a beautiful morning.

I felt the winds shift. *Gravity* shift, at least on the aetheric level. A heavyweight had arrived.

When I looked over my shoulder, I saw that Lewis had made his way out onto the deck. Behind him was the Warden army—faces I knew and some I outright hated. *Ah, good.* Finally, we were at the showdown. Time to rumble.

I turned to face them.

"You're getting off the ship," Lewis told me. "I'm sorry, Jo."

"Oh no. Mutiny! Whatever shall I do?" I put the back of my hand dramatically to my forehead. "Wait. I know. Kill you."

He didn't look especially petrified. Lewis had healed

up some overnight—faster than I'd have thought, but he'd probably had tons of Earth Warden help to accelerate the process. He looked badass and focused, and whereas I was clean, scrubbed, and dressed for sexy success, he hadn't shaved, showered, slept, or changed clothes.

I was ahead on style points, but I wasn't counting the Wardens out. Not yet.

"You can't win this," Lewis said. "Don't push me, Jo. I'm telling you the truth: You can't."

He sounded confident, but then, Lewis always did sound confident when it came to crunch time.

I felt the whispers of wind tease my hair, and the storm—my own personal pet now—yawned and began to spin its engine harder, preparing for battle.

"You going to talk, or are you going to fight?" I asked. "Because the alternative is hate sex, and I'm kind of over you right now." I noted, on a highly academic level, that I was starting to sound more and more like Bad Bob, even to the ironic dark twist in my tone.

Lewis took a step toward me. Just one. But I felt my skin tighten, and something inside me turned silent and watchful, all humor gone.

"You're talking a good game, but I'm still waiting for you to back it up."

I laughed. "Are you *begging* me to kill you? Seriously? Tactics, man. Look into it."

"No," he said softly. "I'm telling you that deep inside, there's a part of you that's still protected. Still fighting. If there weren't, you'd be walking around this ship like the incarnation of Kali, destroying everything crossing your path. Think about it. You haven't killed anybody. And what is your master evil plan? You're taking us to Bad Bob. That's where we wanted to go."

I froze, staring at him. It was true. I'd lashed out at him, but I hadn't killed him. Hadn't killed anyone, yet. Lots of talk, no action.

And he was right, something inside me had convinced me that the ship *should* be taken to Bad Bob ... but it was the old Joanne, struggling to push me in the direction she considered right.

I opened my right hand, and a tiny pearl of light formed, flickered, and grew, expanding into a white-hot ball.

"Talk's over," I said. "It's time to play."

I threw the ball of fire into the middle of them. Lewis hit it with a blast of cold air along the way, shrinking it, and then casually batted it out over the railing when it reached him. "Going to have to play harder than that."

I was aware that while my attention was fixed on Lewis, the other Wardens were trying to get to me. Not physically, but the Earth Wardens were messing with my body chemistry. All kinds of ways the human engine can go wonky—they weren't trying to give me cancer, but they were trying to crash my blood sugar, give me blinding headaches, and disrupt nerve impulses.

I snapped a lightning bolt down. One of the Weather Wardens stepped out and flung up both hands, intercepting the thick, ropy stream of energy and deflecting it, but it left her limp and moaning on the deck, with a black burned patch on the wood that stretched a dozen feet around her in a blast pattern.

I felt an odd tug at my leg and looked down. The decking was growing green shoots, and they were twining up my leg in thick, twisted strands. I hissed in frustration and snapped the plant off at the root, but while I was occupied with that, more fast-growing tendrils erupted up around me, anchoring me in place. It was stupidly annoying, and I finally summoned up a pulse of fire to burn them away from me.

Then I pushed the wave of flame out at the Wardens.

A Fire Warden named Freddy Pierce stepped out and shoved the attack back at me. Then, surprising me, he rushed *through* the flame and hit me in a low tackle. As attacks went, it wasn't subtle, but it caught me completely off guard, and the man was stronger than he looked. I slammed down on my back, and Freddy flipped me over and held me down with one sharp knee digging into my spine.

"Come on," Lewis said, and stepped through the guttering flames to stand over me. His voice was low, kind, and a little sad. "You're not going to kill us. You won't, Jo. And that makes things tougher, because I can't kill *you* if I know you're still in there somewhere."

I laughed and turned my cheek to one side, staring up at him through a mask of tumbling hair. "Do you really think so?" I asked, and blew Freddy off my back.

I blew him *off the ship*.

Into the water.

Then I lunged up, wrapped my hands around Lewis's throat, and called fire. It wrapped around me in a dripping mantle, and Lewis's clothes ignited instantly. He controlled that, but I was attacking him on multiple fronts; while he was putting out the flames, I was turning his breath toxic in his lungs, turning his blood to sludge in his veins. Earth Wardens knew a million painful ways to kill, and it was hard to fight, especially when you were on fire.

But Lewis managed, somehow. He batted me away, sending me reeling back to crash against a metal rail. Somewhere out in the churning iron gray sea, Freddy—

a Fire Warden, with no power over either the water or the living things in it—yelled for help with panic in his voice. Something about sharks.

As Lewis staggered and fell, the bottle that held David's soul entrapped fell out of his pocket and skittered across the deck. I reached out for it.

Cherise got to it first.

She backed up, fast, both hands clenched around the small glass form. She pulled it in to her chest.

The Wardens closed ranks between her and me.

"Back off," Kevin said, pushing his way to the front—and Cherise.

"*You* back off," I snapped. "I saved your life, you rancid little murderer. You owe me."

"I owe Joanne," he said. "I don't know who the fuck you are, and I don't care. You make a move against Cherise and—"

"And what?" I asked, and took a step forward. "You'll cut me? Oh, shut up. Get out of my way if you want to live."

Venna misted into place next to him. She didn't speak. She didn't have to. I got the message well enough.

"I've fought you before," I said.

"You lost," she pointed out. "The poisoned water may sustain you, but it's still poisoned. Don't make the mistake of thinking you're my equal. Ever."

"*Boo*yah, bitch," Kevin said. Someone else, with more sense and better self-preservation instincts, muttered for him to shut up.

"I'm going to kill you all," I said. I meant it. I felt it coming, a kind of inevitable darkness. "I have to." I was still just a little sorry about that, but it really was necessary. Lewis had been right that somewhere deep inside me, the old Joanne was still struggling—poisoning my thoughts, driving my actions.

No more.

I flung my arms wide, felt the storm roar and answer, and shouted, *"Now!"*

The Djinn Rahel erupted from out of the ocean.

No, *not* Rahel—Rahel as commanded by her master, Bad Bob, the Black Warden.

Rahel was as large as the cruise ship. Her hair was a nest of writhing eels. Her face was distorted, pointed into an extreme triangle, and her mouth was full of rows of teeth. She was dressed in rags and weeds and pearls and fish scales, and in both hands she held swords as long as the hull of the ship.

"Oh, Christ," someone said, appalled, and then the screaming started. Not among the Wardens, who instantly began pulling up every defense they had.

It really wasn't going to do them any good at all.

Venna, pretty and fresh in a sparkly pink shirt with a unicorn on it, jumped flat-footed from the deck to balance on the railing. The storm winds hit her like the wave front of an explosive blast, blowing her hair back in a rippling blond flag, but she was absolutely steady as she balanced. Rahel saw her, and that shark-toothed mouth gaped in a menacing smile.

Venna executed a perfect dive, and before she hit the waves, she'd changed into something else, something vast and dark that swam straight at the terrifying sea-hag that Rahel had become.

Rahel's shark teeth parted on a shriek, and she was yanked down under the waves. The *Grand Paradise* rocked violently as the water churned, and the storm winds lashed the ship in swirling gusts.

Rahel wasn't the attack, of course. Just a diversion, something to help get attention away from me. While the Wardens were focused on the water, I concentrated on the metal of the ship's hull, below the water line.

Metal bent and screamed, and the entire ship *twisted* as if it had been T-boned. It rolled starboard, then over-corrected to port, sending people flying and rolling and screaming.

Rahel broke the surface of the water and was yanked under again. The battle continued, not that it mattered to anyone on the ship anymore.

I could feel the damage.

It wasn't containable.

I smiled.

Lewis left the deck in a sudden burst and went airborne—a trick that few Weather Wardens could manage under stress, even at full power. *Formidable,* I thought, filing it away for future reference.

Then something hit us hard on the side, and the ship, already dying, rolled all the way over.

Disaster can be oddly beautiful. It seems to happen in slow motion, like ballet, and if your emotions aren't involved, then it's only input.

All I was feeling, as the ship died around me, was a quiet kind of satisfaction.

It took about ten seconds for the *Grand Paradise* to capsize, and then I was in the water, floating away from the ship. It looked exactly like it had ten seconds before, only now it was upside down and wreathed in so many cascading bubbles that it was like some wild New Year's Eve party gone badly wrong.

There was a ripped section of hull below the waterline, extending nearly half the length of the ship. I could see inside to hallways, storerooms, and the complicated mechanics of what was probably the engineering section.

I had done that. Just me.

I saw people flailing amid the strangely serene wreckage of what had been our only salvation out here in the middle of this watery desert.

Rahel's massive sea-monster body dived past me, driven by a tail that was as much eel as mermaid, and disappeared into the gloomy depths. She was followed by a pink, sparkle-skinned unicorn with eyes of fire, gills, and flippers instead of legs. Its horn was shimmering crystal, lighting up the dark as it shot away in pursuit of Rahel.

The water was shockingly cold, or at least that was my impression. I instinctively reached for power and warmed myself, oblivious to the screaming people bobbing around me in the waves. Weather Wardens were quickly reacting, encasing people in protective bubbles and popping them to the surface if they'd been unlucky enough to end up sucking sea. I supposed they'd be all about saving those who were trapped, too.

I felt the suction of water rushing into the ship.

Rahel and Venna broke the surface again, two giants now screaming and ripping at each other, far less human than I'd have ever imagined; Venna had given up her My Little Pony sparkles and was fish-belly white now, and Rahel's body was a dark mesh of scales and teeth, too confusing to identify individual features.

Venna drove Rahel back under the surface again, and bubbles geysered in their wake.

Lewis rose out of the water. Levitated, like a freaking superhero, dripping gallons of seawater.

"Everybody, move close together!" he yelled. "Grab on to each other. Kevin, you're in charge. Count noses!"

The noses were still bobbing to the surface, like corks. Kevin swam to the center of the chaos and forcibly dragged people to form the first tight layer of the circle, then ducked beneath them to form up the next ring, and the next. "Hold on to each other!" he yelled. "Just like you're in a huddle! And keep kicking!" Now the survivors looked like a giant skydiving stunt, concentric rings of people floating with their arms around each other. Scared, sure, but human contact helped, especially for those who couldn't swim or were too terrified to remember how.

I bobbed in place, watching them for a moment, and then I called sharks.

Lewis felt the pulse traveling out through the water, and he knew what it meant. I saw his head snap around, his eyes widen, and the shock and horror on his face set up a warm, liquid glow deep inside me.

"Now I've got your attention," I said. "Don't I?" There weren't enough Earth Wardens to control big predators like sharks, not if they had to be focused on not drowning at the same time. The Fire and Weather Wardens would be completely vulnerable.

There were thousands of sharks out there. *Thousands.*

And now they turned and headed our way, drawn by an imaginary smell of blood in the water.

Something in Lewis's face changed. He'd made a decision, not one he liked. I wondered what it was.

Between the two of us, a vividly painted craft suddenly erupted through the waves. It was reflective yellow, bright as a traffic sign, and it was completely enclosed, sleek as a science fiction submarine.

A lifeboat.

More of them were popping up now, all around the

Wardens. Lewis—or Venna—had broken them free of the sinking wreck. "Ladders at the back!" Lewis yelled. "Last row of the circle boards first! Each one of these will take about forty people. Wardens, I want a minimum of three of you per boat, and try to evenly distribute the powers!"

The railings around the ship were studded with these strange little craft—fiberglass, highly buoyant, with diesel engines and very little chance of being swamped even in high seas. I assumed they'd have life vests and provisions inside.

It was a race to see if he could get the Wardens into the boats before my sharks arrived for their feast. Lewis correctly deployed his forces, keeping the Earth Wardens focused on repelling attacking predators as the Fire and Weather Wardens, staff, and crew boarded their ships. Then he evacuated the last of them.

I bobbed in the pounding waves, cold and shivering, watching.

The *Grand Paradise,* that floating castle, rolled like a dying whale, heeling in the direction of its fatal wound, and then the stern rose at a ninety-degree angle out of the water, exposing the massive propulsion pods and steering mechanisms. I could see, very briefly, the entertainment area of the ship that I'd never had time to visit—the rock-climbing wall, the pools, the spas.

And then it all slipped beneath the waves with a deep, gurgling death groan, churning foam and debris, and was gone in less than a minute.

I put my face beneath the water and watched its freefall descent into the dark, and laughed, because even if the Wardens survived all this, that was going to be one *hell* of a security deposit problem.

I was still laughing when something suddenly lunged

up from the depths at me. I had one flash of a second to recognize the gaping maw, the dead eyes.

Shark.

Sometimes, no matter who you are, or how powerful, Mother Nature still wins.

I floated on my back, bouncing on the churning waves, watching clouds fly in black, menacing swoops overhead. My storm circled in thwarted, anxious fury.

I was bleeding badly, and I couldn't seem to stop it. I'd blown the shark into bloody meat, but too late; it had gouged a giant chunk from my thigh, and although I'd shut down the pain receptors, I knew how bad it was. The power I had at my command wasn't meant to heal. It was meant to destroy.

Maybe it was a hallucination, but I could have sworn Bad Bob was standing on the wave-tops, looking down at me. He was wearing that same crappy, loud Hawaiian shirt, and his thin white hair blew in the same wind that blew spume from the water into my mouth as I struggled for air.

"What is it the kids today say, Jo? Epic fail?" He crouched down next to me. I could see the water rippling over his toes, but he could have been standing on concrete, while my struggles to stay afloat were getting weaker and weaker. "I think you let this happen. I think you were so damn guilty, you thought a shark bite was what you deserved."

"Fuck you," I whispered, and coughed. God, I hated him. The darkness inside me had filled me to bursting, and I needed to gag it out before it choked me. "I killed the ship for you."

"Yes, you did. Not a bad job. But you let the lifeboats survive. That's a whole lot less impressive."

I blinked away burning salt in my eyes. "Help me."

"Wait, what was the pithy phrase you just used? *Fuck you,* Jo. You kill Lewis Orwell for me. Then we'll talk about how I can help you." He smirked down at me, his pale eyes as vicious and shallow as those of the shark that had come after me. "Consider it the fairness doctrine in action."

And with that, his image turned into a black mist and blew away.

But I didn't think he'd ever really been there anyway.

There were more sharks coming. I'd drawn them here, and now there really was blood in the water—mine. My wounds were pumping out more all the time, and the shark I'd destroyed was functioning as bait too. The next one to arrive wouldn't be so tentative. He'd just rip me in half.

I wondered if it was shock that was making me so fatalistic about that.

The lifeboats were all heading off to the horizon now.

All except one, which peeled off and turned back.

I was unconscious before it arrived.

I woke up lying on the floor of the lifeboat, with two Earth Wardens healing up my bites as best they could.

It hurt.

It hurt a *lot.*

Cherise, Kevin, Cho Chu Wing, and the remaining crew were on this lifeboat, as well as the *Grand Paradise*'s Captain Miller, a sturdy gentleman who retained his military dignity despite his waterlogged uniform. He didn't say much. I didn't suppose he was regretting not going down with his ship, but maybe he was thinking about all the inevitable paperwork.

Or, if he knew I was responsible, he was thinking about finishing up what the sharks had left undone.

"We need to split up the boats," Lewis was telling the captain as I drifted in, out, and around consciousness. "We're like ducks in a shooting gallery out here on the open water."

The captain nodded, but not as if he really understood or cared. I didn't think he cared about much anymore. "I've already sent out distress calls," he said. "Six freighters are heading our way, including a Saudi tanker. They'll start rendezvousing with the other lifeboats within the hour."

Lewis nodded and walked over to take a seat near me. The benches were fiberglass, with cushions that doubled as flotation devices. Among the supplies already broken out were insulating blankets, one of which was already wrapped around my damp, shivering body, and boxed drinks. They were trying to coax me to drink apple juice, but I couldn't choke anything down. Not yet.

I'd learned a startling new lesson: no matter how badass you think you are, having a shark latch on to your body and break a piece of you away will put a dent in your self-confidence.

Cherise was playing Red Cross nurse; she draped a blanket over Lewis's damp shoulders and handed him a juice box, which he mechanically sipped as he stared down at me.

"What?" I asked, and tried to smile. "You never saw somebody trying to kill you get their ass kicked before? Because I know you have."

No answer.

"You want some advice? Pull the Wardens together. If you split them up between the rescue boats, you're screwed."

"Thanks for the tip," he said. "Wardens stay on the boats. I want them protected in case you and Bad Bob decide to play Battleship."

I almost managed a shrug. "Hazards of the sea. They all know what could happen."

"Yeah," he agreed. "I'm sure that'll be a great comfort to their kids back home. I want Wardens behind us, guarding our retreat, as well as with us, guarding our asses up close. You got a problem with that, take it up with—oh, nobody, because at this point, you've got nobody." He raised his head and fixed me with red-rimmed, fiercely focused eyes. "What am I supposed to do with you?"

A week ago, if he'd asked that question, it would have been with an undertone of longing and some heavily suppressed fantasies involving schoolgirl uniforms. Not now. He was looking at me like I'd looked at the shark that had bitten me.

"I can still get you to Bad Bob," I said. "If you want."

"I can't trust you."

I winced and closed my eyes as one of the Earth Wardens laying hands on me did something particularly painful. "I'm serious. I will take you to Bad Bob. I need to get there myself."

"Why?"

I opened my eyes and locked stares with him. "Because he left me to die in the ocean and get eaten by sharks. Because you came back."

"Bullshit."

I blinked.

"Don't tell me you've had a change of heart. I can see you didn't. You're just pissed that he didn't keep his promises to you. The enemy of my enemy is not my friend."

I closed my eyes. I was too tired, too hurt, and too sick to care about his philosophy right now, and the darkness inside me _ached_, impatient with my body's weaknesses. Soon I wouldn't be vulnerable. Soon I'd be like the storm itself—unstoppable, unfeeling, a force of nature.

Lewis had chosen his healers well. They did their job, whether they wanted to or not. It took time, and I slept in between the exhausting bouts. I could feel the life-boat moving, but I no longer cared where it was going. It didn't matter. The storm would follow me, pouring power into me, filling me with darkness.

When I woke up, _really_ woke up, the Wardens had finished their work.

I was healed.

I looked at my jeans, which had a ragged hole ripped most of the way through them, and beneath the bloody cloth, my leg was mostly there. Scarred, yes, but it would heal. The new muscle and flesh felt weirdly tender.

I looked up and saw them all watching me.

"Thanks," I said, and tried to stand. It wasn't as hard as I'd expected. I actually felt fairly good. Better, as the storm above us purred and rained down its darkness into me, reminding me who I was. What I wanted.

Lewis was right not to trust me, but I knew I didn't need to tell him that.

"Jo," he said, "sit down."

I didn't. I looked at him. There was a tingle of fire in my fingers, and as I rubbed them together, I saw sparks jumping. "Time to change course," I said. "I'm taking the boat. The rest of you—you can either come along and shut up or I can leave you behind. In pieces."

He took in a deep, resigned breath. "I didn't save you just to fight you."

"No, you saved me because your delicate conscience

couldn't stand thinking about me getting ripped apart by sharks," I said. "Your mistake, man. Not mine."

"You don't want to do this."

I smiled. And he saw that I really, really did.

Kevin wasn't surprised. He was grimly staring at me with a bleak expression, as if he'd known it all along. *Back at ya, punk.*

"You're not going to hurt anybody else," Lewis said. "I'm not going to let you."

That made me want to prove him wrong. "We knew this was coming," I said. "So go on. Try and stop me. It's time for the lightning round, Lewis. Go for the actual lightning. It's a small, enclosed space, but some of them may not die right off. The sepsis from the burns, that'll probably kill them in the end."

He didn't move. "Don't make me. Please, I'm asking you, don't."

I called fire in my hand.

Lewis grabbed my arm, but instead of fighting me power for power, as I'd expected, he yanked me close, pinning me against his body. Putting my palm directly against his chest.

"Please," he said. There were tears in his eyes. "Jo, I know you're in there somewhere. *Please stop.*"

"No," I said, and let the fire go. It flamed through his shirt, charred his flesh.

And I felt *nothing.*

Lewis let out a soft, agonized moan, but he didn't let me go.

"I'll kill you," I growled, and I meant it. "Every one of you if I have to. But I'm taking this ship."

"No." Lewis grabbed my face in his hands and—kissed me. There was desperation in it, and fury, and pain, and anguish . . .

... and death.

I felt something go very, very wrong in my brain.

Click.

Lights going out. A burst of pain, of surprise, of *knowledge* ...

Fail-safe. He'd put a fail-safe in my brain and he'd made me forget about it and now I'd forced him to trigger it, at long last.

"You're not taking the ship," Lewis whispered. I could hear him, and I could feel the fading sensation of his lips against mine. A benediction into the dark. "Good-bye, Jo. God, I loved you."

Pain exploded through my nerves like flares. I couldn't move, couldn't blink, couldn't take a breath. *Not fair, this shouldn't hurt, death should be quick* ... The fire sank deeper, bone-deep, as if my internal organs were charring and baking.

All the pain was on the inside, shimmering like lava. On the outside, I remained limp. Apparently, already gone.

What was keeping me here?

Lewis lowered me to the deck. I could sense what he was feeling. He was full of horror and guilt for what he'd done to me, even though he'd known that it was necessary. It was toxic in its intensity, truly shocking. I didn't know how he could live with it.

Or if he could.

In the breathless silence, Cherise's voice sounded very small. "What did you do to her?"

"I killed her," Lewis said, and closed my eyes. I felt tears slide down my temples as he did—could the dead cry?—and felt his fingertips brush across my forehead in the old familiar gesture. "I *had* to kill her." It sounded like he was trying to convince himself of that.

Nobody spoke. Cherise pulled in a deep, trembling breath, then let it out in a rush. "You're lying. She's not *dead*. No way. Not Jo."

One of the Earth Wardens who'd just wasted all that time and effort on healing me knelt down and pressed cool fingers to my neck, then bent over to listen to my chest. He checked my eyes, which were fixed and out of focus.

"She's gone," he said. "Christ, Lewis."

"She's not *gone*," Cherise insisted. There was a rising tide of alarm in her voice. The river Denial, flooding its banks. "She can't be *gone*. Check her again."

"Cherise—" Kevin tried to head her off.

"No! Check her again!"

They did. One of the other Wardens even tried reviving me—pumping my chest, breathing for me.

My body was an inert lump of clay, and inside it my mind was shrieking, trapped and unable to get free.

"She's gone," Lewis repeated again dully, with a hitch of agony in his voice. He thought I was dead, I could feel that. Whatever was anchoring me here, in this dying shell, was something he couldn't touch. "We have to let David say good-bye."

"You can't do that, man. He'll kill you," Kevin said. He sounded absolutely sure of it. "No. I'm not letting David anywhere near this. There's no way he won't rip us all into meat for doing this to her."

"Give me the bottle."

"*No.*"

"I'm not going to ask again. *Give it to me.*"

"No!"

There was some kind of struggle, and then Kevin cursed in an unsteady whisper. Cherise was weeping as if her heart was breaking. From everyone else in the small boat came silence, rapid breathing, waves of distress and fear.

God, please, let me go, I begged. My brain should have been off by now, letting me escape into the comfortable dark, but instead I could feel my nerves slowly dying, my cells screaming for oxygen. Nothing I could do to stop it, either.

I was feeling my body die on a cellular level. God, would I be around for the rest of it? Feeling the dead cells turn into sludge and soup? *Decomposing?*

I didn't want to be trapped in this body as it slowly decayed, with no hope of release or rescue.

I realized, very slowly, that what was binding me here was one tiny thread of silver, stretching through the navel of my body and out through the aetheric.

David was holding me here, but he couldn't save me. His power wasn't mine to touch, and it wasn't his, either, not as long as someone else held his bottle and he was trapped inside it.

"Lewis—don't do this, man," Kevin said. I'd never heard that tone in his voice before, so pleading. "I'm begging you. Don't. It's not fucking *fair.*"

"I'm not doing it because it's fair," Lewis said. "I have to do it because it's right. It doesn't matter how long we wait; when we let him out of that bottle, his grief will be exactly the same. So let him out now. Please."

The darkness that Bad Bob had put inside of me battered at the prison of my dead body, fighting to reactivate it. To stay alive.

Without the energy of my body sustaining the darkness, it was growing weaker. Dying along with me.

I felt a whisper of power scent the air as the cap came off of David's prison. I felt him battering furiously at the glass, trying to shatter his way free.

Oh, you fool, Lewis. He'll destroy you.

"David," Lewis said. "Come out."

Wind blasted through the boat, pinning people against the walls, and a wild-eyed angel dropped out of heaven to gather me in his arms.

The sound that came out of him was some horrible cross between a scream and a growl—inhuman, furious, insane with grief. I couldn't move. I couldn't control my eyes to focus on his face, so his expression was mercifully blurred.

Suddenly, I fclt the pressure of darkness inside me ease. Bad Bob had lost interest in me. Dead, I was of no use to him, none at all. The thick, toxic sludge of power inside me began to bleed away.

But it wasn't gone. Not yet.

Lewis said, "David, please understand. You can't bring her back. Not this time."

David's voice was a raw, bloody scream. *"She's not gone!"*

He could touch me. See me. Feel my ghostly presence. He hugged my limp form to his chest and rocked back and forth, his face hidden in my hair.

"Let me save her," he whispered. *"Order me to save her."*

I felt Lewis shudder. "No. David, you have to let her go. She's damaged. She can't fight him off anymore. It's time to let her go." He paused, and then said, with absolute precision, "I'm ordering you to let her die, David."

The silence in the boat was as deep as the ocean. So was the sense of pressure. Even my dead flesh could feel it.

"I'll kill you for this," David said. There was nothing in his voice—no emotion, no hate, no grief. Nothing but simple declaration of intent. "I'll rip you apart one cell at a time, and you'll live a thousand years through the pain. I might even let you scream, if you beg me."

He was utterly serious. He would torture Lewis. He'd do it with the kind of cold distance that the Djinn reserved for those they truly, deeply, madly hated.

He'd do it for me.

"Listen to me," Lewis said, and if he was afraid, it didn't show in his voice. "I'm ordering you not to save her. I'm ordering you to cut the cord and *let her go.*"

"Well, that's a paradox," David said. He still sounded eerily calm, almost relaxed. "Because if I let her go, it destroys the vow that binds me to the bottle, and that means I'm free. Free to pull you apart, Lewis. Free to order the brutal, screaming death of every last one of your kind. Do you really think I won't?" There was madness in him, I realized. Terrible, burning madness, and Kevin was right—letting David free was a death sentence for Lewis. Not just for him, though. For the Wardens. For *everyone.*

In this moment, David was a bigger threat to humanity than anything Bad Bob had ever dreamed.

I didn't want to linger like this. I wanted to tell him it was all right, that Lewis had done it for a reason, a good one, and I didn't really mind. The darkness was dripping out of me in an invisible stain on the deck. I felt . . . clear, at last. Finally, myself again.

I couldn't bring myself back to life; it violated all the laws of the universe. All I could do, now that I was clear of Bad Bob's influence again, was choose to die. But if I did that, if I severed the cord holding me and David together, the result would be the same; he'd be lost, and alone, and mad with fury and grief.

I could feel Lewis working all of that out, and realizing that he was in a trap he couldn't escape.

Just like David.

"Let me have her," David said. "Let me have her and I swear I will not harm you."

Lewis's voice came back stripped raw. Bloody. "You think I'm afraid of *that*?" He stopped and took a deep breath. "She's too dangerous. *You know that.*"

"No," David said softly. "I don't know it. You fear it. There's a difference. Let me have her, or I will teach you fear. *All of you.* You think you've suffered at the hands of the Djinn? *You have no concept of how much I can do to you.*"

Lewis knew the minutes were ticking away, and after a certain point, life wouldn't return to the decomposing tissues of my body. Not any kind of life I'd want to have, anyway.

He also knew that forcing David to kill me was even worse.

"Do it," Lewis said. "Save her."

Before the words were out of his mouth, David acted. A silver cascade of power flooded me, pounded on my heart, drowned my brain. This was the pure white light of the Djinn, bathing me from the inside out. And where it met the fading black tangle of Bad Bob's tattoo . . .

. . . the silver light went out.

There was still a deadly core there, hiding inside me. Under the skin. Not even death had taken it away.

I took in a convulsive breath and sat bolt upright, still held in David's arms, and then I relaxed against him, even through the pain. My eyes spilled over with tears of agony, liquid screams that were the only thing I had to give voice to what was raging inside.

If I couldn't come back all the way, come back *clean*, I didn't want to come back at all.

I shuddered, and my eyes rolled back in my head, and

for a precious moment I blacked out as my nervous system simply refused to conduct any more pain.

I returned to consciousness slowly, with the distant awareness of pain but unable to feel it directly. My back was numb again, all the way down to midway on my thighs. I couldn't feel the back of my head, either. Or the tops of my shoulders.

Out of nowhere, I felt the soft press of lips against mine. I felt the exhale of David's trembling sigh. I felt the burning drops of his tears on my face. "That's all I can do," he said. "Jo. Please. Come back to me."

I blinked, and my eyes slowly focused on his.

"It's all right," I whispered. It wasn't. I felt sick and wrong, and the light seemed too bright for my eyes. "I'm so sorry."

David's eyes widened. Instead of bright copper sparks dancing in them, there was ash, as if something inside him had burned itself out. "Nothing to be sorry for," he said. "You saved their lives. If they'd let you die . . ."

The look he gave Lewis was utterly black with fury. I couldn't imagine being on the receiving end of that much hatred. David really *wanted* to kill him, slowly and horribly. Even now, I felt the conviction of that echoing inside him.

I wound my fist in David's shirt, pulling back his attention. "No," I said. "Don't you dare. Don't use me as an excuse." My voice was a parody of its usual tones, and I had no doubt he could see the sincere fright and dread in my eyes. "No matter what happens. Promise me. He did that for a *reason.*"

He lifted a hand and traced the line of my cheekbone, light as a breath. "No."

"Promise me, David."

"No."

"Promise me."

This time he said nothing at all. He was serious about this. Very damn serious indeed.

Lewis was still holding David's bottle. Now, he gestured to Kevin and handed it over. As Kevin's fingers closed over the glass, David's body shattered into mist and re-formed.

Taking on the appearance imposed by his new master.

As he re-formed, I saw the differences, not the similarities: His hands were too broad. The arms were too muscular, and stained with colorful flaming skull tattoos. His jeans acquired leather motorcycle chaps, and his shirt vanished to reveal a broad, muscular chest beneath a fringed leather jacket.

His head was shaved.

The only things about him that didn't really change was his face, and his eyes. Those remained his.

Those remained the ones that I knew.

Kevin cleared his throat. "Okay, order number one, you will not kill, or allow to be killed, any Warden not actively fighting with Bad Bob Biringanine in the current war. That includes Lewis. Order number two, you will not kill any human, or allow one to be killed, for any reason, unless saving them would put more people at risk. Three—" He sighed. "Especially don't kill me, yo. And get back in the bottle."

David took all that without a flicker, and then he was gone. His eyes were the last thing to leave, and they never wavered from mine.

I felt sick down to my soul. He had come so close, so close to doing worse than I could imagine . . . and for me.

Just for me.

"So what now?" I asked Lewis. My voice sounded

scratchy and uncertain. I felt stretched as thin as rice paper, and just as fragile.

Lewis slid down to a sitting position and rested his head in both hands. "I don't know," he said. "He's put blocks around the mark to keep you from being taken over, but it won't be enough, not for long. This thing is vicious, Jo. It's fatal. We're back where we started, and I think you know I can't let that stand."

My hands were shaking. I pressed them down on my thighs. "I'm listening."

"I need you to get off the boat," he said. "I need you to let us leave you behind."

In the open water.

With the sharks.

I swallowed hard and didn't answer. I was too busy reliving what that had felt like—the teeth hot in my flesh, pieces of me coming off.

Blood.

Lewis didn't blink. "I'm taking everyone else to land-fall. I need you to go on, alone."

"Alone," I repeated, because I could *not* have heard him right. "You want me to go after Bad Bob all by my-self. Swimming. Through shark-infested seas. Are you fucking *insane*?"

He hated himself. I could see the loathing, but I could also see the cold steel underneath it. He knew what he had to do, and he wasn't afraid to do it.

He never was. I loved that about him, and I hated it, too.

"I can't keep you here," he said. "You're a bomb. Sooner or later, you're going to go off, and I can't risk what you're going to do. If you want to save yourself, you need to do it alone."

"Don't feed me crap and tell me it's chocolate," I said.

"I'm, what? A Trojan horse? Bait? Your own personal suicide bomber?"

"You're what you need to be. The way you always are." He reached over and smoothed a hand down my tangled, damp hair. His long fingers felt cool and strange on my skin. "The hardest thing I've ever had to do was kill you. Don't make me do it again. I'm already going to die for it; we both know that. He's never going to forget."

I leaned into the comfort of his touch, closed my eyes, and said, "David will forgive you. Eventually."

"No, I really don't think so." He kissed my forehead. "Especially after I do this."

I felt his emotion spill into me, Earth Warden to Earth Warden—complicated waves of painful guilt, staggering responsibility, and love. So much love it hurt. He shouldn't love me so much. He knew I couldn't love him in the same way.

I started to tell him that, once and for all, but he touched my lips with his thumb. "I know," he murmured. "I just wanted you to remember it. One way or another, this is good-bye, Jo. We're not going to step in the same river twice."

Lewis stood up and spun the hatch. It was a sliding door at the top of the craft, and climbing the steps to get up to it seemed like the march to the gallows.

Lewis held my hand to keep me steady.

I emerged into bright sunlight, blinded by the glitter of the whitecaps and the endless roll of the ocean. By the reflective yellow surface of the fiberglass hull. The storm hung sullenly in the distance, a vast black curtain rippling with wind and power and fury. It couldn't reach me now, but it would follow.

It had to. It was still keyed to the power locked into Bad Bob's mark.

I looked back down as I stripped off the blanket and handed it to Lewis. "Thanks for the apple juice," I said. "The beer's on you if I live."

He didn't smile. There was darkness as thick as the storm hanging around him; his aura was shot through with it.

"Tell David—" I said, and couldn't think of anything to say that David wouldn't already know. "Tell him I'll see him soon." I looked past Lewis's hard face and saw Kevin hovering behind him. "Don't treat David like your slave. If you do, I'll make sure you regret it. Just—leave him in the bottle. Promise me."

Kevin blinked. "You don't want me to let him go?"

"Not yet," I said. "You can't take the risk. If anything happens to me— Well, you saw. I don't want you guys to pay for it." I was condemning David to life imprisonment, if—as was very probable—I died. Not exactly the happy ending I'd been hoping for, but it could have been worse.

I'd seen how bad it could get. Our devotion to each other had a horrible dark side. I'd been willing to call fire, burn twenty innocent people alive to make my point. David had been willing to destroy millions to avenge me.

It wasn't David's fault that he could never, ever forgive; it was just his Djinn nature. Now I had to protect him from his own worst impulses.

I blinked away tears and focused on Kevin, with the bottle in his hand—and Cherise, clinging to Kevin and crying. "Keep David safe for me," I said. "I love all of you. I won't forget."

And then I turned and dived off the boat, into the water.

Chapter Nine

So.

It was just me and the sharks. I was acutely aware of the vast, complicated landscape of predator and prey beneath me as I floated; I'd drawn a whole lot of sharks here, and the Great Whites in particular alarmed me, because I'd seen *Jaws*.

I couldn't feel my back at all, but the rest of my body was chilled from the water. Still, I wasn't likely to die of exposure, or even hunger or thirst. I could maintain my body's electrolyte levels, heat, and general health; I could desalinate water to drink. I could eat raw fish that I could call into my hands, if I wasn't especially fussy. Wasn't looking forward to that part; sushi prepared by a brilliant Japanese chef is a far cry from munching on something fresh out of the sea and spitting out the scales and bones.

I floated and watched the rescue craft fleet sail away. The hatch remained open on the lifeboat I'd left, and I heard arguments pouring out of it until the wind carried it away. Cherise had tried to jump out, twice. I could still hear her screaming at the top of her lungs long after other sounds had faded.

"Bye, sweetie," I whispered, and bobbed in the waves

for a while, until the boats were just dazed smudges on the horizon.

I wasn't a good enough Earth Warden to control several hundred sharks, all operating under their natural instinctive programming. What I *could* do—and did—was create conditions that made it less fun for the sharks to come near me, basically administering electrical shocks to anything that came closer than ten feet.

It was terrifying. Eventually, though, the sharks lost interest or found other prey to follow. A few continued to circle, but I couldn't wait; the longer I delayed, the less likely it would be that David's containment of Bad Bob's torch would hold for me. I started to swim. It was fun at first, and then boring, and then difficult. The human body is designed for only so much wear and tear without periods of rest, and my Earth Warden powers could maintain it, but repairing overly stressed muscles took time.

Time I wasn't going to have.

I kept swimming. After a while, pain took on a lulling sort of normality. You really can get used to just about anything, especially if you don't have any alternatives.

The sun began to dip toward the horizon, and I thought about being out here at night, with a sky full of stars. It was oddly peaceful. I was still myself—rescued from the abyss into which Bad Bob had dragged me, though he hadn't exactly dragged me there kicking and screaming, to be perfectly honest about it. I had a wide streak of darkness inside, all my own, and it wasn't just the scars left over from my earlier Demon Mark; I'd always been ambitious. I'd always pursued power.

I guess I wasn't so different from Bad Bob after all, except that I knew all that was both a strength and a weakness. And I knew it had to have limits.

I felt none of the power or fury that had thundered through me when the torch had been active, but sooner or later, David's containment field would fail, and without him here to renew it, the torch would burn hotter than ever. I was a Warden. I wouldn't be that easy to kill, even stranded out here on the ocean.

I'm working too hard, I thought. *If I swim all the way to him, I'll have nothing left when I get there.*

Depression set in. It does that when your friends sail off and abandon you, and when you have to say a probably permanent good-bye to the one man in the world you'd not only die for, but live with. *Maybe it's not worth it. Maybe I should just take myself out of the game. That'd throw a curl in Bad Bob's tail.*

It had a seductive, petulant sort of sense to it. If I died, his plans were screwed, at least the ones I'd seen. He wanted me. He might even need me to make his small-A apocalypse come true. Without me, he had his Sentinels, but they were second-raters, and we'd already taken out the real threats.

Then again ... if I died, that left David snapped into that state of frenzy and rage, and I couldn't count on him staying imprisoned.

I didn't *want* him to stay imprisoned.

But I didn't want to stay apart. Or go back to the cold, evil bitch I'd become.

I considered all the ways I could make my marriage work while my burning, screaming muscles stroked away at the endless ocean. Nothing solved itself, but I hadn't really expected it to. Eventually, the effort whited out my problems more efficiently than anything else could have. They weren't gone, they were just ... under the surface.

The sun went down. It was a beautiful sight, unbounded by the rules of land—nothing but waves and sea, and an endless bowl of sky. I had to stop more and more frequently and just let myself float. My body hurt so much I cried involuntary, hiccuping tears. Every deliberate movement felt as if my nerves had grown cutting edges and were slicing themselves right out of my skin. My skin felt rubbery and ice-cold, except for my back, which just felt like it wasn't there at all.

Keep going.

I tried, but my efforts came slower, my rests more frequent. I just couldn't keep moving. My energy reserves were gone, and although the world was rich in it all around me, I couldn't tap it like a Djinn could.

I'm going to die out here. Except that I couldn't die, not without breaking the tie to David.

Not without setting him on a path of destruction that would annihilate everything.

The stars came out in thick white veils of light, and I floated on my back in the bobbing waves, too tired to keep moving at any cost.

I slept for a while. I floated.

I think I went a little insane, as the endless, isolated hours passed. Then I swam again, and then I slept.

Eventually, I dreamed I heard a ship's horn.

My ride's here, I thought. It was crazy, but somehow it all made sense, the way dreams sometimes do when you're stuck in the middle—life was an ocean, death was a ship to take me away to lands unknown. I'd bought the ticket, right? So why not take the ride?

I heard the blast of noise again, mournful and musical at the same time.

A spotlight appeared out of nowhere and hit the water, so bright I yelled and covered my eyes.

"We've caught ourselves a mermaid," someone said, from behind the blaze of light. "Fish her out. Let's see what we've landed."

I didn't realize how much of the sea I'd swallowed until I was out of the ocean. I promptly fell to my hands and knees and vomited up enough foamy water to fill a goldfish bowl or two. I rolled onto my side, and continued hacking up frothing mouthfuls. My lungs were on fire from the inside, and my throat felt like I'd gargled with Clorox.

My head throbbed like thunder. My skin felt rubbery and soft, and I was incredibly dizzy.

"Huh," somebody said, and I threw up clots of white foam on a pair of sturdy-looking black paramilitary boots. "She don't look like much, Josue."

The hot searchlight was still beaming down on me from a stubby upper deck. In comparison to the majestic cruise ship, this looked like a stunted dwarf—a working ship, some kind of smallish freighter. Not very well kept. The metal deck around me was spotted with rust, there were careless piles of rope and haphazardly stacked boxes, and the men standing over me didn't look like the shipshape type, either. There were four of them, all in filthy, grease-stained T-shirts, cargo-type pants or shorts, and nonskid work boots.

And they all carried knives and guns. Two of them had their firearms shoved casually into waistbands; the other two had what looked like automatic machine pistols slung on bandoliers across their chests.

I was pretty sure those weren't standard issue for guys on board most cargo ships.

I coughed some more. I tried to sit up. I was, instead,

yanked all the way to my feet, where I wavered and nearly went down again. Gravity seemed like a very strange concept to me, after all that time in the water.

I tried my voice, which came out as rusty as the ship I was standing on. "Thanks for the rescue."

One of them laughed. He was the one who'd declared me alive, I thought, a big, muscular guy the color of mahogany. He looked like he could bite a metal bar and spit bullets. As rescuers went, not exactly comforting.

But I couldn't help but be relieved that the whole survival thing had been taken out of my hands.

"Hola," the big guy—apparently, Josue—said, and aimed his machine pistol somewhere in the direction of a number of my more important internal organs. "Is your name Joanne Baldwin?"

I frankly stared at him. *"What?"*

"Yes or no, mermaid. Joanne Baldwin?" He had an interesting accent to his English—thick, not quite Spanish, more lyrical and unpredictable. Close cousins, though. Portuguese, maybe. "If you're not, I throw you back. I don't have room for pets."

"In that case I'm definitely Joanne." I swallowed another cough. "Somebody told you to look for me. Who?"

"Why? Enemies would have left you sucking water, eh? Must have been friends."

He had a point. I couldn't imagine these guys doing anything without a profit motive, and I hadn't pissed off anyone bad enough to make them spend a lot of money to kill me. Easy enough to just let me drown.

Wait . . . that meant it was someone who'd known I would be in the water.

"You didn't come all the way out here to find me," I said. Josue raised his eyebrows and smiled, not in a comforting sort of way.

"Came for the salvage on the ship that went down," he said. "Stayed for the profits. You're worth a lot of money, mermaid."

"Alive, I guess."

He shrugged. "Apparently."

This ship was far from an honest sort of vessel. They'd picked up the maritime distress calls from the *Grand Paradise*—I assumed the captain had sent them—and of course the lifeboats would have transponders on them, probably sending out automated rescue calls. And in these waters, that would draw two kinds of vessels: well-meaning Good Samaritans, and the kind of ship I'd just been fished onto.

In other words, pirates. And somebody had co-opted them to search specifically for me.

"Look!" said one of the crew, stationed at the railing. He called for light, and the beam burned out into the water, turning it from black to a muddy, sullen blue. At first I didn't see what he was looking at, and then I caught a glimpse of bobbing wood. A few bits of debris from the ship had followed the same currents I'd used. There was plenty of small, buoyant wreckage still around, though the debris cloud had long since dissipated and spread itself out over dozens of miles of open water. Not much of a grave for such an enormous vessel.

"Everybody get off?" the pirate captain asked me, and shoved me with the barrel of his gun when I delayed my answer. "Everybody in those little boats, yes?"

"You bet," I said. "Everybody's been rescued. Well, everybody but me, obviously."

He seemed disappointed. I guessed he'd been hoping to fish out some rich Americans he could ransom back at a significant profit. I didn't blame him; I didn't look like a rich payday, regardless of what his patron had told him.

"How come you didn't end up on a rescue boat, mermaid? You not fresh enough?"

A couple of his crewmates offered helpful commentary about how yummy I looked. Charming. I was starting to feel like today's catch, still wiggling on the line.

I took a deep breath. That was a mistake; it resulted in more lung-wrenching coughing, and I spat up some more foam and mucus. "Let's just say I missed my boat," I said.

"What makes a woman stay behind when a boat is sinking?" he asked. It was a rhetorical question; he was showing off for his crew. "You have a kid on the ship?"

"No."

"Money, then." He flashed me a vulpine grin. "Always money."

"Speaking of money, who hired you to find me?"

The laughter died out on the man's face, and left it watchful and dangerous. "Don't think I want to tell you that," he said. "Not yet."

"Why?" I was starting to believe I'd been better off with the sharks.

"Americans, they're always talking about money. *I give you money if you let me go. My family has money. I got important friends who will pay you.* That sort of thing. They think they can buy their way out of anything." He gazed at me for a long, cold few seconds. "You don't offer nothing. That makes me nervous."

"Maybe I'm poor."

He snorted. "Even the poor offer. You don't even try to make a deal."

"Maybe I'm crazy."

He showed me teeth. "Maybe. Maybe you just think we won't hurt you 'cause you're so pretty."

"No," I said, and held his gaze. "I'm sure you'd try like

hell to hurt me, for any reason or none at all. I'm sure you've slit throats and raped and tortured if you felt like it. Probably just yesterday."

That woke a lot of murmuring among the rest of the crew. I heard the slap of boots—more men arriving from other parts of the ship, drawn by the tinfoil smell of trouble in the air.

"Huh," the captain said. "So what you got to stop me if I want to do the same to you?"

"I'm pretty sure you don't want to know." The tingle on my back that I'd felt as I was drowning had subsided, but the nerves were waking up, and I could feel the outline of the torch forming again, black and steady. I could feel the black well of power opening, ready to flood into me if I opened the door. "You guys know comic books? *The Incredible Hulk?*"

Josue looked blank. He looked around at the others.

"Bruce Banner," one of the crew piped up. *"You won't like me when I'm angry."* In any group of people, no matter how hard-assed they might appear, there's always a geek. I was just surprised that, in this company, he'd admitted it.

"It's like that, only I don't have to wait to turn green," I said. "I'm trying to help you out here, gentlemen. Don't push me, and I won't push back, and we'll all be just fine. Somebody's paying you to keep me alive and in one piece. Let's just all get along."

The captain was no longer amused. "Shut up, bitch," he said, and shoved the barrel of his pistol under my chin. "You don't threaten me. Not on my own ship. I'm not being paid enough for *that.*"

I didn't reach for power. It reached for *me*, a black tidal wave that pounded into me like surf to shore, immense and burning.

No! I rejected it, slammed the door shut and held it closed as the power thundered on the other side. I felt small and pitiful and ridiculously weak, and I knew I was only a second from death at the hands of these men, these *pirates*—but my other choice was worse.

"Sure," I said. Josue hadn't noticed a thing, from the outside; he thought he was still in control, not one heartbeat away from being a red stain on the deck. "You win."

If he pushed that gun into me any deeper, we were going to be engaged. "I always do," he said. "Tell me who you are."

"Joanne Baldwin."

"No. Who you *are.* You're not afraid of me."

"I just gave up."

"Not because you're afraid." Josue was way too smart. It was a little creepy. Then he took it too far by saying, "I like women best when they're afraid. They shut up more."

"You're a real charmer, did you know that?" He flashed me his pirate smile. "All right, so you're going to put me in the hold. What then? You turn me over to whoever paid you to come get me?" I had an awful feeling I already knew who that would be, and his initials were Bad Bob Biringanine.

"Something like that," Josue agreed. "Unless you plan to make me a better offer."

"I'll pay you twice what he's paying you," I said. I *did* want to get to Bad Bob. Just not as his helpless captive. Much better if I could hire myself a hard-bitten pirate crew and take the fight to him unexpectedly.

Josue slowly showed his teeth in a smile. He had two gold-plated incisors, both on the bottom, and it gave him a glam vampire look that must have been pretty effective in his line of work.

"Where you got all that money hidden, mermaid? In your panties?" He made a grab, as if he was about to make a withdrawal. I fended him off.

"No, idiot. I keep my money in a bank, like every other criminal who isn't a complete moron. Look, I was on that ship with some of the wealthiest people on earth. I'm not just some casino rat. I know people."

Josue looked unimpressed. "What people?"

"Cynthia Clark. The movie star?"

Pirates started naming movies with the geeky enthusiasm of film obsessives everywhere. From the breadth of their knowledge, I figured they must have the biggest DVD collection ever somewhere belowdecks. Not that they'd ever paid for any of it, of course.

"Famous friends doesn't mean you have money. How you expect to pay me?" Captain Josue asked, and spread his hands to show how unencumbered I was by those phantom millions.

"Electronic transfer," I said. "It's how business works these days. People don't carry cash, they carry personal identification numbers and ATM cards."

He wasn't convinced. "And how does this help me? Do you see any computers on my ship?"

I gave him a very slow smile. "If you take me where I want to go, I promise you, I'll fill your ship so full of dollars you won't be able to sleep without restacking bundles of cash."

"Then give me your account number and PIN code. I'll check it out."

I raised my eyebrows. "I thought you didn't have a computer."

"That's not what I said." He laughed. "You give me the information and I'll verify that you're not a lying whore. That seems fair."

"Sorry. It's all I have to bargain with. Guess you'll just have to trust me."

"I was born at night, mermaid. Not last night," he said. I didn't like the confidence of his smile. "You show me cash, and then I believe you. Not before. Thiago, take her below."

The guy who'd copped to being a comic book geek grabbed my arm and hustled me down the narrow space between the wheelhouse and the railing, toward the stern of the boat. "Hey, Thiago?" I asked. "I could use some help here. Talk to your boss, would you?"

"Shut up," he said. "You won't like *me* when I'm angry."

So much for geek solidarity.

Two hatches later, I was shoved across a rusty threshold and into some kind of ship's hold. It was nothing like the vast, spacious warehouse of the *Grand Paradise*; this was a cramped, hot, stinking metal box that gave mute evidence that the ship had once been a fishing vessel.

I swore I'd never eat tuna again.

"Hey!" I yelled, as the hatch banged shut behind me. "You're really going to regret this!"

And that sounded so stock B-movie that I shut up and found a place to sit and rest my aching head on my aching crossed arms.

The burning torch on my back throbbed in time with my heartbeat, and I could feel it stretching back through the aetheric, a slimy tether that kept pulling on me, trying to drag me to the dark side.

"Keep your shirt on, Bob," I murmured to the dead fish. "A girl's got to sleep sometime."

I curled up in a nest of burlap and old packing material from one of the crates, and fell completely unconscious.

Not a care in the world, strangely enough. Too tired to have one.

When I woke up, my whole body ached less, but that only meant the alert level had gone down from red to orange, damage-wise. No way could I swim far in my current state. I needed the ship if I intended to stay alive.

Well, if I couldn't buy it, there were other ways. They were as dangerous to me as to the captain, though.

I banged on the hatch until I got attention, and was dragged back up on deck. It was midday, and the sun was dazzling on the water. I blinked against the glare.

Josue was once again lounging at the rail. "Don't you ever work?" I asked him.

"Don't you ever shut up?" He nodded to the crewman holding my arm, and another gun dug into my ribs. "Now, maybe you're willing to tell me the account number of all this mythical money you have to share?"

I shook my head.

"Wrong answer." He turned to Thiago, who was holding me. "Shoot her and put her over the side. Do it in the stomach. That way she has time to change her mind before the sharks come."

Damn. I was glad this guy wasn't a Warden.

Thiago tried to follow orders, but when he pulled the trigger, it resulted in a dry click. He tried again, frowning.

"Here, let me see," I said. I took the pistol from him, held it in my hand, and melted the barrel into dripping slag that ran through my glowing fingers and in streams across the deck. "Oh, there's your problem. Man, they really don't make these things like they used to."

I heard more clicks as other pirates joined the hunting party, but I'd disrupted the firing mechanisms of every single gun aboard the ship in one fast burst. So many delicate parts to a gun, really. Not like a good blunt object. "Don't make me blow up your ammunition," I said. "It'll take your hands off with it when it goes up. Classic choice, though. Who wants a hook to complete the whole pirate image?"

Guns hit the deck and tumbled, metal on metal. Weapons skidded from side to side in the pitch and roll of the waves, and an Uzi nudged my foot. I kicked it to the rail, where it hesitated on the edge, then tipped over.

"Good boys," I said. The captain—no coward, even if he didn't understand what was happening—pulled his knife, the better to fillet me. "Okay, not you, obviously, and I'm voting you off the island. Thank you for playing. Say hello to the sharks."

I blew him over the side of the ship, out into the water. He hit with a tremendous splash and came up screaming.

I ignored him. "Right," I said. "Your captain had an attention problem. Who wants to be in charge now?"

They all looked at each other. Nobody dared make a move to rescue Josue, who was flailing like a gaffed fish, although their gazes frequently cut in his direction. One man stepped forward—Thiago, who I suspected was the second in command anyway. "You are," he said. "Miss."

I smiled at him—my best, most winning smile, fueled by a wild edge. "You're a smart guy. Thiago, do you want to make some money?"

"Sure."

"Same deal I tried to make with your ex-boss. You take me in that direction"—I pointed toward where I knew Bad Bob was, as the torch on my back throbbed when I faced that way; no clue what the nautical course was, and I didn't much care—"and I can promise you that you'll get one hell of a great payday out of it. Better than holding up unlucky pleasure boaters, anyway."

He exchanged looks with his fellow scavengers—okay, pirates—and one by one, they nodded. The sound of their captain's increasingly desperate calls for rescue off the port bow probably had something to do with their quorum.

"Can we pick him up, please?" Thiago asked, like it was an afterthought, and pointed toward their captain. I turned my head and looked at him. The dawn wind blew my damp hair over my face, but I was pretty sure he could see my expression even at that distance, with that concealment.

"If he points so much as a dirty look in my direction, I'll shoot him in the stomach and let *him* tell it to the sharks," I said. "Make sure he knows that. I don't feel like giving second chances right now."

Thiago nodded. He had a good poker face, but there was a shadow of uneasiness in his dark eyes. "What do you want us to call you, miss?"

I smiled. "You can call me whatever you want, buddy. This isn't going to be a long-term relationship. Believe me."

Thiago gave some orders, the content of which was lost on me, but the ten or so men that crewed this rusty scow snapped to it. Somebody fished the captain out of the ocean and got him safely out of my sight. I felt the engines growl, shift, and surge beneath my feet as we got under way. The bow turned, heading toward a destination that wasn't visible in any way on the horizon—except to me.

After enjoying the view for a while, I went down to the hold, where I found the captain enjoying the hospitality of the rotting tuna. I pulled up an empty crate.

"So," I said. "How about you tell me who hired you to fish me out of the water, Josue?"

"Vai pro Inferno," he said. *"Foda-se."*

"Want to see a magic trick?" I asked, and put my hand out, palm up. Nothing in it. I turned it palm down, then over again.

Lightning danced along the skin, clung to my fingertips, and dangled from my knuckles like a handful of tangled string.

Josue sat back.

"You know anything about Tasers? This is the same thing, only without the delivery system. Oh, and the batteries. And you know the best thing?" I leaned forward and smiled. "It never runs out of juice."

There's no such thing as a loyal pirate. "He was a man," Josue said.

"Name?"

"I don't ask names. He gave me cash money."

"White hair? Big, blue eyes? Red nose? About this tall?" I indicated Bad Bob's height, but Josue was shaking his head.

"No, never seen that one. This one, he was weird. Shaved head. Wearing leather like out of some motorcycle movie. Scary."

My heart took a running leap. "How'd he pay you?"

"You won't believe it: gold. Sunken treasure. He said he'd just found some." Josue laughed and shook his head. "Crazy people out here. All crazy. I thought I'd find you, see if you were worth keeping. He shows up again, I shoot him if I like you and keep the money anyway."

Josue had no idea what a bad idea that would have been. "Did he say what to do with me when you found me?"

"Yeah." Josue's smile was a model of impish delight.

"He said tell you Kevin said hello. And to take you back to port and let you go. Crazy. Like I said."

I let out a slow sigh. "And you figured you'd threaten me into giving you something else? Or just rape and kill me?"

Josue shrugged. "It's the way things are."

"You are such a lucky man that things didn't work out your way," I said. "If they had, you'd be screaming your way to hell right about now, along with everybody else on this ship."

He didn't believe me, but he should have. I was in no mood to be Ms. Nice Guy, but compared to the fury that David would have unleashed on them if they'd hurt me, there was literally nothing I could do to them that would be anywhere near as horrible.

"My offer's still open," I said. "You take me where I want to go, and I'll pay you enough money to make you king of the pirates forever."

He tried not to look interested. "How do I know you'll keep your promise?"

I turned my hand over again. Lightning flashed and crawled. "You know I'll keep this one."

Josue sat up straighter, his eyes flicking around as if he was trying to figure out an exit strategy. He finally nodded. "It's a deal," he said. "Just—put that away, *bruxa.*"

"Hey, Josue? Call me a witch again, I *will* Taser the holy shit out of you." I felt the black exhilaration creep over me once more, the stealthy march of Bad Bob's influence running through my veins. "Oh, hell, maybe I'll just do it anyway."

I didn't, but it was fun watching him think I would.

I paced the bridge as Josue ordered the crew around. I had nothing to do, really, except wait and think.

Think about Kevin sneaking around behind Lewis's back to let David out of his bottle, sending him to pluck me out of the ocean.

Why?

Cherise, I thought. I couldn't imagine Kevin getting the initiative to come running to my rescue any other way. We'd always cordially hated each other.

I was even more surprised that David hadn't tricked his way out of the bottle again by now. It wouldn't take much slack for him to snap the rope that bound him; Djinn had been doing it for millennia, and they were very, very good at finding loopholes to exploit. Either Kevin had been very specific about what he wanted him to do, or David didn't really want to get free just now.

Maybe because he knew that if he did, he might end up fighting me, and neither of us wanted that. He'd wanted to save me. Kevin had allowed him to do it.

Kevin, you're a romantic. That made me smile. I supposed I'd have to thank him some way.

Maybe by not killing him. That was a gift that kept on giving, right?

The sun was putting on a spectacular evening display, all clouds and blood, when the lookout called a warning. At least, I thought it was a warning—Portuguese wasn't exactly my strong suit, but the tone definitely sounded urgent.

"What is it?" I asked Josue, as he left the bow rail to head toward the stern.

"A ship," he said. "Coming up behind us, and moving fast. Big, maybe a military ship or a tanker."

"Tankers don't move that fast," I said.

Josue continued to stare over the stern rail, frowning. "Could be more trouble than you're worth, mermaid. I'm thinking I throw you back."

"You want to go downstairs again, talk it over?"

He gave me a scornful sneer. "You can't sail the ship alone. My men won't work for you."

"Want to bet? Just do what I tell you, Josue. If I feel this ship slow down, you're over the side, and your crew goes with you. That's a promise."

He knew I meant it. He nodded. I had no doubt that later on, he'd try to stab me in the back, maroon me, or otherwise screw me over, but for now he was treading carefully—partly because I was a potential payday, but equally out of sheer morbid fear. He'd seen a sample of what I could do, and he didn't want to see more.

I didn't really blame him for that. I wasn't wild to see it, either.

I locked my hands behind my back and kept my legs spread wide, riding the bucking of the waves with the ease of a long-practiced sailor. We both watched the dim shape on the horizon take on edges and definition.

Definitely a ship. Big.

The lookout called another warning. Josue looked up, frowning, and blinked. He cursed in Portuguese—no, I didn't recognize the words, but the flavor's the same in any language. "Storm," he said. "Coming on fast from the south."

My friend the storm had hung back, content to let me run; I wasn't sure anymore whether I was holding its leash or it was holding mine. But something had changed. Maybe it sensed that the containment around the mark on my back was fading again, or that I wasn't following my approved script.

It was heading our way. Fast.

The blood sunset had disappeared behind a boiling, rising mass of clouds—iron gray ones, with greenish-black underpinnings. It was already crawling with lightning inside. Power had been poured into it—an awful lot of power.

"Hold course," I said. I didn't think all that effort Bad Bob was putting out was meant solely for us. We weren't that hard to sink, frankly.

As we sailed steadily toward it, the storm spread out, flattened, swirled, consolidated, gained density and deeper color.

Then it started to spin around a center axis—slowly, majestically, unevenly at first, then spiraling out like a deadly galaxy. The blender of the gods, taking shape right in front of me.

"We need to get out of its way!" Josue shouted. I felt the first breath of wind sweep over us, vivid with the smell of rain. The clouds were whipping toward us. He cursed me in Portuguese, and ordered his men to follow his instructions.

I locked the rudder in place with a burst of Earth power. They worked frantically to free it, but they weren't getting anywhere.

As the wind increased, so did the amplitude of the waves, and the small ship was nowhere near as able to crush through the turmoil as the *Grand Paradise* had been. The vessel was battered, and when it slammed bow-first into the rising waves, the spray fractured into foam and coated everything on board in slippery, unpleasant slime.

Then came the rain, hammering in sheets that felt like needles. Josue's crew broke out battered rain slickers. I ignored the offer, and stood at the bow, watching the storm's progress. I could feel its blind menace, its anger, but it wasn't directed downward at me, not even as the rain intensified into a heavy, strangely hot downpour. The wind speed increased, and the clouds rotated faster. It intensified as the ship crashed and fell through the waves. I tethered myself to the rail and resisted the waves that crested the bow and washed the decks, trying to pull me over.

Something wild inside me broke free as we rode through the storm, and in the blaze of lightning and pounding surf, I felt at home. Finally, completely at home. All those years of fighting the storms, and I'd never realized how much a part of them I was. How complete I was when I was with them.

I was almost sorry when we hit the eye of the storm and calm fell over us— but I looked up into the primal heart of the enemy, and it looked back at me with a kind of affectionate recognition.

Good dog.

When we hit the trailing side, the winds lashed us so viciously that we lost two of the crew, even though they'd been tethered. The seas swamped the decks, shattered glass, woke terror from seasoned pirates who picked their teeth and yawned at the idea of a normal tempest.

After a white-knuckled eternity, the storm was past us, and heading for its *real* victim.

The ship closing in on us from behind.

The seas continued heavy against us, and Josue wanted to slow our pace. The engines were laboring, and the crew was exhausted and sick.

"No," I said. I didn't need them anymore. They'd served their purpose, both ship and crew, and I no longer had to worry about their breaking points. "Just keep the throttle open. We'll be fine."

I wrapped energy around the straining pumps and valves and increased their speed. It wouldn't last long, but it would give us more of a lead against our pursuer, who had the full weight of the storm to deal with now. I looked back to see its forward progress stalling, as if it had met cooler air to slow it. The storm was lashing that other ship with all its supernatural fury.

Josue, also watching, crossed himself.

The moon rose, but it was quickly veiled by clouds. As night descended on us, it was thick and black and claustrophobic. Only the shattered reflections of our running lights spoiled the illusion of sailing through empty, limitless space.

"*Mãe de Deus,*" Josue murmured. "It's still coming, that ship. Like a ghost out of the grave."

It *was* a ghost.

The *Grand Paradise* had gone down, I'd seen it. It had been too badly damaged and too thoroughly flooded to float, and yet there it was, gaining on our tail. The running lights were all working, blazing merrily in the darkness, and it was charging at a speed that didn't seem natural for such an enormous ship.

It was trying to get to me before I reached my destination.

"Hold on," I told Josue, and opened the throttles even more on our nameless little pirate ship, sending it leaping and slamming through the waves like an oversized, wallowing speedboat. The hull wouldn't take it for long, but it didn't have to.

Out there in the darkness was my destination.

I felt a Warden grabbing for control of our engines, and whipped a black scythe of power across the lines of force. It must have hurt, and badly. "Do it again, and you'll pull back a stump," I muttered, and gripped the rail tighter. "Back off."

I didn't think they would. If they were strong and confident enough to make it through the hurricane, they'd be more than competent enough to tackle me.

A Djinn breathed into focus on the deck a few feet away, and I prepared for the fight of my life . . .

. . . but it was David.

David.

My David, perfect in every line. Not Kevin's incarnation of him.

He didn't say anything. Neither did I. Josue drew a knife and stabbed at him, but David didn't even bother to cast him a look, just flicked his fingers and sent him flying across the deck.

"Are you here to stop me?" I asked.

"No," my husband said, and took a step toward me. Then another. I was in the V-shaped well of the bow, pressed against the rails—nowhere to go but over the side, into the black waters. "I'm not here to stop you."

"Then what?"

He took another step, risking a full attack. I could feel the urge, the *need* vibrating through me like plucked strings. *Don't let him fool you. Don't let him stop you. You need to reach Bad Bob. If this goes badly, you know what will happen. The two of you will be responsible for destroying the world.*

In the ripping light of a lightning strike on the cruise ship looming slowly up behind us, David's face was serious and very calm.

"I'm here to help you," he said.

He opened his hand, and in it were fragments of glass.

The broken pieces of his bottle.

I stared at them for a moment, into his eyes. "How—?"

"Cherise," he said. "She wants you to live. So do I. She got the bottle away from Kevin. She—trusts me."

Cherise was a romantic idiot, in this one sense: She

simply didn't understand how dangerous David really was. I wasn't even sure I understood . . . although I was starting to get a really good idea.

I tightened my grip on the rail as the ship pounded into a particularly deep trough, then painfully plowed up the leading edge of the next wave. "I see. And did you stop for anything else along the way?"

"You mean, did I kill Lewis?" he asked. "Not yet." He took one more step, and we were body to body, soaked with rain, blinded by lightning. Sealed together by storms. "That doesn't mean I've forgotten him. Don't ask me to do that."

I couldn't begin to try. "How did they raise the ship?"

"Who says they did?" David's smile was knowing, and a little bitter. "It's not the *Grand Paradise*. Lewis lied to you from the beginning. The *Grand Paradise* was a decoy, designed to lure Bad Bob into showing his hand. He sent the other Wardens out of Fort Lauderdale, aboard the *Grand Horizon*. It's a sister ship—a little smaller, a little faster. Crewed entirely with Wardens and Djinn. It's been making good time and staying off of Bad Bob's radar. Until now."

That son of a bitch. Lewis really had suckered me, every step of the way. He'd known I was a risk, if not a ready-made traitor. He'd used me as a stalking horse, although I had to admit he'd put himself on the line, too.

But he'd also exposed Cherise and dozens of other innocents who had no place in this. And an unforgivably large number of Wardens, although I supposed for any kind of a feint to work, he had to commit himself to it.

I would never forgive him for risking so much, no more than David would be able to forgive him for the kill switch that Lewis had put in my brain.

"So by suckering Bad Bob into kicking the living crap out of us, the *Grand Horizon* got a virtually free ride," I said. "Right?"

"As far as I know."

"How could you not know?"

"It's crewed by Ashan's Djinn. Everything was compartmentalized from me. Deliberately so."

We'd both been cut out. Well, I'd been hoping Lewis had fallback positions, in the beginning, and it looked like he'd done a hell of a lot more with a hell of a lot less than I'd have managed in his place.

"They're in for it now," I noted, as three lightning strikes crawled the *Grand Horizon*'s deck, searching for something to destroy. "But we're still going to get there ahead of them."

"I know." He cupped my face in both hands, and he studied me closely. I knew what he was looking for.

"I'm all right," I said. "Seventy-five percent all right, anyway."

He seemed to calculate me at about the same rate.

"If we succeed," he said, "we will have another problem to consider."

I hadn't actually thought past the consequences of failure, which were fairly horrific. "Like what?"

"You may inherit his power. And you may be tempted to use it."

"I could use it for good."

"So did he. Once. It isn't a power you can use, Jo. It's a power you must destroy."

I looked back at him. "So if I grab it from Bad Bob, you're going to take it away from me. Or die trying."

"Maybe," David said. "But first we have to live to get there, don't we?"

I turned to face him. The next lurching drop sent him

into me. Our lips found each other, hot and hungry and damp, tasting of salt and desperation. For a moment even the storm seemed to stop, suspended between heartbeats.

I felt the darkness in me trying to reach out to him, and slapped it down hard. *No. Not yet.* David might be here, he might be with me, but he wasn't *with* me. And I wasn't going to be the one to enslave him yet again, not until I had no other choice.

I turned to face south, toward the empty horizon. "He's not far now," I said. "One thing at a time, right?"

David's arms gripped the railing on either side of me, bracing me against the violent bucking of the ship as we plunged toward the darkness. "Right."

Chapter Ten

The Wardens on the *Grand Horizon* had learned from our mistakes, it appeared; we saw them break through the storm, and they must have set up a series of Djinn/Warden cooperative alliances to maintain their bubble shield, because I could see the glistening curve of it from the deck of our ship as the waves broke and foamed over the smooth round surface.

I wished them luck in keeping that up. It was brutal, soul-shredding work. "How long until they catch up?"

David handed me a plate. Our pirate cook had made some kind of meat, finely chopped and spiced, with spongy bread. It was delicious, and surprising; I'd somehow expected wormy crusts and rum. I gobbled down the lunch with gratitude.

"Good?" David asked, amused, and shook his head at my garbled reply. "They're gaining. They'll catch up to us by midday."

"Can't let that happen," I mumbled. "Lewis was very clear. This needs to be me. Not them."

"Bad Bob and his storm didn't slow them down. How do you propose either of us stops them, short of destroying them?"

I chewed and swallowed. "Ask them."

He evidently hadn't thought of that. I winked and carried my plate to the wheelhouse, where Josue was dozing on a stained old cot at the back while his navigator did the hard work of steering the tough little vessel on the course I'd set. I asked about the radio and was pointed belowdecks, to a small, claustrophobic closet of a room with bad ventilation and a crew member who evidently liked beans and hated baths. I evicted him from his battered chair and rolled up to check out the radio. It was old, but highly complicated.

"Hey!" I yelled through the closed door. David opened it. "Help me out a little. I'm not Sparky the Wonder Horse."

That earned me a full, warm smile. "I wouldn't say *that*."

"Watch it." I meant that; he was looking at me like I was the old Joanne. The less demented one. "Keep your guard up. I mean it, David. Bad Bob can be funny, too. That doesn't make him any less of a monster. Don't you dare trust me. I can't trust myself, not anymore."

The smile faded, and the sparks in his eyes turned ash-dark. "Yes. I understand." David looked at the radio, and the dials turned. "There. That should put you in touch with the *Grand Horizon*'s bridge."

"Thanks." I slipped on the headphones as he shut the door between us—less to provide me with privacy than to give me elbow room. There wasn't enough space in here to breathe. "Merchant vessel—" Oh, hell, what was this ship's name? "Merchant vessel *Sparrow* for the cruise vessel *Grand Horizon*. Please respond, over." I expected I'd have to repeat myself, but instead I got an immediate crackle of connection.

"*Sparrow,* this is *Grand Horizon*." I knew that voice. "You made it."

"Lewis." I kept my voice neutral, although I was glad he'd made it, too. Even if he had tried to kill me. "You're lucky David hasn't made a lampshade out of you."

"Time will tell." Lewis obviously knew all about how much trouble he was in on that front. "You're heading straight for Bad Bob."

"I have a plan. Obviously, it won't be as good as yours," I said, "but I make one hell of a good distraction, right? So I go in, do as much damage as possible, and you guys land for the cleanup."

"That would be great—if I thought for a second we could actually trust you." Lewis's voice was bleak and dry, even through the distortion of the radio waves. "You brought us this close. That's enough, Jo. Break it off. Whatever happens, don't let him finish what he started in destroying you."

"What makes you think he can't do it from a distance?" I asked. "I'd rather go down fighting for you than against you."

"Jo—"

"Maybe you didn't get that I wasn't asking your permission. I was informing you, that's all. You can not love it all you want, but it's what's going to happen, and—" I felt the laboring engines of my little ship begin to struggle. "Don't you even *think* about it, man. You start screwing with me and you are in a world of trouble."

He covered the mike, presumably to warn off the Earth Warden or Djinn who was trying to shut me down. "I'm not interfering," he said. "I'm just advising, and I advise you very strongly to break this off and run, Jo. Now."

"You sent me out here," I said. "You put me on the hook for bait. *Let me do this.*" No answer but static. "Fine. Joanne Baldwin Prince, signing off—"

"Wait," he snapped. I did. "Don't take David with you. We're not allowing any of the Djinn to make landfall. Too dangerous for them."

I was a bit unclear on the concept of how one stopped Djinn from doing something, if they weren't bound to a bottle, but I didn't bring it up. "And what do you suppose I'm going to do about stopping David?"

His sigh rattled the speaker. "You're not going to love the idea."

"Try me."

He did. I heard him out, although my first impulse was to blow the radio up in a satisfying shower of sparks. I thought about it.

After a long, quiet moment, I agreed.

"Jo?" I was so deep in thought that Lewis's voice startled me. "Still there?"

"More or less. Look, I can't trust anyone on this ship, not with what you're asking. Send me someone." I thought about that for a second. "Send me someone who isn't going to take shit from some fairly scary pirates."

"I've got just the guy," Lewis said. "We're going to slow down, to give you time to get to the island ahead of us. But we'll be coming when you need us."

"I hope so," I said. "Let's not say our good-byes this time. Last time was a real bitch."

He seemed to think so, too. "*Grand Horizon,* signing off."

"*Sparrow,* signing off." I put the old click-to-talk mike down and sat for a moment in silence, staring at the equipment.

Then I rummaged around in the desk drawers. It was a battered old thing, looked like it had seen service in the First World War, and I surprised a long-tailed rat in the top drawer, who stared at me with beady little eyes and an entire lack of alarm. A pet, maybe. Or maybe this was his ship, and I was the infestation.

I shut that drawer and tried the next one. The rats had made nests of the paperwork that had once been in there; it was nothing but shreds.

The third drawer yielded an almost empty bottle of Cutty Sark.

"Score," I said. I unscrewed the cap, wiped the lip of the bottle with my shirt, and threw back the rest of the booze in one long, thirsty pull. When there were no more threads of amber snaking their way down the glass to my mouth, I lowered the bottle and set it on the desk.

"David?"

He opened the door.

It's not that easy to catch a Djinn who's alert for treachery, and David—even though he loved me—knew better. I'd just told him not to trust me.

But he gave me the benefit of the doubt, even with the empty bottle open on the desk in front of me.

I looked up at him and said, "We need to talk, honey."

Lewis sent Brett Jones, Fire Warden, former Special Forces. He was bigger than Josue, and after a dick-measuring initial meeting, Josue evidently accepted that Brett was meaner as well. I didn't know Brett that well, but Lewis did, and if Lewis sent him to take care of us, then we could trust him.

"Watch your back," I whispered to Brett as I passed him. He'd come armed to the teeth, which made him fit right in with all my pirate crewmates; on him, though, it looked like professional accessories. He nodded to me. It seemed like a thousand years since we'd sat in the movie theater on the *Grand Paradise,* watching as our colleagues were carried off in body bags after that first clash with Bad Bob's storm.

Brett looked as hard and tired as I felt. He also looked very alone, standing at the bow with his arms folded, watching the speedboat head back to the distant cruise ship. The weather was still foul over in that direction. The storm just wasn't about to give up its prize, no matter how hopeless it was.

Standing in the filthy confines of Josue's tiny captain's cabin, I brushed the worst of the tangles out of my hair, and used a burst of power to clean my clothes and remove the worst of the grime from my skin. As accommodations went, even temporary accommodations, these earned zero stars; the bed was filthy, the floor was littered with toenail clippings, and the walls were pasted over with hard-core porn actresses in action shots.

David opened the cabin door and stepped in. He watched me in silence, not touching me. We'd talked about all this, but convincing him was another matter altogether. And even when he bowed to necessity, he did it grudgingly.

I wished I could really tell what he was thinking, but then, he probably was wishing the same thing.

"One good thing about this," I said. "This time, we get to do it right."

He shrugged. "As far as I'm concerned, the first time was good enough for eternity."

That made me smile. "You *must* be a romantic. I mean, what with all the mayhem and the chaos and the not finishing the ceremony—"

"If I wasn't a romantic, I wouldn't be here."

He had an excellent point. I decided not to pursue it. Instead, I put down Josue's comb and did another critical review. I looked . . . surprisingly good, actually. The sun and sea had given me a blush of bronze, and my eyes seemed clear and cool as the Caribbean waters. My hair had, for a change, taken its glossy curls to a style, instead of to a mess.

David slid his hands over my shoulders, and I looked up at him. "It's time," he said. "Wouldn't want to keep the guests waiting."

The guests were, of course, the assembled pirates of the ship I'd recently, and randomly, named the *Sparrow*. None of them had made any effort to change clothes, splash water on their faces, or brush their teeth, but they were seated cross-legged on the deck, clearly happy with slack-off time.

Josue had donned a ridiculous coat. A tuxedo jacket, obviously ripped off from some prior victim on a yacht. I hoped I wouldn't notice any bloodstains.

"Hurry your asses up," he said. "We don't have long."

Not exactly the wedding march, but it would do. I exchanged a look with David, and he gave me his hand, and we walked the short length of the deck to the bow, where Josue was standing. The sun was behind clouds again, and the air smelled heavy with brewing storms. David's best man—and, I supposed, standing in for my maid of honor—was the Fire Warden, Brett Jones. Big and foreboding as a Djinn, only armed like a pirate and watching Josue and everybody else, including me, with smart, cold focus.

I felt both protected and unsettled.

"I don't have no holy books," Josue said. "So I make it up as I go along. You don't like it, you go get married in hell."

"As long as you get the important stuff right," I said. "Go ahead."

"I get paid first."

There was a brief pause, and then David reached into his pocket and brought out a small handful of very large bills. Josue grabbed them and flashed a highly inappropriate smile, then asked, "What's your name?"

"David Prince."

"David Prince, you come here with this woman to be married. Right?"

I didn't dare throw a glance at David, because there was something so weirdly hilarious about this that I was already choking on it. After a beat, he said, "Obviously."

I coughed.

"You sure you want to do that?" Josue said. "Because you got to take care of her, love her, never look at another woman. Even if she's sick or gets old and fat."

My coughing turned into a full-fledged fit.

"If you mean will I stand by her in sickness and in health, for richer or poorer, for all the days of our lives—yes, I will," David said, very quietly. The urge to laugh left me suddenly, and I squeezed his hand. "I vow that I will."

I felt no corresponding surge from the aetheric, the way I had the first time we'd done this, but then, David had completed his side of the vows the last time we'd done this.

I hadn't, not officially. Which was why Lewis and I had decided to go through with this. It was an experiment— probably doomed to failure—to see whether or not it would make any difference in the way Djinn and humans were bound together . . . if *we* were bound together by ritual, completely.

"You're sure about this," Josue said. He continued to stare at David. "I give you some time to think."

David didn't smile. "I'm sure. Move along."

"Well, okay." He turned to face me. "How about you?"

"You suck at this," I told him. I got a slow leer in return. "Come on, at least make an effort!"

"You dump this guy, come back to my cabin, I'll make an effort."

"To clean up the toenails off the floor?" I asked sweetly. "Come on, Josue. Today."

He clasped his hands, and tried for a pious expression. I doubted he'd ever seen one, except maybe in the DVD collection belowdecks. "Do you—what's your name again?"

"Joanne Baldwin."

"Joanne Balderwin, take this—uh, Prince David, to be your husband? Do you swear to honor and obey him, and to never look at another man, even if this one gets—"

"Sick, old, and fat, yes, I know."

"What would that matter? He's a man, yes? It is the prerogative of a man to get sick and old and fat." The crew laughed raucously behind us. "Do you swear to honor and obey him, even if this one gets poor and lazy?"

I closed my eyes and fought a cage match with my temper. *"Ask it right."* He heard the echo of darkness in my voice, and the laughter of the crew died away. "I mean it."

Josue cleared his throat. When he spoke again, the mocking tone was gone. "Do you take this man as your husband, forsaking all others as long as you both live?"

Close enough. I felt something happening, a stirring in the aetheric like a soft breeze. It swirled around me, lazy and gentle, and then solidified into a silver mist.

"Yes," I said. "I vow it."

The mist fell like soft silver rain on the aetheric, and I felt it sliding over my skin in warm threads.

And then it hit the black torch, and all hell broke loose.

"Jo!" David grabbed me as my knees folded. "What—?"

I had to make this work. *Had to.* Holy crap, Lewis had been right the whole time. Because our wedding vows hadn't been finished, I'd made myself vulnerable to the invasion by Bad Bob. The equations had been out of balance, and on the aetheric that was a very bad thing.

We were setting it right.

The connection between us went wild, power flooding from him into me in a silver torrent. Power straight from the bloodstream of the aetheric, pure and white-hot.

"Take it out of me," I panted. "Hurry. *Hurry!*"

David rolled me over on my stomach and ripped my shirt open, exposing the rippling, angry tattoo on my back. The thing under there was being forced to the surface.

David's power was acting in self-defense, because I was now part of him. Flesh of his flesh.

I heard his breath rush out, and then he put one hand on the back of my neck and said, "Hold still. It's coming out."

I felt blood sheeting over my back, and heard the pirates scrambling backward to get away from the thing that was thrashing its way out of me.

I had enough control left to block the nerves before the pain got unbearable. I couldn't see what was happening in the real world, but on the aetheric there was something that looked like a cross between a squid and a virus flailing its way out of my silver-shining body.

David fried it into grease and smoke on the deck beside me, and then burned it again.

The change was immediate, and dramatic. Calm flooded me, and confidence, and power—the power of the Djinn.

I directed it to my back, and sealed the ravaged muscles and torn skin—something not even Lewis could have done, as powerful as his talent for things like that was.

I'd just become something else. A bridge between the Wardens and the Djinn . . . and something of both at the same time.

And Bad Bob's mark was *gone*.

I was free.

David picked me up and cradled me in his arms. I felt warm and relaxed, contented as a drowsy cat in the sun.

"It worked," he said. He sounded surprised. "You were right."

"Damn straight," I said. "It's why he wanted to stop us at the wedding. Bad Bob knew that once we exchanged vows, he wouldn't be able to control me anymore." I felt drunk on silver bubbles, and I laughed. "Free. We're free of him."

David captured my hands and kissed them. "Not quite yet," he said. "He can't control you. That doesn't mean he's helpless." He pulled me back to my feet. My shirt was a disaster, so I tied the rags together in a makeshift halter top. Not so bad, really, all things considered.

Josue had prudently retreated as far as he could from us. Brett Jones was still standing there, looking focused despite the sight of an alien critter ripping out of my flesh.

I nodded to Josue. "Finish it."

"Hell with you, crazy bitch!"

"Finish it!"

From all the way across the deck, he made the hasty sign of the cross. "Then I declare you married," he said. "*Mazel tov.* Kiss the bride before we do."

He picked up a half-empty bottle of cheap rum, pulled out the cork, and swigged down a gulp, then passed it around. Our version of cheap champagne.

David pulled me into his arms, and what would have been a symbolic kiss turned deep, hot, and thoroughly suggestive. I helped with that part, thinking of nothing except the moment, the sensation of his body against mine.

We'd won. At the very least, we'd won my freedom from becoming Bad Bob's slave.

Now I had to make sure that David didn't suffer that fate, either.

We broke the kiss and clung together, panting. He was whispering things to me, quiet wonderful things. Promises.

And then he closed his eyes and said, "I don't want to do this. Not this way."

"I know," I said, and kissed him again, gently. "But it's important. Tactics and strategy, right?"

"Tactics and strategy." He sounded resigned, not happy. "All right. I'm ready."

I nodded over his shoulder to Brett, who unzipped a pocket on his tactical vest and pulled out a small glass bottle with a cork. A little more ornate than I was used to seeing—probably something they had in the stores on the cruise ship, although the cork would have been a new addition.

"I've got your agreement to do this, right?" Brett asked. He was asking David. After a long moment, David nodded. "Be thou bound to my service. Be thou bound to my service. Be thou bound—"

"Wait," I blurted, and took both of David's hands in mine. "If this is the last time I see you, I need you to hear this."

He waited, amber eyes glowing like suns. I fumbled for words. "I—just— David, if something happens to me, if this doesn't go right, you have to promise me, *vow* to me, that you will look out for humanity's good, not just the Djinn's. Don't punish the Wardens if I die. Please."

He knew why I was asking that. "Lewis tried to kill you," he said. "He *did* kill you. Are you asking me to forgive him?"

"I'm not going to ask the impossible. I'm asking that you not take revenge for something that turned out not to work anyway, that's all."

There's something very unsettling about a Djinn that doesn't blink when he's talking to you—even one you love with a deep, desperate intensity. "You *are* asking the impossible," he said. "Lewis hurt you. He did it as part of a plan. I can't allow that to go unanswered."

"You have to," I said. "Please. I need a vow."

"You know that I can't say no to you, don't you?" He wasn't smiling, though. "Yet this time, I have to. The answer is still no, Jo. He can no longer be trusted by the Djinn."

That really wasn't good. "But you'll still work with him? With the Wardens?"

"To a point," he said. I could tell he wasn't going to be more specific about where the point *was.*

That was all I was going to get from him, even now, even at this most vulnerable moment.

I nodded to Brett, who repeated the binding phrase again—three times, just to be sure.

David's hands misted out of mine as the binding took effect. I felt the hammering blow of it shatter the aetheric between us, and then he was exploding into mist, and the mist was sucked into the bottle in Brett's hands. He corked it with calm efficiency, and I watched him put the bottle in a special padded case, and then into the pocket of his tactical vest.

"With your life," I told him. "You know that, right?"

"Yes," he said. It was a simple answer, and it left no room for doubt at all. He'd do it. I couldn't ask for better than that.

I fried the ship's engine with a burst of pure Earth power, fusing metal parts together, gunking up everything that looked remotely important. The *Sparrow* sputtered and began to drift, dead in the water.

Josue stopped looking afraid and started looking alarmed, then angry. "You do something to my ship?"

"Why, is something wrong with it?" I kept my expression as innocent as possible. That was probably what made him glower at me as if he'd like to take me apart but wasn't sure it was safe to try. "My friends on the cruise ship will help you. Oh, and I wouldn't try any other guns you might have stashed. Serious mistake on so many levels."

He gave me his most dangerous look. In earlier days, I might have actually been intimidated by it. Today ... not so much. "Worst day of my life, the day I fished you out of the ocean, mermaid."

"Really? The sad thing is, it wasn't the worst day of mine." I stepped up on the railing at the vee of the bow, balancing on the balls of my feet. He backed away, watching me. Not quite certain of what I was doing. "Good luck."

He crossed himself. "Go with God, so long as you go." His sudden piety didn't convince me he wouldn't stab me in the back if he could get a clear throw when

I turned around. I gave Josue one last look, and then I dived from the railing of the *Sparrow* into the open ocean water, heading south.

Bad Bob wasn't on an island, after all. Well, to be accurate, he *was* on an island—but the island was floating and he was moving it wherever he wanted.

Neat trick. First, most islands aren't all that prone to float, since they're really the tops of underwater mountains. This one was able to drift, withstand the full force of a Category 5 hurricane, *and* navigate at will.

It also explained why he was so crazy hard to track down. I wasted time and frustration until I figured out that I was heading not for a specific spot in the ocean but a *mobile* spot. I found it as the sunrise spilled over the long, rocky key of the island, which was moving away from me at a fairly rapid speed. I had an embarrassment of choices for first impressions, but *you've got to be kidding me* was certainly in the hunt for first place.

The entire island was *turning*, the mirror image of the mouth of a black-and-green hurricane that was hovering above it, just . . . spinning.

Not even Bad Bob—I hoped—had the power to do this alone. No, he had to be augmenting it somehow . . . And then it occurred to me. I was filled with silvery aetheric light now, thanks to my connection to David; Bad Bob had a Djinn, too. Rahel. He'd taken her by force, and that explained the negative energy in what I saw hovering over the island.

Of course, Bad Bob himself was no Prince of Positive Thinking, either.

The scary thing was that with that much power, he could do almost anything he liked, and this floating fortress was just demented enough to amuse him.

I kept swimming. I'd been at it for hours, and I was very, very tired, but I also wasn't about to give up. Besides, I was building up some fierce quadriceps.

Jo, a voice whispered in my ear. I gasped, startled, and sucked down a lungful of water. I paused, treading water. *Jo, can you hear me?*

It was Lewis's voice. I shook my head and bopped myself in the ear, hoping I was just having a hallucination.

Stop hitting yourself. Yes, it's me.

"How do you know I'm hitting myself?"

I can hear the pops in your eardrum. It's an old Earth Warden trick. Works great for covert ops. Lewis was making an effort to sound like nothing had passed between us the past few days. Like it was all just the same old. *How's the swim?*

"Long," I said. My teeth were chattering. "You didn't dial me up on the ear-phone to chat."

He paused for a few seconds. With Lewis, that was weighty. *Did David agree? Is he in the bottle?*

"Yes." Better not to overshare on that, I decided. "Could we speed this up? Water cold. Body tired."

Can you do this? Are you sure?

What a dumb-ass question. "No, I'm not sure," I snapped. "Of course I'm not sure. Why? Second thoughts?"

Yes. We've got one shot at this. He may not even let you get close. He may kill you before you get anywhere near him.

Cheery thought. "If he does, you've still got a shipful of Wardens and Djinn ready to bring the wrath of God down on him and—" It occurred to me suddenly why Lewis was taking the trouble to say these things. "David."

You and I know that he'd stop at nothing to destroy what killed you.

Oh Christ. "You cannot be serious with this. Lewis. Please, tell me you're not asking me to go and deliberately get my ass killed so that it will trigger David into a homicidal rampage against your enemies?"

It would work.

Sure it would. It would leave Bad Bob and whoever was around him radioactive dust. Including, probably, the cruise ship, which would become collateral damage.

The hideous thing was that as a nuclear option, it was not bad. So long as you accepted that the pile of bodies would be unthinkable, but at the end of the day, the enemy would be gone....

No. "Not happening, Lewis," I said. "If I get killed anyway, fine, all bets are off. But I'm fighting all the way down. Get me?"

Yes. You understand that I had to ask.

Not really. But I was starting to think that in some ways David was right—I never would truly know Lewis. Not at his core.

"I'm signing off, Lewis," I said, and spit salt water as a wave slapped me. "Hey. Thanks."

For what?

"Letting me say no."

I got a dry, tinny chuckle in my ear. *How could I ever stop you?*

"See you on the other side, then."

Yes.

That was it. Our big good-bye. As romantic scenes went, it lacked, but that was all right. We were past all that now.

After a good half hour of chasing down the floating island, my flailing hand finally slapped a boulder on the island's rocky shore—whatever sand there once was had long ago been scoured away, so there was nothing left to this beast but slick, water-smoothed stone. I grabbed at the rock, but my hand slid off. I kicked, gritted my teeth, and lunged up out of the water as far as I could.

My rib cage thumped down painfully on the smooth surface, and I started to slip back, but more kicking and clawing paid off. I found a handhold, at the cost of the last memory of my French manicure, and hauled myself out of the pounding surf to lie exhausted and dripping, draped like Josue's proverbial drowned mermaid over extremely uncomfortable terrain.

"Damn," I whispered. "Why am I doing this again?" Oh yeah—because I was probably the only one who could, with anything like certainty.

And because sometimes I just had to face my own demons—and Demons—head-on.

I spent several moments just letting my muscles shake and cry out in relief, and then rolled up to a sitting position to take a look around. It wasn't much of a garden spot—lots of black basalt and granite. This place wasn't more than a few dozen millennia away from the lava flows that had built it in the first place. It still had most of its sharp edges.

That wasn't great for me, of course. I'd worn heavy boots, but my battered shorts probably weren't going to protect me from gathering some new and interesting scars as I scrambled across the edgy landscape.

I climbed up on the tallest boulder I could find and did a quick survey. The island was bigger than I'd expected—maybe a solid mile across—and toward the middle there was an unlikely small collection of jagged palms, all dying now. Whatever fresh water had nourished them was long gone.

This island was a rotting hulk, and I wondered uneasily how Bad Bob had kept sixty Sentinels—that I knew about—alive on such a bare span of rock. I supposed he'd laid in supplies, but he didn't seem to be a logistical kind of guy.

Maybe they were eating each other. It wouldn't surprise me, given the level of devotion he inspired in people.

This was not the place I'd have picked as my home away from home if I had to choose a portable island paradise, that was for damn sure. No beaches, no living trees, no water, no shade. Just razor-edged rock and the odd crab scuttling by. The surface of Mars, only at least fifty percent less hospitable.

If I hadn't been doing such a careful survey of the island, I might have missed the first attack that came at me. There was nothing to give it away but a faint shimmer against the rocks, like a reflection of waves—but it didn't move with the waves.

It was bending light, and it was moving fast, heading my direction.

I'd never seen one in full daylight before. That was a crystalline skeleton, barely visible without the human disguise its kind had adopted back on the *Grand Paradise*. I knew now why it had gone for the skins; the creature made a vibration on the aetheric as it moved, a kind of ringing like a finger tapping an ice-cold crystal glass.

The skins had muted the vibrations, hidden them in the natural noise of human existence.

The crystal shimmer disappeared, lost in the glare of the sun for a second, and then I saw the blur of it against the piles of rocks only about three feet away from me.

I didn't have time for fancy moves, just dived out of the way. It was fast, but the rocks were just as hazardous to its footing as to mine, and I saw it stumble and try to catch its balance as it checked its momentum. Instead, it tumbled off into the water.

It sank below the surface in seconds, pulled down by the density of its bones.

Well, that was great news, but as I looked up, I counted three more shimmers against the rocks, heading in my direction. I calculated frequencies. I didn't have time to try very many, but the good news was that I'd already killed one of these things on my own. Well, with help, but close enough. I knew the theory, and even without the direct access to the aetheric that I'd have had with David free, I wasn't starved for power. I was almost shining with what had spilled into me at our wedding ceremony.

The next creature lunged for me, and I opened my mouth and picked a note. Nerves forced the amplitude of the sound too high, and the creature just kept coming. I adjusted the range of the note, holding it steady, and fine-tuned it as the beast came closer, and closer, and—

—and then it burst into a powder-fine shower of disrupted crystal. Instant sand.

Gotcha.

Two more on the way, bounding over the rocks. I dug deep into my diaphragm and half-remembered old singing lessons. I kept the note going, and amplified it a thousand times, sending it in a shock wave out across the island from end to end. The intensity of the sound swept out like a bomb blast. I was immune to it, but across the island, a dozen crystal ghosts exploded into dust and shards as the wave of sound rolled over them.

The note did more than take care of them; it also brought Bad Bob's other allies out of hiding. Farther inland, near the stunted, mummified trees, Bad Bob's former Wardens were coming out of camouflaged tents and starting to get organized. The shock wave rolled over them, and dozens more went down—not dead, but stunned and probably deafened. I'd caught them by surprise.

They returned the favor.

As I took a step forward, stone softened under my boot, and I sank in to my ankles. A rival Earth power was trying to harden the matrix again around my body, which would have not just trapped me but pulverized flesh and bone, if I was lucky—or amputated both feet at the ankles, if I wasn't.

I held her off, and found some weedy grass struggling to survive between the rocks near my opponent. I added a giant shot of power to send it growing and weaving between the stones. It slithered out of a crevice and wrapped around her ankles, yanking her flat on the ground, then dragged her out into the open where I could see her.

I knew the woman. She was a thin little thing, older than many of my peers in power—a veteran, someone who'd ruled with an iron hand in the old days. A contemporary of Bad Bob's. Her name was Deborah Kirke. She'd been wounded in the Djinn rebellion, I remembered, and she'd lost most of her family when her Djinn had destroyed her house around her. She had cause to believe Bad Bob's anti-Djinn agenda, but that didn't mean I could give her a pass. She'd taken up arms against me and the other Wardens.

That meant she had to be stopped.

"Deborah," I yelled. "Just stay down, dammit. I don't want to hurt you!"

She didn't. I suppose, from her perspective, she really couldn't.

I trapped her under a clump of boulders and reinforced it by melting the top layer into a concrete cage. She could breathe, and in time she'd probably dig her way out of it. I was heartsick doing this to an old lady, but I had a war to fight, and mercy wasn't going to win me any consideration from their side in return.

Another former Warden had emerged from cover as well. I knew this one, too—Lars Petrie, a Fire Warden. He liked to form whips out of living flame, and sure enough, one hissed through the air and cut a burning path down my right arm. It wrapped around my wrist and yanked me off balance. I wasn't prepared, and the burn bit deep, charring skin and muscle. That was bad; burns created distractions, made it harder to concentrate, channel, control the forces I needed to balance.

I grabbed water out of the sea. It rose in an arc into my hand, frozen solid, and compacted into a spear. I barely paused before sending it arrowing at Petrie's chest.

He dodged. The spear hit the rocks behind him and shattered into snow, but it distracted him. While it did, I formed another blade of ice and slashed it through the whip. The flame fell apart on my side of the cut, leaving ugly black spirals up the skin of my arm, with red exposed muscle.

I tried not to think about how much that was going to hurt once the nerves woke up.

I started running for him, knife clutched in my uninjured hand, and while I was at it, I shook the rocks under his feet, a miniature earthquake that sent him stumbling. He wrapped his fire whip around a boulder to steady himself, but I was there when he straightened, already cutting at him with the knife.

I got it under his chin and held the cold edge there. Our eyes met, and Petrie's widened in shock and horror.

"Listen to me," I said. "Lars, we have no fight here. None. You can't win, and he doesn't expect you to. You're nothing but compost and cannon fodder to him."

"Yeah? And what the hell am I to you?" he demanded, and shoved me backward. "I watched four Wardens die while Djinn ripped them apart, and where were you? *Screwing* one of them. You don't care about us, any of us. Don't pretend we're the same."

The fire whip formed in his hand again, and I moved my right foot back for better stability as I tried to anticipate which way I needed to dodge. He trailed the whip on the ground, snaking it this way and that, hissing the burning edges of it over stones. A tiny alarmed crab scuttled out of a tide pool and toward the sea. A second later, the whip touched the pool and turned it into steam, baking whatever was unlucky enough still to be trapped there.

"I'm not your enemy," I said, and held out empty hands toward him. "Come on, man. Let's not do this."

Petrie, like Deborah, was a post-traumatic survivor of the Djinn attacks. I didn't know what had happened to him, but I remembered that the review team had removed him from his duties, and that Miriam, the head of the internal security team of the Wardens, had put in precautions . . .

Petrie had a fail-safe in his brain. *Dammit.* Standard Earth Warden procedure was to put a two-stage fail-safe in place. The first one stunned, and the second one killed. If I knew the stun code . . .

But I didn't. And I had no time to find out, because even if Lars was damaged and irrational, he was one hell of a master of that whipping loop of fire. It flared at me without warning, and I dropped to a crouch. That saved my neck, most likely; he'd been aiming to decapitate me, and I felt the scorching heat as the living flame snaked over my head.

I lunged forward and pulled up seawater with both

hands, forming a massive wave that shattered over the rocks and hit Lars from behind, sending him flying and dousing his fire whip in a hot blast of steam.

I threw myself on his chest as he sprawled on top of the rocks. "Stop!" I screamed at him, and banged his head against the rock. "Stop fighting me!"

I put a forearm over his chest to hold him down as he struggled. My arm was bloody and torn from the fight, dripping on his chest, and I felt savage. So much for the black torch being responsible for all my darkness; Bad Bob had been right, I'd had some of it all along.

And I always would.

He got an arm free and put it to use by landing a right hook to my jaw—but not hard enough to break free, or to break my bones.

"Just stop," I said. "Please stop." I didn't know if I was talking to Lars Petrie, or to myself.

I let Petrie go, and he sat up, exultant triumph lighting up his plain, middle-aged face. I backed away.

I heard a dry, ironic sort of clapping behind me. "Impressive." Bad Bob's voice. "Damn if you aren't still a do-gooder, after all this effort."

Petrie's face twisted in fury, and his fire whip formed in his hand, then snapped toward me.

From directly behind me, Bad Bob said, "Duck."

I did. Well, I was going to do that anyway.

A sheet of ice the thickness of a razor slashed through the air, spinning like a saw blade. It sliced feathering hairs from the top of my head, bit into Petrie's neck, and kept on spinning.

I gasped as Petrie's hot blood splashed over me in a wave. That blade hadn't been aimed at me.

It had been intended for Petrie. I whirled around while Petrie was still falling.

Bad Bob was sitting in a battered deck chair behind me, right out in the open, on top of a pile of rocks that I'd have sworn had been empty a few seconds before. He grinned and waved at me, and made a discus-throwing motion. "Hell of a shot, eh? I should turn pro."

Petrie's head and body hit the stones separately, spattering me with even more blood.

I couldn't turn to look. I didn't dare take my gaze away from Bad Bob, who was no illusion, not this time. He was *here*. Within striking distance.

Victory was at hand . . . for one of us.

"You look tired," Bad Bob said. "Rough trip?" He sipped a beach drink. He was wearing a Hawaiian shirt in vomit yellow and pinkeye pink that clashed with his skin and hair. He also was wearing old man shorts, socks, and flip-flops. If I hadn't known who and what he was, he'd have looked like any old pensioner roaming Fort Lauderdale or asking directions at Disney.

"Why?" I blurted. He knew what I was asking, so I didn't even look at Petrie.

"Thought I'd give you a helping hand, since you seemed to be having some crisis of conscience. Tell me, why is that, anyway? I figured you'd be well on down the road to not caring about anyone but yourself by now."

I tried slow, even breaths. The burn on my arm was getting worse, and shock was setting in. I needed to heal myself, and I had the power to do it; I just didn't dare spare the concentration it would take to build the matrix of energy and direct the healing.

Bad Bob didn't blink. "Oh, where are my manners? Have a seat, kid. You look just about done in."

And with a wave of his hand, there was another beach chair, this one shaded by a ruffling yellow awning

fringed in white. There was even a little side table, and a
fruity cocktail with a blue folding umbrella.

"No, thanks," I said. It was only three steps to the
chair, but I wasn't at all sure the chair wouldn't turn out
to be a spring-loaded bear trap. Messy, and undignified,
as a way to exit stage left. "I think I'll just stand. It's
great for the calf muscles."

"Suit yourself, but your calf muscles have always been
top flight, especially in those heels you like to wear." He
smacked his lips, just another leering old geezer. "Come
here all by yourself, did you?"

"Sure. Why not? You're not going to hurt me, are
you?"

"Never in a million years, sweetness."

Oh sure. I remembered being forced down on my
back, and Bad Bob handing a bottle to his Djinn, and a
Demon sliding its black tentacles down my throat.

No, he'd never hurt me at all.

"Turn around," he said. "Let me see the progress."

He meant let him see the black torch.

Moment of truth. I'd spent time in the water forming
an illusion, one that had all the weight of reality to it.
The twisting shadow on my back looked and felt like
the real thing.

I hoped Bad Bob couldn't tell the difference at this
range.

My shirt was knit, and sleeveless. I pulled it up so that
my back was revealed. "Satisfied?" I didn't wait for an
answer, just dropped it back down again. "I'm still on
your team, Bob. You saw to that, whether I like it or not.
I was your first-round draft pick."

Had he bought it? I couldn't be sure. He sat there
looking at me, nothing in particular showing in his expression, and then nodded. "Just wanted to be sure," he

said. "You wouldn't believe all the crazy crap people pull trying to get into the VIP section these days. Some Djinn came in here about three hours ago, pretending to be you, if you can believe that. Talk about your Trojan horses. That was a dumb idea. They think I can't tell the difference?"

I felt my throat go tight and my guts clench. "Who was it?"

He shrugged. "Didn't ask. She looked just like you, though, right down to the sassy attitude. Good copy. If I hadn't known that tattoo was a fake, I might have just let my guard down for her."

Was he taunting me? I was afraid that he was, but I didn't want to force things until I knew for sure. "So where is she now?"

"Why?"

"Because I'm not on great terms with them anymore." That was almost true.

He lit a cigar, a big Cuban thing, and puffed until he was satisfied with the draw. "What do you think happened? I've got dependents, you know. People got to eat."

Whatever I'd expected, it wasn't that. "What?"

He gave me more of that horrible grin. "Sweetheart, you ever order a Djinn to become a pot roast for dinner? Unbelievable, the things you can do when you've got power over them. It's a real education."

I felt an actual wave of sickness travel through me, like the blast from a bomb of nausea. And he kept on smiling.

I couldn't stop the words that rolled out of my mouth. "You fucking sick awful evil—"

"Ah, that's the old Jo," he said, and winked at me. "You know what's wrong with all my old friends, the ones I talked out here to the middle of Buttcrack, No-where, with me? I tell them how to humiliate and mu-tilate a Djinn, and they dive right in. They think it's payback. I hate to say it, but the human race is starting to completely disgust me, sweet pea, and that's why I'm so glad you're here. You, I can still shock. You restore my faith in humanity."

That logic was so twisted it ought to be served salted, with a side of mustard. "You just killed your own guy," I said. "That can't be good for morale."

Bob dismissed it with a shrug. "Petrie was nuts. Ev-erybody knew it. But I'll tell you what, sugar, I was really amazed at how many Wardens I got to turn their coats. I didn't even work that hard at it. Talk about morale, you guys need some team-building retreats or something. Then again, you'll all be dead, so that problem solves itself, really."

This sounded so much like Bad Bob that it lulled me into believing that he'd keep on talking, forever . . . and then a thick black tentacle burst up out of the rocks be-neath my feet and writhed its way up my ankle, my calf, my thigh.

"Oh, damn," he said, and sipped his drink. "Try not to move. It'll take your skin clean off if you struggle."

The thing was like an octopus tentacle, and I could feel the obscene, cold suction of hundreds of tiny cups against my skin. I froze. It didn't read as alive on the aetheric, and it wouldn't respond to any kind of Earth power that I could wield.

"Let me go," I said. Bad Bob tilted his head, eyes burning an incandescent, almost Djinn shade of blue.

"Nope," he said. "Did you really think I wouldn't know you slipped the leash? Nice trick, by the way. I can always try it again, but I have the feeling you won't be all that easy to screw with again— Hold still or you'll lose that leg, you know."

I gave up struggling. "Fine. So what are you going to do with me? I don't make a very good pot roast, I'm just telling you right now."

Bob sighed and pinched the bridge of his nose, like I'd given him a monster headache. "What the hell am I gonna *do with you*?" he repeated. "You're kidding. This isn't remedial school for half-assed criminals. I'm going to kill the holy hell out of you, but first, you get to help me get what I need out of the Wardens."

I winced as my boot slipped against the rocks, and the tentacle wrapping my leg gained a couple more inches and got very, very friendly. "Lewis won't deal."

"Of course he'll deal. That boy loves you, always has. I know him. I picked him for the Wardens." Bad Bob looked positively malevolent for a second. "Lewis never did want responsibility. He isn't going to step up to it now, with your life on the line."

I blinked. Bad Bob, the all-knowing and all-powerful, was talking like an old man, set in his ways, reciting out-of-date facts. Lewis certainly had once been like that, but like Bad Bob himself, he'd changed. Bad Bob hadn't bothered to find out how much.

"So what am I worth?" I asked. "What are you going to ask?"

"He's not stupid. He grabbed all the Djinn he could find and bottled them. My folks back on the mainland couldn't find much, and what they did find got them killed. So I'll trade you for a cargo full of bottles. How's that? Make you feel any better?"

Not really. But I didn't believe for a second that Lewis would trade *one* Djinn for me, much less a boatload. Besides, rescue was on its way.

Rachel Caine

Right?

It had been maybe ten minutes since my arrival on the island. The *Grand Horizon* was supposed to be visible by now, but I couldn't see its distinctive outline anywhere on the open seas around us, and it was way too big to miss. Had something happened? Had Bad Bob managed to sink the second ship, too?

Was I all alone here, at the end?

Well, if I was, I was going to go down fighting.

God, please, don't let him kill me.

Because David really would destroy everything.

Chapter Eleven

Bad Bob talked. He loved to talk, and I let him, because I learned a lot.

Bad Bob, I was starting to realize, really didn't have much. While we'd been sailing around the Atlantic as a big, juicy target, he'd been conducting a multifront war. Those never work; ask Napoleon. He'd had operatives back home who'd gone after the remaining Wardens, on the theory that if they were any damn good, Lewis wouldn't have left them behind. That got him a big fat score of fail. The Wardens didn't lose a single person, or any Djinn.

The Sentinels, who were getting increasingly desperate, had been taken down not by the Wardens themselves but by Homeland Security. They couldn't even defeat a bunch of *government* men.

That was kind of rich.

What remained of Bad Bob's threat to the Wardens was here, on this island, which meant a bunch of fanatics in rags with the aetheric equivalent of a nuclear device.

Not great, but at least isolated.

I couldn't move much, thanks to my mutated octopus friend, but I could pay attention to Bob's manic ramblings, in case there was something useful to be learned.

I didn't know if the thing inside had driven him mad, but it certainly didn't know how to flip the OFF switch.

Eventually, Bad Bob got impatient. He'd expected my rescue to heave over the horizon, but if it was out there, it was smart and very patient.

That was good.

It just wasn't good for me.

"You're sure they got the message?" I asked. I'd managed to find a position sitting on the stones, with my pinned leg carefully held straight out. I didn't want to look too closely at what was happening to me; it felt very much like that tentacle was sinking into my leg, and I'd really had enough of that kind of thing. "Maybe your ransom demand went to voice mail. Sucks when that happens."

"Oh, they know I have you. They just need some incentive, that's all," Bad Bob said cheerfully. The sun was beating down on my unprotected head, and while I wasn't going to get delirious from the heat, or the lack of water, it wasn't the most comfortable I'd ever been.

And I didn't like the sound of *incentive*.

I liked it a whole lot less when Bad Bob got out of his chair and walked toward me, because as he did, he reached into empty space at his side and brought out the Djinn Ancestor Scriptures.

I stared at it wearily. It wasn't of human origin, this thing; as far as I knew, it wasn't of Djinn making, either. The Ancestor Scriptures probably wasn't even a book, in the strictest sense, although it certainly had that appearance here in this plane—leather binding, wrinkled ancient pages, metal flaps to lock it shut.

What it really was I couldn't say, but I was pretty sure that it had been written by a higher power than the Oracles, and the Oracles of the Djinn had been entrusted with its care and feeding.

Whether this was one of the three originals or a copy, I couldn't say—the copies were just as deadly, if maybe not imbued with as much power.

"How'd you get your hands on that?" I asked Bad Bob as he opened the metal latches and began to flip crackling, translucent pages. "Garage sale at the Villain Supply Company?"

"I took it from an Oracle," he said, but absently, as if it really didn't matter. He wasn't bragging. "Air Oracle. Years ago."

That, I could believe. The Air Oracle had always struck me as hostile, guarded, angry at the world in general and humans in particular. I'd certainly gotten little to no love from him/her/it.

That kind of made sense, if Bad Bob had gotten there first. He'd given bipeds a bad name.

"Hmmmmm." Bad Bob looked down at a page, considered it, and shook his head. "No, too subtle. This—too messy. Ah, here we go. I'll just turn on old DNA inside you, see what we get. Maybe you'll grow a tail, shark teeth, chicken skin ..."

Well, I definitely wasn't waiting around for *that*.

I stole Petrie's specialty, and formed a whip of pure plasma out of the air, igniting it with a burst of silvery power out of my special Djinn reserve. It burned hot blue, and where it slithered over the rocks, it left melted trails behind.

I snapped it toward Bad Bob.

He caught it in one hand, wrapped it around his fist, and yanked. I slid forward on the stones; the tentacle wrapped around my left leg tightened, and I felt flesh tearing under the strain.

Dammit.

I let go of the whip, and the fire guttered out, leaving

just a trail of greasy smoke between us. Bad Bob, for a change, didn't say anything. He walked over to where I was pinned in place, blood streaking down over the tentacle anchoring me.

"You just don't lie down, do you?" he said. "I always said you were way too good for the Wardens. You made the rest of us look bad." He turned and yelled toward his watching followers. There were a lot fewer than I remembered—maybe twenty, if that. Granted, I'd taken some down earlier, but I didn't think I'd grounded quite that many. He'd probably lost some to incursions and his own craziness—like Petrie—plus I figured that those who could think logically enough to escape had grabbed transportation and taken their chances.

That probably meant they were dead, out there on the ocean, but at least they'd died cleanly, off this black hunk of stone.

His remaining troops scrambled to assemble at his silent wave of command. They were terrified, and they were realizing—all too late—that the savior they'd imagined him to be was all in their heads. He'd used their fears against them.

I imagined he would continue to do that, right up to the end. They had to follow him now. Where else was there to go?

"Get over here!" he yelled. "Bring our friend along!"

The Sentinels began crossing the distance. Some of them were old, some were wounded, none of them looked entirely compos mentis.

They all looked at me like I was dinner—which, considering Bad Bob's earlier pot roast revelation, was a truly sickening thought.

"Moira," Bob said, and held out his hand. A spritely

little pixie of a young woman stepped out from the others and came forward to lock fingers with him. In her left hand, she carried an old green wine bottle with an equally ancient cork stuffed in the top.

I didn't know her. She was younger than I was, which surprised me—a lovely young girl with fair skin and full lips and a head of thick, lustrous red hair that glinted gold in its highlights.

She held the bottle up to Bad Bob as if seeking his approval on a choice to serve with dinner. He nodded.

Her eyes were the same blue as Bad Bob's. "Hey, Da," she said. "What can I do to help?"

He pecked a kiss onto her perfect milkmaid's cheek. "Oh, just stand there and look pretty."

I felt a step or two behind the curve. *"Da?"* I said. "Unless she's speaking Russian, you've got to be kidding me. You've got a *kid*? Wait—more importantly, some woman actually slept with you? Without a condom?"

"Shut up," the girl said, and temper blazed up in her like magma. That, more than anything else, convinced me of the paternal bloodline.

"Wow," I said. "I don't know whether to say congratulations or condolences. That probably goes for both of you."

"Moira, meet Joanne," Bob said. "Moira's my pride and joy, the fruit of my powerful loins. Isn't she beautiful?"

Moira, like daughters everywhere, looked annoyed. "Oh, can it, Da."

"I'm very proud of her. But you know how that feels, don't you, Jo? You're a mother. More or less."

That made me flinch, as he'd known it would. I wanted to demand that he leave my own child out of this—a half-human/half-Djinn hybrid who'd become one of the three Djinn Oracles. The Earth Oracle, in fact, which was how I'd gained access to that particular set of powers—through her.

Imara had been born full-grown, and she was a lot like me—she could, and did, take care of herself. Besides, the Djinn would have closed ranks around their Oracles, protecting them at all costs.

Imara was safe. I was the one at risk. He wanted me to fear for her, but I just stared him down.

"Nothing?" Bad Bob watched my face. "Huh. Well, okay then. Cross that one off my list." And he pulled the cork on the bottle. "Oh, wait. Let's revisit that."

A ghost misted out of the air. My own body, mirrored. My own dark hair. Everything the same, except her golden eyes, and the brick-red layered dress that swirled around her body like smoke.

No. It couldn't be.

"Damn," Bad Bob said, and turned to Moira. "I thought I told you to bring the *white.*"

She smirked. "Sorry."

I didn't pay any attention to their playacting. My brain seemed stuck, unable to move past the word *No* to any kind of possible outcome to this moment.

My daughter Imara was *here*. And she couldn't possibly be here. There was no way Bad Bob or any of his minions could have captured her, stolen her from her chapel in Sedona, without triggering an all-out war with the Djinn. They'd fight to the last of them for her, no matter whose daughter she'd been in the beginning. Not only that, but David would have known. There was no way that he and Ashan *couldn't* have known, if something happened to Imara. The Earth Herself would have fought back to protect an Oracle.

My daughter looked at me with desperate fear in her

eyes, and I couldn't stop a pulse of maternal anguish from traveling like lightning through my body.

And then I pushed it away. "Nice try," I said. "But no sale. That's not my daughter."

Moira gave her father a harassed look. "*Told* you she'd never buy that malarkey," she said, and grabbed the bottle back from him. The form of the Djinn shifted away from Imara's reflection of my face, took on darker shades and harsher angles. Long, cornrowed hair with gleaming bits of gold beaded in. This was a Djinn I knew.

Rahel.

The Djinn had fought to keep that part of her appearance the same—at what cost, I couldn't quite imagine— but she'd lost the war on clothing. Moira dressed her like a Barbie, and the effects were ridiculous. Rahel was wearing a wine-colored evening gown, sleeveless, with a plunging neckline and a slit up the side. White opera gloves. Dangling diamond earrings.

Rahel was a beautiful creature, but this looked wrong on her. Deeply, stupidly insane.

"Wait," Moira said, and giggled. She added a tiara on top of Rahel's head, a ridiculously ornate confection of chrome and fake diamonds. "Wave to the adoring crowds, Miss America."

Rahel's right hand came up and did a mechanical, empty wave.

Her eyes were locked on mine, and I hated what I saw in them, because it was a very close cousin to the madness that I'd recently seen in David, when he thought I was gone. A desire to crush and destroy and kill everything in her path. She'd been tormented, forced to do horrible things. And she, like David, was not inclined to forgive.

"Hey," I said to Moira. "Seriously, is that the best you can do? Because that's not even original. Honestly, I used to be a Djinn. I had a teenage boy for a master. Now, *he* had an imagination. You're just—sad. But then again, like father, like daughter . . ."

I got that pulse of fury out of her again. "You shut your whore mouth!"

"Wow. Like I said. Sad. When you have to quote a MySpace graphic, you've just given up." I ignored Moira and looked at her father. "What's the point of having the kid here? Were you just lonely for somebody who had an extra helping of crazy in the veins?"

The girl smirked at me, turned, and skinned up the edge of her thin white shirt.

She didn't have a torch mark. Instead, her back was a mass of writhing fire, moving just below the skin—worse than mine had ever gotten, even at its most painful. "I'm one of the chosen," she said, and dropped the fabric. "Like you used to be, before you gave it all up."

"Jesus," I said. "Just when I thought you'd hit rock bottom, Bob. Congratulations on tunneling down."

"It's the family business," he said. "Bringing an end to this travesty we call humanity."

I checked the horizon. No ships breaking the smooth outline of the sea.

I was starting to sweat.

"So what now?" I asked. "Not that this isn't fun, but my leg's falling asleep. Can we move the end of the world along a little? Or at least work in a nap?"

Moira laughed. Bad Bob shrugged. "Sure," he said. "For you, sweetness, I'll kick it into high gear. But you know that means you're going to suffer, don't you?"

"I figured," I said, and shrugged. "I'm already suffering. These rocks are really uncomfortable."

He laughed. "What a girl," he said, and elbowed his daughter. "Right?"

By her expression, she found me a good deal less charming. "She's nothing," she said. "You never needed her, Da. You always had me." *Oooooh, jealous. Very jealous.* I could use it.

"That's true." He kissed her forehead, but his eyes never left me. "That's very true. I've been taking out her bones, one at a time. What do you think, princess?"

"Too boring." She wasn't even looking at me; she pulled free of Bad Bob and walked a slow circle around Rahel, inspecting her Miss America impersonation. "Make her work for it."

"Hmmmm. There's an idea. Two birds and one very big stone." Bad Bob slammed the book closed and put it under his arm. "All right, then. Let's see what you can do, my child. Impress me."

Moira sat down on a handy boulder, open wine bottle in both hands on her lap, and tossed glossy red hair back over her shoulders. "Rahel," she said. "I want you to break Joanne Baldwin's right leg in two. Use your hands. Do it now."

She knew the rules of commanding a Djinn—be specific about intent, method, and time frame. And I could see that they'd had plenty of practice with Rahel—she hadn't gained that traumatized fury without cause.

"Do it slowly," Moira said. "Make her feel every second of it."

Rahel's eyes focused on me, and she began walking across the stones toward where I sat. Not a hell of a lot I could do to stop her; if I tried to resist, my *other* leg was sure to be crushed, and maybe even pulled off by this tentacle thing Bad Bob was using for a tether. She still looked ridiculous in her getup, but I didn't let that fool me for a second. I'd seen the Djinn in the grip of truly evil people, and they were no more to be reasoned with than the blade of a knife.

I looked past Rahel at Moira. "I guess you hate me for being the daughter he never had. Daddy didn't trust you, did he? That's why he came after me in the first place. Because you weren't measuring up. Either that, or he wanted to screw me. Your choice."

Bad Bob's face went very still, and I knew I'd guessed right.

So did Moira. She surged to her feet. "Rahel! When I tell you, you're going to kill that bitch for me!"

One rule of commanding an embottled Djinn: *Never* give your orders angry. Moira had just forgotten to explicitly frame her order as to *whom* to kill. *Bitch* could apply to, oh, more than one of us standing here, and unless she caught that error later on, Moira was in for a nasty surprise.

I saw the light flare gold in Rahel's eyes, and I took a deep breath. *Wait,* I mouthed. The desire to strike was almost primal in her, and she knew she was close, so close to having the freedom to exact her revenge.

I knew I could push that button anytime I wanted to—but first, I had to endure a little more. Moira would think of her mistake if I gave her the time.

I needed to keep her engaged.

Rahel bent down and put her hands on my outstretched right leg, the nontentacled one. Her opera gloves felt cool and smooth against my skin. "She did say to do this slowly," she said, and I let out a slow breath, then nodded. Rahel was telling me, without wasting words, that she had identified the gaps in Moira's original order. To a Djinn, the word *slowly* meant something entirely different than it did to a human. Their time-scales were vast, and that instruction was not nearly as specific as Moira might have believed it was.

Now it was up to us to hide that fact.

Rahel froze, with her hands on my leg. I waited. I didn't feel anything—no increase in pressure, no pain, nothing. She'd taken the freedom Moira's instructions offered to simply stretch this out so long that it might take a lifetime for her grip to increase its force enough to crack a bone, much less break it.

"Nice," I murmured, and got a brief, cold parting of her lips. Her teeth were filed to points. "Don't panic, whatever I do."

Rahel raised one arched eyebrow, and I began to struggle against her grip, panting—selling the idea that she was hurting me, when in fact she was doing nothing but pinning my right leg to the stone.

As performances go, this one probably was a bit over the top even for high school melodrama, but Moira lapped it up like cream. I tossed in some begging and bargaining. She loved it. Pretty girl, but either Bad Bob's genetics or Bad Bob's black tattoo had rendered her broken and sick. I remembered someone else like her—Kevin's stepmother, Yvette Prentiss. The avid shine in Moira's blue eyes as I threw myself around and shrieked in simulated agony was almost exactly the same.

Then again, Bad Bob had been involved with Yvette, too. I had the feeling all the sickness came from one poisoned well.

Behind her, seated on his plastic throne, Bad Bob looked less focused on my performance. He scanned the horizons restlessly, frowning. His attention was on the effect, not the cause—he wanted my pain to draw my hypothetical rescue out from hiding.

I could have told him that it wasn't coming. Lewis was too careful for that.

I wasn't sure how long Rahel intended to carry on our little drama, but my voice was getting hoarse from all the screaming, and even Moira's attention was starting to wander. When you're losing your torturer's focus, it's probably time to wrap up the play.

I let out a heartrending shriek of utter agony, and went pitifully limp, weeping like my heart would break. I didn't have to simulate being exhausted. Throwing yourself into something like that takes a sweaty, aching toll.

Ah, she liked that. I had Moira's full attention once more. "Rahel, break Joanne Baldwin's other leg," Moira said, and her pale tongue came out to lick her lips. "Do it just as slowly."

Really, you can't spell sadist without the word *sad*. She'd just forgotten that my other leg was the one wrapped in Bad Bob's tentacle tether.

Rahel might not have normally been able to take the tentacle from my left leg, but she'd just been ordered to do something that allowed her to freely interpret method, and in one lightning-fast move, she reached down, plunged her fingers deep into the base of the tentacle, and ripped.

Oh *Christ* that hurt. The tentacle fought back, clamping down on my leg with all its muscular strength, and I felt things pop and move that really shouldn't be shifting around inside. Rahel ripped at it again, digging her sharp fingernails into dark flesh and ichor, and tore the thing loose from its roots deep in the rocks.

I rolled free, still wrapped in the black coil.

"What the hell are you doing?" Moira screamed. "Rahel, *stop!*"

Rahel froze, still crouched over the thrashing remains

of the tentacle. I had seconds, at most, to make this happen, and I knew it.

Strangely, Bad Bob hadn't reacted at all. I saw his face in a blur as I rolled behind the shelter of more stones, and it was impassive and watchful.

Assessing.

I didn't have time to try to remove the tentacle, but I didn't need to; cut off from its body, the thing was already dissolving into slime. When it drained away, it left my skin pallid, wrinkled, and torn, like old paper soaked for too long. I was losing blood, too much of it. I slammed Earth power through my nerves and pinched off broken capillaries, set up a healing matrix, and shut off the pain.

I couldn't afford it right now.

"Hey, Moira!" I yelled. "How old arc you? Maybe nineteen? Twenty? I was about your age the first time your dad tried to screw me!"

No girl wants to hear that about her father, especially when it comes from the daughter-rival that Daddy loves more.

Like I said, I could push that button anytime I wanted.

"Rahel!" Moira's voice was a raw, vicious snarl. "Kill that bitch *now*!"

Again with the lack of specificity.

I felt the energy shift, darken, and as I peered around the edge of the boulder, I saw Rahel streak straight for Moira.

It's possible that Moira might have recovered in time to order her to stop, although Rahel's attack clearly caught her totally by surprise.

To make damn sure it wouldn't fail, I reached out with a burst of power and filled Moira's mouth with seawater. She choked, gagged, and then it was too late. As the water rippled down from Moira's open lips, Rahel's claws sank deep into her throat.

In her thrashing, Moira let go of the wine bottle, and it rolled toward the edge of the boulder.

Bad Bob calmly reached over and caught it as it fell.

Shit.

Moira was sputtering blood, and her face was shockingly pale, her eyes desperate. Rahel remained where she was, claws in the girl's neck, and I saw her flash a look at Bad Bob.

He didn't react at all.

I was gripping the edge of the rock too hard, but I needed the sharp reminder of where I was, what the stakes had become.

Rahel ripped her claws free in a contemptuous gesture, and blood misted and spattered in an arc around her. She willed away the Miss America costume in favor of her more usual tailored pantsuit—in bloodred, not neon.

She turned her back before Moira's pallid, dying body toppled.

Bad Bob was holding her bottle, and unlike Moira, that evil old bastard knew every trick. "Freeze until I tell you to move again, Rahel," he said. "That was a goddamn stupid waste." There was no genuine emotion left in him, not even for his own child. He saw it as a waste, all right—because Moira hadn't measured up, in the crisis. "Jo. Come out."

"Yeah, not likely!" I yelled. I tried to slow down my breathing, order my thoughts. "This isn't going well for you, Bob. Maybe you should just give up now."

He laughed. "No."

He still had the book, and even though he hadn't

bothered to bring it out yet, he also had the spear, the Unmaking. I hadn't even managed to free Rahel, dammit, and if his daughter's bloody end hadn't been enough to distract him, I couldn't think of much else to try.

"Fair enough," I said. "Want to call it a draw? Lose/lose?"

"I want to call the game," he said. "On account of the death of the world."

I'd have liked to think he was just being grandiose, but there was a dark undertone to his voice now. Seeing Moira die had destroyed his fun, apparently; he was ready to just skip right to the end, which in his book was *and then the universe blew up. The end.*

"That really what you want?" I slowly got up, hopping on my good right leg, and braced myself on the boulder I'd been using for sparse cover. "Come on, Bob. If the world ends, so do you. I thought you wanted to destroy the Wardens and savor your victory first."

"As long as we all go out together, I'm fine with it," he said. I expected him to reach for the Ancestor Scriptures, but instead, he stretched out his hand, which disappeared in a tingle of blue sparks and reemerged holding a thick, matte-black cylinder like a spear, sharp on both ends.

The Unmaking. Its presence set up a horrible crawling repulsion in me, an itching all up and down my nervous system. I wasn't sure if the scientists were right, and it was stable antimatter, or if it was something even more exotic, like dark matter. Whatever it was, it did not have a place here, not in this world.

It was *wrong.*

It was also radioactive as hell, and it had almost destroyed me the last time I'd come anywhere near it. Now I was so closely connected to David, sharing the same well of power, that I didn't dare risk it again. If I was poisoned, he might be, too. And through him, half the Djinn.

Bad Bob rested one end of the shaft against the stones at his feet and leaned on it. The thing was a little taller than his head now, wickedly pointed. "You really bamboozled me, you know. I never thought you'd come alone. Never thought David would let you."

"He didn't," I said. "Nobody lets me do anything. You know that."

He nodded, but the look in his eyes was far, far away. "I liked you," he said. "Back in the day. Before things went wrong."

"I liked you, too." I hadn't, exactly, but I'd admired him. We'd all admired him. "I know you took the Demon Mark on for the right reasons—you wanted to save lives. You just weren't strong enough, in the end."

"Neither were you," he said. We weren't accusing each other now; there wasn't any heat to this exchange at all, just simple fact. "You'd have hatched out a Demon in the end, if you hadn't gotten all tangled up with the Djinn. But look what it did for you—all the things you've seen, all you've done. I made you stronger."

He wanted my approval.

I felt a hot breath of wind, then a gust off the ocean. Something was stirring out there. It blew my hair into a writhing cloud, and waves crashed the rocks at my back, dousing me in spray.

"Whatever doesn't kill you makes you stronger," I said. "And whatever *does* kill you—"

"Makes you invincible, if you're lucky," Bad Bob said, and smiled. I sensed a kind of good-bye in that smile, because it was real. Not a manic stretch of his lips, but a genuine expression of feeling and warmth. "You'll always be my kid, Jo. My crazy, brave, stupid kid."

And he'd always, in some sense, be my father. My mentor. The man who'd pushed me over the edge and made me grow wings to survive. The most abusive bastard father in the world.

I nodded, not trusting my voice.

"Here it comes," Bad Bob said, and looked up.

Something fell out of the eye of the hurricane. It was like a glass ball, soap-bubble thin, and it hit the rocks of the island and smashed into smaller spheres, each of which bounced and rolled over the rocks, uncoiled, and stood on two or four legs.

Crystalline skeletons, creatures out of drug dreams, that vanished like ghosts against the sunlight.

The Sentinels—those still standing—were unprepared. A few of them defended themselves, but most died, ripped apart on the rocks. My old colleagues, who'd lost their way and followed a false messiah.

I couldn't help them. Worse: I didn't *want* to help them.

Here at the end of the world, we were all going to have to settle up our debts.

"They're parasites," Bad Bob said. "Like dust mites. Bugs crawling through a crack in the wall. Vicious little things, though."

He slammed the Unmaking down onto the rocks, and a ringing vibration rippled out from its quivering length—the same frequency I'd used before, but a thousand times more powerful. Every crystalline skeleton exploded into powder.

Another glass ball fell, but it exploded well before contact with the ground when he slammed the point down again and woke that awful sound.

I'd clapped my hands over my ears. I couldn't help it.

"I thought you'd welcome their help," I said. I kept

watching Rahel, hoping that she'd be able to somehow break out of her paralysis, but she was as still as the rocks around me, and just about as lifeless. My only ally was completely out of commission. "Since it looks like it's just the two of us."

"What would they be good for? You can kill them. I've seen you do it." He shook his head. "We're on to bigger things. You feel the lines of force under us? This is a nexus point, Jo. It's the thinnest space between the planes, and between the worlds."

The island hadn't come to this place by accident. I could feel the humming power underneath my feet, and in the air around me. He'd been very careful about his choice of location for this. A born manipulator.

Like Lewis. *Where are you, Lewis?*

"Basic principles of magic, Jo," he said softly. "Like calls to like. And sacrifices have special weight here."

He threw the Unmaking to me—not *at* me, but *to* me, a low underhanded pitch.

I dodged it easily, but it didn't fall; it turned and hovered in midair, pointing at me. Menace radiated off of it like black light. I backed up, carefully, not taking my eyes off it.

It darted straight for my chest. It was too fast, and I had no room to maneuver.

My body reacted instinctively, and wrongly.

I put out my hands and grabbed it to hold it back from my exposed chest.

It was like plunging my hands into a vat of dry ice—instant, agonizing cold.

The pool of Djinn power inside of me turned toxic and black, poisoned at its source, and I felt myself begin to rot from the inside out. I was just enough Djinn to be vulnerable, and just enough human to be corruptible.

He'd counted on that. And on my survival instincts.

The spear felt hot and heavy in my hands. It had burned me, before, but now its touch felt different—almost like flesh. I could hear it singing to me, a fascinating whisper of noise that had nothing in common with the music of our world, *any* of our worlds.

It made me sick and dizzy at first. I tried to drop it. I gagged and tried to throw up the darkness inside, but it wasn't the kind that sat heavy in the stomach. This darkness filled me to the brim.

It took me over, completely.

When I opened my eyes again, I saw things differently. Literally. Holding the Unmaking made colors shift and burn, the whole structure of matter and light twist around me. It was beautifully destructive.

"We need more," Bad Bob said. He was a pillar of blazing darkness in front of me, alien and somehow not alien at all. "You know how to make more of it, Joanne."

I knew. I'd seen the process at work. The antimatter incubated inside the body of a Djinn, converting the power into its raw, black opposite, stabilized into a form we could handle and use.

Rahel knew it, too. I saw the fatal acceptance in her face, and the haughty courage, even though she was trapped in place by the bottle that Bad Bob held in his hand. *Come, then,* she seemed to be saying. *If you can.*

If I'd been myself, any version of myself, I wouldn't have done it. Couldn't have.

But holding the Unmaking had taken all that away from me, just as Bad Bob had intended.

I heard myself scream, a raw sound that fused oddly with the music of the Unmaking as it crawled through my nerves.

I lifted the spear in both hands and plunged it toward Rahel's chest.

It never got there.

A pulse of pure hot Earth power rolled up through the rocks and blasted them into knife-edged fragments under our feet, sending me flying in one direction, Rahel in another.

The attack came from underneath us.

Bad Bob was caught by surprise. He staggered, leaped for stable ground, but it dissolved underneath his sandals. He fell. The Ancestor Scriptures skittered across stone, and the bottle dropped toward a fatal impact with the edge of a piece of lava rock.

I got to Rahel before the bottle hit stone. I felt the firm impact of the spear hitting her flesh, and then— then she was gone, and the spear was broken off at the tip, vibrating like a tuning fork in my hands.

Rahel's bottle had shattered into pieces, and she was gone.

Rahel was *free*.

The Unmaking howled at me. It was angry at being cheated.

"Son of a *bitch*!" Bad Bob clawed his way out of the hole in the island, and jumped again as another hole was blasted up through it from beneath. Water geysered into the air between us. I held the spear in both hands and cast my own awareness out, too.

It was an impossibly stupid thing to do, but Lewis had taken the *Grand Horizon* down, like the world's most unwieldy submarine. It floated in its protective, glistening bubble right below the island, and as I looked down into one of the holes, I could see people on the decks looking up at me a dozen feet below.

Something hit me from behind with stunning force,

and I toppled into the water. The spear was as heavy as an iron bar, and it dragged me down toward the ship below.

Rahel wrapped her arms around me and pulled me back before the spear could touch the fragile surface of Lewis's protective shield that kept everyone on the ship alive beneath the waves. I fought to get free, and when that didn't work, I tried to move the spear around to stab her from behind.

She pinned my elbows and dragged me back, swimming like a dolphin at attack speed.

The protective dome sparked with golden light, and I saw Wardens emerging. Lots of them. They were accompanied by the bright silver glow of Djinn, and it was all bright, and weirdly beautiful, and I realized that I was running out of air. The screaming of the Unmaking in my head was so loud it blotted out everything.

Rahel wouldn't let me breathe. I fought with everything I had, trying to throw her off, and for a moment it seemed like I'd succeeded.

I seized the opportunity and shot myself through the water at cannon speed, heading up. I blasted a path through the rocks and came up in the middle of the floating island, gasping and shuddering. I grabbed the husk of a dead palm tree and pulled myself from the water just a second before the hole sealed itself over beneath my boots. I used the Unmaking to lever myself to my feet. Where it touched, the rocks blackened and dissolved as if I'd doused them with acid.

My hands were black now, and my forearms were the gray of dead flesh, but I didn't hurt at all.

Bad Bob slid down a small mountain of rubble, and it exploded into flame and shrapnel behind him. He thumped down next to me, and we both looked up.

The storm circling overhead had taken on a thick darkness, pregnant with menace. As I watched, the clouds inverted their colors—a negative image, just a flash, and then emerald lightning tore through the sky, breaking in all directions.

"Time," Bad Bob said. "Take that up, Jo. Take it to the other side."

Now I knew what he wanted from me. The Unmaking had made it clear to me, in ways that nothing had ever been clear before. None of this mattered. None of this was real. I'd been living an illusion all this time, a sad little nightmare of a life that started nowhere and ended in darkness.

Beyond that portal lay the *real* world. The *only* world.

This was just a fiction, and it needed to end so that we could all go to a better place.

I took a firmer grip on the spear, and rose up into the aetheric, into the heart of the storm.

Chapter Twelve

At the center of the slowly rotating mass of energy was the portal to the other world. The *real* world.

It was like a drop of pure darkness, maybe a dozen feet across—space made liquid. I could feel a kind of pull coming from it—not gravity, not force, nothing so simple as that. It was aware, and awake. It was hungry and endlessly patient, and I realized that it was like the slow, vast intelligence of the planet below me . . . like, but so much *more*. The Earth was a virus, a microbe. What lay on the other side of the portal was *God*. Not ours, though. A jealous, angry, hungry God.

In the aetheric, the spear I was carrying was tremendously heavy, and the higher I tried to rise, the heavier it got. It was like swimming with an anvil.

Then a truck full of anvils.

Then the world in my arms.

I screamed in soundless frustration and gained another few feet.

Then another. *I was so close.* I could see the shimmering waves in the portal, feel its draw. I could feel the answering vibration in the Unmaking, the key for the lock, and the lock that wanted to be turned.

My whole aetheric body was on fire. My senses had

shifted, changed into a different spectrum, and I could finally see what was holding me back from completing my mission . . .

The Djinn.

They were all around me, grabbing on to me, pulling me down. So many of them. Between me darted human forms—Wardens, trying to stand between me and the destiny of everything.

It was the magical weight of the world, and it was all against me.

I snarled and surged forward, again. I tried stabbing at the Djinn with the spear, but they easily avoided me.

The Wardens did, too.

I was being dragged backward, and as I was pulled, I gouged bloody holes in the aetheric in my fury. The spear left a gaping black trail, a scar between worlds—not enough to open the door, though.

I reversed my efforts, and instead of trying to break free and go up, I charged down, arrowing through the unprepared Djinn line, and used a burst of hot black power to brake myself back into my body.

Bad Bob was on his back, trying to crab-walk away from the Djinn who was advancing on him—who had already hurt him, from the burns and scars on his face and arms. His hair was half burned off, and his eyes glittered with absolute insanity.

I didn't recognize the Djinn, because it was shining like a golden sun, power incarnate. It reached down and picked up the Ancestor Scriptures from where Bad Bob had dropped them.

The Djinn's back was to me. I didn't think, I just acted.

I raised the spear.

He turned.

It was David. David standing there, facing me. Facing his own death at my hands. I couldn't identify what I saw in his face, in his eyes, except that it was not anger, not at all.

I snarled and lunged for him. The Unmaking had me now, dark and cold and certain, and it was going to take us both.

He said, *"Fides mihi,"* and touched his hand to his chest, over where a human heart would be.

And suddenly, the world went quiet. Time stopped.

The Unmaking swallowed its unending shriek.

And I *remembered*.

I was an observer to the past.

The lifeboat, where Lewis had killed me.

I was dead on the floor, lying in David's arms. Pale and limp and open-eyed. Done, and yet still trapped inside the shell.

My old self took in a convulsive breath and tried to fight her way free. I knew this moment. I recognized the agony that rippled through her body as Bad Bob's torch fought her for control.

I watched her pass out, head lolling against David's body as he poured energy into her to seal off the mark and cut her off from the black influence of the thing, one last time.

I didn't remember anything else, but the scene played on, a bare few seconds that changed everything.

"The containment won't last," Lewis said. "You know it won't. I used one fail-safe on her. We can put in a second one while she's out."

"Not without her consent."

"She already gave consent." That was lawyering the point, but David allowed it to slip past. "We can't kill her.

We can't save her. The best we can do now is to make sure that she can be controlled if this goes bad."

David bared his teeth like a wild thing, and I thought for a second that he really would lunge right for Lewis's throat. "*You're* not deciding when she lives or dies," he said. "Not *you.*"

Lewis closed his eyes in what looked like gratitude and relief. "I don't want to," he said. "I never wanted to. You have to be the one, David. You're the only one she trusts enough to get close at the last moment. If it's Joanne or the world, you have to choose."

David froze, and the people clustered around the edges of the tableau shuffled. Cherise was the one who finally spoke.

"She'd want it to be you," she said. "She really would."

There were tears shining in my friend's eyes.

"I'll put the fail-safe in place," Lewis said. "You choose the codes."

It was a combination, of course. Words, and deeds.

Fides mihi. Trust me.

And his hand, giving me his heart.

Fides mihi.

David's use of the fail-safe should have killed me. If I'd been myself, only myself, it would have turned me off like a light, gone forever.

The Unmaking deflected it from shutting down my body, but it couldn't stop the memory from returning, and the memory brought its own clarity. Its own powerful, unstoppable force.

In the second that passed, the terrible certainties that had filled me since Bad Bob put the Unmaking in my hand began to unravel. *No. This is wrong. This is all wrong. I can't do this.*

David wasn't the enemy.

This life wasn't a fiction. It was the only reality I had. The only one I wanted, no matter what the creature beyond that portal promised me.

But even though my brain caught up with the realities and horror of being taken over, I couldn't stop the physics of what was already in motion—me. I was already lunging for him, and I was too close to miss him.

David put the Ancestor Scriptures between us.

The Unmaking hit the book, and for a second it pushed deep into the pages, tunneling through toward David's chest. Then it stopped moving, as if it had hit an impenetrable wall.

Then it began to shake in my hands. Not vibrate. *Shake*.

And then it exploded.

Shards of it flew everywhere—powdery bits, larger fragments. Some hit the rocks around us and gouged out massive craters as they skidded. The powder whipped away on the wind, a radioactive cloud that glowed hot green in the aetheric.

And one fragment—the largest one—flew straight up, into the eye of the storm.

It shrieked its way through the portal in our world, then the aetheric, and then through every plane stacked above it, ripping a hole just large enough for a single drop of darkness to squeeze through.

It trembled pendulously, then fell from the portal—a dozen feet across, maybe.

Directly above us.

I lunged toward David, trying to push him out of the way. He did the same, trying to save me.

We collided at the center, and the black drop came crashing down on us.

I wrapped my arms around David, felt his go around me, and power flared silver through and around us.

Then the darkness hit us, and the world ended.

I never expected to wake up, and I was really sorry I did. I must have been lying on the rocks for hours, cold and wet and cramped; my muscles were so stiff and strained that I whimpered even before trying to shift my position.

Overhead was a clear night sky, thick with constellations, and a bright yellow moon, three-quarters full.

Wind rustled over the island.

"David?"

No answer. I pushed myself up to a painful, staggering walk. In the moonlight, I saw nothing but black rock and sea spray.

"David?"

There was a body lying a few feet away, half hidden behind a boulder.

Bad Bob, not David. He'd died hard and ugly. Something had blown his torso in two, dividing him neatly in half from the crown of his head to somewhere around his navel. He'd been dead for hours. The blood was mostly dried on the stones around him, and he smelled lightly of decay.

More dead Sentinels littered the landscape. Moira was still draped over the stones where Rahel had left her. Lars Petrie's severed head rocked gently in the tropical wind.

There was a cruise ship standing off the island, all its lights ablaze, but it was too far to swim, feeling as cramped and cold as I already was. God, I felt *awful*.

It was a mystery to me how I was still alive, or why.

"David?" I fumbled around, trying to find that silvery cord that connected us on the aetheric.

I couldn't *find it.* Or the aetheric.

I'd gone completely headblind; I was unable to feel anything beyond my own normal human senses.

I'd lost my access to power.

"David!" I screamed it in panic this time, desperate to find him. I felt like I was suffocating, trapped inside my own skin.

So *alone.* I scrambled over rocks and bodies, looking for him with single-minded intensity, getting more and more panicked with every silent second.

I found him sitting on a boulder at the very tip of the island. He was naked and shivering.

"David? Oh God—honey—"

He was different. Very different.

When he raised his head, I saw that his eyes had gone plain brown.

Human brown.

I crouched down beside him and wrapped him in my arms. He tried to speak, but nothing came out. "My God. What happened to us?"

He couldn't tell me.

I needed to signal the ship anchored out there, let them know we were still alive, but when I reached out for a spark of power, I found nothing. Nothing at all. Not a single tingle of energy that wasn't fueled by the rapidly diminishing level of my own blood sugar.

I had no supernatural power at all.

Neither did David, as far as I could tell.

He got over a little bit of his violent shivering—enough to talk again. "B-b-black corner," he whispered.

I knew what that meant. There'd been damage to the

Earth Herself—damage that had destroyed the ability of the planet to channel energy to this part of the world. Most black corners were small; a few measured as much as a city block, but those were rare.

This one . . . there was no way to know how far it extended, but inside it Wardens wouldn't have power, and Djinn wouldn't be anything more than human—helpless, and ultimately dying as their stored energy ran out.

We had to get off the island. *Now*.

I gathered up dried palm husks and whatever I could scavenge from the bodies and ripped tents of the Sentinels that was burnable. I found some waterproof matches in a backpack and got a signal fire going. It wouldn't burn for long, but it didn't need to, and while it was burning, I wrapped David in the cast-off clothes of dead men and sat with him at the fire, trying to get him warm enough to stop shaking.

It seemed to take forever for a boat to arrive. When it did, it was full of Wardens, and Lewis was the first to step off the craft and onto the rocks.

He didn't exactly rush to our aid. He looked ill, and almost fell as he made his slow, careful way over the rocks. He wasn't the only one. All the rest of the Wardens looked just as bad.

"What's happened?" I asked. "Lewis?"

He coughed, as if something was broken inside. He wiped blood from the corner of his mouth and leaned his weight against a boulder as if he was too weak to keep standing.

"When the portal leaked, you and David took the hit. You absorbed it and stopped it from going any deeper into the earth. If you hadn't, we wouldn't be here right now." He stopped to cough again, and this time I wasn't sure he'd stop. When he finally did, his voice was scratchy and thin. "But because you were joined when you took the hit, the shock bounced both ways. Through the Djinn, and through the Wardens."

Oh dear God. "How bad is it?"

"It's turned this whole part of the ocean into a giant black corner," Lewis said. "We've got to get under way. If we run the engines hard, we might make it out of the dead zone before the Djinn start to die."

David raised his head for the first time. "Won't help us," he said. "You and me." He nodded to me, and I knelt next to him, my knees digging painfully into the edges of the stones.

"What are you talking about?" I asked. "What about us?"

"The blast—had to shift everything away to keep us alive—"

Lewis was getting it now, that bad feeling. I saw it as he straightened and looked more intensely at the two of us. "What is he talking about?"

David grabbed my arms. "Our powers are gone," he said. "Had to destroy them. Had to."

I wasn't sure I could even dare to speak. I finally, slowly shook my head. I wanted to reject this. I wanted to believe that we were just wounded, maybe, temporarily stunned. *Something.*

"You mean the impact left the two of you human," Lewis said. "No powers. Nothing but—human."

David nodded, relief flooding over his face. He hadn't been able to put enough words together, in his shattered state, to make sense out of it.

Human.

The two of us. *Human.*

I was suddenly aware of him in ways I'd never been before—of anxiety that I'd never felt before.

He was *mortal.* And I couldn't protect him, or myself, from anything that could fly at us—weather, fire, earth. Demons. I couldn't even bat away a simple tornado.

We were *fragile.*

"No," he whispered, and put the warmth of his palm against my face. "No, think it through, Jo."

It was hard to push past the fear, the knowledge that we were so much at risk, but I looked into his eyes for a long moment, and then I saw what he meant.

We were both human.

We could have a life together. A normal life.

We could have children of our own together.

"But—" My trembling fingers touched and traced his lips. The same lips, and different. "But you used to be—"

"I used to be human," he said. "Long, long ago. And if I have to be human now, I can't imagine a better partner for my life."

He kissed me. It was a real, human kiss, intimate in ways that even our most amazing kisses hadn't been, somehow. Bordered by our own awareness of mortality.

"Hate to interrupt this tender moment," Lewis said, "but we're fucked if we stay here. And by the way, your powers aren't gone. They're still out there, somewhere. Basic conservation of energy."

We both looked at him. I saw a weary flash of utter hatred in David's face. No, being human hadn't taken away any of that antipathy. Definitely not. "Someone else inherited our powers."

"The problem is we don't know where they went," Lewis said. "Or who's got them. If we survive outrunning the black corner, we've still got to find out where your powers went. Worst-case Warden scenario—someone just woke up with enough power to destroy half the world and hasn't got a clue what to do with it."

"And the Djinn?"

"Ashan," he said. "Worst-case scenario is that Ashan is now the sole Conduit for all of the Djinn, and he's going to be very, very pissed off about Wardens in general."

I pulled David to his feet, and realized that I could barely walk. My left leg and arm were covered with the scars that hadn't had time to heal since the battle. Nothing was bleeding, but everything hurt, and hurt badly. I fought back tears and braced David as he took careful, halting steps.

He stopped, breathing hard, shaking his head. Overwhelmed.

"Hey," I said, and grabbed his face in both my hands. "Don't you give up on me now. We're alive. We're together. Don't let him get to you. *Our* worst-case scenario is that we end up together. Human. Alive. That doesn't sound so bad, right?"

He nodded, and a convulsive shudder went through him. He put his arms around me, and his head rested on my shoulder. The last of the Wardens boarded the rescue craft, and then it was our turn.

I didn't want to let go.

"Fides mihi," he said. "I said that, didn't I? To get you back in time to save both of us?"

"I will always trust you." I kissed him gently on cheeks that tasted of sweat and sea. "And I will always bring you home, my love."

Fides mihi.

Now I had to make it count.

Sound Track

As always, I had plenty of musical help to get me through the complicated journey of *Cape Storm*. Enjoy ... and please, support the artists by buying the music—otherwise, they might have to stop making it.

So Long.. Stereoside
Hole in the Middle................................Emily Jane White
Black Is the Color of My
    True Love's Hair ....Nine Simone & Jaffa
Light It Up... Rev Theory
Count to Ten... Tina Dico
Silence ....Delerium & Sarah McLachlan
Let It Die ....Foo Fighters
Get Free .... The Vines
Electrofog ....LeCharme
Electric Feel...MGMT
Alive and Kicking ....Nonpoint
The End Is the Beginning
    Is the End....................................Smashing Pumpkins
Kill, Kill, Kill.................................... The Pierces
Bad Girlfriend .... Theory of a Deadman
Every Day Is Exactly the Same .... Nine Inch Nails
Don't Trust Me ....3OH!3
Our Time Now... Plain White T's
I'm Not Over ....Carolina Liar
Strange Times...Black Keys
Better Brother...Madita
The Bomb ....Bitter:Sweet

The Best Revenge.......................................Fischerspooner
My Mistakes Were
   Made for You ....Last Shadow Puppets
Tomorrow .... Ladytron
Pocketful of Sunshine.......................Natasha Bedingfield
Violet Hill ....Coldplay
At Your Side...Lionel Neykov
Sour Cherry..The Kills
Salute Your Solution ....The Raconteurs
Walk Like an Egyptian (Kairo Mix) ....Wilman de Jesus
Could've Had Me ....Lex Land
Sitem..Candan Ercetin
Retreat ....The Rakes
Mercy.. Duffy
It's Not My Time ....3 Doors Down

About the Author

Rachel Caine is the author of more than twenty novels, including the Weather Warden series. She was born at White Sands Missile Range, which people who know her say explains a lot. She has been an accountant, a professional musician, and an insurance investigator, and still carries on a secret identity in the corporate world. She and her husband, fantasy artist R. Cat Conrad, live in Texas with their iguanas, Popeye and Darwin, and a *Mali uromastyx* named (appropriately) O'Malley. Visit her Web site at www.rachelcaine.com, and look for her on MySpace, LiveJournal, Facebook, and Twitter.

Available Now
From Rachel Caine

THE WEATHER
WARDEN NOVELS

ILL WIND

HEAT STROKE

CHILL FACTOR

WINDFALL

FIRESTORM

THIN AIR

GALE FORCE

CAPE STORM

"You'll never look at the Weather Channel
the same way again."
—Jim Butcher, author of the #1 *New York Times*
bestselling Dresden Files novels

**Available wherever books arc sold or at
penguin.com**